# Love Just in Time

## FLORA SPEER

LOVE SPELL BOOKS     NEW YORK CITY

*For my aunt, Sylvia Tuft, and for my brothers,
David and Ralph De Groodt, with thanks for your
help with the research for this book.*

LOVE SPELL®

December 1998

Published by

Dorchester Publishing Co., Inc.
276 Fifth Avenue
New York, NY 10001

ISBN 0-505-52289-6

The name "Love Spell" and its logo are trademarks of Dorchester
Publishing Co., Inc.

Printed in the United States of America.

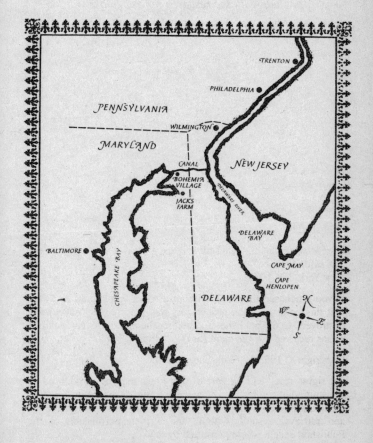

# Love Just in Time

# *Prologue*

*Huntsley Hall, Kent, England*
*Spring, 1823*

"Hah! Here you are at last." The Marquess of Huntsley looked up from the papers spread out on the huge library desk to fix a cold glare upon his second son. "I am gratified to see you have finally managed to remove yourself from your mistress and your gaming."

"I left London as soon as I received your message, sir, and rode here as fast as I could without killing my horse." Justin Neville Benedict Martynson advanced into the room as far as the chair that had been placed in front of the marquess's desk. There Justin stopped, one hand resting on the carved back of the chair. He tried not to grip the wood so tightly that the marquess would notice and comment, but he wanted a barrier, however flimsy, between himself and the father who despised him for a wastrel. "I assume

9

the matter must be of some great moment, or you would not have summoned me. The last time we met, you said most clearly that you hoped never to see me again."

"Look at you," the marquess sputtered. "Dressed in the height of fashion while the rest of your family is hard pressed to keep food on the table and this old house intact. How much did your tailor charge you for that coat, you young fool? I'll wager you can barely move in it. And as for your cravat—"

"I am fortunate to have an excellent valet in Gilbert," Justin remarked quietly. "He ties my cravats for me."

"D'you bathe every day? I've never seen a man so clean or linen so white." The marquess's own clothing was wrinkled and spotted, and the library in which he sat was in chaotic disarray and obviously had not been dusted for weeks.

"I am of a tidy disposition, sir," said Justin, who was accustomed to these complaints from his parent. "In that I am much like my mother."

"She would be ashamed of everything else about you!" the marquess shot back. "Drinking, wenching, gaming, phaeton racing—you are a disgrace to your mother's memory, and to my name!"

Justin's mouth tightened. The death of Aurelia, Marchioness of Huntsley, some four years earlier had left a deep and aching emptiness in his heart. Justin's mother had always understood him, whereas his father made

no secret of his preference for the older son, William.

"Sit down," the marquess ordered, pointing to the chair behind which Justin had barricaded himself against the inevitable parental fury. "I have a task for you."

"I am astonished to learn that you think me capable of anything other than winning a phaeton race," Justin murmured. At a snarl from his father he sat down, but he would not keep silent. In London he was considered an intelligent man. Only in his father's presence was he reduced to an inept child. "Since you regard me as a fool, why don't you set William to this task, whatever it is?"

"Because William is newly married and I will not separate my older son from his wife until they have bred at least two heirs to my title. Nor would I send Lady Chastity with him into a dangerous situation until she has fulfilled her marital duty to your brother and there are children in the nursery. No, you are the only instrument available to me, so I am forced to use you."

"Danger?" Justin's eyes gleamed. "What danger? What is this task?"

"The danger lies in the journey, rather than in the task itself." The marquess paused for a moment before continuing. "I do not expect you to remember my younger brother Roger, who was also a ne'er-do-well like yourself."

"He was the one who went to America to seek his fortune." Justin chose to ignore the insult

to his character. "Didn't Uncle Roger bankrupt himself in an unfortunate investment before he died in poverty?"

"Do not interrupt me, boy. As it happens, Roger's foolish investment may turn out to be his family's financial salvation. Twenty years ago he put all his savings into shares in the Chesapeake and Delaware Canal Company. Work was begun on the canal, then stopped for lack of money. I do not expect you to know aught of the geography of that area—"

"Oh, but I do." Despite his father's admonition, Justin dared to interrupt, for his interest was piqued by what the marquess was telling him, as it had been piqued a week previously by the somewhat drunken discourse of an acquaintance who was recently returned to London from Baltimore. Justin was glad that he had taken the time to sit in his club and listen to what George Feathercraft was saying, and now he repeated much of that information to his father. "The rivers of southern Pennsylvania empty into the Chesapeake Bay, which makes those waterways useless as transportation routes for the farmers and manufacturers of western Pennsylvania who wish to sell their products in Philadelphia. Building a canal between Chesapeake Bay and Delaware Bay would make it easier and much more profitable to get goods to Philadelphia. It would also shorten by some five hundred miles the sea passage between Philadelphia and Baltimore or Washington."

"Precisely." The marquess regarded his son with surprise. "I had no idea you were so well-informed. But you cannot know the contents of the letter I received three days ago from Mr. Benjamin Wilmot, the agent in Philadelphia who has attended to my affairs in regard to that American property my brother Roger left to me when he died. The project to rebuild the Chesapeake and Delaware Canal has been reactivated, which means that I have hope of realizing a large profit from those old shares that Roger bought. I trust you are aware that our family has fallen upon difficult times?"

"I have heard of it, sir." Justin did not respond to the heavy sarcasm in his father's voice. Justin's own income was secured by a small inheritance from his mother, which he husbanded with greater care than his father suspected. "I will do anything I can to help. What is it you want of me?"

"You are to go to America. In Philadelphia, you will meet with Mr. Benjamin Wilmot. You will make every effort to extract as much money as possible from those old canal company stocks and also from the small farm that Roger held in Maryland."

"The canal company may need to use its available funds for construction costs rather than paying large dividends to the shareholders." Justin was thinking rapidly as he spoke. "I may have to remain in the United States for some time. Would it be possible for me to live on Uncle Roger's farm? Then there is the

matter of transferring funds from Philadelphia to London."

"You may live on the farm or not," the marquess responded. "I do not care. Your task will be to see to it that the moneys owed to me are sent to England as quickly as possible. Mr. Wilmot will attend to the details of the transfer. As for the time you will have to spend away from England, I would rather have you in the wilds of America than in the stews of London. There must be less trouble for you to get into in America."

Justin knew better than to try to argue with his father, and it had at once occurred to him that a trip to America might be just what he needed. Justin's life had become a bit too exciting in the last few days since his dearest friend, Percival Cadell, had been forced to flee London after killing the son of a powerful earl in a duel over the honor of Percy's sister. Justin, who had acted as Percy's second and then helped him to a safe hiding place to escape the vengeance of the infuriated earl, could all too easily imagine what his own father would have to say when he heard about his son's part in that particular scandal. It was a miracle that the marquess did not already know. Justin had thought the duel was the reason his father wanted to see him so urgently, and he was greatly surprised to discover that he had been called to Huntsley Hall on another matter entirely.

A long journey across an ocean to a new world far from London and scandal, Justin thought.

There were fascinating possibilities inherent in the mission he had just been given, and his facile mind went to work immediately, laying plans.

"Very well, Father." Justin tried to sound as serious as he knew the marquess wanted him to be, but his thoughts were dancing down avenues that would have shocked his father—and perhaps would have made him refuse to send Justin to America after all. "I will need a week or two to settle my affairs in London. As soon as that is done, I will make arrangements to sail to America."

"You will leave in one week. You will give these to Mr. Wilmot." The marquess pushed a packet of sealed papers across his desk toward Justin. "I have booked passage for you on a ship leaving Bristol next Tuesday on the morning tide."

"One week?" Justin repeated, stunned by this news. He had hoped for a bit more flexibility in his schedule.

"You will want to return to London at once, to begin settling your affairs, as you call it. I suggest you begin by handing your latest mistress over to someone who is willing to assume the lease on that house you rented for her."

"You know about that? Sir, I had planned to stay here at Huntsley Hall for one night, at least. My valet is following in the coach with my clothing and other belongings."

"Then meet the estimable Gilbert on the road and turn him back to London. You will both have work to do in the next few days. Well,

what are you waiting for? Take those papers and leave. Now."

"Yes, Father." Justin stood up and held out his right hand to his parent. The marquess ignored the gesture. "I hope you remain in good health until I return, sir. I will do my best for the family."

"See that you don't fail me," the marquess said, his gaze once more lowered to the papers he had been studying when Justin had first arrived. "I will need every farthing you can send to me if I am to avoid selling Huntsley Hall."

Justin looked down on his father's bent head for a moment more before he turned on his heel and left the library.

# Chapter One

*Chesapeake City, Maryland*
*January, 1993*

"Laid off?" Clarissa stared at her boss, one hand arrested in the act of tucking an errant curl of glossy black hair back behind her ear. "I never expected to hear this from you."

"I wish I didn't have to do this." Dr. Bucknell's eyes were sad behind his thick glasses. "You have been a wonderful assistant and the patients like you. I wouldn't let you go if I could possibly avoid it. But you know how it is. With the latest rent increase on the clinic building and malpractice insurance premium rates going up every year, the only way I could keep a second medical assistant on my staff would be if I raised my fees, and I don't want to do that. It wouldn't be fair to my patients."

"I understand your reasoning. I even agree

17

with it. But what am I going to do now?" Clarissa turned away so Dr. Bucknell wouldn't see the tears filling her eyes. "We have mortgage payments to make on the house, and Rich has been out of work for six weeks."

"This recession has been hard on everyone. I'll give you the best possible reference and I will keep you on until the end of the month. You might get lucky and find a new job before then."

"Thanks." Afraid she would break down completely, Clarissa left the doctor's private office and made her way to the clinic's small laboratory. There Betsy, the other, older medical assistant, awaited her.

"It's a tough break," Betsy said before Clarissa could reveal her unhappy news.

"Did you know about this?" Clarissa asked.

"He told me last night after you left. He feels just awful about it, and so do I. I'll keep my ears open, and if I hear of any jobs—"

"That's what he said." Clarissa tilted her head in the direction of Dr. Bucknell's office. "But where do either of you imagine I'll find another job in this area?"

"There's always Wilmington," Betsy offered. "Lots of doctors have offices there near the hospital."

"If I have to drive all the way to Wilmington on the highway every day I'll need a new car, and I can't afford to buy one. After paying the monthly bills we can barely afford to buy food. Now I'll have to go home and tell Rich what

has happened." Suddenly Clarissa was unable to say anything else and even more unable to contemplate telling her husband about this latest economic blow.

"Is he still giving you trouble?" Betsy asked with her usual sympathetic air.

"I don't know what I'm doing wrong. I try so hard to be a good wife, but he's so damned cold and distant. At first I believed it was because he lost his job just before Thanksgiving, but when I think about it, I know the trouble started long before the holidays. I'm really worried about his reaction to this piece of news. Oh, Betsy, why is everything so hopeless?" Clarissa stiffled a sob.

"Surely one of you will find work before long," Betsy said encouragingly.

"If only Rich would be a little less quarrelsome. If he would just put his arms around me and tell me he knows we will get through this bad time. I knew marriage would have its ups and downs, but I never imagined it would be so damned lonely. Lately, I feel as if I'm carrying the entire relationship on my shoulders and Rich isn't contributing one little bit emotionally."

"Men," snorted Betsy. "Never there when you really need them, and who can figure them out? I sure can't. Both of my husbands were real bastards and the guy I'm seeing now isn't much of an improvement. Sometimes I think they're all alike."

\*    \*    \*

It was after dark when Clarissa left the clinic run by Dr. Bucknell. The rain had turned to sleet and her car slid several times before she reached her small, one-story house. She had been so proud of the house when she and Rich bought it, so full of plans to decorate and improve it, to plant a garden and build a deck where she and Rich could eat their dinners during the warm weather. She had envisioned the children she and Rich would have—two boys and two girls, all playing in the fenced-in backyard while the grown-ups drank their coffee on sunny weekend mornings. Those dreams seemed very far away on this bleak evening, and she dreaded hearing Rich's comments on the loss of her job.

So deep in gloom was Clarissa as she pulled into her driveway that she scarcely noticed the car parked in front of the house. The sleet was heavier now, and there were pellets of ice bouncing off the hood of her car. Fumbling with her keys she rushed to the back door, which was nearer than the front entrance.

"Rich?" The kitchen was empty, but there was a light on in the living room. "Rich, why haven't you started dinner? I left the casserole in the refrigerator. Did it look too inedible? Would you rather get a pizza?"

There was no one in the living room. Hearing a sound from the direction of the master bedroom, Clarissa went to the bedroom door and pushed it open. The light on the bedside table was lit, so she could see into the room quite clearly.

20

She wished she could not see at all. If only it were dark, the ecstatic moans would have told her what was happening on the bed she shared with her husband, and the darkness would have spared her the sight of his blanket-covered back and his unmistakable movements. But the room was not dark, and she could see that on this evening her husband was sharing their bed with someone else. Clarissa advanced into the room, her feet silent on the carpet. She was numb, in a state of shock, but she knew one thing: she had to find out who was with Rich.

"I love you, love you," Rich whispered softly to his companion. His words tore at Clarissa's heart. Once Rich had spoken to her like that, when they were newly married and deep in love. At least, she had been in love.

"Harder. Harder," Rich's lover cried, still unaware of Clarissa's presence. "Oh, Rich honey, don't stop now or I'll die."

Clarissa thought she recognized that voice. Aching with disgust and revulsion at the lovers and at herself, yet unable to prevent herself from making certain, she took another step and then another, tiptoeing toward the side of the bed. She looked down at the couple there, noting with the eerily detached precision of severe emotional shock that Rich was pumping violently in response to his lover's demands and noting, too, the wriggling encouragement he was getting from his partner. Rich gave a strangled cry and went rigid—and now Clarissa was close enough to see who was in bed with him.

21

"How could you?" she screamed. "My friend! Friend? What kind of friend would betray me like this? What kind of husband would? Damn you! Damn you both!"

Clarissa was not aware of leaving the bedroom or of passing through the living room or the kitchen. She only knew that she had to get away from the scene in the bedroom where Rich, the man she had married and planned to spend the rest of her life with, now lay in a passionate embrace with her dear friend. She had to get out of the house she and Rich shared. After what she had just seen, it was her home no longer.

She went through the kitchen door so fast that she slipped on the ice-covered back steps and fell, cracking her knee on the sidewalk. She felt no discomfort from the injury. The pain in her heart was so great, so all enveloping, that nothing could supersede it. Sobbing bitterly, Clarissa wrenched open the car door and collapsed into the driver's seat. She saw the kitchen light go on, and then the porch light, and she knew Rich would come after her. If she saw him she would probably kill him.

Slamming down the gas pedal, she skidded back down the driveway. When she shifted into drive, the car slid sideways on the slippery road. Then she was slipping and sliding down the street, heading away from the house, heading anywhere that was far from Rich and his lover, and far from Clarissa's pain.

But the pain went with her, misting her eyes, dulling her brain. She knew she ought to stop,

or at least drive more slowly, but something in her demanded speed. Before she stopped driving she wanted to put as much distance as possible between herself and Rich, and the faster she did it, the better.

"How could you hurt me like that?" Clarissa asked her absent husband. "How could you care so little about me or about what we had together? How many times have you done that in our bed and I never guessed it? In our bed, Rich, where you were too tired to make love to me, or too upset about being out of work for so long. Oh, God, all those days when I was at the clinic and you were home alone—were you really alone? And those overnight trips to job interviews—what wonderful excuses they must have been for you. What's wrong with me that I didn't see what was happening, that I never guessed?"

Clarissa reached the bridge over the canal. Still uncertain just where she wanted to go, she floored the gas pedal, increasing her speed as she ascended the steep grade of the arch of the bridge. When she reached the top she kept her foot on the pedal. The sleet and rain had frozen solid on the upper reaches of the bridge so that she was in effect skating, rather than driving, on the downward slope.

Clarissa saw the truck coming toward her just as she roared toward the bottom of the bridge. With a sudden jerk, she turned the steering wheel sharply to the right.

Clarissa never knew what happened next, whether she actually hit the truck or missed

23

it by inches. She felt the car making a right turn, but after the truck went past she could not straighten out the wheel. She continued in the same sharp turn until the right front fender of her car hit something solid. The sound of ripping metal assaulted her ears, followed by a flash of blinding blue light. She suddenly realized that her foot was still jammed down hard on the gas pedal. She knew she ought to take her foot off the gas, but she couldn't seem to do it. Then she and her car were sailing through the air. The car door next to her tore open. In her anguished haste to leave her house she had neglected to fasten the seat belt, so when the car tilted to the left, Clarissa fell out of it.

The night was black and cold, like the water toward which she was plummeting. She heard herself scream. . . .

# *Chapter Two*

It was considerably warmer, but still raining hard at dawn when Rich Brown stood with his friend and a police officer, the three of them staring down at the murky gray water of the canal.

"When we got the car out," the policeman said, "we found the registration in the glove compartment. That's how we knew it was your car, sir. You say your wife was driving it and she was alone?"

"That's right." Rich shook his head, the very picture of a grieving husband. He passed a hand across his face as if to wipe away tears. In the heavy rain no one could say that he was not crying. "She went out last evening to get cream for my morning coffee. I told her the weather was too bad for her to drive and I'd make do with milk, but she insisted."

"We had a report from a trucker who said he passed a car matching the description of Mrs.

Brown's. The trucker said she seemed to be out of control and was driving much too fast. Like a bat out of hell is how he put it. He said she only missed him by a few inches. Apparently, she swerved to the right and crashed through both the guardrail and the fence."

"It certainly looks like sturdy protection," Rich's friend remarked.

"It is," the policeman replied. "It was intended to prevent exactly this kind of accident. We can't figure out how Mrs. Brown got through it."

"By going like a bat out of hell," Rich's friend murmured.

"However it happened, we still have to find the body." The policeman sent a sympathetic look Rich's way. "You may not want to stay, sir. Is there anyone else who ought to be notified?"

"No," Rich said. "Clarissa was an only child and her parents are dead. Except for a few distant relatives who live out of the country, there is no one but me."

"You shouldn't be alone at a time like this," said the policeman.

"I'll stay with him. I know what he's going through. Clarissa was my friend, too." His companion put a hand on Rich's shoulder, and the policeman moved away. Rich did not speak until the officer was beyond hearing distance.

"I was planning to tell her last night that I got the job in California and that I wanted a divorce before I left," Rich said. "I didn't want to hurt her anymore than I had to. I didn't want her

to know about us. And I never wished for her death."

"But this does simplify things," his friend pointed out. "Now she can't tell anyone that she saw us together."

"I guess you're right." Rich heaved a deep sigh. "Poor Clarissa. She loved me, you know."

"We'll arrange a nice funeral service for her." His friend spoke in a bracing tone. "Then you can sell the house and move to California. After a decent interval, I'll join you there."

"Yes." With another sigh, Rich turned away from the canal. "I guess things have worked out for the best, haven't they? Let's go now. I don't want to be here when they bring up her body. I couldn't deal with that."

"I understand, dear." But as they walked off the bridge, Rich's companion added quietly, "If you ask me, I think this happened just in time."

# *Chapter Three*

*Light, brilliant and golden, blinding Clarissa. Too bright . . . too painful to open her eyes into that light. Better to stay in the darkness.*

"Turn her over again, boys," said a rough masculine voice. "Push hard on her back."

Hands turned her unprotesting body as ordered. Hands—there seemed to be dozens of them—pressed down upon her ribs and spine. She struggled to draw air into her lungs and could not.

"For God's sake, man, do you intend to break her every rib?" A new voice, more commanding and with a distinct English accent, interrupted the would-be helpers. "Here, let me try."

The pummeling hands ceased their painful work. Two strong male arms went around her waist, lifting her and pressing her back against a firm body. Without warning, the arms tightened, joined fists slamming into her just below her rib

cage. Water poured from Clarissa's throat and lungs. With the water gone, there was room for air to enter. She gasped, greedily sucking in the air her body craved. The fists tightened for a second time and more water erupted from her mouth. Clarissa began to fight against the man who was holding her.

"Enough." She coughed, spewing water and air.

"Can ye breathe now, girl?" the first man asked, stooping down to peer into her face as she hung limply over the second man's arm. He glanced upward, looking beyond Clarissa. "Jack, me lad, I think she'll live. Ye can put her down now."

The man holding Clarissa lowered her to the ground. Kneeling, he supported her in a sitting position against his thigh, with one of his arms across her shoulders.

"Someone bring us a blanket," he ordered. "She is shivering."

"And just where in the name of all the saints would ye be thinkin' a man'll find a blanket in this weather?" his companion demanded.

"Then we will use my coat. She cannot remain like this, wearing only her shift."

"Aye, and that's another thing. Why would a female be floatin' in the canal wearin' only her shift, may I ask ye? Did someone try to murder her? Or—Mother of Heaven preserve us—did the poor thing try to kill herself? We cannot have females drownin' in the canal. It'll give the place a bad name."

"We can ask questions later, when she has had

time to recover from her ordeal. Now, get my coat, Sam. And my boots and hat, too, if you can find them."

"The boots'll be just where ye dropped them, my lord, when ye were preparin' to jump in to rescue her, but yer hat is lost."

"Don't call me my lord!"

"Men," Clarissa muttered, still with her eyes closed, still not sure what was happening or why. "Always men causing trouble."

"I take it you are not overly fond of the masculine gender?" murmured the man who was holding her.

"I hate men." Clarissa tried to turn her head away from the painful brightness that penetrated her lowered lids. The only shadow available to her was the area next to his broad chest. When she moved toward that shade she immediately found herself lying with her cheek against damp fabric beneath which thrummed a steady heartbeat.

"Surely you cannot hate all men?" Her rescuer responded to her weary statement with barely disguised humor. "It would be a pity if you disdained every one of us, for you, madam, are plainly made to delight and please a man."

"That's what you all say at first," Clarissa told him, her cheek still pressed on his chest.

"Here's yer coat, my—er, Jack, and yer boots as well, but ye lost yer hat when ye jumped in after her."

"Thank you, Sam." A heavy garment was draped around Clarissa's shoulders. The motions

involved in this procedure roused her completely from the stupor that was holding her in thrall.

"You are the one who pulled me out of the water?" By a great effort she finally managed to get her eyes wide open. Immediately, she was compelled to squint against the glare of the sun so that she could see the man who was still holding her.

He was remarkably handsome, with finely chiseled features and a long, high-bridged nose. His eyes were gray behind dark lashes. His hair was wet, dark, and straight. It was worn pulled back into a low ponytail and fastened with a dripping wet black ribbon. His white shirt—a poet's shirt, she noted, with wide sleeves and an open, slashed neckline—was also wet, as the skin of her cheek had earlier informed her.

"Aye, girl, he's Jack Martin, yer rescuer," the man called Sam said. "And right happy we'd be to hear ye say just how ye got into the canal."

"I fell," Clarissa said. She frowned, trying hard to recall exactly what had happened. She remembered sleet, darkness, her car traveling much too fast on the downward arc of the bridge.

"Fell where?" Sam asked.

"I came off the Chesapeake City Bridge and sideswiped a truck. My wheels locked—did something happen to my brakes? It was so icy, such a terrible storm." She floundered to a confused halt when the man holding her tightened his arms around her in a way that conveyed a stern warning. The message was immediately reinforced by his low, urgent voice in her ear.

"Madam, I suggest that you be silent," he advised, "else these men will think you are a madwoman."

"I am beginning to wonder about that myself." Clarissa shrugged off Jack Martin's arms to sit up and look around. A group of a dozen men—half of them black and the other half white, but all clad in the same type of wrinkled, dirt-streaked blue overalls and work shirts—stood nearby, watching her and the two men with her. Clarissa assumed that these workmen were the owners of the many hands that had tried to force the water out of her lungs and start her breathing again. With one of her own hands on Jack Martin's shoulder for leverage, she got to her feet a bit unsteadily to face the men.

"Thank you," she said to them. "All of you. I appreciate what you did for me."

A few of the men grinned at her, a few shuffled their feet in the dusty ground. Several looked pointedly at Clarissa's legs, which extended well below the hem of Jack Martin's coat. Following the direction of their glances, Clarissa looked down at her own legs and feet.

"Oh, my God!" The white shoes she wore every day were gone. Her panty hose were laddered with runners, and she suddenly realized that the white uniform in which she dressed for her work at Dr. Bucknell's clinic was also missing. Beneath Jack Martin's coat she wore only the remains of her panty hose, her briefs, bra, and the opaque white slip that she had worn under her uniform. "What has happened to me? Where am I?"

Turning away from the men, Clarissa stared at the unfamiliar surroundings. She stood on a spit of land bounded by water. On one side of her flowed a lazy greenish river. On the other side lay a ditch about 60 feet wide, its sides shored up by stout timbers. Clarissa could not tell how deep the ditch was, because it was full of water. A short distance away on the same spit of land sat a square, unpainted building from which issued a sound she thought she recognized.

"Is that a steam engine?" she asked.

"It is in the pump house," Jack Martin answered her. He was watching her closely. "They are testing the lock."

"The lock?" she repeated. "But there aren't any—not anymore."

She looked around again, getting her bearings and taking in more details on this second scanning of the area. On the south side of the river stood a two-story house and a few shacks. All of the buildings were unpainted and the shacks looked as if they would fall down in the slightest wind. Beyond these buildings Clarissa could see workmen carrying long boards and what looked like heavy wooden beams. She thought they were putting up another house. A narrow wooden bridge connected the settlement on the south side of the river with the land where she and the men were standing.

"Where am I?" she asked again in utter bewilderment.

"Ye just came out of there," Sam replied, pointing to the ditch.

"Exactly what is there?" Clarissa demanded.

"Why, girl, 'tis the western end of the great Chesapeake and Delaware Canal, the finest work of engineering ever seen in the modern world," Sam informed her proudly. "To yer left is the first lock. The river ye see is Back Creek, a branch of the Elk River."

"That's not—this can't be." Clarissa stopped. She remembered seeing pictures of the old canal taken before the federal government had bought it in the early twentieth century and turned the Army Corps of Engineers loose on it to widen and straighten the waterway so large ships could use it. What she saw before her closely resembled those old photographs. "Is this some historical exhibit you're building?"

"It will be a fine exhibit on the official opening day," Jack Martin answered her, "though I doubt if the investors will be greatly pleased by the final cost of building the thing."

"The canal isn't opened yet?" Clarissa tried hard to make sense of this. Then she remarked on another anomaly, one she had actually been aware of since first regaining consciousness. "Why is the sun shining so brightly? Why is it so warm?"

"Because it's mid-July," Sam said. He was a short, burly man with sandy hair and blue eyes that might, on some more joyful occasion, have twinkled at her with easy laughter. At the moment, Sam's eyes were filled with concern

for her. "Wouldn't ye expect warm weather at the height of the summer?"

"But it's not summer." She stopped herself from declaring that the month was January, warned again by a frown and an almost imperceptible shake of the head from Jack Martin. "Of course I would expect July to be hot and sunny," she said to Sam. "My confusion must be the result of nearly drowning."

"How did ye get into the canal?" Sam asked once again. "And where are yer clothes?"

"Leave off, man," Jack Martin ordered. "The lady has endured a terrifying experience. She needs dry clothing, a cup of wine, and a chance to gather her wits together."

"Yes, please." Clarissa agreed to these most welcome suggestions with fervor.

"And where are ye thinkin' to take her to procure such refinements?" asked Sam. "Not to Madam Rose's house, I'll be bound."

"For the moment, it seems the only place to take her," Jack Martin responded. "We will think of something more suitable later. Madam, are you able to walk across that bridge you see or shall I carry you?"

"I'll walk." The thought of being lifted into those strong arms a second time and carried such a distance was too unsettling to contemplate. Clarissa did not want any man to touch her unless it were absolutely necessary. She was finished with men, those treacherous and undependable creatures.

Still, she could not help admiring the way the

damp gray fabric of Jack Martin's trousers clung to his long, muscular legs. While she had been trying to decide exactly what had happened to her, he had taken the opportunity to pull on a pair of high black boots. When he lifted his head from this task, his drying hair gleamed dark reddish brown, like fine mahogany in the sunlight. A wide black leather belt circled his slim waist. He rested his hands at his belt and she saw how long fingered and graceful they were. Clarissa could easily imagine those hands holding a sword and quelling some fierce opponent—or rescuing a lady in distress.

"Damned romantic nonsense," she muttered to herself and started toward the bridge.

The wooden planks were like a boardwalk at the seashore, hot in the July sun and so rough hewn that she had to step carefully to avoid gouging her feet full of splinters. Tiptoeing along in the shattered remnants of her panty hose, guarded on either side by Jack Martin and Sam, Clarissa slowly made her way across the river. Several of the workmen trailed behind them. The bridge ended at a rutted, baked-mud street.

"This is Bohemia Avenue," Jack Martin informed her. "The town is Bohemia Village."

Clarissa was about to reply that she knew Bohemia Avenue and that, according to her high-school history teacher, Chesapeake City had not been called Bohemia Village since the middle of the last century, but she bit back the words, deciding not to offer any more information until she discovered exactly what

was going on. Nothing she saw resembled the canal or the Chesapeake City that she knew. This Bohemia Village wasn't even a village; it was just one dilapidated building, some shacks, and a mud road.

To be fair, there were several new houses in the process of being erected and it looked as if there would soon be a few shops if she was right in her guess as to the future of the construction now under way. Clarissa could hear the sound of hammers, and the clean smell of freshly sawn or shaven wood drifted on the air, almost overcoming the less pleasant odors of stagnant water and human refuse.

"'Twill be a fine town once the canal is fit for constant use," Sam said, having noted her interested glance toward one of the building sites. "All the ships coming through will have to stop here and pay their fees before they enter the locks. We'll soon have a general store and houses for the canal pilots—and a bank to safely hold all the cash."

"You are a hopeless optimist, Sam," Jack Martin told his friend. "If there are many more landslides, you will have to start digging the canal all over again."

"Just wait and see if I'm right," Sam responded cheerfully.

The men conducted Clarissa to the large, two-story building. The moment they stepped across the veranda and through the unpainted door, she knew what the place was. All sounds in the main room stopped when they entered, and every eye

turned to Clarissa. There were only about 20 or so people present, lounging on settees or upholstered chairs or sitting at tables, and at that hour of the day most of them were women in various stages of undress. The smells of tobacco and alcohol reached Clarissa's nostrils, along with the unexpected fragrance of roses.

"This is a whorehouse," Clarissa said bluntly.

"A saloon," Sam amended.

"A tavern," Jack Martin said. "A place for the men who work on the canal to come, to eat and drink and be entertained."

"I'll bet." Clarissa glared at the two men. "Just what kind of woman do you think I am anyway?"

"Well, as to that," Sam said, "we're not quite sure. It has crossed me thoughts that ye might have run from this very house to throw yerself into the canal."

"There is nothing," she informed him, "nothing in this world that would ever make me commit suicide. I have recently proven that to myself by surviving a heartbreaking emotional blow and then an accident that left me nearly drowned in that ditch out there. And never, Mr. Sam, have I ever been anything even vaguely resembling a prostitute. Quite the opposite, in fact. I want nothing to do with disgusting men."

"MacKenzie," said Sam, grinning at her.

"What?" She was so angry she thought she had not heard him correctly.

"It's not Mr. Sam. It's Samuel James Mac-Kenzie. At your service, madam." The words

were pronounced with only the faintest trace of a Scottish accent, and he bowed with a courtly flourish.

"You didn't say yer," Clarissa noted.

"That's for the men out there"—Sam waved a hand in the general direction of the canal—"and for the women in here. They all expect the supervisors to sound more like the workmen than like our friend Jack here. I try to oblige them; it makes my work easier."

"You must understand, madam," Jack said. He stopped short. "I beg your pardon. We do not know your name."

"Clarissa Jane Cummings," she said, meeting his probing gray eyes with a level gaze. She would not use her married name any longer. The very thought of Rich Brown made her feel ill. She would divorce her errant husband at the first opportunity.

"Why does your own name make you so angry?" Jack Martin's question made Clarissa realize that her thoughts must be mirrored on her face. But she did not want to explain to him about Rich.

"What about you?" she countered.

"What about me?" His sharp eyes made her distinctly uncomfortable.

"Jack is sometimes a nickname for John," she said. "Is John your actual name?"

"Jack will do very well." Never had Clarissa encountered such haughty disdain written across any man's features. Further personal questions about him died on her lips, unspoken. "Now,

Miss Cummings, you must understand that we enjoy few amenities in this rough place."

"I had noticed," she murmured.

"Therefore, since you came to us undressed, you will be compelled to make do with whatever clothing is available. Perhaps later we can arrange to send you to Wilmington, where you will be able to purchase the raiment to which you are apparently accustomed, but for the moment, you will have to accept what Madam Rose can supply, or else you will go naked."

"I have no desire to go to Wilmington," Clarissa said. "I live in this area."

"There, madam, you lie." Jack spoke in a low, deadly voice. "I know everyone who lives within twenty miles on either side of the entire length of the canal, and you are not among the citizens of this locale, either in Maryland or in Delaware."

So assured was his tone of voice that Clarissa could only gape at him, dumbfounded and unable to think of anything to say in response to his accusation that she was lying. How could he know everyone he claimed to know? And how could he be so damned sure—and so mistaken— about her?

"Well?" he said after a long moment's pause. "Will you allow Madam Rose to dress you?"

"Do I have a choice?" Clarissa snapped.

"You may not believe it," he said with a glance at the lounging women in their flimsy wrappers and low-cut chemises, "but there is respectable clothing to be found in this house."

"Sure there is," Clarissa spat back, "for the

pleasure of men who want to pretend they're raping innocent, old-fashioned schoolgirls."

She was delighted to see that both men actually looked shocked by this remark. Clarissa was fast growing tired of the game they were playing. She wanted a rational explanation for her presence in this canal-building theme park, and then she wanted to find a quiet place where she could take a hot shower, put on a clean bathrobe, and lie down on a comfortable bed in air-conditioned coolness and sleep until she was rested enough to cope with the mess her life had become.

It didn't look as if she was going to get that kind of break. Jack Martin's intriguingly shaped lips parted, almost certainly to scald her with some snooty, English-accented quip about her apparent knowledge of brothels—as if she had ever seen one except on television—but he never said whatever he was planning, because their little group was joined by a remarkable-looking woman.

"Ah, Madam Rose," Sam said. "Just the person we wanted to see."

"Hello, Sam." Madam Rose was close to six feet tall and the masses of pale blonde hair piled on top of her head made her look taller still. She wore a floor-length gown of rose silk, cut with a rather high waistline, long tight sleeves, and a modest neckline that ended in a narrow lace ruffle at her throat. The skirt of the gown was trimmed with an abundance of ruffles, lace, flowers of matching silk, and heavy rose cording.

Madam Rose's height, strong facial bones, and cool blue eyes gave her the appearance of a Viking goddess and she had the dignity to fit that role—with one aberration. Sam MacKenzie barely reached her shoulder, but the smile she bestowed on him suggested that Sam's lack of physical stature was no problem at all so far as their relationship was concerned. After her warm greeting to Sam, Madam Rose turned more formal with Clarissa's other escort.

"Good day to you, Mr. Martin. How can I help you?"

"Miss Cummings fell into the canal and her clothing was swept away before we could rescue her," Jack Martin said.

"I heard the commotion." A faint glimmer of humor lit the cool Scandinavian eyes. "What a pity that the undertow in our still uncompleted canal is strong enough to rip the very garments off a poor woman's back."

"She needs something to wear until she can make new clothing," Jack Martin said.

"Something simple," Clarissa put in, refraining from adding that she had no intention of sewing any clothing at all. Sewing was not her thing, not when there were plenty of shops in the nearby mall.

"You can put it on my bill, darlin'," Sam said, giving Madam Rose a heated look.

"Your bill, when you finally bother to pay it," Madam Rose rejoined, "will buy me a new house and furnish it besides."

"Let the bill rise a little higher and it'll buy yer freedom from this line o' work," Sam suggested, sliding an arm around Madam Rose's waist. "And I'll begin yer new life by makin' an honest woman of ye."

"You could begin by laying aside that ridiculous and patently inaccurate accent." The words were spoken in an affectionate tone, but Madam Rose went back to business at once, turning her full attention to Clarissa. "If you will come upstairs to the wardrobe room, Miss Cummings, I will endeavor to find something to fit you." She gestured toward a wooden staircase.

"This is not Sam's responsibility," Jack Martin said. "I will pay for Miss Cumming's clothing in cash."

"I don't want to owe anything to a man," Clarissa said to him, rather ungraciously. "I'll repay you as soon as I can get things sorted out."

"I have no objection to any arrangements you wish to make, Mr. Martin." Madam Rose nodded toward Clarissa. "Come with me, Miss Cummings. If you gentlemen would care for a drink while you wait or a slice of cold roast beef or some bread and cheese, Dancy will be happy to serve you."

"I'd rather be served by yerself, Rose, in yer own special way," the irrepressible Sam said with a wink, "but I'll make do with Dancy just this once."

"We will await your return in the taproom, Miss Cummings," Jack Martin said, turning

toward the huge black man who came forward to take the men's orders.

"Is Dancy your bouncer?" Clarissa asked Madam Rose as they ascended the rickety stairs to the second floor.

"My what?" Madam Rose looked puzzled.

"The one who removes obstreperous patrons from the premises," Clarissa said, trying to suit her language to the surroundings. She was too tired to argue that anyone in Madam Rose's business should have known what a bouncer was. "The person who maintains order in your establishment."

"I maintain order here," Madam Rose said. "Dancy is cook, dishwasher, barman, and yes, he does occasionally remove a customer who has imbibed too heartily. He is also a full partner in my business. Do you find that objectionable, Miss Cummings?" She suddenly sounded defensive.

"No," Clarissa answered. "Why should I object?"

"Because Dancy is a freed slave."

"Slave?" Clarissa nearly tripped on the top step. She recovered in time to hurry after Madam Rose into a small room crammed with clothing that was piled on chests, chairs, and a bed with a badly sagging mattress. The walls of the room were unpainted wooden planks. There was one window covered by a wooden shutter, also unpainted. This Madam Rose threw open to admit more light.

"Good heavens." Clarissa stared around her,

unbelieving. "This room looks like a theatrical costumer's vault. I've never seen so many spangles or feathers or gaudy colors in one place before."

"In a way, the girls who work for me are actresses," Madam Rose responded. "The customers often require them to play a part. It makes the process more enjoyable, you see, which encourages the customers to return often, so that we all make more money."

"This is crazy. I don't believe this is happening. Where the hell am I?"

"You ought not to curse, Miss Cummings. It is most unladylike. I do not permit my girls to curse. Refinement of speech is vitally important."

"I usually watch my tongue," Clarissa confided. "At the clinic where I work, we deal with a lot of elderly patients and they don't like to hear a young woman swear, so I try not to do it. It's just that this has been one god-awful—excuse me. I mean, this has been a most peculiar day. Oh, Lord, just listen to me. I'm babbling like an idiot." She collapsed backward onto the creaking mattress, giving way first to uncontrollable giggles and then to equally uncontrollable tears.

"I don't know what's wrong with me," she wept, burying her face in a ruffled red satin petticoat.

"Please don't dampen the costumes. Here, this will help." From somewhere amongst the voluminous folds of her pink silk skirts, Madam Rose produced a tiny vial. She pulled out the

stopper and then held the vial under Clarissa's nose. "Breathe deeply of this."

Clarissa choked and gagged on the ammonia scent that wafted from the bottle, but her tears stopped.

"*Sal volatile*," Madam Rose explained, replacing the stopper in the bottle. "Smelling salts. I always keep a vial handy. Some of my new girls become hysterical when they first begin to work here."

"I shouldn't wonder." Clarissa yearned to ask Madam Rose how an apparently intelligent woman had become involved in such a career, but she lacked the nerve to pry so deeply into the affairs of someone she did not know.

"If you are feeling quite recovered," Madam Rose said after a few minutes had passed, "let me look at you and judge your size."

When Clarissa sat up, Madam Rose pushed Jack Martin's coat off her shoulders and stood gazing at her figure with a professionally considering eye.

"You are much too slender to suit any but the most degenerate of my patrons," she told Clarissa.

"I'm glad to hear it," Clarissa responded. "Prostitution would not be my first career choice."

"I can tell. You don't have the look of a girl who would enjoy this kind of life," Madam Rose said. "Some girls do enjoy it, you know, at least for a short time. They like the attention men pay to them. Others take to this life out of desperation to keep themselves from starving. There

is little else an uneducated young woman can do, if she has no family to feed and house and protect her."

"Is that how you got into the business?" Clarissa asked, curiosity finally overcoming her manners. She asked the question in a sympathetic voice and Madam Rose did not take offense, but she did favor Clarissa with a long look before she answered.

"I was betrayed by a man," she said.

"I can identify with that," Clarissa told her. "The same thing happened to me. I came home from work last night and found my husband— found him—" She gulped. Madam Rose again offered the vial of smelling salts, but Clarissa waved it aside.

"And so you ran away from him," Madam Rose said. "Did you throw yourself into the canal?"

"No. Rich isn't worth dying for. The miserable bastard."

"I approve of your sentiment, though I do wish you would moderate your language." Madam Rose pocketed the smelling salts. "Anger is always better than grief. Now let us find clothing for you before Mr. Martin storms up the stairs and pounds on the door and commands us to be done with this business."

"You don't have to give me any of these fancy costumes," Clarissa said. "I'll be perfectly content with an old pair of jeans and a work shirt."

"Why in the name of heaven would an attractive woman like yourself want to look like a

workman?" Madam Rose appeared to be genuinely horrified by this idea. "You cannot think to disguise yourself and thus hide from your searching husband?"

"No." Clarissa sighed. "Rich probably isn't looking for me. After what he did, I wonder if he ever cared about me, and he must know that I don't want anything more to do with him. I just want to forget I ever had a husband."

"In that case, you need not concern yourself about serious pursuit on his part. Nor will I mention to anyone in Bohemia Village that you have a husband." Madam Rose turned brisk. "Let me see. What would fit you?" Searching in one of the trunks, she pulled from it a soft gray cotton dress, the fabric sprigged with blue and yellow flowers and tiny green leaves.

"How pretty." Clarissa touched the skirt. "But it's so long."

"No, it is not. It's too short," Madam Rose declared. "Your ankles will show, but you could add a flounce at the hem to lengthen it. Here is the fichu to go with it, and this is the petticoat. You will want another chemise to replace the one you are wearing. Since Mr. Martin is paying for all of this, I will try to find a second dress that will fit you."

Clarissa held up the sheer white cotton fichu, which had a narrow ruffle all around its edges. She had seen enough pictures of Martha Washington and Betsy Ross to know what a fichu

was and how it was worn. It was intended to be draped around the neckline of a dress and knotted so the long ends would hang down the front of the dress.

"Here." Madam Rose held up a long gown with a blue-green bodice and a white skirt. "You will need another petticoat for this dress and a second chemise. Then, stockings, garters, shoes, a night rail and wrapper, and a hat and gloves." She began piling the items on the bed as she verbally listed them. When she lifted what looked like a big straw sunbonnet out of a round hatbox, Clarissa lost her patience.

"Stop it!" she cried. "I am not interested in all this fancy dress stuff. I just want something to cover me decently until I can get out of here. I'll buy some real clothes at the mall, and I promise I'll pay you back for whatever I wear when I leave here. In fact, if you'll take credit cards, I'll pay right now. Oh, sh—I mean, oh, good heavens, I've lost my purse."

"Mr. Martin has said he will pay me in cash, and he will do so before you leave my house. You may settle with him for the bill, if you wish." Madam Rose was unperturbed by Clarissa's emotional outburst. "As for the dresses, I do assure you they are the simplest ones I have. Both of them will be most becoming to you, with your dark hair and those remarkable blue-green eyes. If you need a purse, I can supply one. Nor will I tell anyone who comes looking for you where you have gone, if that is why you are so eager

to leave Bohemia Village. I am an expert at concealing the whereabouts of young women who want to disappear quietly. You appear to be a most unusual young woman with your own secrets to hide. Now, after your plunge into that dirty canal, I expect you would like a bath, wouldn't you?" she said, the sudden change in subject stopping Clarissa from making another hasty and ill-considered speech.

"I don't want to inconvenience you." The thought of Clarissa Jane Cummings taking a bath in such an establishment as Madam Rose's was absolutely incredible.

"Convenience has nothing to do with it. Mr. Martin will pay for your bath. Come with me."

Madam Rose kept a tiny room set aside exclusively for bathing. Once the copper tub was filled with buckets of steaming water carried in by two young black girls who looked like twins, Madam Rose handed Clarissa a bar of soap and a cotton bathrobe that had a double ruffle down its front.

"When you have finished, go back to the wardrobe room," Madam Rose instructed. "The girls will help you to dress. I must attend to business downstairs."

Clarissa was hot, sticky with partially dried canal water, and ready to break into tears again at the slightest provocation. She looked after Madam Rose's departing back, then at the tub of lovely clean water. The soap in her hand was, of course, rose scented.

"Oh, what the hell," she murmured, sniffing at the soap. "Whatever is going on, I may as well enjoy it."

Half an hour later, feeling greatly refreshed and with her skin and hair smelling of roses, Clarissa allowed the two black girls, who told her their names were Emmie and Lucy, to help her into the gray sprigged-cotton dress.

"But no corset," Clarissa insisted, rejecting the heavy white linen garment with its buckram stiffening and narrow stays. "I refuse to be that authentic for this Early American pageant."

"You scarcely need a corset." Madam Rose rejoined her at that point. "In fact, you are much too thin, Miss Cummings. You will have to eat more if you wish to fill out your dress."

"This is the first time I've ever been given that advice," Clarissa said. "I've been dieting all my life."

"Emmie, Lucy, pack up the remainder of Miss Cummings's belongings in that bandbox and put them into Mr. Martin's cart. It is waiting outside the front door. And be quick about it," Madam Rose added. "He is growing impatient."

"Mr. Martin's cart?" Clarissa repeated.

"It has been decided that you will stay with him at his farm for a few days," Madam Rose informed her.

"Who decided this? Did he?" Clarissa's eyes flashed. "I won't do what any man says just because he says so. From now on, I make my

own decisions. Where is he? I'll tell him so myself and save you the trouble."

"I would not cross him if I were you," Madam Rose advised. The cool statement gave Clarissa pause.

"Just how well do you know Jack Martin?" Clarissa demanded, the question making Madam Rose smile as if she understood a secret to which Clarissa was not privy. "I thought you and Sam MacKenzie—"

"Sam is an old friend," said Madam Rose.

"And does Jack Martin come to visit you, too?" Clarissa did not know why she was asking so many impolite questions. She was usually much more discreet. It was no business of hers if Jack Martin slept with every girl at Madam Rose's house twice in each week and with Madam Rose herself on Sundays. Madam Rose did not seem at all surprised by her heated words.

"I no longer work in that way," she said to Clarissa. "I am too busy with the management of this establishment. Most of the men who labor on this end of the canal come here, and the contractors, too, but Mr. Martin less often than the others. He has no particular girl of whom he is fond, though the girls like him because he is kind to them and always pays them a little extra when he is finished."

Her face red with embarassment for having asked the question, Clarissa went through the open door and headed toward the steps, and Madam Rose said softly, "Be careful, Miss Cummings. You are an innocent, and he is not."

"I hate men," Clarissa said. "I am not interested in Mr. Martin in that way."

"Of course not." Madam Rose smiled at her. It was a real smile, not the carefully calculated smile the madam of a whorehouse routinely bestows upon her best-paying customers. "I recognize your type of woman, Miss Cummings, because I was like you myself, wounded and full of pain. I do not know everything your husband did to you—I suspect it was more than mere unfaithfulness—but of one thing I am certain. You have never known real pleasure with a man. When you do, you will fall into love with that man. Therefore, choose your partner carefully. Do not allow your heart to be broken; once broken, it may never mend."

"My heart has already been broken. I don't plan to give any man the chance to do it again. And in case you haven't noticed, not everything in this world depends on sex."

"On sex, no," Madam Rose said, her blue Viking eyes oddly soft. "But on true love, everything depends. Guard your heart well then, Miss Cummings. And beware of Mr. Jack Martin."

# Chapter Four

"If you refuse to return to your own home," Jack Martin said to Clarissa, "and you have no wish to join Madam Rose's girls, then you have no choice but to go with me."

"I don't think that is such a good idea," Sam said. "It would ruin her reputation, and your own, Jack."

"Be quiet, Sam." Jack Martin spoke through his teeth without looking at his friend.

"It doesn't matter what you think, Sam," Clarissa told that worthy personage, "because I am not going anywhere with anyone."

"Just what do you intend to do?" Jack Martin demanded.

Clarissa wished he were not so imposing a man. From his almost dry, tied-back hair to his still-damp poet's shirt to his long, straight legs and his booted feet, he presented a romantic figure designed to thrill any woman. Were Clarissa

not so disgusted with men, she might have been more appreciative of his physical assets. Were she not so tired and confused, she certainly would have coped better with his chauvinistic insistence that he knew what was right for her.

"Since you claim to have no relatives, and since I am the one who pulled you out of the canal," Jack Martin said to her, "I am responsible for your welfare. I have never yet failed in my duty to family or to friend."

"I am neither a relative nor a friend of yours," Clarissa snapped. "I am perfectly capable of taking care of myself."

"Do you really think so?" Her handsome tormentor gave her a dazzling smile that revealed a set of perfect teeth, but there was no humor in his gray eyes. "Where will you sleep tonight? How will you find food?"

"I'll take a room in a motel," she said. "I'll rent a car. Then I'll visit the mall to buy dinner and some modern clothes. People will stare at me if I walk around in this old-fashioned dress."

"Madam, you sound like a madwoman. You are making no sense at all," Jack Martin said, frowning. "To begin with the most trivial of your statements, your dress will not be considered much out of style in this part of the world. In London, yes. It might raise some uncharitable comment there among members of the *ton*, but not here in America."

"Oh, thank you very much," Clarissa retorted. "I suppose most of you Brits of the *ton* still refer to this country as the Colonies!"

"These United States have not been British colonies for more than half a century," he replied.

"For half a century?" Clarissa repeated, trying to ignore the growing chill of fear at her heart. She refused to believe the implications of everything that had happened and all that had been said since she had first regained consciousness. It was easier to quarrel with the man standing before her than to accept the mounting evidence of her own eyes and ears. "Are you crazy?" she demanded of him.

"I wonder if you are the one who is crazed," he responded. "Tell me, Miss Cummings. Assuming that you are able to reach the road that runs between Philadelphia and Baltimore, which is the only place where you might find a suitable inn, and assuming that you do locate such a roadside inn—both of which are highly unlikely achievments for a woman alone and on foot—how do you then plan to obtain a room if you have no money?" That obvious question brought Clarissa up short, preventing her from giving him another sharp answer.

"You are right," she admitted. "My credit cards are at the bottom of the canal, along with my car and my purse."

"There is no cart at the bottom of the canal," he said. "If there were, I would know about it. Furthermore, if you ever possessed a letter of credit, you should have deposited it at once into a bank in Wilmington, which is the nearest settlement able to provide such a service. Did you

have a letter of credit, Miss Cummings?"

"Don't be silly," she said, her voice suddenly trembling. "I know what you're talking about, and no one uses those old-fashioned things anymore. Credit cards are much more convenient."

"Are they indeed?" His glance was frosty. "You have no ready money. From what you say, you also have no family, no friends, no letter of credit, and no means of proving you are who you claim to be. You came to Bohemia Village wearing only a chemise and a pair of badly torn stockings. What do you expect us to think of you, Miss Cummings?"

"You don't understand."

"No, I do not. It is incomprehensible to me why you would refuse an honest offer of hospitality when you so obviously have no other options. I give you my word of honor that you will come to no harm while you are in my care, madam."

"Word of honor?" Clarissa gave vent to a cynical laugh. "Boy, is that line out of date!"

"Do you dare to impugn my honor?" His voice and his eyes were so cold, his anger so evident that Clarissa took two steps backward.

"I still don't like it." Sam's measured tones eased the strained silence spinning out between Clarissa and Jack Martin. "But when you put it in just that way, Jack me boy, and considerin' the lack of available accommodations in this area for a respectable young woman, I can see ye do have a point. Miss Cummings, I'm thinkin' ye ought to go wi' him. If he says ye'll come to

no harm, ye can be sure ye'll be safe wi' him."

"I don't like or trust men," Clarissa began.

"So you have stated repeatedly, ever since a group of men saved your life," Jack Martin said. "I, for one, am growing weary of your constant protestations. For the last time, madam, will you accept my offer? If you say no, I warn you I shall leave you here to fend for yourself." With that, he stalked out of Madam Rose's house.

"Go with him," Sam urged.

"I thought you didn't like the idea," Clarissa said to him.

"I didn't. I still don't. But he has the right of it. There is no other choice. Ye don't want to have to sleep beneath a tree, where ye'll be available to hungry mosquitoes and wanderin' snakes, and the occasional canal worker who's lookin' for a bit of excitement, do ye?"

"No, I don't want that." Clarissa shuddered.

"Then tell him ye'll go wi' him."

"Sam, your accent keeps slipping," she told him, once more using irrelevance to avoid thinking about overwhelming, terrifying facts.

"Aye, lassie, I know it," Sam said. "'Tis a sad situation when a man cannot remember whether he's Irish or Scottish."

"If you are trying to make me laugh and feel better, you aren't succeeding." While she might find Jack Martin difficult to deal with, Sam MacKenzie was another matter. In his kindness and his honest concern for her welfare he reminded her of certain of her male relatives. In her childhood she had been blessed with a

father, two grandfathers, assorted uncles and male cousins—all of whom had been good and decent men. It wasn't right for her to blame every member of the male sex for what Rich had done to her. Sam MacKenzie was trying to help her in the same way that one of her uncles would have done. For all she knew, Jack Martin might honestly be trying to help her, too. Clarissa let out a long breath. "All right, Sam, you can stop worrying about me. I'll go with Mr. Martin."

She found him standing beside an open cart supervising the loading of several wooden crates in addition to the bandbox containing her new wardrobe. From somewhere he had acquired a low-crowned straw hat to replace the one lost in the canal.

If they were going to drive for any distance, he was going to need that hat. The sun was so bright that Clarissa was grateful for Madam Rose's insistence that she wear the straw sunbonnet. She did not much like the yellow and blue flowers that decorated it, nor the green satin ribbons that were tied into a big bow beneath her chin, but the wide, scooped brim did shade her eyes. She wished for sunglasses, but something warned her not to ask for them. Everyone in Bohemia Village seemed to be so determined to keep up the Early American theme that she just knew they wouldn't have anything as modern as sunglasses, not even in the souvenir shop. That thought reminded her of an interesting fact.

"I haven't seen any tourists," she said, hoping Jack Martin would dispel all her rapidly growing fears by telling her that Bohemia Village was closed to visitors on whatever day of the week this was.

"I beg your pardon?" He looked at her as if she were a complete idiot.

"Visitors," she translated for him. "Except for workmen and Madam Rose's girls, the village is deserted."

"The visitors will arrive on the day the canal officially opens," he said. "May I assume from your presence at my side that you have decided to accept my invitation?"

"Just until I figure out what the hell—I mean, until I understand what has happened," she answered him.

"You do seem to be a bit confused. Perhaps I can be of some assistance to you in clearing your thoughts," he offered.

"That would be very kind of you, Mr. Martin." Thinking that Madam Rose would approve of her refined language, Clarissa repressed a giggle and let him help her up onto the seat of the cart. He then leapt up beside her. The cart was made of wood, the single board seat had a matching board back, and the whole contrivance was pulled by a sturdy-looking farm horse.

"Hold on," Jack Martin said and flicked the reins over the horse's back. The cart lurched forward, the motion rocking the cargo in the rear and nearly bouncing Clarissa off the seat. When she yelped in surprise, her companion

slanted a glance in her direction. "I told you to hold on."

"Do you always travel in this thing?" Clarissa discovered that, not only did she have to hold on to the seat, she also had to hang on to her bonnet to keep it from falling off the back of her head and strangling her with green satin ribbons.

"I deeply regret that I cannot provide you with a well-sprung coach," her companion responded. "No doubt you are more accustomed to such conveyances than to farm carts."

"As a matter of fact," she revealed, "my own car could use new shock absorbers."

Jack Martin did not answer her. Setting the horse to a steady trot he drove along the single, rutted baked-mud road of Bohemia Village, calling out greetings to the carpenters and other workmen whom they passed. Leaving the village behind, he kept to what looked like a cattle path through a dense green wilderness. Clarissa could tell it was supposed to be a road because the trees and underbrush had been cleared away on either side, but there was no other traffic to be seen.

"Where exactly are we going?" she asked with as much dignity as she could muster while being jolted and bounced on the hard wooden seat.

"To my farm."

"I know that. Where is it? What is it like?" Did the man never offer information freely? Clarissa studied him. He did not look like a farmer to her. It was true that his hands bore calluses from

hard work, but there was something about Jack Martin that made her think of elegant drawing rooms and ladies in satin and lace gowns with fans in their hands. She wondered what his real name was. No man who looked the way he did could possibly bear the pedestrian name of Jack Martin. Clarissa was certain that, if she asked him, he would only evade her question. She let her gaze travel from his hands to the profile dominated by that long slash of nose. Perhaps sensing her interested regard, he turned his head to look directly at her. Their eyes held for a moment, and each silently attempted to search out the secrets of the other.

"You are a most intriguing woman, Miss Clarissa Jane Cummings," he said softly. He smiled, and Clarissa, unable to prevent herself, smiled back at him. "If you know any Welsh," he said, "you will understand why I named my home Afon Farm. In Welsh, the word afon means river, and my land borders the Elk River."

"Are you Welsh?" she asked.

"My mother was." His smile disappeared and he returned to the original subject. "It is good farmland, and it will be remarkably profitable before much longer. Once the canal opens, Bohemia will grow into a larger village—some would tell you it will become a city—and those who live there or who pass through on the canal will gladly buy the produce from Afon Farm."

"You keep talking about the canal opening," she said. "When will that happen?"

"There has been water along the entire route since the Fourth of July," he said. "Unhappily, there is still a lot of work to be done, mostly in shoring up the sides. There are altogether too many landslides to allow shipping to move freely as yet. Landslides or not, however, the formal opening, complete with speeches, fireworks, and visiting dignitaries, is scheduled for mid-October."

"October of what year?" Clarissa could scarcely breathe for tension. She knew she could not continue to deny mounting evidence just because she did not want that evidence to be true. Suddenly, she was determined to know the truth, no matter how terrifying it might be.

"Why, in October of this year," Jack Martin said in answer to her question.

"Which is what year?"

"Miss Cummings, are you telling me that you don't know what year it is?" A smile flashed across his handsome features, then faded when he saw her sitting there with her hands clasped tightly together in her lap. The straw bonnet she wore lifted with the breeze of their forward motion; the green ribbons blew against his sleeve. Clarissa did not move to press the hat more firmly onto her head or to catch and control the ribbons.

"Please just tell me the exact date of the official opening of the canal," she ground out.

"The canal should be opened on the seventeenth day of October," he said, "in the year 1829."

"This is actually 1829?" Her voice was a broken whisper.

"That is so." He gave her a hard look. "Have you lost some time, Miss Cummings? Have you been seriously ill? Or have you suffered a head injury, so that there are days, or perhaps weeks, that you cannot recall?"

"Thank you for not asking if I'm insane. I know you have your doubts about me, but I am generally acknowledged to be a competent and reasonably sensible person." Clarissa took a long, shaky breath. "Mr. Martin, I am going to trust you, because I have to talk to someone about this, and there isn't anyone else."

"I will keep whatever confidence you care to entrust to me," he promised.

"Something is terribly wrong here, and I don't know what it is or how it happened. When I fell into the canal, the year was 1993," she said and paused to observe his reaction. So far as she could tell, there was none. He looked briefly at her, then turned his attention to the road ahead. Unable to read his thoughts, she went gamely on with her story. "You tell me that the year is now 1829. I am, naturally, a bit upset by the discrepancy."

Wishing she had Madam Rose's vial of smelling salts, Clarissa sternly repressed a mad desire to burst into wild laughter. But she knew she couldn't afford to lose control now. If she did, Jack Martin would surely decide that she really was crazy, and she needed him to believe her.

"Are you quite certain about this?" he asked with every appearance of perfect calm.

"Of course I'm certain! I know when I was born, and I know what day yesterday was. Ever since you pulled me out of the water, the evidence has been mounting that I am now in some previous time."

"What evidence?" He was remarkably calm.

He's a true aristocrat and a leader, Clarissa thought, not entirely irrelevantly. Absolutely nothing will upset or frighten him, or if it does, he will hide his emotions so no one will ever guess what he's feeling. He'd be a good person to have on my side in a fight.

"In my time," she said aloud, "the canal is much wider and the locks have been eliminated. Back Creek is just an inlet used for mooring pleasure boats. And at Chesapeake City there is a very high bridge over the canal. That's what we call your Bohemia Village," she added.

They rode on in silence for a while through sun-dappled shade. Jack Martin guided the horse with skilled hands. Clarissa sat watching him, waiting for some comment and trying to control a fear that could easily become hysteria.

"Well?" she prodded, unable to be patient any longer. "Tell me what you're thinking."

"That you do not behave in the way a well-bred young woman should," he said.

"I don't doubt that in the least. In my time, women are much less restricted. I can tell you," she added, grabbing at her bonnet, "that our

65

clothing is much more comfortable. You would probably find it indecent."

"Have you no idea by what means you came into the past?" he asked her.

"You do have a talent for sticking to the subject," she told him. "When I get upset, I tend to wander all over the place, conversationally speaking, and I babble. No, I don't know how I got here. I just went into the water in one century and came up one hundred sixty-four years in the past. This is so unbelievable!" She gulped back the scream she wanted to let loose. She knew that acting like a crazy woman wasn't going to help the situation. She had to try to stay calm.

"When you first regained consciousness, you mentioned ice and sleet," Jack Martin reminded her.

"It was January. There was an ice storm. That's why I couldn't stop my car and why I went over the edge and into the canal."

"I see."

"Do you? Mr. Martin, do you really believe me?" It seemed to Clarissa that her very life depended on his response.

"My every instinct tells me that such a story cannot be true," he said. "Yet if you are mad, then it is a remarkably consistent form of madness. While your behavior seems strange to me, everything you have said and done today makes sense when viewed in the light of your claim to be from the future. My God! The future!" He broke off, staring at her.

"Boggles the mind, doesn't it?" It was a stupid thing to say, but Clarissa was too badly shaken to care. Badly shaken—hell, she was on the verge of real hysterics.

"Indeed it does," he said. Then, after a moment's thought, he added, "Miss Cummings, let me warn you of something. I have a personal reason to be aware of the way in which unscrupulous men may exploit women."

"So have I." Clarissa lifted her chin, wondering what was coming next. In her heart she knew that one major reason why she wasn't screaming or crying or banging her fists on the cart seat in abject terror was because the man beside her was taking all of this so calmly. She clung to his calmness and self-control and obvious common sense as though those qualities were a lifeline he had tossed to her in the midst of a raging torrent.

"Then you will understand the advice I give you now," Jack Martin said. "I beg of you not to confide this amazing information to anyone else. Most people will not believe you. They will think that you are mad and that can only be to your detriment. Some few will believe you, and of those few, some will want to use you. If you are truly from the future, then you can provide valuable information about coming events."

"I hadn't thought of that. Until now, I've been too busy telling myself there must be some simple, rational explanation for what has happened. I haven't spared a minute to consider what it would mean if what I feared was actually true."

"Consider it now," he said, "and guard your speech and your actions."

"Yes, I think you are right. Does this mean you do believe me?" She looked at him with a hopeful gaze.

"I do not know what to believe," he told her. She noted his tightly drawn mouth and the set expression on his face, and she knew he was not really convinced.

"What should I do now?" she murmured, half to herself. "If I don't know how I got here, then I probably can't get back to my own time again, can I?"

He took her rhetorical questions as a request for more advice. "It seems to me that the only course for you is just what we have already agreed upon," he said. "You will stay at my farm for a while. No one will annoy you, and you will have freedom in which to decide what you want to do next. If you wish, while you are there, we can discuss your situation further, which ought to help you put your thoughts into better order. It will also help me come to some conclusion as to the truth of your claim to be from the future. In any case, I will not lock you up like a madwoman, nor will I harass you for more details until you are ready to divulge your entire story—for I do believe there is more to be said on this subject than you have yet revealed to me."

"I have told you everything I can remember about the accident," she responded. "Thank you for your generosity, Mr. Martin."

Forgetting that she did not want to be told by a man what to do, or that she did not want to touch any man ever again or to have any man touch her, she laid one hand on Jack Martin's arm. When he covered it with his own hand, she did not pull away.

# *Chapter Five*

They reached Afon Farm in late afternoon, when the lowering sun was sending shafts of mellow golden light through the thick vegetation, setting trees and bushes and wildflowers aglow. The farmhouse sat high on the crest of a hill, having been deliberately located by the builders in a spot where it would catch the cooling breezes from the river. On the gently sloping sides of the hill all but a few trees had been cut down and the land turned over to crops, corn on one side of the road leading to the house and wheat on the other. Both were tall and lush in the midsummer heat. In the orchard, peach and apple trees were heavily laden with ripening fruit. A rough-cut meadow surrounded the house itself.

The house was white, built square and low with a veranda across the front supported by wooden columns. A row of bright yellow marigolds bordered the veranda, enlivened by a clump of

orange tiger lilies at one corner, the lilies just beginning to burst into bloom.

They did not stop at the front of the house as Clarissa expected, but drove instead around the side to a large barn, its walls neatly white-washed like the house. In a paddock next to the barn, several horses raised their heads at the sound of cart wheels on the gravel drive. Just as the cart pulled to a stop, a middle-aged black man emerged from the barn.

"Good thing you're back on time, Mister Jack," the man said, grinning. "Sarah's just about got your supper ready, and she don't like keepin' food too long past the correct moment to serve it, as you and I both have cause to know."

"Sarah can stop worrying. I have brought both my appetite and a guest." Jack Martin helped Clarissa out of the cart. "Miss Cummings, this is Moses, who is stable master, field hand when needed, and all-around helper at all times."

"Hello, Moses." Clarissa could tell by the way he looked at her that Moses was wondering in what capacity she would act while at Afon Farm. Her host made no explanation, but launched instead into a series of instructions.

"Moses, you had better call Luke to help us unload those crates. I want to do it at once, before I eat. We can put everything into the barn and open the boxes tomorrow. I will take Miss Cummings's baggage myself."

"I'll see to the horse before I get Luke." Moses picked up the reins and led the cart through the large barn door.

71

With Clarissa's bandbox in one hand, Jack Martin took her by the elbow with his other hand, guiding her toward the back of the house, which was shaded by a veranda identical to the one across the front, except that here there was no row of flowers. Instead, a cluster of morning glory vines twined up two white columns and moonflower vines up the remaining two. From the edge of the veranda outward a brick courtyard had been laid as a way to keep mud and dust out of the house, for the kitchen was separate from the main building and there was a great deal of traffic through the rear doorway. The brick kitchen building sat at the far corner of the courtyard, reached by a covered walkway. Beyond the kitchen was the kitchen garden, enclosed by a low brick wall. Farther down the hill, close to the trees that formed a natural boundary between the cleared land and the river, stood two white cottages.

Clarissa wanted to see more, but her host hurried her into the main house. This building consisted of four rooms, two on each side of a wide center hall.

"It will be easy enough for you to find your way around," Jack Martin told Clarissa. "Here on your right at the back of the house is the dining room. Just in front of it is the parlor. Across the hall are two bedrooms. Mine is at the back. You will have the guest room at the front."

"I've seen old houses like this one," Clarissa said. "They have so many doors and windows that it's difficult to furnish them."

"The doors and windows are to let the breezes circulate." He stood back to allow her to pass into the guest room.

It was simply furnished. A low rope bed on a wooden frame was covered with a thin mattress and a colorful quilt. A blanket chest stained in bright swirls of green, red, and brown stood against one wall. Next to the chest a washstand had been placed, with a basin and pitcher on the top shelf. A small bedside table held a china candlestick in a blue-and-white pattern to match the basin and pitcher. Beneath the bed Clarissa saw a chamber pot in the same blue and white. There were three windows, each with plain white curtains. There was also a door connecting the room directly to the bedroom used by the master of the house. To Clarissa's relief, it was closed.

"You should be comfortable here," Jack Martin said, setting down her bandbox. "If you need anything, ask Sarah where it is. She will be glad to help you, though I am afraid at the moment she is busy preparing our evening meal."

"I can manage by myself," she assured him. "Can I get some water? The ride was dusty and I would like to wash up before eating."

"The pump is at the side of the courtyard, just next to the kitchen. The privy is in the field down the hill and well beyond the kitchen. There is an enclosed outside bath stall built against one kitchen wall. You can get warm water in the kitchen, but you will have to carry it yourself. Sarah is too busy to act as lady's maid."

"I told you I can manage on my own."

"Good. We are completely informal here. Make yourself at home, Miss Cummings."

Clarissa closed the bedroom door after him. She untied the ribbons and removed her bonnet, then stood paralyzed by the churning emotions she had valiantly kept under control since regaining consciousness beside the canal. Fear, confusion, horror, and a deep weariness all combined to keep her from thinking clearly. She stayed as she was for a long time, her hands clutching the ridiculous bonnet. She was unable to move, unable even to weep.

Then the quiet of the house began to seep into her perceptions. She could hear birds calling to each other outside the windows and men's voices in the distance briefly raised in laughter, but the house itself was empty and quiet. There was a profound peacefulness in the absence of noise. So much of her life had been spent against a background of sound, of piped-in music, of the noise of her aged automobile or the hum of other machinery, and the incessant chatter of radio or television. The lack of artificial sound was remarkably soothing. A knot deep inside her, a tightness of which she had scarcely been aware, slowly began to loosen, and with its unclenching, her ability to function as a thinking human being returned.

"All right," she said to herself at last, speaking in a whisper so as not to disturb the lovely quiet. "I have to stay here until I figure things out, and I can't say anything about being from the future

to anyone but Jack Martin. That means I will have to act as if I belong in this time. Therefore, if I want to clean my face and hands before eating, I will march right out to the pump and fill that old pitcher with water as if I know what I'm doing. I wonder if it's safe to drink the stuff? No, I'm not going to worry about it." She lifted the pitcher, which was surprisingly heavy, and hurried down the hall and out the back door.

The pump was easy to find. Getting water out of it wasn't so easy. Clarissa had never used a pump before. Hoping to avoid wetting her long skirt and soft, ballet-type slippers, she bent over from the waist, holding the pitcher under the spout with one hand, while with the other hand she tried to lift the pump handle.

"Put the pitcher on the ground and use both hands on the handle," a familiar male voice said behind her. Clarissa looked around to discover her host, stripped to the waist, a towel in one hand. His feet were bare and he was wearing a clean pair of tan breeches that fit him like a second skin from his waist to the curve of his calves. His hair was damp. He was obviously fresh from using that bath stall he had mentioned.

"Like this, Miss Cummings." Slinging the towel over his shoulder, he took the pitcher from Clarissa's unresisting fingers and set it down under the spout.

"I just used it, so it is primed. Now, pump," he ordered, stepping back a pace. "You must learn to do it on your own."

For a moment Clarissa could do nothing but stare at him. He was magnificent, hard muscled and sleek, like a finely bred stallion. On that thought she swallowed hard and reached for the pump handle.

"Pump smoothly and steadily," he instructed. "Up and down. Up and down. Keep on. It is easy once you find the rhythm."

Clarissa had already caught the motion and she fervently wished he would go away. His powerful, half-naked body, the steady pumping motion, the hypnotic sound of his low voice, and his repetitious words were all conspiring to threaten her shaky self-control. Between strokes of the pump handle she glanced at his face. She saw laughter in his eyes, and far worse, she thought she detected masculine erotic interest.

"Up and down," he said. "Up and down again."

"I understand!" she cried. "I can do it."

"Of course you can. Just don't give up. Now up and down again."

"Stop saying that!"

"Here it comes." His voice became almost a caress as water spurted from the pump spout, then began to emerge in a steady stream. "It always comes. After a certain number of strokes, it is inevitable."

"I'm sure it is!" She gave the handle one last downward push and watched water running over the edge of the pitcher.

"There you are," he said in the same caressing voice. "You learn quickly, Miss Cummings."

She fancied she could still see that dangerous glint in his eyes. Clarissa ran her tongue across dry lips and made herself look away from him.

"Thank you for your help." Seizing the handle of the pitcher, she attempted to lift it. The full pitcher, heavy when empty, was too much for her to carry in one hand. Releasing the skirt she had just lifted out of the dampness, Clarissa bent down, using both hands to pick up the overflowing pitcher.

"If you try to hold it out in front of you like that, it will only seem heavier," said Jack Martin, still watching her.

"If I hold it against my body, my dress will get wet," she pointed out. "My hem is already wet, my shoes are soaked, and I am hot and tired." She stopped, realizing that she was beginning to sound like a spoiled child. "Sorry," she said. "I didn't mean to scold."

"Just this once, I will help you." He took the pitcher from her and led the way to the guest bedroom. There he poured water into the basin. "I trust you will find the pitcher a little less unwieldy now that some of the water is gone."

"Thank you." Her voice was small and filled with the embarrassment she felt. His bare arm brushed against her as he turned toward the door. Some laughing devil dwelling deep inside her mind made her look full at him while his head was turned for a second, and she noted the bulge at his groin. He saw. She knew he had seen and noted her quick downward glance.

"Hurry and wash," he said. "You don't want to keep Sarah waiting when the meal is ready to serve."

Clarissa barely resisted the impulse to lift the pitcher in both hands and hurl it at him in retribution for the faint, knowing smile that lifted the corners of his mouth. She wondered how nineteenth-century ladies ever kept their tempers if all the men were like this one. Surprisingly, she kept her own temper under control.

"I will be as quick as I can," she told him sweetly.

"No more than half an hour," he said, his face impassive once more.

After he was gone, Clarissa began to wonder if she had only imagined the emotional content of the scene at the pump. Very likely she was seeing sexual interest where none existed. Jack Martin was only being kind and trying to help her adjust to a difficult situation. After all, her own husband had not been especially interested in sex with her, not after the first few months of marriage, and she had never been bothered by the kind of propositions that other women claimed to have received. A year or so after her marriage, Clarissa had finally come to the conclusion that she was a sexually uninteresting person. Thus, though the act of infidelity had been her husband's, she was all too ready to assume a large share of blame for the failure of her marriage. If she had been more interesting, more womanly, perhaps Rich wouldn't have looked elsewhere.

*Should have seen—should have done—failure—failure. . . .*

The words tumbled over and over in her mind each time she thought about Rich and the scene in their bedroom upon which she had stumbled. The rhythm of pumping, the spurting of the water, and above all, the caressing tone of Jack Martin's voice had brought that shameful scene back to her, and with it, a crushing sense of guilt.

It was not Jack Martin's fault. He knew nothing about Rich. He didn't even know that Clarissa was—had been—married. In this time, only Madam Rose knew, and Clarissa did not think she would tell anyone. Men were Madam Rose's business, so she would be an expert in keeping secrets from them. In any case, Madam Rose did not know all the details.

*In this time.* With a sense of relief Clarissa splashed cold water on her face and then looked up into the mirror on the wall behind the washstand. In this time her marital problems didn't exist. She wasn't even married, for how could there be a marriage with a man who would not be born for another one 134 years?

"It's gone," she said, smiling at her reflection. "Wiped out. It hasn't happened. As long as I stay in this time, I'm free of all that pain and I don't have to feel guilty anymore."

Refusing to listen to the quiet inner voice that told her the scars on her heart would not heal easily, she washed her hands, tidied her hair, and went to dinner with Jack Martin.

\*     \*     \*

Sarah was a handsome black woman in a dark blue calico dress and a spotless white apron. An orange-and-yellow printed scarf, twisted into an intricate pattern of folds, completely covered her hair. She arrived at the dining room door a minute or two after Clarissa had entered the room.

"Oh, my God—er, my goodness." Clarissa stared at the tray Sarah was carrying and then at the second tray borne by a slim teenager, who, from his resemblance to Sarah, was obviously her son. Clarissa looked from the food to her host. "Are the two of us expected to eat all of that?" she asked.

"Once you taste Sarah's cooking, you won't be able to restrain yourself," Jack Martin responded. "I found a true jewel on the day I discovered Sarah."

This compliment was greeted by a throaty chuckle from the woman in question. Sarah finished unloading her tray onto a polished mahogany sideboard that almost matched the color of Jack Martin's hair.

"Some men think of their stomachs before anything else," Sarah said.

"Gluttony is my besetting sin and you, Sarah, are my primary temptress." Jack Martin bent over a roasted chicken, sniffing appreciatively.

"Shame on you, Mister Jack. Sin is serious." But Sarah's chuckle rose again.

"Sarah, Luke, this is Miss Clarissa Cummings, who will be staying with us for a while," Jack

Martin said. "She is unfamiliar with farm life, so she may have questions for you about the way in which things are done here."

"We'll help you all we can, ma'am." Sarah gave Clarissa a long look, then nodded her head as if she approved of what she saw.

"Mama?" Luke was still holding his tray of food.

"Put that pie down at the end of the sideboard," Sarah instructed him. "Mister Jack, I'll bring the hot water for your tea in a short while so it won't be too cool when you're ready for it."

"Thank you, Sarah. Enjoy your own dinner." At Jack Martin's nod, Sarah and Luke departed.

"Miss Cummings, will you sit?" Clarissa looked around to discover her host holding a chair and looking at her expectantly. There was a place set at the head of the bare, gleaming table, where an armchair awaited the master of the house. On the master's right the place of honor had been set for a guest, and it was there that Jack Martin stood, the back of a smaller, armless chair in his hands.

Clarissa recalled Sunday dinners at her grandparents' house when she had been a girl, events at which all the men and boys were expected to hold chairs for the ladies present—and one particular cousin who used to push Clarissa's chair in so far that she was crushed against the edge of the table. No gentleman had held a chair for her since she was 11 years old. She slipped into the chair Jack Martin was holding. Unlike her mischievous cousin, he did not push it in too far.

"Do you prefer the leg meat or the breast?" he asked. Clarissa was gaping at the fine china and elegant silverware, so she did not answer him at once. "Miss Cummings?"

"Oh, the white meat please, but I can get it myself." She made as if to rise again, but his hand on her shoulder stopped her.

"You must learn our ways," he said. "I will serve you."

She wanted to protest that she liked the outside pieces of breast meat best and that she wanted the luscious-looking gravy ladled over the dressing, not the meat, but with a sense of abandon she leaned back in her chair and let him arrange her dinner plate for her. While he was at the sideboard she recalled another of her grandmother's rules. She took her elbows off the table, straightened her spine, and adjusted her shoulders so she was no longer lounging.

"Here you are." The plate set before her contained three narrow slices of rosemary-scented chicken breast taken from the outside, a scoop of cornbread dressing, a small pile of saffron-colored rice, and green beans with bits of bacon scattered over them. The gravy had been dribbled over the dressing and the rice, but not on the meat. Jack Martin's plate was heaped a good deal higher than Clarissa's and before the meal was over he had emptied it and filled it again and eaten all of the second helping of food.

Considering the many subjects they might have discussed, their dinner conversation was oddly impersonal, consisting mostly of delighted

comments on the food and Clarissa's questions about the farm, which her companion answered as briefly as possible.

In addition to the main course, there were incredibly light biscuits with fresh sweet butter, and then a salad of mixed greens and herbs followed by large slices of warm peach pie for dessert.

"Is this a special feast in my honor?" Clarissa asked.

"Sarah likes to cook," Jack Martin replied.

"It's wonderful. I haven't eaten this well in years."

"You have another enthusiastic admirer, Sarah."

Clarissa had not heard her come into the room. Sarah set a china teapot down on the sideboard before responding. "It's just fresh food, simply prepared," she said.

"That's why it's so good," Clarissa told her. "Some people think fancy sauces can disguise inferior food, but there is no substitute for fresh ingredients. At least, that's what my grandmother used to say. I can't tell you how many dreadful meals I've eaten that were supposed to be gourmet delights."

"I don't know what that means, Miz Cummings, but your grandmother sure was right about usin' fresh food."

When Sarah left them alone again, Jack Martin rose from the table to open a door in the sideboard and bring out a wooden tea chest lined with metal. He spooned leaves into the teapot,

gave the brew a stir, then replaced the little chest in the sideboard.

"When I first came here, I discovered that a family of field mice had moved indoors," he said, having noticed her questioning look. "They were connoisseurs. They ate most of my first packet of tea before I could evict them. I decided a metal-lined chest would keep out both mice and the summer dampness. I forgot to ask if you want cream or sugar for yours. Do you like tea?" He placed a silver tray containing the pot and two dainty china cups in front of Clarissa.

"I like it. I drink it plain, too." He obviously expected her to pour the tea for them. Feeling very much the grand lady, Clarissa did so.

"Madam Rose said I am too thin, but if I eat like this at every meal, I soon will need a corset after all," Clarissa noted. "Oh, dear. Somehow, I am absolutely certain that real ladies of this time do not mention corsets at the dinner table."

"They do not," he said, but she could tell he was trying not to smile. "Upon whatever subject you choose to discourse, Miss Cummings, allow me to tell you that I find your company most pleasant. Despite Sarah's fine cooking, I do not entirely enjoy my solitary evening meals."

"Then you live here alone?" Clarissa discovered that she was unaccountably pleased by this idea.

"Yes, except for my employees and the occasional guest. Do you care for Madeira?" he asked when the tea was finished.

"I don't even know what it is," she admitted.

"Then you must learn. Even the most delicate elderly ladies have been known to sip a glass on occasion." He poured the straw-colored wine from a crystal decanter into two stemmed glasses that looked awfully small to Clarissa. "Shall we enjoy it on the veranda?"

Again he held her chair for her. Then, with the wineglasses in hand, he led the way along the center hall to the front of the house.

"How quiet it is." Accepting the wine from him, Clarissa took a small sip. "Oh, that tastes nice." She stepped off the veranda onto the gravel path. There was still a faint glow low in the western sky, but overhead the stars were beginning to shine, and the sounds of a summer night gently charmed her ears. Insects chirruped, frogs peeped down by the river, and tree leaves rustled in a passing breeze.

"No boom boxes blasting away," she murmured, taking another ladylike sip of wine. "No fire sirens or train whistles. Just peace. It's so restful here. If I stay at Afon Farm for very long, I will learn to love it."

"Miss Cummings," he began.

"No." She stopped him. "You will probably tell me it's highly improper, but you cannot go on calling me Miss Cummings. Nor do I intend to call you Mr. Martin."

"I have known ladies married for years who still called their husbands mister," he said, moving to stand just a little too close to her. "What do you propose to call me?"

85

"I would like to use your real name." Clarissa stepped off the gravel and onto the rough grass, moving away from him.

"Jack will do nicely then." He joined her on the grass.

"We both know Jack Martin is not your real name." She felt him go absolutely still beside her. A long moment of charged silence grew between them.

"What do you mean by that?" His voice was quiet and even, but Clarissa wasn't fooled. She had made a guess about his name and she knew she had struck a nerve.

"You don't look like a Jack. Jack is a plumber, a mechanic, a man who works with his hands." Certainly not a man who ate off fine china and silver and who served Madeira wine at the end of a meal. Such a man ought to have a long and elegant-sounding name.

"I am those simple things," he said. "In addition, I am a farmer, a contractor of supplies to the canal project, a hunter, a carpenter, and a physician to the horses and cows when necessary. In short, a jack-of-all-trades. Therefore, I am in truth Jack."

"You aren't going to tell me, are you?"

"I am Jack Martin."

So sure was she that his name was not Jack Martin that she almost called him a liar, until she remembered the blazing anger he had displayed in Madam Rose's house when she had dared to question his word of honor. She looked up at his stark profile against the western sky and

knew instinctively that he would never break down under feminine questioning. He was too elusively mysterious to give up his secrets until he was ready to do so.

"Have it your way," she said. "I'll call you Jack. You may call me Clarissa. I give you permission, sir." She tried to sound lighthearted.

"I find Clarissa much too formal for so informal and unusual a lady." Unmistakable humor warmed his voice. "I shall call you Clary."

"Clary." She tested the sound of it, swallowed a little more wine, and said it again. "Clary. Yes, I like it."

"It suits you," he said. "Soft and light and quick. And not at all formal."

"You mean, not well behaved."

"Say, rather, unaccustomed to our ways. That will change if you remain here long. You are too clever not to adapt yourself quickly."

"No one has ever called me clever before." She finished her Madeira. "As for staying here, on a night like this, remaining in the past doesn't seem so terrible. I just wish I knew whether I can stay here or what will happen if I have to go back." She fell silent when he laid a hand on her shoulder.

"Have you considered the possibility that in the other time, in the future, you may be dead? If, as you claim, your cart fell into the canal, you may have died in that accident."

"Not cart. Car," she said, not wanting to think about his suggestion. "It was a car with an internal combustion engine. Don't ask me to explain

it to you, because I don't know how it works. There are a lot of things in the twentieth century that I don't understand."

"Clary."

"I can't be dead." Her voice rose on a frightened note. "I'm here. I'm breathing and talking and you can feel my shoulder beneath your hand."

"Yes," he murmured, his hand sliding around to the back of her neck. "You are here, and you do appear to be solid. Perhaps I ought to perform an experiment to make absolutely certain of your apparent presence." Before Clarissa could pull away, his lips brushed lightly across hers.

"No," she whimpered.

"Yes," he whispered. "Now, once more, just to be sure."

This second kiss was not a test. It was the real thing. Her hand with the wineglass still in it was crushed between them, but that didn't stop him. He held her head so she could not pull away while his mouth worked a long, slow magic on hers. Clarissa was so amazed by her own welcoming reaction to him that she did not try to stop what was happening until his tongue slid along the edge of her lower lip. Only then did she begin to fight him. He released her at once.

"How dare you?" she cried. "I do not want to be kissed or handled in any way at all by any man."

"Now you begin to sound like a woman of my time," he said. "What a pity."

"Here. Take your damned wineglass!" She thrust it at him. "Don't try to ply me with liquor a second time, because I won't fall for it again."

"Ply you with liquor?" He was laughing at her. "'Twas but a single, very small glass of wine. A baby could drink it and feel no ill effect."

"Just keep your hands off me!" She was shaking so hard that she was afraid she would fall to the ground, thus giving him an excuse to touch her again. She was horrified to realize that she wanted him to touch her. But she couldn't trust—not ever again, not after what Rich had done, not after what she had seen.

"At least we both know now that you are truly alive," Jack said. "Clary, if I offended you, I apologize. I thought you were willing to be kissed."

"Well, I am not willing!"

"I did not force you, Clary. I stopped the moment you resisted. Your reaction to what happened is greatly exaggerated." He paused, as if considering. Then, he asked, "Why is that? Did someone hurt you once? Or more than once? Is that why you are afraid of men? Or is it just me you find repulsive?"

"Yes. No. It's none of your business. I don't want to talk about this."

"It seems we both have secrets," he said. "Shall we agree not to question each other too closely? In that way, we ought to be able to continue a pleasant association while you are here."

"Why do you want me here anyway?" she demanded.

"I have told you why. There is no other suitable place for you to go."

"I don't believe that for one minute. There must be a town where I could find a room."

"You have seen Bohemia Village. There is another town just a bit larger at Newbold's Landing, which is the eastern end of the canal, and there are other settlements south of here. Most of the land in this area is forest or farmland. I fear you have no choice but to remain with me, Clary. I have promised that no harm will come to you, and I will keep my word."

"You still haven't explained why you want me here."

"How could I fail to be intrigued by a story such as yours? I would like to help you unravel the mystery of your sudden appearance at Bohemia Village."

"Is that really all that interests you?"

"I do confess to a certain sympathy toward young women who find themselves alone and abandoned through no fault of their own. Such women need the protection of a strong man."

"I don't!"

"Do you not?" When she made no response to his softly uttered question, he added, "Go to bed, Clary. After a day such as this one, you must be exhausted, and morning comes early at Afon Farm."

"I am tired." In fact, suddenly she wasn't sure she would be able to walk across the veranda

and into her room. She could not remember ever being so tired in all her life, and her head was aching. She moved slowly, heavily, dragging her feet.

"Good night, Clary."

She did not answer. She felt too drained to speak. It took all of her remaining energy to close her bedroom door and pull off her dress and underwear. Someone—most likely Sarah—had emptied and dried the basin on the washstand and unpacked her bandbox. The covers on the bed were turned down, and the white cotton nightgown and robe Madam Rose had given her were draped across the snowy sheets. Clarissa pulled the pins out of her hair, but she was too tired to brush it. She slipped the nightgown over her head. She was asleep before she fell onto the bed.

She wakened much later to the sound of a booted foot crunching on the gravel at the front of the house. The smell of tobacco came to her on the still night air. She heard a sigh, a footfall on the front veranda, a step in the hall, and then all was silent and she slipped back into sleep. She did not open her eyes again until a rooster crowed just before dawn to start the new day.

# Chapter Six

"You don't need to come to the kitchen for breakfast, Miz Clary." Sarah looked up from the biscuit dough she was rolling out on the scrubbed pine table. "I'll gladly carry it to you in the dining room."

"I like it better here." Clary smiled to herself at the way Sarah addressed her. Apparently, Jack had informed his staff that they were to use his new name for her. She didn't mind a bit. With a new name she felt almost reborn, fresh and clean, with no unhappy past to shadow her days. She looked appreciatively at the whitewashed kitchen walls and the yellow-and-white-checkered curtains. A pot of chives sat on the wide windowsill next to a peach pie fresh from the oven, set there to cool. "The kitchen is so pretty with the morning sun coming in the window."

"The sun'll be hot later." Deftly, Sarah cut the

biscuits into rounds and arranged them in a pan. "The men started work early, while it was still cool. They'll be back soon, hungry as wildcats in winter." With the biscuits safely in the brick oven next to the fireplace to bake, Sarah began to slice a slab of bacon into thin rashers.

"Let me help you." Clary glanced around the kitchen, trying to find something that needed doing, that she would know how to do. She took a step toward the bacon, but stopped with one hand still outstretched when the knife Sarah was holding plunged downward point first into the tabletop.

"This kitchen is my domain," Sarah declared, fists on her hips. "I don't need outsiders in here, tellin' me how to do my work."

Clary burst into laughter. She laughed so hard she had to sit down. She dropped onto one of the sturdy wooden chairs on the other side of the table from Sarah and held her sides, laughing until she was in tears. Sarah leaned across the table, both hands spread out on top of it.

"What's wrong with you?" she demanded.

"I wish I knew," Clary answered, wiping tears off her cheeks. "Perhaps it's delayed hysteria. Weren't you told how Mr. Martin pulled me out of the canal yesterday?"

"I heard. That don't explain what you're doin' here or why you're tryin' to push me out of my kitchen."

"I'm not. I was hoping to make myself useful and also hoping that you would be willing to teach me how to cook in a kitchen like this. I

93

don't know anything about it. I'm a terrible cook at the best of times."

"Can't cook? Why not? Didn't your mama ever teach you anything a grown woman's supposed to know?"

"I guess not, because I seem to be seriously lacking in womanly accomplishments." In kitchen and bedroom alike, Clary added silently to herself. "You see, Sarah, I have no family, no friends in this area, and no home, which is why Mr. Martin invited me to stay here for a while as his guest. But it seems to me that everyone at Afon Farm has work to do, so I think I ought to try to make myself useful, too."

"You want to be useful," Sarah repeated. Her eyes narrowed. "Are you one of the girls from Madam Rose's?"

"Far from it." Clary stifled renewed laughter at the thought. It was a minute or two before she could continue. "I have only the most basic idea of what those ladies do to earn their living."

"It's just as well." Sarah pulled the knife out of the tabletop and went back to slicing the bacon. "From what Dancy says, you don't want to know too much about the goings-on in a place like that."

"You know Dancy?" Clary asked in surprise. She was even more surprised by Sarah's answer.

"Dancy is Moses's brother. He's not suited to farm work. He didn't want to stay here, so Mister Jack convinced Madam Rose to take him on at her place. It's close enough that we can see Dancy from time to time, and he's done quite

well there, though I wish there were another place where he could get honest work."

"Madam Rose told me that Dancy is her partner," Clary noted.

"You want to be useful? Then don't just sit there and talk. Use this cloth to wipe off the table and then set it before those starvin' men arrive. The dishes are in the cupboard in the corner, cutlery's in the drawer underneath." Sarah arranged bacon slices in a black iron skillet, then put the skillet on the wood-burning cookstove. Thinly sliced steaks went into a second skillet. The coffeepot sat on a lower level of the cookstove, where it would stay hot until the coffee was wanted.

Clary busied herself with dishes, spoons, and knives, and while the two women worked, Sarah talked. Clary had the impression that Sarah was lonely for female company. The fact that her companion at the moment was a stranger and a white woman didn't seem to matter.

"Madam Rose made Dancy her partner after he saved her life and her business," Sarah said. "Those men diggin' the canal drink an awful lot of beer and whiskey, and Madam Rose's is the only place around here to buy it. There was a terrible brawl one night. The house was nearly destroyed, all the furniture broken, and one of the men involved held Madam Rose with a knife at her throat. But before he could hurt her, Dancy crept up behind the man and hit him over the head with a shovel. Then he tossed out the rest of the brawlers and helped Madam

Rose to clean up the place and stood guard for the remainder of the night so she could sleep."

"So Madam Rose made Dancy a partner out of gratitude?" Clary was wide-eyed at this story.

"She calls him her partner. I'm not sure just what the exact arrangement is. There's all kinds of laws about black folks ownin' property, so it may be that Mister Jack is the legal partner, but if so, he sees to it that Dancy gets the money that's due him. And to give her credit, Madam Rose has always been fair to Dancy, too."

"She struck me as a fair woman," Clary agreed, "but awfully tough. I guess she has to be to survive in her business."

"She ought to get out of that business before she gets killed. Or put in jail." Sarah began turning the bacon slices with a long-handled fork. "You want to put the butter and the honey on the table, Miz Clary? There's strawberry jam, too. Mister Jack likes it on his biscuits."

"Sarah." Clary paused, honey jar in hand, watching Sarah to see what effect her words would have. "Madam Rose said Dancy is a freed slave."

"That's right." Sarah checked the steaks, which were sizzling in their own pan.

"Forgive me if I'm overstepping a boundary I don't see," Clary said, "but are you a slave? And what about Moses and Luke?"

"We used to be."

"But you're not now?"

"Not since Mister Jack bought us."

"He bought you?" Clary sat down hard on the

nearest chair. "He actually went to a sale and bought human beings?"

"Happens all the time. Lots of people think black folks aren't human."

Clary almost bit her tongue. There were a dozen things she wanted to say, but she reminded herself that this was the early nineteenth century when slavery was not uncommon. Even a man as obviously well educated and cultivated as Jack Martin might own slaves and think nothing of the human cost.

"Sarah, would you tell me about it? About the sale and how you came to be free?"

"It happened about five years ago. Mister Jack went down to Carolina lookin' for strong laborers 'cause he needed help on the farm. Nobody round here wanted to hire out to work on a farm, 'cause there was much better pay diggin' the canal.

"Dancy was up for sale first. You've seen him. He's big and strong and looks like he'd be a good field hand. But Dancy can't stand bein' out in the sun all day. It makes him sick. Anyway, Mister Jack didn't know that, and if the auctioneer knew it, he wasn't talkin', so Mister Jack bought Dancy. Then Moses went on the block."

"Just Moses?" Clary was horrified. "You were going to be sold separately? I've read about this kind of thing. How awful for you."

"Luke was just a little boy then, and he started cryin', 'cause he thought he was never goin' to see his daddy again," Sarah said, continuing in the same matter-of-fact voice in which she had

related all of her family's history. "Mister Jack noticed Luke and came over to us and asked what the trouble was and if we were bein' mistreated. When he learned we were a family, he asked me just one question. 'Sarah,' he said, 'can you cook and clean house?' I told him, 'I'm the best cook you'll ever get.' So he bought all four of us and brought us back here. Treated us real good on the trip, too."

"When were you freed?" Clary asked, enthralled by what she was hearing.

"I'm comin' to that. Here, the biscuits are done. Watch your fingers. The pan's hot. Put a napkin into that basket and pile the biscuits into it. Then pour some cream into the blue pitcher.

"When we got to the farm here," Sarah said, "Mister Jack showed us around and told us we could live in those two cottages just down the hill. Then he offered us a bargain. He said the farm hadn't been worked for years, but he wanted to make it profitable and he needed help to do that. He said he didn't believe slaves would work as well as free men and women who had something to gain from their efforts, so he'd give us each our freedom and a plot of land for our own. In return, the men were to work in the fields and with the livestock, and I was to be housekeeper and cook. Then, when each harvest was in, he'd pay us a portion of the profits in cash."

"He didn't have to do that, did he?" Clary wondered where Jack Martin had acquired such enlightened ideas. For the time in which he lived,

his generosity to people he could have kept as slaves was truly astonishing.

"No, he didn't have to be so good to us," Sarah agreed. "'Course, Dancy didn't last too long. Like I said, he can't stand bein' in the sun all day, which is why Mister Jack arranged for him to work for Madam Rose, so he could be indoors most of the time. Mister Jack is in Bohemia Village quite often, so he keeps a sharp eye on Dancy to be sure he's all right. Dancy needs a bit of extra help, you see, 'cause he's not as strong as he looks. Moses, now—Moses is the strongest man I've ever known." Sarah's mouth curved in an affectionate smile as Moses walked into the kitchen.

"Strong," he said with a deep, rumbling laugh, "and half starved after puttin' in a full day's work before breakfast."

Behind Moses came Luke. Jack followed a minute later, doffing his hat as he came through the door. He was dressed like the other two in boots, denim overalls, and a blue work shirt.

"Did you all wash up?" Sarah demanded. "Nobody sits at my table with dirty hands. Luke, let me see your hands. You, too, Moses."

"Don't you want to see my hands?" Laughing at his cook, Jack held his own hands out for inspection along with Moses and Luke.

"I guess you'll do." Sarah nodded her approval. "Sit down now. It's almost ready."

Jack's eyes met Clary's with a question. She knew he was thinking about the way he had kissed her the night before, because that kiss

was uppermost in her mind, too. But after hearing Sarah's story, she had a very different opinion of him. Whatever else he might be, Jack Martin had a heart big enough to be generous to many different kinds of people, including a desperate slave family. Including herself, too. Perhaps he had a thing about helping people in trouble. Clary gave him a bright smile. She thought he looked relieved.

"Since time immemorial," he said with a wink at Clary, "cooks have ruled their kitchens with iron hands."

"Clean iron hands," Sarah said, breaking eggs into the skillet next to the bacon. She flashed a quick look in Clary's direction. "And sometimes cooks take on apprentices. Miz Clary, you better get those steaks before they burn, 'cause I only have two hands here. You can pour the coffee, too."

They all ate together, sitting around the kitchen table. There was no point in separating the master of the house from his workers, for they were all too busy to consider social distinctions. And while Clary knew that racial distinctions would have kept most white landowners of that time from eating with their black farm workers, Jack seemed oblivious to that particular difference.

"You think today and tomorrow will be enough for the peaches?" Sarah asked.

"It'll take another three days at least to get the earliest ripening ones picked," Moses answered her. "After that, half a day every other day should

do it, so we can work on the other crops, too. Sarah, you goin' to help us?"

"Soon as I clean up the kitchen," Sarah said.

"Well," Clary put in, "if everyone else is going to be out in the orchard picking peaches, I'm going to be there, too."

"It's hot work," Sarah cautioned.

"If it's not too hot for the four of you, then it's not too hot for me," she insisted.

"You'll need a big hat." Jack was watching her intently but he made no objections.

"And some work clothes," Clary added. "Sarah, are there any old overalls I could wear? I don't care how ragged they might be. I just want something I can move in easily. This long skirt is very hampering."

"No." Jack sent her a look that she was sure was meant to make her give up at once her outrageous idea of wearing men's clothes.

"Yes," she said, lifting her chin and trying to appear stern and determined. "There was a *time*, Jack, when I practically lived in blue jeans."

"Was there?" Hearing the emphasis she put on the word time, he nodded. "Very well, then. If it is what you are accustomed to wearing, I will not attempt to stop you. Sarah, outfit her as best you can, and we shall see how long she lasts in the heat."

Clary lasted longer than the rest of them expected. Clad in a pair of clean but threadbare overalls that Luke had outgrown, a pair of boots discovered in the house when Jack first had come

**101**

there, one of Jack's own shirts with the sleeves rolled up, and a pair of his thick winter stockings to pad out the too-long boots, she worked beside Jack for the greater part of that day, stopping only to help Sarah carry a cold midday meal out from the kitchen so they could eat beneath the peach trees.

"What do you do with all of these peaches?" she asked in the late afternoon as she and Jack lifted yet another basket into the cart. "We can't possibly eat every one before they spoil."

"Moses and I will take a couple of cartloads into Bohemia Village," he answered. "There will be boats picking up goods to take to Baltimore to sell. They will be eager for fresh peaches."

"Is that how you usually dispose of your extra peaches?"

"Until the canal is fully useable." Jack's eyes were gleaming at the prospect. "Sam MacKenzie and I have talked about buying our own boat. We could load it with produce from Afon Farm and fill out the cargo with smaller loads of goods that people will drop off at Bohemia. It will be a while before the canal is safe for larger boats, but when it is finally completed, we will be able to sail through to the Delaware River and then upriver to Philadelphia in only three or four days."

"Where you and Sam will both immediately become fabulously wealthy peach barons!" Clary teased. Seeing Jack relaxed and laughing, with his blue shirt open at the neck and the gleaming sun on his dark hair when he doffed his hat for a moment to wipe his brow, she

decided to take a chance. "I'll bet you never picked peaches in England, did you?"

She wasn't sure what kind of reaction she expected from him. He might ignore her comment or accuse her of intruding into his mysterious past, where he had warned her not to go. Or he could just laugh off her remark and go on picking peaches. What he did was meet her eyes squarely before he gave her a direct and simple answer.

"I never picked peaches or anything else from a tree in England. I never did any useful work there." Clapping his straw planter's hat back onto his head, he adjusted the overloaded basket they had just moved so it wouldn't tip over and spill the peaches, and then he straightened up to gaze over his land, taking in the sun-drenched fields and the blue river just visible here and there between the trees. The look on his face was one of deep contentment.

"I have learned a lot in these last few years since I came here to live," he said. "I like America. There is a sense of great freedom here. I feel as if I could explore to the very horizon and beyond and never meet an obstacle I could not conquer. This is good land. There is great satisfaction in farming it."

Clary saw that he was perfectly serious and not the least bit annoyed with her. "You've become an American," she said softly.

"Perhaps I have, in spite of myself." He grinned at her, reaching out to push her wide-brimmed hat down farther onto her head. "Watch out for

the sun. It's turning your nose red. Let us get back to work, Clary. We must take advantage of the good weather."

"We could eat in the kitchen," Clary said. "It's not right to expect Sarah to work in the fields all day and then come back and cook our dinner and serve it to us."

"Don't even suggest it to her," Jack warned. "Sarah's sense of what is right and proper would be deeply offended. It is bad enough that I—and now you—eat breakfast in the kitchen during the harvest. Trust me, Clary. I know her better than you do."

"All right. You're the boss."

"See that you don't forget it."

Clary laughed and headed for her bedroom. Jack's mood had lightened even more as the day wore on, until his eyes were dancing with mischief and his teasing had Sarah chuckling and Luke cracking up with youthful laughter. Clary had the feeling that this was the way Jack and his employees usually worked together, with good humor and hard physical effort. They appeared to be perfectly comfortable with each other and their easy acceptance of her felt wonderful to Clary. Her arms and shoulders ached, she knew her nose was sunburned, she could hardly wait to get out of her dusty work clothes and into the bath stall next to the kitchen—and it had been a long, long time since she had been so content.

She pulled off her clothes, folding them into a pile to put on again the following morning when

the peach harvest would continue. After shrugging into her wrapper, she grabbed her towel and a cake of soap. Madam Rose had included a bar of rose-scented soap in the bandbox she had made up for Clary, but Clary thought after a day in the fields she would need something stronger. Sarah's homemade soap would be just the thing.

She pumped two buckets of water and took them to the bathstall. Then, after hanging the towel and robe on the hooks outside the entrance, she began to soap herself. The bath stall was just a J-shaped curve of brick with a clean gravel floor and no roof. The bricks looked different in color from those that made up the kitchen wall to which the stall was attached. This made Clary think the bathing arrangement was a later addition, probably built after Jack had arrived at the farm. Even without a door, she had a certain amount of privacy, for anyone wishing to enter could see the towel and clothing hung on the hooks and would know the stall was already occupied. It might be cold to take a bath there in winter, but on a hot summer evening it was just fine. Clary didn't even mind using cold water. Her hair and body lathered to her satisfaction, she dumped a bucket of water over herself to rinse off the soap. With her hair dripping into her eyes, she blindly reached around the corner of the entrance, groping for her towel. It was put into her hand.

"Give it back when you are dry, and I will hand you the wrapper next," Jack said.

"You aren't supposed to be here," she told him.

"Madam, I am next in line."

Quickly she dried herself, then wrapped the towel around her wet hair. When she put her hand around the corner again, Jack gave her the wrapper.

"Go away," she ordered, "and stay away until I have finished."

"Am I an inadequate assistant?" She could hear the laughter in his voice.

"I don't need an assistant. I can take my own bath and dry myself. Go away!"

The silence following this command made her assume that he had obeyed her. With the sash of the wrapper tightly knotted about her waist, she lifted the long skirt off the wet ground and clutched the neckline up to her chin. Then she stepped around the curve of brick. He was waiting for her, one arm braced on the wall.

"I trust you are feeling better now," he said, his gray eyes twinkling.

"Much." She tried to step around him but he was too big and the bath stall entrance was too narrow.

"Thank you for today, Clary. You were a great help."

"Even though I shocked everyone by wearing men's clothes?"

"Did you really wear them frequently in the other time?"

"Almost every day."

"You must have driven to madness every man

106

who saw you in such garb." He took his hand off the brick wall. With one finger he tilted her chin upward. She saw his mouth soften and knew he was about to kiss her. With a hiss of sharply indrawn breath, she stepped backward and his hand dropped. "You need not fear me, Clary. I would never do anything to hurt you."

"So you say. Prove it. Let me out of here."

He moved aside so she could pass him. She stepped out of the shadow of the curving brick wall into early evening sunlight. He followed her.

"While there is a certain piquant charm to the sight of a lovely woman in men's clothing," he murmured, "I find that I much prefer to see you in more feminine attire."

It was then that Clary realized how the slanting rays of the sun must be shining through the thin cotton wrapper, outlining her figure. To make matters worse, she was holding the skirt at knee height. She was more completely covered than she ever was at the beach, and certainly more covered than when Jack had pulled her out of the canal, yet she felt indecently exposed. She dropped the fistful of cloth she was holding, letting the wrapper fall down to her ankles, and then she stalked away to the house without looking back to see if he was still watching.

"Infuriating man," she muttered, safe in her room and rubbing her hair so hard with the towel that she almost made her head ache. "Those long looks, those innuendos—who the hell does he think he is? Oh, no—pardon me, Madam Rose—

forgive me, Mr. Jack Martin. I meant to say, who in heaven's name does he think he is to treat a lady in such a shocking manner?"

She began to laugh at herself. She couldn't help it. She couldn't decide whether she ought to be an outspoken, crude-mouthed, late-twentieth-century woman or an overly genteel nineteenth-century lady. Furthermore, if she were perfectly honest with herself she would admit that she found Jack Martin's open interest in her flattering, and although she ought to know better than to trust any man, she believed him in her heart when he said he wouldn't do anything to hurt her.

That night Sarah served up a baked ham, sweet potatoes, greens, and fresh corn bread for dinner with a warm peach cobbler for dessert. Jack was the perfect host, humorous, relaxed, and only mildly, politely flirtatious. Clary enjoyed herself so much that she was more than a little disappointed when he suggested an early bedtime. Then she was annoyed with herself for being disappointed. She had made it clear to him that she did not want anything romantic to happen between them, and he was taking her at her word. There was no logical reason why her feelings should be hurt when he did not suggest an interval beneath the stars with glasses of Madeira wine. On this evening he didn't even bring out the wine; he just escorted her to her bedroom door and bid her good night.

Tired as she was, she could not fall asleep. She lay with her eyes closed while scenes from the

day just past replayed themselves like a movie through her thoughts: Sarah's story of slavery and freedom, the backbreaking work of picking peaches, Jack's laughter and easy manners with his employees, the way he treated Clary, herself. Who was he, this strange Englishman who had bought and then freed an entire family, who had dragged a half-drowned and desperately unhappy woman out of a canal and taken her home with him and treated her as if she were someone fascinating and desirable and yet did not force himself upon her?

She heard a footstep on the gravel in front of the house. Recalling the sounds of the previous night she got out of bed and on silent bare feet went to the open window. Jack was standing a few paces beyond the veranda with his head thrown back, gazing up at the stars. He held something in his hand, and when he put it in his mouth she realized that he was smoking a pipe. A trace of tobacco smoke drifted her way.

"I ought to tell him what twentieth-century medicine has discovered about the dangers of tobacco," she murmured. She almost climbed over the windowsill to warn him right then. She had one knee on the sill when she stopped herself. "Clarissa Cummings, what are you doing? This is an excuse to go out there and stand under the stars with him until he kisses you. And then you'll tell him that you don't want him to touch you. And he'll know—and you'll know it, too—that all you want is for him to put his arms around you and hold you tight and tell you that he'll never

let anything hurt you again. And you know you can't trust or depend on any man, not even this one. Not ever again."

She made herself go back to bed and forced herself to stay there, lying stiff and breathless, listening for the slightest sound Jack produced as he strolled on grass or gravel. When she heard his step on the wooden veranda floor she closed her eyes, feigning slumber as if he could see her through the bedroom wall and the closed door. She did not sleep until long after his own bedroom door had clicked softly shut and all movement in his room had ceased.

The next day, they picked peaches again, not stopping until it was nearly dark, and the evening was a repetition of the previous one. On Clary's fourth day at Afon Farm, she and Sarah did not go to the orchard to pick. Instead, they sorted the peaches, keeping the ripest ones for immediate use and packing the less ripe fruit into the baskets in which they would be transported to Bohemia Village to be sold. In late morning Jack and Luke drove the loaded cart into Bohemia Village, not returning until dark.

While they were gone Moses attended to various farm chores before going into the orchard to pick peaches by himself. Meanwhile, Clary and Sarah made peach jam in a huge old kettle. When the jam was finished they moved on to another method of preserving summer's sweet gifts. Jack kept a barrel of Kentucky whiskey in the pantry that opened off the kitchen, and the

women used some of it to mix with honey. Then they packed the peeled, halved peaches along with whole cloves and sticks of cinnamon into crocks and covered them with the honey and whiskey mixture.

"This is bourbon." Clary dipped a finger into the whiskey and licked off the drop that clung to her fingertip. "It's pretty raw stuff, too."

"Just you wait," Sarah told her. "What's in the crocks will be nice and mellow by Christmastime, with all the peach juices bein' drawn out by the honey and those spices flavorin' everything. Mmm, I can almost taste it now."

"I wonder if I'll still be here at Christmas." With the crocks full and the edges wiped clean with a damp cloth, Sarah put the lids on and they carried the crocks into the pantry.

"Where else would you go?" Sarah asked.

"I don't know. Even if I went back, I don't have a home anymore."

"Then you just stay here. There's few better places. And," Sarah said, handing Clary half-a-dozen ears of corn to husk, "you've turned into real good kitchen help. I'd hate to lose you. Now take those ears outside so you don't get scraps all over my clean floor. And be sure you pick off all the silk. Then bring them back here and scrape off the kernels into the big bowl while I fire up the oven."

It seemed to Clary that every crop on the farm needed harvesting at the same time, but Jack and Moses appeared to have an agreed-upon

schedule, so they worked methodically. Peaches, corn, wheat, beans, early apples, and even a small crop of tomatoes were gathered, though Sarah informed Clary that few people cared to eat tomatoes, fearing they might be poisonous.

"Black folks know better," Sarah said. "Tomatoes never hurt us, and Mister Jack likes them." She added the vegetable to a tasty rice dish and did not laugh when Clary insisted on eating raw slices as a salad.

Sarah showed Clary how to cut the herbs that grew in the kitchen garden, how to tie them into bunches and hang them from the storeroom rafters to dry for winter use. Every third or fourth day Jack took a cart laden with produce into Bohemia Village. Each day Clary and Sarah worked together in the kitchen or, when they were needed, in the fields with the men.

The hot, sunny days fell into a pattern of early rising, long hours of work broken by a cold midday meal, and brief, cool evenings when Clary was too tired to care that Jack never talked about himself or mentioned his past or his family or friends—but then, she didn't talk about her past life either. Nor did Jack make any further romantic overtures toward her. He was doing what she wanted him to do—he was obeying her order to leave her alone—and for that she told herself she was grateful. For the first time in years no one was making any emotional demands of her. Thus, for the better part of a month, she existed in a timeless world of steady work and dreamless sleep in which she rarely

thought about her old life. If she recognized that certain deep and bitter wounds from that life were beginning to heal, she did not dwell on the thought.

On one particularly hot afternoon Jack returned from Bohemia Village early and walked into the kitchen, where Clary and Sarah were working.

"I can scarcely believe my eyes," he said. "Clary, you are wearing a dress."

"My overalls are in the laundry." She looked down at her flower-sprigged gray cotton dress, which was somewhat faded after several washings.

"What do I smell?" Jack looked around the kitchen, then at Sarah.

"Bread fresh from the oven," Sarah told him, "and three pies just put in to bake. Two apple and one peach, so you'll have a choice. The ham'll go in next for a nice, slow baking, since tomorrow's the Sabbath." The nearest church was too far away for regular attendance, but Sarah refused to cook or bake on Sundays, and she spent the day quietly in the neat white cottage down the hill, where she and Moses and Luke lived.

"Clary," Jack said, "would you like to go on a picnic?"

"You're not plannin' to take her out in that leaky rowboat, are you?" Sarah asked. "You thinkin' of spendin' the evenin' fishin'?"

"If I catch anything, I shall ask Clary to clean it down by the river," he promised solemnly, ignoring Clary's disgusted gasp of refusal. "Your

113

kitchen will remain spotless until Monday morning, Sarah. Clary, get your hat."

"I'm not sure I want to go," she said. She could see Sarah looking from her to Jack with an expression that reminded her of a mother worried about teenagers about to go off on a date.

"I was only teasing. I promise not to make you clean the fish," Jack said to Clary. "It will be much cooler by the river. You will come to no harm in my rowboat. I am an accomplished sailor."

Clary stood in the hot kitchen, thinking about cool river water and the shade provided by the tall trees that edged the water. If she spent an hour or two alone with Jack, away from the farm and his constant chores, perhaps she could coax information out of him about his own past and why he was living alone in Maryland. It was also possible that together they might be able to think of a reason for her presence in the early nineteenth century. She had put such questions aside for weeks. Now that she had a few minutes to think about them, they began to nag at her mind once more.

"Go on," Jack said to her. "Find your hat while I supervise the packing of our meal to be sure we don't open the basket later to discover we have been given something I don't like."

"Supervise, huh?" Sarah gave vent to a hearty chuckle. "There's nothin' you don't like. You eat everything I set in front of you, and you know it."

"That is because you are such a marvelous cook. Now let me see what treasures you have stored in the pantry."

"Mister Jack, you come out of there! Don't you go disturbin' my arrangements."

Shaking her head in amusement at Jack's teasing and Sarah's affectionate fussing, Clary headed across the brick courtyard to the house. In her room she snatched up the straw hat she usually wore when working in the fields, then paused to take a quick glance in the mirror. That morning she had tied her long dark hair back with a ribbon, but in the heat of the kitchen, curls had escaped to cluster about her face. Thanks to the herbal concoctions Sarah insisted she use every day, her skin was only lightly tanned in spite of long hours in the sun. Her cheeks were flushed, her eyes sparkling. She looked like a woman on her way to meet her lover.

She ran all the way back to the kitchen.

# *Chapter Seven*

"Sarah was right." Clary walked across the narrow sandy beach to examine the rowboat in question. "This thing doesn't look seaworthy to me."

"Obviously, you are unacquainted with the finer points of shipbuilding. This thing, madam, is an excellent little craft. She handles beautifully. You will be perfectly safe in her." While he spoke Jack flipped the dilapidated-looking boat right side up, spread the blanket in the stern, and deposited the picnic basket in the bow. He gave the bow a shove, sliding the rowboat off the beach and halfway into the water. His preparations completed, he put out his hand to Clary to help her into the boat.

"Can you absolutely guarantee that it won't sink?" Clary was still regarding the rowboat with trepidation.

"You have my word of honor on it."

She saw the smile in his eyes and knew he would tease her for at least a week if she refused to go with him. She took his hand and let him guide her over the side. After making certain that she was comfortably seated on the blanket with her back against the stern, Jack pushed on the bow again, sending the boat into the river. When he jumped in Clary came bolt upright, clutching at the sides, afraid they would tip over. She wasn't afraid of the water—she knew how to swim. It was just that she felt helpless while wearing long skirts. She was used to a bathing suit or a pair of shorts when she was around boats. She was sure that, if she fell in dressed as she was, the weight of her skirts would drag her down and she would drown.

There was no question that Jack knew what he was doing. After a few minutes Clary sat back and relaxed, watching the easy motions of his arms as he rowed upriver. His ever present planter's hat shielded his face from the sun and shaded the expression of his eyes from her, so she had no hint as to what he was thinking. As for herself, she was all too aware of his masculine presence and of the fact that they were completely alone. There were no other boats to be seen and no sign that humans lived anywhere near the river.

"This is a tributary of the Elk River," Jack said, breaking the long silence between them with neutral conversation. "Afon Farm is on a point of land between the two."

"Were you serious about fishing?" Trying to

appear less nervous than she was, Clary let one hand dangle carelessly into the water. When she looked over the side she could see that it was remarkably clean water.

"Not really. I was only teasing Sarah. We can make another excursion to fish if you like on some later day. I thought this would be a good opportunity for us to talk without interruptions." Having reached the middle of the river some distance upstream from where they had embarked, he shipped the oars, then reached around to lift the picnic basket out of the bow. He set the basket on the bench next to him before, with a graceful movement that barely rocked the boat, he slipped off the bench to sit beside her.

"Is this safe?" Clary wasn't talking about the boat rocking too badly and dumping them into the river. She was more concerned about Jack's disturbing nearness. There was so little space in the stern of the rowboat that his right arm and thigh were pressed against her left side.

"That depends," he said. "If you bounce around and try to move farther to starboard, we may very well tip over and capsize. If, on the other hand, you have the good sense to sit quietly and eat the cold collation I have provided, you should stay dry."

But not necessarily safe, she thought, accepting the napkin he handed to her. Jack pulled a wine bottle and two stemmed glasses out of the picnic basket.

"Uncorked while still safely ashore," he said, showing her that the cork had been pushed part-

ly back into the bottle. "Now, my dear, if you will hold the glasses steady."

"Wine in a rowboat, served in fine crystal?" Clary shook her head. "Jack Martin, you are crazy." Nevertheless, she held the glasses as ordered while he poured a pale wine into them.

"I am cut to the quick by your assessment of my mental capacities. How can you so cruelly insult the very person who has made this charming meal possible?"

"Just bad manners, I guess." She tried the wine and found it delightfully refreshing.

"On the contrary, I perceive nothing wrong with your manners." Jack quirked an eyebrow at her. "No, 'tis rather some unhappy event in your past that has made you so mistrustful of men, a matter which I plan to investigate this very evening."

"Why spoil a lovely picnic by talking about unpleasant subjects?"

"Then you do admit this open-air feast was a good idea?"

"So far it is." Clary was thinking furiously. If she could make Jack talk about himself she would divert his attention from her own past while at the same time learning more about him. She was continually fascinated by the way he could change in a moment or two from a serious, practical farmer who was not afraid to get his hands dirty working side by side with his black helpers or with women to a charming, carefree man of the world who at times barely missed coming off as a shallow playboy. Most definitely,

Jack Martin was an interesting personality. "Did you do this sort of thing very often in England?" she asked him.

"Now and then." He unwrapped a napkin from a plate of cold chicken and offered the plate to her. Clary selected half a breast. Jack took a leg and bit into it with evident relish. Clary was about to ask where in England he had conducted his picnics when he spoke first.

"Did you often do this sort of thing?" he asked.

"No. It's too bad. I like eating out of doors."

"I am glad to hear it. I will make certain that we do it again soon."

"Jack, tell me—"

"Here is some of Sarah's fresh bread, sliced and buttered," he interrupted. "We also have wedges of tomatoes, some of that cheese I bought from a trader in Bohemia Village last week, and a napkin full of sugar cookies. Sarah refused to give me the peach pie. She claimed it would be too messy to eat with our hands. Somehow I think she was wrong about that."

"Jack—"

"Was there something else you would like? It is not an extravagant feast, I admit, but it seemed adequate to me."

She regarded the man sitting next to her and knew he wasn't going to reveal anything about himself that he didn't want her to know. He lounged at his ease, his hat tilted over his forehead to keep the westering sun out of his eyes, his crossed, booted feet resting on the oarsman's

bench, their two wineglasses and the picnic basket crowded next to his feet. He gnawed on the
chicken leg he was holding as if he hadn't eaten
all day.

"It's a lovely feast," she said.

"Thank you. I thought so, too." He slanted a
quick look at her. "You seem to be content at
Afon Farm."

"I am." If he was going to be secretive about
his life before coming to Maryland, then she
could be just as closemouthed about her own
life and about her feelings.

"I have noticed no indication that you may be
suddenly called away," he said.

"Neither have I." She met his level gaze. "Perhaps we would not recognize those indications
if we saw them. Then again, perhaps I am in this
time to stay."

"Would that make you unhappy?"

"No, it wouldn't."

"You sound surprised, Clary."

"Someone from the twentieth century would
probably point out all the material advantages I
would be missing by remaining here," she said
slowly. "Certainly I work harder and live more
simply than I ever have before."

"There is a deep pleasure to be found in sim-
plicity. I have experienced it myself."

"And in quiet," she agreed. "That is the difference I notice most. Almost all the sounds I hear
now are natural ones."

"Then you have no real desire to return to
your original time?"

"I think it's out of my control. Coming here was certainly not my doing." When he offered her the sugar cookies, she took two of them. "I eat twice as much as I ever did before, but I don't seem to gain weight, and I am developing new muscles."

"Still, you are softer than when you first came here. You are more at ease. I assume that is in part because you were unhappy in the other time."

"I try not to think about that time. Or about your suggestion that in the twentieth century I may be dead." She leaned forward to pick up her wineglass, and when she sat back again, Jack's arm was around her shoulders. Clary tensed, but did not try to move away from his casual embrace. In the cramped boat, there was no place for her to go.

"I have noticed," he murmured, "that you have a lamentable tendency to avoid any subject that distresses you. Thus, you deliberately do not think about your unhappy past. It was unhappy, was it not?"

"I am not avoiding anything."

"No?" He took the wineglass from her hand and set it down on the bench. "Prove the truth of that statement."

"I don't have to prove anything to you."

"Perhaps the person to whom you need to prove something is yourself." His hand touched her cheek only briefly, yet it was as though she was imprisoned in bands of steel. He turned her face toward his and his eyes captured hers. Clary

was aware of a most disturbing heat sweeping through her body. She told herself it was caused by the wine.

"How can a woman so beautiful be so untouched and yet so afraid?" he whispered.

Even if there had been some place for her to go, Clary could not have moved. There was a trembling deep inside her that made her incapable of any action. Jack pulled off her hat and tossed it into the bow of the rowboat. His own hat sailed after it.

"I am not beautiful," Clary protested.

"You truly think not?" He smiled at her. "Therein lies a sad mistake of perception, madam." His fingers moved from her cheek into her hair. She felt the hair at the back of her neck loosen as he unfastened the ribbon that secured the full weight of her locks. He lifted the dark curls, pulling them forward to frame her face, while he spoke in a soft, caressing voice. "Hair like the finest, blackest jet. You must allow it to grow longer than shoulder length. I can easily imagine it cascading downward to your hips or lower still.

"Eyes like pure aquamarine crystals." His fingertips lightly touched each eyelid. Clary sat immobilized while one long finger moved to outline her lips. "And a mouth designed to drive any man mad with passion. Oh, Clary, your beautiful mouth may well prove to be my undoing."

Still holding her only gently, his fingertips barely touching her chin, he gazed at her for

a long moment, then slowly lowered his face to kiss her lightly.

"Don't." Clary caught her breath, frightened by the haunting sweetness of his mouth. "I can't."

"I thought you were beginning to forget your fear," he said. "I hoped in time you would learn to trust me."

"I do trust you," she whispered. "About everything except—except—"

"Except this?" His mouth touched hers again briefly, just long enough to make her want him to kiss her a third time.

"Please—" A tear trembled at the corner of her eye. She blinked it away.

"Gladly, my dear." He kissed her cheek where the tear lay.

"Jack, I—" She prepared herself to tell him why she could not allow him to continue. She would explain all the reasons. He would understand and row the boat back to shore and escort her to the farmhouse and never trouble her like this again. She drew in a shuddering breath and opened her lips to speak.

"Oh, Clary. Clary." His mouth was a sweet enchantment on hers. The arm that lay around her shoulders tightened, drawing her closer to him.

She raised a hand to push him away, but when her fingers touched his shoulder they did not push. They gripped, her nails digging into the hard muscle beneath his shirt.

He did not allow her to catch her breath long enough to offer any coherent protest against his

lovemaking, though soft cries and moans he permitted. Nor did he object when her hand crept upward from his shoulder to his cheek and then to his smooth mahogany hair. His own hands were busy, too. Clary cried out when he covered her breast. He stifled the sound with a renewed onslaught upon her mouth. A moment later she was pressing herself upward into his hot palm, straining against the cotton bodice of her dress. She felt the boat rock a little as he shifted position, but she was no longer concerned about being dumped into the water. She was instead totally focused on what he was doing to her.

It was magical, incredible, beyond anything she had ever experienced. His tongue teased around the edges of her mouth until her lips parted and he plunged into her in a surge of velvety heat. Clary was drowned in pure sensation. Forgetting distrust and fear, she gave herself up to kisses that drugged her senses, yet stimulated them at the same time.

She scarcely noticed when he removed his hand from her breast and reached down to lift her skirt, but she was immediately aware of his fingers creating upward-moving heat along calves and knees and then on her thighs.

"Clary." He tore his mouth from hers to whisper in her ear. "Don't be afraid. Let me show you—no, don't be afraid of me, sweetheart." This last admonition was murmured as his fingers reached the place between her thighs and she went rigid and tried to clamp her legs together. He stopped her cry of alarm with his mouth,

kissing her until she began to relax again. He did not remove his hand from between her thighs, and after a few minutes he began to caress her. Clary whimpered against his mouth, stiffened a second time, then made herself go limp. She was quaking in the very depths of her being, but she did not want him to stop what he was doing. In fact, if he were to stop, she thought she would go mad, because there was a heavy, throbbing need building steadily in the area where he was stroking and massaging. If he would just—just touch—there! His finger circled, pressing against the exact spot, and Clary shivered into erotic awareness.

"What are you doing?" she cried.

"Hush, love. It's all right." His mouth took hers again. And then the most amazing thing began to happen. His tongue slipped into her mouth again, while in the same way his finger slid into a more intimate place. Clary felt her body tighten around him. She winced when he withdrew, and she sighed with pleasure when he came back into her. All the time his mouth was on hers and his tongue was inside her, too, surging and withdrawing in her mouth. She felt a second finger stroking her most sensitive place, stroking and stroking until the rippling convulsions began and drove the breath from her lungs and sent her mind reeling far beyond thought into sensation so intense that she screamed aloud in exultation.

When she was able to think again, she was lying crushed against Jack's chest, with her skirt

still up around her thighs and her arms wrapped about his waist.

"Dear God in heaven!" she exclaimed. "I mean, good heavens, what did you do to me?"

His arms tightened and she felt laughter rumbling through his chest. She sat up, risked a quick downward glance, then looked into his eyes.

"You haven't finished," she said, preparing herself to accept what he would probably want her to do for him.

"That doesn't matter. I will survive the discomfort, for a while at least. There is no need for us to rush matters." The look he gave her was deep and searching. "Clary, we must talk. You cannot evade my questions now."

"No, I guess not." She sank back into his arms and lay quietly for a while before speaking again. "That never happened to me before. It was lovely." An inadequate word to describe what she had felt during those soaring, ecstatic moments, but her mind seemed to be as relaxed as her body, so she could not think of anything more profound to say.

"I am glad I was with you for your first time," he said. "However, Clary, when I touched you so intimately, I discovered to my surprise that you are not a virgin. I assume that your distrust of men is the result of having been badly used and then abandoned."

"That's pretty close to the truth," she admitted. "Emotional abandonment is every bit as

127

bad as a man physically walking out of a woman's life."

"Who was he? Did you love him?"

"I thought I loved him very much," she said slowly, trying to gather her thoughts so she could decide how to tell Jack the truth without making him angry or revealing too much. "We knew each other as children and we were always friends. He was kind and gentle during those first years, and he never gave me the hard time other boys gave their girlfriends."

"Hard time?" Jack looked puzzled.

"The pawing," she explained. "The heavy kissing and groping and wanting more than a girl wanted to give."

"Ah, I understand. He treated you as a gentleman ought to treat a lady, hoping thus to lure you into dropping your guard. Very clever of him. When did his behavior change?"

"After we got married."

"You have a husband?" He sat up with so abrupt a movement that the boat rocked and tipped.

"Not anymore," Clary said. "If I were still in the twentieth century, I would divorce him. As it is, in this time, I am not married yet, because Rich hasn't been born yet. Believe me, if I ever have the chance to marry him again, I will say a loud, clear no."

"I can see some distinct advantages to your unusual situation. Of course you are not married." He came down beside her once more, but he did not put his arms around her. "Am I cor-

rect in believing that your distrust of men stems from Rich's ill treatment of you?"

"Neglectful treatment would be a better word for it. I don't think he ever loved me. I think now that he married me because everyone we knew expected us to marry."

"That does happen," Jack agreed. "So it was not a happy marriage?"

"At first I thought it would be, once we both had a little time to adjust, but after the first couple of months Rich began to grow more and more distant. Whenever I tried to be romantic he told me I was a bore. You know, Jack, I really shouldn't be telling you this. It's not in very good taste for me to lie here with you after what we've just done and say these things about Rich."

"On the contrary, I think it is vitally important for you to tell me everything," he said. "It is the only way I am ever going to understand why you feel the way you do about men."

"I can tell you all you need to know in just a couple of sentences." A bitter note crept into Clary's voice. "Rich and I were married for two years, and for much of that time he made me feel guilty because I wasn't exciting enough for him. Then one evening I discovered him in bed with someone else—with a mutual friend, to be precise."

"You should not have seen that." His touch on her cheek was soft and reassuring. "You must have been deeply hurt."

"I was furious. It was like being hit by a bolt of lightning. In that one moment I understood

that all my efforts to be a good wife were futile and always would be. That was when I ran out of the house and got into my car and drove away as fast as I could. As I came off the canal bridge I sideswiped a truck and the car must have flipped over or my foot jammed on the gas pedal. I'm not sure what the exact mechanics of the accident were, but that was when I went into the canal. The next thing I knew, you were pumping water out of me." Clary hoped that the information she had just provided would satisfy him and that he wouldn't try to probe more deeply into her life in the twentieth century. She did not want to relive the humiliation of her marriage and its ending. But she should have known Jack better than to imagine he would stop until he knew everything.

"I am beginning to understand," he said. "I take it your intimate relations with Rich were not pleasant?" When she did not answer, he added, "You did suggest a few minutes ago that you never fully enjoyed yourself with him."

"No." Clary took a deep breath to strengthen herself for further revelations. "It was always very fast and usually rather uncomfortable. I was prepared for that at first, and I thought it would get better with time. We talk openly about sex in the twentieth century, so I did know what I was missing, and I tried to correct the situation. I used to read books on the subject and make delicate suggestions to Rich, but I only annoyed him. He refused to go to a marriage counselor. He said that, if there was

any problem, it was all in my head. He was the only man I had ever been with, so I didn't have anyone to compare him with. I finally decided that he must be right and that my unhappiness really was all my fault."

"Self-centered brute," Jack muttered.

"He wasn't really a brute," she said. "He never hit me and he was always reasonably polite. Our problems were all in the bedroom, and he didn't seem to be the least bit upset by them, possibly because I made a point of never refusing him."

"As I said, a self-centered brute," Jack repeated. "Clary, I am not without experience in such matters. If I told you just how much experience I enjoyed in my younger days, you would probably be shocked. I have been more continent since becoming a responsible landowner." He gave her a wry little smile. "I am not boasting about the life I lived as a very young man. I only mention it so you will know that I am aware of the responses of women in the bedroom, and thus I hope you will believe me when I say that you are one of the most deliciously responsive and potentially the most passionate woman I have ever known."

"I have never thought of myself as a passionate woman," she murmured.

"I am not at all surprised to hear that," he said. "I stand ready to teach you anything you want to know in such matters."

It was Clary's turn to sit up. "You are a dangerous man," she told him.

"Possibly." He ran a finger along her right calf,

the touch sending renewed tremors through her. She brushed his hand away and pulled her skirt down to her ankles.

"Probably," she told him, "you will break my heart, too, if I let you."

"Rich did not break your heart. He damaged the image you once had of yourself, and he badly injured your woman's pride. I would not blame you if you were never able to forgive him for that. But your heart he did not even crack, let alone break."

"You may be right," she admitted after a moment's consideration of this theory. "Rich was my childhood friend and my teenage crush, but the last two years destroyed any tender feelings I once had for him. That doesn't mean, however, that I will easily trust another man."

"You can learn to trust," he said. "You are learning already, or else you would not be here with me."

"Yes, and look what happened when I trusted you for a few minutes."

"Are you going to pretend that you did not enjoy it?" A smile tugged at his lips. His finger was running up and down her arm. Fighting back the urge to return his smile, Clary shook off his hand.

"I will begin to trust you," she told him, "when you tell me as much about your past as you now know about mine."

His fingers closed around her wrist, holding her tightly. His laughing mouth hardened into a firm line.

"You know as much as you need to know. Judge me by what you see of me every day." His voice dropped a tone or two. "Judge me by the fact that I have not ravished you, though I have wanted you badly since the first day I met you. I could make you want me, Clary. With what I have learned about you this evening, I could make you ache with desire for me until you came to my bedroom at night and knelt down and begged me to take you. And though my need for you would be far greater than yours for me, and you lay naked and panting beside me, still I would not possess you if doing so would mean harm to you or if I thought you would regret it afterward."

"Don't talk like that." She could not free her arm, nor could she take her eyes from his.

"That is how far you can trust me, Clary. Other men you may find untrustworthy, but not me."

"Then tell me who you are," she whispered. "Tell me your real name."

"I cannot."

"You want me to trust you, but you won't trust me."

"There are other people involved."

"Are you married?" she cried, frightened at the thought.

"No." His hand on her wrist loosened. "After hearing your story, I can understand why you would ask that. I am not married, nor have I ever been married. You have my word on it."

"Why won't you tell me your name?"

"Because six years ago I made a promise. Since I am an honorable man, I cannot break that promise. Would you want me to break a promise I made to you?"

"No, of course not, but—"

"In this you must trust me, Clary. That is what trust is: belief without demonstrable proof of what I say."

"I don't know if I can do that." She looked down at her hands, twisted together in her lap.

"With your history, it will be particularly hard for you. Will you make the effort? Will you give me the chance to prove to you day by day that I am an honorable man and worthy of your trust?"

She did not answer him at once. Instead, she raised her eyes to the glorious sunset painting the western sky with molten gold and suffusing the earth with a soft, shimmering light. She looked around at the green trees growing close to the river and at the pale, sandy beaches that showed here and there along the river's edge. The rowboat had drifted slowly downstream until they were almost level with the beach from which they had set forth. Clary saw a fish leap out of the water to catch a hovering insect and watched the ripples spread outward after the fish sank back into the water. She had grown to love the farm, and the land and river around it. She cared deeply about the people who lived on Afon Farm. She knew that she was perilously close to falling madly in love with the master of Afon Farm and that in letting herself

love him she would be taking the biggest risk of her life. Was he honest? Or was everything he had said to her since the first day she had arrived at Bohemia Village a lie? She shivered a little, thinking of what he had done to her in the hour just past and of what they might do together in the future. And then she gave all her qualms and all her fears to the river and let it take them away. Only when she had made her decision did she meet his eyes once more.

"Yes," she said. "I'll give you the chance. I will trust you."

Clary knew that, if Luke had not come running onto the beach just as Jack helped her out of the rowboat, she and Jack would very likely have spread out the blanket and lain down on it to make love. She was trembling with renewed need for his touch and he, after a deep and passionate kiss upon hearing her declaration of trust, had climbed onto the bench and rowed them to shore with his eyes locked on hers, save for an occasional quick glance over his shoulder to be sure he was heading in the right direction. As the rowboat ground softly into the sand, Clary licked her parched lips, thinking of Jack's kisses and of his hands caressing her. She was certain that her heated emotions must be written upon her face for him to see. Furthermore, seated where she was, she could hardly avoid noticing the evidence of his continuing desire for her.

"Jack," she whispered.

"Yes, Clary. I know." His voice was weighted with meaning. He leaned toward her, letting his hands move from her shoulders to her breasts and downward to her waist. There his hands remained, urging her upward. Then he was standing on the damp sand and she was balanced in the boat with one hand on his shoulder, expecting him to pick her up and carry her to drier ground.

Luke chose that moment to race out of the trees and onto the beach.

"Mister Jack," he yelled, panting, "my daddy says to come quick. The chestnut mare's taken real sick. Daddy thinks it might be a bad case of colic."

"It's all right, Luke. Stop and catch your breath." Turning to Clary, Jack added in a lower tone, "I am sorry, but this is important."

"Of course it is," she agreed. She could see how regretfully he was setting aside passion, and she felt that she could do no less. She, too, was sorry they would not make love, but she was not hurt or angry about it. This was not Rich trying to avoid her. This was Jack, and she could tell he wanted to be with her and that it was an effort for him to resume so quickly his role as responsible gentleman farmer. The knowledge was like balm to her none-too-secure feminine ego. "We can be together another time. I know how valuable the horses are. You can't afford to lose one. Tell me what I can do to help."

"You could dispose of the remains of our picnic." As he spoke, Jack was pulling the rowboat

out of the water. He handed the basket and her hat to Clary and gave the blanket to Luke. "Forgive me for leaving you so abruptly, but I ought to get to the barn at once. Moses does not call for help without good reason."

"I do understand," she said, adding with a laugh that she hoped he would find encouraging, "I will leave Sarah's kitchen as clean as I find it."

"Thank you, Clary." She knew it wasn't just the promise about the kitchen for which he was thanking her. He was grateful to her for agreeing that he ought to do what his position as owner of Afon Farm required of him and for not raising petty objections over his departure. Jack spoke to Luke. "Escort Miss Clary safely to the kitchen and help her there for as long as she needs you. Afterward, you may join your father and me in the barn." With a quick smile for Clary, Jack set off on the path between the trees, followed at a more leisurely pace by Clary and Luke.

"Go on, Luke," Clary said to him as soon as they came out of the trees and onto the open farmland. "I know you want to be in the barn with the other men."

"You sure, Miz Clary?" His youthful face lit up when she linked him with the men. He stood bouncing from foot to foot in his eagerness to be gone, yet she knew he would not leave her unless she urged him.

"I am positive." Clary took the blanket from him. "Tell Mister Jack that I will make a pot

of coffee and leave it on the stove in case you need something later to help you stay awake. Now, go."

"Thanks, Miz Clary. You know, we men might have to stay up all night long with that horse." Luke took off across the fields at a run.

An hour later, with her kitchen chores completed, Clary pumped water for a quick bath. Hoping that Jack would soon join her, she used the rose-scented soap. But he did not appear and after a while she got into her bed to wait for him. Her mind still filled with memories of his lovemaking, she fell asleep listening for his familiar step in the hall.

# *Chapter Eight*

As Luke had predicted, the menfolk were compelled to spend the entire night in the barn with the ailing chestnut mare. Thus, Clary suspected that exhaustion might have caused the accident, for it was not like Jack to be careless about his work.

Clary was in the house straightening her room when she heard Luke's voice raised in excitement, followed by Moses's quieter tones. Hurrying to the back door she saw Jack walking across the brick courtyard between the other two. She did not at first notice the bloodstained cloth wrapped around Jack's left forearm below his rolled-up shirtsleeve, but she could tell that something was wrong.

"What is it?" she asked. "What's happened?"

The men paused when she left the veranda and approached them.

"Mister Jack was trimmin' a piece of harness

while we were sittin' with the horse," Luke explained, still in that high-pitched, excited voice. "The knife slipped and he stabbed himself. There's blood all over the stall."

"It was nothing," Jack insisted. "The horses were more upset by the blood than I am."

"No wound inflicted in a barn could possibly be called inconsequential," Clary told him. "Moses, take him to the kitchen. I have a pot of water heating on the stove already. We can use it to wash out the wound. Luke, bring some more wood for the stove."

"I thought I could just go to my room and wash it off in the basin," Jack said. "Or perhaps beneath the pump. All it needs is a little fresh water and a tight bandage."

"I was right about you, Jack." Clary took him firmly by the left elbow, ignoring his wince of pain at the sudden gesture. Relentlessly, she steered him toward the kitchen door.

"Right about what?" he asked, trying unsuccessfully to pull away from her.

"You are crazy. Either that or you have no common sense at all," she said as she pushed him into the kitchen. "Sit down and put your arm on the table and let me look at the wound."

"Yes, madam." Meekly, Jack seated himself.

"Miz Clary, I thought all ladies fainted at the sight of blood." Luke dumped an armload of wood onto the floor and began feeding the logs into the cookstove.

"Not this woman," Clary said. "Nor would your mother faint either. Luke, as soon as you get that

fire burning well, fill another kettle with fresh water and put it on the stove to heat along with the first pan." She pulled the cloth off Jack's arm and looked at the gash.

"You did a bang-up job of it," she told him. "Moses, hand me the big basin from the shelf over there. That's right. Now, Jack, I am going to let you bleed into the basin for a while to help clean out the wound before I scrub it with soap and water. Let's get rid of this bloody cloth."

"You're right about cuttin' human flesh in a barn, Miz Clary," Moses said. "I've seen smaller cuts than that fester up till a man's arm had to be taken off."

"At least this isn't a puncture wound," Clary said. "If it were, I'd be scared to death about tetanus."

"It sure is bleedin' steady like." Luke peered over Clary's shoulder to see.

"All right, guys, pay attention now." Clary straightened to look at them one by one. "This is a problem I do know something about because a long time ago I used to be a medical assistant, so you men are going to follow my orders on this. Luke, your job is to keep that stove going and at least two kettles of water boiling. Moses, where is Sarah?"

"Most likely in our cottage," Moses said. "She always stays quiet on Sundays."

"Well, we are going to have to interrupt her. She's a sensible woman; she'll understand. Find her, Moses. Tell her I want a large needle, a spool of strong white thread, and the cleanest white fabric she has for bandages. Come back

141

here as soon as you deliver my message, Moses, and bring the supplies with you."

"Yes, Miz Clary." Moses did not question the way she was taking charge.

"Mistress Clary," Jack said, "I do not wish to seem overly squeamish, or to complain when you are trying to help me, but I do have a certain aversion to watching my lifeblood draining away into a kitchen basin. Perhaps if you were to replace the cloth Moses used and allow me to press down on it, I could stop the bleeding and save you the trouble of having to sew up my arm."

"Not on your life," Clary told him. "That cloth came from the barn, so it must be loaded with germs."

"Germs?" He gave her an amused look. "What, pray tell, are germs?"

"Bacteria," she replied. "Microbes. Organisms too small to see with the naked eye, yet powerful enough to cause a massive infection. What you need is a couple of shots of antibiotics. Not to mention a tetanus shot, just to be on the safe side."

"Fascinating," he murmured, still amused in spite of her seriousness.

"What you are going to get instead is a couple of shots of Kentucky whiskey," she informed him. "Some of it you will drink to numb the pain, because the stitching-up process is going to hurt like hell, and some I will use to wash out the wound. It's harsh stuff, but it's the best disinfectant we have."

"Couldn't I just drink it all?" he asked. "It does seem a pity to waste any of it on my arm when water will do as well."

"This isn't funny, Jack." She glared at him, her fear for him transformed into anger. "I'll just bet you and your friends back in England all say idiotic things like that before you ride into battle. And no doubt, sick jokes along that line are also required before you fight a duel—or better yet, afterward, while you lie bleeding to death on the grass at dawn."

He went perfectly still for a minute or two before he responded. When he spoke his voice held an odd note of despair beneath the continuing, defiant humor.

"I have never ridden into battle," he said. "I fear I was a triffle too young for the Napoleonic Wars."

"Be serious, Jack," she admonished.

"Will seriousness heal my arm or prevent the infection you dread?" he asked.

"No, it won't." She sat down across the table from him, clasping her hands together on the pine surface. "Jack, I'm going to be perfectly honest with you. I am worried. In my time, with good care and antibiotics, a wound like this wouldn't be a life-threatening problem."

"I know you will do your best for me." He reached out to her with his right hand, laying it over her clasped fingers, where they rested on the tabletop. "You see, I trust you, Clary."

"My best may not be good enough." Her voice was tightly controlled because she was afraid her feelings for him would get in the way of what she was going to have to do in the next hour. He didn't deserve any of the crippling possibilities that Clary could foresee. Jack Martin ought to continue to be whole and in vital health, striding across his fields and giving orders to Moses and Luke. He ought to sit tall and strong at the head of his mahogany dining table, pouring out Madeira wine at the end of a meal. And he needed two good arms to put around her when they made love—because they were going to make love. Only his death or her return to the twentieth century could prevent them.

"I understand your apprehensions. I share them." The warm smile he bestowed on Clary made her wonder if he could read her mind. "I put myself into your hands without reservation and without fear."

"I have never actually sewn up a wound myself," she admitted, "but I have assisted the doctor I worked for lots of times. Jack, I want to warn you again: with only whiskey for anesthetic, it is going to be terribly painful."

"I know that. I can bear it. I have borne worse."

"All right, then." There was no one else on the farm who understood the real dangers as well as she, and no one else who knew the methods to use to prevent a severe infection. There was no point in wishing for the twentieth-century equipment and medicine she did not have. She

could only do her best for Jack and pray that he would recover. She began to rise from the table, but he held her where she was, his hand tight on hers and his voice taking on a new urgency.

"Clary, let me say something while Luke is out at the pump and before Moses returns. If the outcome of this is not as we would wish, you will find papers in the bottom drawer of the chest in my bedchamber. They will provide proof that Moses and his family are all free, if any proof is needed beyond what they already have in their own possession. You will also find in the chest my will and instructions on what is to be done with the farm."

"I'll see to it." There was no point in protesting that he would be just fine; they both knew his prospects might be grim. She lifted the hand that covered hers and pressed it to her lips. "I'm glad we met, Jack Martin."

"Not half so glad as I am," he responded. "Now do you think you could repair my arm without further delay?"

"I have been waiting for Sarah," she said, just as Sarah came through the kitchen door.

"I'm right here. I've brought the needle and thread and the clean bandages you wanted—oh, Mister Jack, what have you done to yourself?" Sarah shook her head over his wound before sending a worried glance in Clary's direction. She said nothing at all about the disorder in her immaculate kitchen. "Tell me what you want me to do, Miz Clary."

"Thread the needle with a doubled length of thread," Clary instructed. "Make it three times longer than the gash in his arm. Put the needle and thread and the sharpest knife you have into the boiling water. Then wash Jack's arm with soap and hot water, while I wash my hands."

Quickly they made the preparations. Clary scrubbed her hands with the hottest water she could bear and Sarah's strongest soap. When she thought the needle and thread had boiled long enough, she told Moses to give Jack two big glasses of whiskey.

"If you want more, just say so, and Moses will give it to you," she said to Jack. "Now, Sarah, pour whiskey over the cut and the surrounding arm. Do it slowly. I don't want to touch anything yet myself because my hands are clean."

Jack groaned when the whiskey met the open flesh, but he kept his arm over the basin.

"Now, Jack," Clary said, "take your arm off the basin and lay it down on the clean cloth Sarah has arranged. Moses, hold his shoulders. Sarah, hold his hand steady, but don't touch him above the wrist."

"There is no need to hold me. I will not move," Jack promised.

"You won't be able to stop yourself," she said. "It's a reflex to pull away from whatever causes pain."

Taking the needle and thread out of the water, she began to lay down sutures, drawing the sides of the wound together, making secure knots and using the sharp kitchen knife to cut the thread

after each stitch. Fortunately, the gash in Jack's arm, though a good four inches long, was not very deep. It involved no large blood vessels, nor was the muscle tissue badly damaged. Clary worked as quickly as she could, not looking at Jack's face at all because she didn't want to see how badly she was hurting him. He made no sound, but she could sense how rigidly he was holding his entire body and once or twice she heard him grit his teeth.

"Miz Clary, why do you keep cuttin' the thread after every stitch?" asked Luke, who was watching what she did with great interest.

"Because after the wound heals I will cut the stitches, then take hold of the knots and pull out the threads one by one," she replied, making her explanation as simple as possible. "That will prevent the stitches from becoming infected later." *If there is a later for Jack,* she added to herself. *If he doesn't die of blood poisoning or lose his arm to gangrene.*

Hearing Jack moan, she paused before taking another stitch and looked at him in surprise. So far, he had endured the pain in silence.

"Do you want more whiskey?" she asked him.

"Not at the moment," he said, "but I fear I will have to order a new barrel in preparation for your future surgical activities. Are you saying that, after I endure the putting in of these stitches, I must also survive their removal?"

"Sorry about that, but it can't be helped." She tried to speak as lightly and teasingly as he had just done. "Look at it this way, Jack: if your

wound heals cleanly, you will be so grateful to me that you won't mind the discomfort."

"Will I not?" he murmured.

"Hold still now. Just another stitch or two and we're finished." A few moments later she knotted and cut the last stitch. "I think a little more antiseptic is in order before I put on the bandage. A glass of whiskey if you please, Luke."

"Yes, ma'am." Luke filled the glass and handed it to her. Clary dipped a clean white cloth into the glass and swabbed Jack's forearm from elbow to wrist.

"What a waste of good whiskey." He spoke through gritted teeth, and she knew he couldn't take much more pain. She was amazed that he hadn't passed out after the first couple of stitches. Quickly she wrapped the wound in one of the bandages that Sarah had provided, and then she looked from Moses to Luke.

"If you two gentlemen would help me get our patient to bed," she said, "then I think we can declare the operation a success.

"Sarah." Clary looked from the mess on the kitchen table to the housekeeper. Sarah waved her away.

"You go on, Miz Clary. I know you'll want to sit with him. And don't you worry about my kitchen. Mister Jack's life is more important."

Jack insisted he could walk unaided, but he was distinctly unsteady on his feet and Clary was grateful to Moses and Luke for staying close on either side of him. Once in his bedroom they stripped him down to his calf-length

linen underdrawers and tucked him into bed. He did not protest the assistance. Clary noted that he was pale and his skin felt clammy. He soon drifted into a light doze.

"Anythin' we can get for him?" Moses asked, sending an anxious look in Clary's direction. "Or for you?"

"A pitcher of fresh water," she said, "and a clean cloth from Sarah, if you please. He will probably spike a fever, so I will want to wipe him down occasionally to keep him cool."

"I'll be glad to do that. Young unmarried ladies shouldn't be handlin' men's bodies."

"I have taken care of other sick men in the past. There is nothing the least bit improper in it." She wasn't going to tell Moses that she was not an unmarried lady as he thought. She patted his arm, understanding his need to do something to help. She felt the same way about Jack. "I will take good care of him, and I'll call you if I need anything. You have been very helpful, Moses. You, too, Luke."

"Could I be a doctor when I grow up?" Luke asked. "I'd sure like to learn to fix wounds the way you just did."

"We'll talk about it sometime soon," she promised. "You will have to learn to read and write first."

She promptly forgot Luke's interest in medicine, for Jack became feverish and restless. Through the night she washed his face repeatedly with cool water and bathed his chest, too, hoping thus to lower the fever. When he began

149

to pick at the bandage on his arm, she took his right hand in hers and sat on the edge of his bed, holding his hand and talking to him. She did not think he heard her. He was lost in his own world of feverish pain and memory.

"Philly," he muttered. "Don't say that. Dead? He can't die. No—best friend I ever—I won't let him—damn it! No—no!"

"Jack!" Clary began to wonder if she would have to call Moses to hold him down. Jack was too strong for her to control. She was practically sitting on his chest and he was still thrashing around, his movements threatening to throw himself and her off the bed and onto the floor. "Jack, wake up. It's me. It's Clary."

"Clary?" His eyes were open but they were focused on something beyond her sight. "Impossible story—shouldn't believe. Mouth so sweet. Skin like silk. I want you, Clary.

"Bloody bastard!" he shouted a moment later. "Use a woman like that. Why? Kill him! Oh, God, it hurts!"

"I know, Jack. I know." She put her arms around him and he turned gentle, nestling his face against her breasts. "Try to sleep, dear."

He lay quietly for a while, and Clary started to relax. She ran a hand through his tangled hair, smoothing it back from his face.

"Damned unfair," he said suddenly. And then he began to shiver. Clary covered him with the quilt from his own bed. When he continued to shake she pulled open the connecting door

between their rooms and hurried into her bed-chamber to take the quilt off her bed. She stopped just inside her room and turned around to look more closely at that door. There was a lock on it, but no key on either side. She had never tried the door, just assuming that it was locked.

Jack could have entered her room on any night. He wanted her, yet he had restrained himself. She recalled his words about not rushing matters, and she knew he had been thinking of her welfare rather than of what he desired.

"I wish you had come to me," she whispered, looking through the doorway to where he lay, shaking on his bed. "If you die now, we will never know what it would have been like. After what you did for me yesterday afternoon, I think it would have been beyond anything I ever imagined."

He cried out again, shouting something about Philly or Philadelphia. Clary hurried to him and tucked the quilt around him. Gradually the shivering stopped, but then he began to complain of the heat, so she removed the quilts and bathed him in cool water again.

Sometime during the silent hours of the night his fever broke and he fell into a deep sleep. Clary watched him for a while until exhaustion caught up with her, too. She wanted to lie down beside him. But she was afraid she might disturb him, and she knew he required rest above all else just then. Leaving the door between their rooms wide open she stretched out, still clothed, on her own bed. Her last waking thought was

that she would do anything to see Jack Martin well and happy again.

He was awake and alert the next morning, though he was pale and, Clary suspected, much weaker than he wanted her to know. She was just leaving his bedchamber with a pitcher in her hand, headed for the pump, when Moses appeared, also with a pitcher, his brimming over with fresh water.

"Sarah says for you to go to the kitchen and eat breakfast right now," Moses said. "I'll stay with Mister Jack while you're gone. There's things I can do for him that he wouldn't want a woman doin'."

"I suppose you're right, but make him stay in bed."

She should have known that Jack wouldn't obey that order. When she returned to his room an hour later carrying a fresh supply of bandages, he was sitting on the side of his bed and he was wearing his breeches.

"He won't listen to me, Miz Clary," Moses said as soon as he saw her. "Maybe you can tell him to lay down again."

"I refuse to be shaved while lying in bed," Jack declared. "No offense to you, Moses, but I can do a better job of it myself while standing upright. If you would just help me with my boots—"

"You get back into bed!" Clary marched right up to him and gave him a hard shove on the chest. Jack did not move. He didn't even waver.

"I have work to do," he said.

"Not in the fields," Moses told him. "It's rainin' hard."

"Rain never stopped me before," Jack replied.

"There's nothin' to pick today 'cept corn, and Luke can do that," Moses argued. "You stay indoors like Miz Clary wants. If you catch the lung fever, we'll all be runnin' around tryin' to save you again."

"There speaks a wise man," Clary said. "As your primary care giver, I must insist that you show some common sense and stay indoors. There is a monsoon going on out there." She waved a hand toward the window, inviting him to see for himself.

"Very well." Jack looked from Clary to Moses and back again, apparently comprehending that they were going to join forces to prevent him if he tried to leave the house. "I ought to spend a few hours working on the ledgers. I will do that today."

"You ought to be in bed," Clary insisted.

"Writin' in books is better than workin' in the fields or tendin' the horses," Moses put in. "'Least he'll stay dry if he's in the house writin'."

"How is the chestnut?" Jack asked him.

"Gettin' better, just like you will if you do what Miz Clary says. Horses have sense enough to stay in their stalls when they're ailin'. I just wish you had the same kind of sense, Mister Jack." With that, Moses stamped out.

"My boots please," Jack commanded Clary.

"I refuse. If you feel ill and have to lie down, I will only have to pull the boots off you again. Don't you own any slippers?"

Looking around she discovered a pair of soft-soled woolen mules tucked beneath a magnificent Philadelphia highboy made of finely grained mahogany. She gave the tall chest of drawers only a cursory glance, since she was more interested in seeing Jack properly clothed against the dampness than in admiring the pediment that topped the chest or the lovely carved shell motifs that decorated its apron and the tops of its legs. However, she did look closely at the slippers when she picked them up, noting that they were handmade. Each slipper had a crest embroidered on the toe in red, green, and gold threads.

"These are very pretty." Clary slid the mules onto Jack's feet. His feet were like his hands, long and slender and elegant. Still in a squatting position, she looked up at him. "Did someone embroider these especially for you?"

"I wear them because they are comfortable." He stood up, leaning against the carved mahogany bedpost for support.

"Take it easy," Clary advised. "Don't move too fast. If you faint, I will have to call Moses back to lift you into bed again, and if that happens, I warn you, I will make you stay there until tomorrow, even if I have to tie you down to force you to obey me."

"Madam, I have never fainted in my life. If you will excuse me now, I intend to shave." Carefully

he moved toward the washstand. "I said you may go, Clary."

"Do you need anything?" Still she lingered, unwilling to leave him alone. She knew what pain and fever could do to a patient, so she did not believe that he was feeling as well as he claimed.

"Moses has provided what I require," he said.

"Call me when you are finished and I'll change your bandage before I help you with your shirt."

He did not answer. He was working up a lather, using a knob-handled brush in a small bowl of soap. Clary suspected that he was weak enough to have to use all of his available energy for what he was doing, leaving nothing to expend on conversation. She went into her own room, pushed the door half closed, and pretended to be tidying her belongings until he summoned her back.

She made him sit on the bed again while she removed the bandage from his forearm. There was some redness along the wound, but overall it did not look badly infected. Clary began to hope it might heal cleanly.

"Hurrah for good Kentucky whiskey," she muttered.

"Well?" Jack asked. "Will it be completely healed by a week from Wednesday?"

"Of course not." She gave him a sharp look. "What's so important about next Wednesday?"

"It is the day I leave."

"Leave the farm?" She gaped at him. "Where are you going?"

"I have business along the canal," he said, "and then in Wilmington and Philadelphia. I should be gone for a little more than two weeks."

"So that's what you were talking about." She began to rewrap his arm with a clean bandage.

"What do you mean?" he asked. "I do not recall informing you of my planned journey."

"You were babbling last night when you were feverish. You mentioned Philly several times."

"Philly?" He looked startled, then puzzled. Then he laughed. "Is that what you call Philadelphia in your time?"

"Haven't you heard the term before?" She stopped wrapping the bandage to look hard at him. "If not, why did you use it when you were delirious?"

"Perhaps you mentioned it, Clary."

"Perhaps. I could have." He was being evasive and they both knew it. But why should he be secretive about the nickname for a city? It didn't make sense to Clary.

"I would like you to remove the stitches before I leave," he said.

"I can't decide about that until I see how quickly your arm heals," she replied. "Jack, may I go with you? I would love to see Philadelphia the way it used to be."

"It is impossible. I will spend several days along the canal, and there would be no place for you to stay. In the cities, I will be preoccupied with business."

"I don't mind camping out at the canal," she said, "and I could wander around by myself in Wilmington and Philadelphia."

"No, you could not. This is not your time, Clary. In this time, gentlewomen do not wander around unescorted."

"Do you expect me to stay here at the farm forever?" she cried. "I am used to being more mobile than that."

"Ah, yes. In your car, the machine you ran into the canal."

"That was an accident. I am not going to stay here while you go off to the big city to enjoy yourself."

"Oh, yes, you are. Philadelphia is an unhealthy place in the summer heat, with yellow fever and the sweating sickness. No, it would be too dangerous for you, Clary." He caught her by the upper arms and pushed her down on the bed. He winced when he bumped his left arm, but the discomfort didn't stop him. She lay beneath him, his bare chest pressing on her breasts, his mouth just a breath away from hers. He smelled of bay rum and Sarah's homemade soap. All of Clary's senses came instantly alive, clamoring for his embrace. Until he spoke again. "While I am gone, I want to know that you are safe here, waiting for me to return."

"Of all the male-chauvinistic comments I have ever heard, that was one of the worst," she told him, disappointment and irritation dispelling any softer emotions. "Why should I have to

157

wait for you? And down on the farm, no less! Why can't I go with you?"

"I have told you why not." He grinned at her. "Tell me, Clary, exactly what is a primary care giver? The phrase suggests interesting possibilities."

"In your case it refers to the fact that I am the one who is seeing to your wound," she said, momentarily diverted from her annoyance with his antediluvian attitude toward women.

"'Tis but a narrow definition. Would you like to hear the activities I would include under that term?"

"I can imagine what they are." She lifted a hand to stroke his freshly shaven cheek. "You are the most exasperating and the most complicated man I have ever met. You tease when you ought to be serious. You won't talk about yourself. You do more work than any two men."

"I want you more than any other two men possibly could," he said.

"You have been injured," she objected.

"What does that signify? It's not my left arm that will be involved in making love to you, Clary."

"In your weakened condition—"

"I do not feel at all weak when you are near." He shifted his position, letting her experience his hardness and strength. Clary slid her arms around his neck and parted her lips, awaiting his kiss.

"However," he said, sitting up and moving away from her, "perhaps it would be advisable

for me to wait a while, in order to prevent the depletion of my vital energies so soon after surgery. Particularly since my primary care giver is seriously concerned about my condition."

"You insufferable tease!" Clary pushed herself off the bed to stand with fists on hips. He caught her right hand, pulling it to his mouth. He placed a kiss in her palm and curled her fingers around it while Clary's irritation melted once more and her frustration level rose by several notches.

"If you will assist me in donning my shirt, Mistress Clary, I feel certain that will be all the seduction my poor, decimated body can bear for the moment." He stood, forcing her to look up at him, and then he bent to kiss her lips quickly and lightly. "You must understand, my dear, that Moses or Sarah or even Luke may appear at any moment, expecting to find me stretched out upon my deathbed. What would they think—Sarah in particular, if she comes bearing tea and hot soup to strengthen me in my weakness—what would they say if they were to discover you making passionate love to a man who is desperately ill with a raging fever? They would believe that you were taking unfair advantage of a dying man and think much less of you for it. For I do assure you, Clary, I have been shaken by a violent fever that rages in my blood day and night."

"It serves you right for teasing me like that, though I must admit I see your point." Clary picked up the shirt lying folded at the foot of his bed. She held it out to him. "I suggest that

you put on the left sleeve first. Jack, you do look pale. Are you sure you feel well enough to get dressed?"

Instead of answering her, he grabbed for the bedpost and stood weaving, his face suddenly chalk white and beaded with perspiration.

"Jack!" Dropping the shirt, she caught him, slinging his right arm over her shoulder. "Come on. Don't pass out on me yet. Get into bed first. Jack, will you please help me?"

"Doing—my—best." But he was too weak to be of much assistance and Clary ended up heaving him forward onto the mattress. She landed beside him with his arm holding her down.

"'Tis but a momentary light-headedness," he murmured. "I shall recover soon and then I will be able to rise again."

"Rise?" She shoved his arm off her shoulder and sat up. "Will you please just knock off the comedy and this macho-man routine? Listen to me, Jack Martin. You are sick. Do you understand? Sick, as in feverish and weak from an injury. You are going to stay right here in this bed until I say you have recovered." She pulled his slippers off his feet and angrily threw them across the room. "If you had listened to me in the first place, this wouldn't have happened. Let me look at your arm."

"Why?" His eyes were closed, dark lashes resting against the pale skin of a curiously youthful face. Clary repressed her desire to stroke his mouth and to push his loose hair back off his forehead.

"Because with all the moving around you've been doing you may have torn a stitch." After assuring herself that no further damage had been done to his arm, she rewrapped the bandage and sat looking at him. Since he had been lying down for a few minutes, his color was much better.

"By your stern expression, I foresee a lecture," he said, watching her.

"You deserve one," she told him. Lifting a warning finger to prevent him from speaking again, she went on. "If you have any common sense at all, which I am seriously beginning to doubt, you will understand after this little incident that you are not well enough to be out of bed. If you will just stay put for today, I may allow you to get up tomorrow."

"What reward will you give me if I obey you?" he asked.

"You will get your health back," she snapped. "That should be reward enough." Sliding off the bed and keeping her back toward him, she added, "However, you can't lie there all day in your breeches. Unfasten them and I will help you to pull them off. But stay flat on your back. If you stand up and get dizzy again, I swear I will let you stay on the floor."

"You could call Moses to help you," he suggested.

"Moses is too busy to spend the entire day looking after a man who doesn't have the brains of a flea," she retorted.

"Would you assist me now?" He sounded remarkably humble and contrite. Clary spun

around, expecting more teasing and nonsense from him, only to find him struggling to push his unbuttoned breeches down over his hips. She caught them at the waist and slid the breeches along his legs, fully aware of his well-developed muscles beneath her fingers.

"Shall I remove my underdrawers, too?" he asked, still in that humble voice.

"Certainly, if you will be more comfortable with them off," she said, her eyes on the breeches she was folding. "Don't be modest on my account."

"You were frightened for my sake, weren't you? You thought I was going to fall and hurt myself. Clary, come here." He held out his right hand.

"I don't think I should." She stayed well out of his reach.

"In my weakened condition, I would be hard put to overpower you, should you choose to resist me," he said.

"Why can't you be serious for more than a few minutes at a time?" she demanded, still refusing to look at him. She laid the folded breeches down on the blanket chest at the foot of the bed.

"I was completely serious on Saturday afternoon," he replied.

She heard him moving around on the bed. Fearing that he was trying to rise and come after her, she risked a glance at him, only to discover that he was wrestling with the pillows.

"Let me do that." She took the pillows from him, fluffed them up, and piled them at the head

of the bed. "Now just slide yourself along until you are sitting against the pillows."

He had apparently decided not to remove his underdrawers, for which Clary was deeply grateful. She did not know what she would do if she were confronted by the naked flesh she could see straining boldly upward against the linen. The instant he relaxed against the pillows she pulled the sheet over him right up to his armpits. She expected a knowing grin from him, but he remained serious.

"Clary, tell me the truth. I know I was miserably ill last night. Do you think the fever is a recurrent thing? Will it attack me every night, weakening me a little more each time until it kills me? I have seen other men die that way. If it is to happen to me, I want to know so that I can put my affairs into order while I am still lucid."

"The fever you suffered last night was a natural reaction to being injured and to having your arm repaired under nonsterile conditions, but the wound doesn't look abnormally swollen or red. If you can get through the next couple of days and it starts to heal well, then I think you shouldn't have any serious trouble. You don't have any problem moving your fingers or your hand, do you?"

"Only a little, when the muscle pulls." He flexed his left hand and wiggled his fingers for her to see. "I ought to be back at work by tomorrow."

"Haven't you heard anything I've said?" she cried, exasperated almost beyond endurance.

"You absolutely must take it easy and keep the wound clean until it heals properly. You have been entirely too casual about this, Jack."

"I am not at all casual. Nor am I unappreciative of your efforts on my behalf. I have no wish to lose my arm or my life. Not now. Not when I have so recently discovered how surprisingly sweet life can be." She had moved closer to the bed, so he was able to reach her hand. "I have not finished with you, Miss Cummings. There is much more we need to say to each other, and more—much more—for us to do together."

# Chapter Nine

As Clary expected, Jack grew feverish again in the late afternoon. Through the night that followed, she repeatedly wiped his hot skin with cool water. She thought the continuous rain and the humid heat were making his condition worse, and there was a time toward midnight when she would have given anything she possessed for a small air conditioner. But as had happened on the previous night, the fever broke and Jack fell into a deep sleep.

In the morning Sarah found Clary curled up at the foot of Jack's bed. "You can't go on like this, stayin' up with him every night!" Sarah exclaimed. "You'll soon be sick yourself."

"The fever wasn't as bad last night," Clary said, stretching her stiff shoulders. "He wasn't delirious. That's a good sign."

"You come to the kitchen now and eat. I'll call Moses to stay with him for a while."

"I am not leaving this room," Clary told her. "If Moses is here, Jack will think he can get out of bed. He will obey me if I insist that he stay where he is."

"That man don't obey no one." Sarah cast a reflective glance toward the sleeping figure on the bed. "Mister Jack always thinks he knows best, and usually he does. If he listens to you, then you are someone special. None of us here on the the farm would dispute that after the last two days."

"Let's just say that I have convinced Jack that I know more about treating wounds than he does. Sarah, if you will bring food for both of us, I'll see to it that he eats a good breakfast."

When he awakened a short time later, Jack argued about wanting to shave, but eventually he gave in when Clary promised that if he would obey her orders he would have to remain in bed for only one day more.

"However, I cannot lie here and do nothing," he insisted. "Bring me the ledger. It is in the bottom drawer of the chest. I will also need my traveling desk, which is in the parlor."

"All right, if it will keep you quiet," she agreed, going to the highboy. The bottom drawer contained not only the heavy bound ledger, but an assortment of other papers. Some of them looked like letters. Restraining her curiosity as to the contents of documents that might reveal at least some of the well-hidden facts of Jack's life, Clary gave him the ledger he wanted, then located his traveling desk. This was a wooden box

with a slanted lid that was intended to be used as a writing surface. In compartments beneath the lid were paper, quill pens, a knife to sharpen the quills, and a tightly closed bottle of ink.

"Don't open that," Clary warned when Jack picked up the ink bottle. "A spill will stain the sheets."

"How, may I ask, am I expected to write in the ledger if I cannot use ink?" His sharp response told Clary better than any other evidence could have done that he was recovering nicely. In her experience, male patients who felt well always resented being forced to remain in bed under female supervision.

"I have an idea," she told him. Hurrying back to the parlor, she returned carrying a small table, which she placed next to the right side of the bed. With the ink and pens on the table in easy reach and Jack ensconced against a pile of pillows, he was able to work in relative ease. Clary left him there and set about her daily chores.

By midafternoon Jack was growing increasingly restless. After checking his arm to be sure it was healing with no sign of serious infection, Clary agreed that he might eat his evening meal in the dining room. She even brought him a pitcher of hot water so he could shave and wash.

Retiring to her own bedroom and closing the connecting door, Clary quickly changed into the only other gown she owned. She had torn the hem of the gray cotton dress, which was her usual daytime attire, and it would have to be mended

before she could wear it again. Her other gown, the one she saved to wear in the evenings, was a more elaborate affair. The tight, wide-necked bodice of blue-green silk had puffed, elbow-length sleeves finished with embroidered ruffles. The white muslin skirt was gathered onto a wide waistband that was set several inches higher than Clary's natural waistline. All around the hem of the skirt a repeating pattern of blue flowers and green leaves was embroidered. Because the skirt was so sheer, Clary was forced to wear a cotton petticoat. She also put on a simple cotton chemise, but she refused to wear either the corset or the long drawers provided for her by Madam Rose.

Clary considered the ankle-length drawers to be an idiotic article of clothing. They were nothing more than twin tubes of white cotton held together at the waist only by a drawstring. The garment had no center seam. Clary supposed this arrangement was convenient when attending to the wearer's personal needs, but the drawers tended to twist and bind around her legs in a hot and irritating way. After her first attempt to be authentic and wear them, she had folded up the drawers and tucked them down at the bottom of the blanket chest in her room. As for the corset, she would have to be a madwoman to hook and lace herself into such an instrument of torture. In spite of all the food she was eating lately, she remained slender enough not to have to restrain her figure in order to fit into the dress.

After completing her toilette by brushing her
hair hard and confining the thick dark curls
behind each ear with matching combs, Clary
took her gray dress and the needle and thread
that Sarah had given her and went across the
hall to the parlor to work on the torn hem until
Jack appeared.

The parlor was not a room that was used
very much in the summertime, and the furnishings did not look as if they had been chosen
with much consideration for what went with
what. Against the plain whitewashed walls and
uncurtained windows the elegant love-seat-size
settee covered in blue silk looked out of place,
as did a wing chair upholstered in multicolored
crewelwork on a pale background. There was a
wooden footstool in front of the wing chair, and
a small round table was between the chair and
the fireplace, as if someone sat there regularly in
cold weather. A pipe and jar of tobacco added to
the impression that this was where the master
of the house spent the cooler evenings. Clary
had moved a second table from the parlor to
the bedroom for Jack to use. She wished she
had that table back, because she needed to put
a lighted candle on it in order to see what she
was doing. The room was so shadowy that she
stabbed her finger with the needle.

"Damn it!" she muttered. "Oh, dear. Sorry,
Madam Rose. I really am trying to watch my
language, but sometimes it's hard."

"Were you speaking to me?" Jack stood in the
hall doorway, looking frighteningly handsome

in pale beige breeches, a white shirt open at the neck, his embroidered woolen slippers, and a blue silk dressing gown. His hair was clubbed with a blue silk ribbon.

"I was talking to myself." Clary hoped he couldn't see in her eyes what she was thinking. Jack Martin was easily the sexiest-looking man she had ever encountered and she was amazed at herself for the way he could make her feel just by coming into a room.

"I hope you will not be offended by my state of dishabille," he said. "I did try to don my coat, but found it difficult to get my left arm into the sleeve while wearing the bandage."

"I am not offended," she replied. "You ought to see the way some men in the twentieth century dress—or rather, don't dress. Compared to bare feet, torn jeans, and a dirty sweatshirt, you are wearing formal attire."

"Yours must be an unusual time, if the gentlemen choose to dress like beggars," he murmured. With one long finger he lifted a corner of the dress spread across her lap. "What are you doing?"

"Mending." Watching his face for the flash of humor she knew would come, she added, "And waiting."

"Indeed?" There it was, just as she expected. He was trying not to smile. With practiced grace he seated himself in the wing chair. Where had he learned to move in that lithe, perfectly balanced way? He was like a cat—or an expert swordsman. That was it, she thought. Jack moved like someone fencing in a costume movie. But for him it

wasn't a movie; it was real life. Suddenly she was tired of playing guessing games about him. If he would not tell her anything about himself, then perhaps someone else would—but not anyone on Afon Farm. She was convinced that neither Moses nor Sarah knew much more about Jack than she did. If she wanted to find out about him, she would have to get away from the farm and talk to other people who knew him. She thought of the perfect excuse to leave for a little while.

"You know, Jack," she said, "this room really needs to be redecorated."

"I sit here so seldom," he responded, "that I have thought more than once about turning the room into an office. It would be more convenient. I spend entirely too much time working on my ledger in the dining room, which makes it difficult for Sarah to serve meals in there."

"You could put a desk in the corner and still have space left for a seating area," Clary offered. "Actually, I was thinking more along the lines of curtains and a rug and some cheerful cushions. You need more light in here, too."

"Do you think so?" He was regarding her with an interested, alert expression, as if he was wondering what she would say next.

"If you are worried about money, it shouldn't cost very much."

"I was not thinking about money," he told her. "Would you like to make a list of what you will require? I intended to ask you if you would like more clothing. I will be happy to purchase

any goods you want in either Wilmington or Philadelphia."

"If you would let me go with you, I could make my own decisions on the spot and get exactly what I want," she suggested.

"I have told you that you may not make this trip with me." It was said politely, but so finally that Clary knew she would not be able to change his mind.

"I still don't understand why I can't go." She knew she sounded sulky, but she didn't care.

"I have my reasons. They are good ones. However, soon it will not be necessary for you to go far abroad to shop. You will be able to buy a great variety of goods in Bohemia Village. Every time I drive into town, some new building has been finished. When the larger boats begin to sail through the canal this autumn, they will all have to stop at the locks. Then the village will become a grand market for everyone who lives in this area. Tell me, Clary, does this desire to travel and to refurbish my home mean that you believe you are in this time to stay?"

"Does that question mean that you believe my story about coming here from the future?" she countered.

"You do appear to be a singularly honest and straightforward young woman," he said thoughtfully. "Amazing as your claim is, during these past weeks, I have seen nothing in your actions or your speech to make me think you are not telling the truth. Your surgical skills alone suggest that you are not a woman of this time. Then there is

your independent spirit. Yes, Clary, after close daily contact with you for more than a month, I must conclude that you have indeed been removed from your own time to this one."

"Thank you." Clary closed her eyes in sheer relief. "You cannot know how much your belief in me means."

"Perhaps I do know," he murmured.

"I am beginning to accept the idea that I will be living in this time permanently," she said in response to his declaration of belief in her. "The funny thing is, after the first few days of adjustment, I really haven't minded being here. I am happier now than I have been for years. I do wish, though, that you would give me a little more freedom."

"You are not a prisoner, Clary."

"The thing is, in my time, women don't just stay at home every day. We go out without a male escort, we have jobs, and we are very independent."

"I have already noted your independence. Yet you claim to be happier here," he said, "under my protection."

"Don't think for one minute that I will stay here contentedly forever. Sooner or later I am sure to develop cabin fever. At which point you will discover just how difficult a twentieth-century woman can be."

What Jack might have said in response to that threat was prevented by Sarah's appearance to announce that their meal was ready. For the next hour Clary directed her comments to the food

173

and to the polite conversation that Jack insisted upon when they were at the dining table.

"I do believe the rain has stopped," he remarked as they rose at the end of the meal. "I would enjoy a breath of air after two long days as a convalescent." Drawing Clary's arm through his, he guided her down the hall and onto the front veranda. There he sniffed the humid air. "It will rain again soon."

"Then you will spend another day indoors," she told him.

"I will not. I have too much work to do."

"Developing cabin fever so soon, Jack?" Her voice was wry. "Then you must know exactly how I feel."

"Touché, Clary." She heard his low laughter in the darkness, just before he caught her face between his hands. His palms were rough with calluses, but his touch was gentle.

"Never before have I met such a determined woman," he said. "You are amazing, Clary, to come here from so far away and make a place for yourself with such speed and apparent ease. The astonishing thing to me is that, for all your determination and your independent ways, I have not the least desire to tame you. I would much prefer to have you remain with me by your own free choice."

"Let me go to Philadelphia with you."

"No, Clary. Do not ask again. I have planned a busy schedule in which there is no time for a woman's presence. It would be most inappropriate for me to take you along. However, I make

such journeys with some regularity. Perhaps the next time you may join me. Would that satisfy you?"

"When will the next time be?"

"I should know the answer to that when I return. The final work has been speeded up on the Deep Cut, to meet the date chosen for the official opening. I ought to return there once or twice more before mid-October, and I may have to visit Wilmington again."

"I learned about the Deep Cut in grade school," she said. "It's in the ridge that makes up the center of the peninsula, where men are digging by hand through ninety feet of solid granite to get down to canal level. There are terrible landslides and other assorted accidents. And the bridge over the Deep Cut—I learned about it, too. I got a very good grade in history class," she ended proudly, to Jack's approving grin.

"Summit Bridge was completed before the workers began removing the earth," Jack added to her story from his own firsthand knowledge. "The engineers of the project decided it would be less expensive, far easier, and much less dangerous to build the bridge first and then dig out the canal beneath it. Unfortunately, no one knew how unstable the earth walls would be in that area, so the men are having to shore up the sides. Nor did any of the engineers expect to have so much difficulty while working through the marshes at the eastern end toward Delaware Bay.

"Sometimes I think this canal will never be finished. And it has been so expensive that I doubt if it will ever earn a dividend for the stockholders." He paused, drew a long breath, and added, almost to himself, "There are men who are most upset about the lack of return on the investment."

"I want to see the bridge, Jack," Clary told him. "In the twentieth century it has been replaced by a new bridge."

"We will all go to see it on opening day," he promised. "Now, hush, Clary. I don't want to talk about the canal anymore, or the bridge either."

"What subject do you want to discuss?" Newly aware that his hands were still holding her face, Clary fell silent.

"On Saturday evening we were conducting a most interesting conversation, which was interrupted entirely too soon," he murmured. "I would like to take up the threads of that talk again now."

"In what way?" She knew full well what he wanted, but she longed to hear him say it out loud.

"I am asking you to share my bed tonight."

"Oh, Jack." She could not breathe. She had the feeling that his hands on her cheeks were all that was holding her on her feet. Without them she would surely collapse.

"You did lead me to believe you were willing," he said. "But I will not force you, Clary. I have seen at close hand the pain and grief that ensue when a woman's true wishes are not heeded. I

would never do that to you. You must come to me freely."

"Will you do what you did out there on the river?" She did not know how she had the nerve to ask him that. She could feel the blood rushing to her face in embarassment.

"Dear girl, what can your past be like that you can ask such a question? No, don't answer. From what you said on Saturday, I can all too easily imagine the kind of treatment you once endured. Clary, I promise you we have barely begun to sample the pleasure we can give to each other."

He hadn't even kissed her yet and already she was aching to feel his hands on her. She could not see his face. His voice was a hypnotic whisper in the dark, yet she instinctively knew that everything he said was true. If she said no, he would leave her alone. It was an incredible promise, but he would keep it. She knew he wanted her, for it had been perfectly obvious during their picnic in the rowboat. She sensed that his need had grown even greater. And she, having tasted the delight of his touch, wanted to repeat the experience. Repeat it? No, she wanted to go farther. She wanted to know everything he could teach her.

"Clary?"

"Yes, Jack. I will spend the night with you." She felt a sudden rush of pleasure sweep through her veins. This was not going to be something Jack did to her; it would be something they did together. In the instant when his mouth closed on hers,

Clary ceased to marvel that he would trouble to ask her permission first, when he might so easily have swept her along on his own passion. Nor did she think at all about her earlier distrust of men. Jack had read her character over the past month, and she had come to know his integrity. She put her arms around his neck, pressing herself against him in silent surrender to what they both wanted.

She thought she would faint before he finished kissing her. His thumb rubbed along the margin of her lower lip until she opened her mouth, allowing his tongue to surge into her with devastating effect on her senses. One of his hands caught the back of her neck, holding her head steady, while his other hand slid downward to draw her lower body more firmly against his harder frame. Clary melted into him, holding on tightly, letting him ignite a roaring blaze inside her.

She knew she was going to find with him the exquisite completion she had known only once before, and that once had been in his arms. He would not stop or let her go until she was as satisfied as he was. This knowledge, this absolute certainty, eliminated her last qualms, so that when he did release her she did not feel abandoned, but waited patiently to discover what he would do next.

He put out his hand and Clary took it. Side by side they walked back into the house and along the hall until they reached the door of his room. The house was quiet and empty save

for the two of them, and Sarah had doused the candles before leaving. Clary stood just inside his bedroom door while Jack lit the candle on the table next to his bed.

"I ought to change," she murmured, looking down at the blue-green silk and white muslin.

"I will undress you." Again he held out one hand, and Clary went to him.

"You are so lovely." He removed the combs from her hair, pushing his fingers through the thick and curly mass. When Clary tilted her head back, his burning mouth descended upon her throat. She clutched at his shoulders to keep herself from sinking to her knees. A moment later his fingers were at the neckline of her gown, unhooking the bodice right down to the waistband.

"Where?" He asked, and she became aware of his hands running along the stiffened waistband, searching for the fastenings.

"Here." She showed him where the hooks were and the dress loosened and fell away from her body. The drawstring of her petticoat gave way at his assault and the garment crumpled downward atop the dress. He pulled her chemise upward over her head. Clary saw the flare of humor in his eyes when he realized that she was wearing no corset or drawers or stockings. Then laughter faded to something very like reverence and his hands were caressing her from throat to thigh and back again.

"Beautiful." His hands rested on her breasts, palms against nipples. Clary moaned softly. She

moaned again when he lowered his mouth and fastened it first on one breast and then on the other. She began to tremble, already aching to feel him inside her.

Slowly Jack eased her down onto his bed and knelt next to her. One hand slid upward, to knee and thigh and beyond. Clary gasped and pushed her hips against his hand.

"Do you know how much I want you, Clary? You are so warm, so responsive to my every touch." He buried his face in her soft belly. Clary caught at his head with both hands, pulling off the ribbon, freeing his mahogany hair from its tight queue. But when she would have lifted him toward her to kiss his mouth, he pulled away, leaving her sprawled upon the bed while he removed his robe and shirt and slippers. His fingers moved quickly on the buttons of breeches and underdrawers, and then he was pushing both garments downward together, revealing firm buttocks and long straight legs. He turned to her and Clary's eyes went wide. He saw her reaction and smiled and came to stand beside the bed. Clary could not stop staring.

"Are you afraid?" He rested one knee on the bed.

"No." Clary licked her lips nervously.

"Then what is it?" He moved closer to her.

"I was thinking how much I want you—all of you—deep inside me." Boldly she met his hungry gaze. "I was thinking what a finely made man you are, and not just physically."

"At the moment, the physical aspect would seem to predominate," he murmured.

"Do you think you could kiss me again?"

"I intend to kiss you everywhere." He stretched out beside her and took her into his arms.

"At first, I was worried that you might still be too sick for this," she said. "You know, weakened by fever and all that. It would be too bad, wouldn't it?" His mouth stopped her words for a long, sweet moment.

"You did warn me once that you have a tendency to babble when you are overly excited," he teased gently. "I shall therefore take your babbling in this instance as a positive sign and proceed to try to leave you quite incoherent." His hands moved on her, touching and stroking, his caresses becoming ever more intimate.

"But—but I—oh, Jack—no one ever—oh, good heavens!"

"I do believe I am succeeding," he whispered.

"Don't tease. This is serious. You're driving me mad." These words ended in a short little screech as his fingertips stroked slowly down her spine and into the cleft between her buttocks.

"You are absolutely right, madam." Jack separated her thighs and knelt between them. "This is no longer a joking matter. Now open your eyes, my sweet, and look at me."

"Oh, please," she whispered. "Jack—you have to—please—do something—I can't—can't—"

"Is this what you had in mind?" He slid into her so smoothly and so swiftly that Clary's eyes

flew open with shock at his sudden entrance. She saw the blaze of triumph in his eyes and heard his whispered, "Beautiful, so beautiful, Clary. You are so tight and so hot."

"Jack." He was balanced over her. Clary wrapped her fingers around his upper arms. She became aware of her inner body adjusting to his presence and tightening around him. And still she could not speak in coherent sentences. Her mind was busy elsewhere, registering the new sensations and the growing demands of her body. "You—don't stop—I need—want—"

"I know. Hold me, Clary. Put your arms around me. I need you to want me as much as I want you."

"I do. I—Jack! I can't stop!" Her arms were around his waist, her fingernails digging into his back. Some force within her demanded that she move, and when she did, he began to move, too, in deep strokes that rapidly led her to the brink of total mental chaos. Then the rhythm changed, intensifying, and Clary went rigid for a long, breathless moment. Locked in Jack's arms, safe and cherished yet still free, she went soaring into an ecstasy so wildly intense that it sent the breath out of her lungs in a long, broken cry.

Even after he separated from her, Jack held her close, kissing and caressing and whispering to her, teaching her what gentleness and tenderness could do, until at last she lay back, gazing at him in near adoration.

"Are you coherent again?" he whispered.

"Don't tease," she began, and he sobered at once.

"I am not teasing you, Clary. I only wanted to know if you are completely yourself again."

"I don't think I will ever again be my old self. Not after that."

"I am deeply honored to hear you say so. I consider your words a great compliment." He turned onto his back, but still kept an arm around her. They lay quietly for a while, until Clary was unable to keep silent any longer.

"You knew I wanted you, yet you asked my permission," she said. Rising on one elbow she looked down at him, waiting for some kind of response.

"It is only fair to ask first," he said. Clary could not be satisfied with that.

"You have mentioned a couple of times that you once knew a woman who was misused by a man." He grew still, as he always did when she pried too deeply into his past life, but this time, emboldened by their lovemaking, Clary persisted. "Is it because of her that you asked?"

"Yes." Nothing more, just the single word. Consumed with curiosity and a need to know everything she could discover about Jack, Clary tried again.

"Who was she?"

"A girl far too young and innocent to know how to deal with a man who refused to believe

her when she said she did not want him."

"You cared deeply about her." Jack remained silent. "What finally happened, Jack?"

"That man will not harm another woman." The tone of his voice chilled Clary, but she would not stop asking questions—not when he was actually answering them instead of turning them away with teasing.

"And the girl? What happened to her?"

"I hope in time she will recover her old spirits and understand that what happened was not her fault. I pray she will learn to be happy again."

"Was this in England, Jack?"

"It happened years ago." There was finality in his voice, and Clary thought it was best to let that particular subject drop. However, she did have one more comment to make.

"Madam Rose told me that you always treat her girls well." With that, she lay down beside him again. He laughed at what she had said.

"I have not been to visit the girls at Madam Rose's house more than five times since I arrived in Maryland," he said. "And not at all since you came into my life."

"I am so glad to hear that. I admit I did wonder a bit about your frequent treks into Bohemia Village."

"All I sell there is produce," he said, laughing again, "and all I buy are supplies for house and farm."

"And what do you do along the canal?" she asked, taking a chance on a new line of inquiry because he was so relaxed.

"I was a contractor for portions of the work," he replied. "I make periodic inspections to be sure the sections dug earlier under my supervision and using material I supplied are holding up well, and to make certain that the work done by my men is not being destroyed by those now in charge."

"And what do you do in Wilmington and Philadelphia?"

"The board of directors is based in Philadelphia. We hold meetings; I make reports. And there is other business to which I must attend."

"And Wilmington? What do you do there?"

He rolled over, looking down at her with eyes in which caution and a deep reserve warred with his usual teasing attitude and a new warmth directed toward her.

"Madam, I do believe you are once more becoming incoherent. Perhaps you will allow me to assist you in reaching rational thought again—after a certain interval of complete madness, of course."

"You are evading my questions."

"Only because you ask too many of them, and most concerning canal business, when what I have in mind for this evening has nothing at all to do with the canal. You ought to be flattered, Clary, and stop changing the subject, for I intend to spend the entire night listening to you babble in uncontrollable excitement."

"Jack—I think—don't—oh, don't stop—Jack!"

"Just as I thought," he said and put his mouth on hers to silence her.

# *Chapter Ten*

For Clary, the next six days passed in a romantic haze. The rain stopped and they enjoyed clear, dry weather, with the sun having grown gentler since the year was moving on toward September. Jack's arm was healing nicely with no sign of the infection Clary had dreaded, so he was soon back at work on the farm and making his regular trips into Bohemia Village. He never made any overt display of affection when Moses, Sarah, or Luke were present, but whenever his eyes met hers, Clary could read in them the desire he would unleash when nighttime came. Not certain what the reaction of the deeply religious Sarah would be to their affair, Clary did her best to conceal her feelings, too. She wondered about Sarah sometimes. Did that intelligent woman really believe that Clary and Jack simply went into their respective bedrooms at night and kept the connecting door closed? Or did Sarah think that

what Clary and Jack did together was their own private affair, something not to be discussed?

During this time, Clary's emotions were in a constant state of delightful turmoil. She was growing steadily more grounded in her new life, until she could not believe that she would ever return to the twentieth century. Nor did she want to return. There was nothing in that other time to draw her back. Her father and mother had died within a few months of each other when she was barely into her teens, and all four of her grandparents were dead years before her parents. The other relatives—aunts, uncles, cousins—who had been a part of her childhood were all scattered around the world and she seldom saw any of them. As a result, for the greater part of her young womanhood, Clary had been starved for love. She realized that what she and Rich had known together was not love at all, but something much less, something trivial and temporarily convenient. For all the years of loneliness and for the pain of her unhappy marriage, this time with Jack was her reward. She went eagerly to his bed each night, where she responded to his skilled lovemaking with increasing passion.

"I was right about you," he whispered into the predawn grayness of Monday morning. "You are the most responsive woman I have ever known."

"I never dreamed that two people could fit together so perfectly," she said. "Or that I could be so happy for so many days in a row."

187

"And so totally incoherent for so much of that time," he teased.

"You weren't exactly making intelligent conversation yourself a few minutes ago," she teased back, adding, "I hope I never have to leave you."

"I could not bear it if you did."

They had not spoken of love, but Clary knew in due time they would discuss the future. For the moment, it was enough that she had cast aside her former distrust of men and opened her heart to Jack.

On Tuesday afternoon, at Jack's insistence, she removed the stitches from his arm.

"It is best to have it done before I leave tomorrow," he said, laying his arm on the kitchen table so Clary could work on it. Luke peered at the healing gash, then at Jack's face.

"You want some whiskey first?" he asked.

"I believe a glass would not be amiss," Jack responded. When Luke gave it to him, he drained it at a single gulp.

"Luke, you get out of Miz Clary's way," Sarah chided.

"I think he wants to watch." Clary smiled at Luke. "I have a feeling that Luke plans to be a surgeon when he grows up."

"Yes, ma'am, I do," said Luke.

"What school would take a black boy?" Sarah demanded.

Clary looked from Sarah's angry face to Luke's hopeful one to Jack's half-amused expression.

"Perhaps Luke could go to school in Europe," she said.

Sarah appeared stunned by this idea. "What place would there be for him when he came home?" she asked.

"I don't know," Clary answered honestly. "We can talk about it later. For now, let's pull those stitches out of Jack's arm."

She used a sharp knife to cut each stitch and, lacking forceps, caught each knot in her fingers to pull out the thread. As he had done during the original repair, Jack made no sound and did not flinch during the somewhat rough procedure.

"Are you all right?" she asked him when she was done.

"Perfectly." But his jaw was set and his face was a bit pale. Clary swabbed the area of the wound with whiskey and put on a fresh bandage.

"That will keep it clean," she said. "Perhaps you ought to lie down for a while."

"I shall instead take this opportunity to make the final preparations for my departure," he replied. "Perhaps you would be good enough to look in on me later, to make certain that I am not lying unconscious on my bedroom floor."

"I'll do that." Clary finished cleaning off the kitchen table and disposed of the dirty bandage. When she looked up again Jack was gone. "Sarah, is Moses taking the cart into Bohemia Village tomorrow?"

"Mister Jack said to let Luke do it," Sarah answered. "He'll ride into town beside the cart, so Luke will only have to travel the one way by himself. Why do you ask?"

"I'd like to go along. If Jack won't let me go as far as Wilmington or Philadelphia, at least I could enjoy a day in the village. From the small bits of information I have been able to drag out of Jack, I understand it has grown since I last saw it."

"I don't think Mister Jack would object." Sarah considered the proposal. "Things in the village have quieted down somewhat since the work at this end of the canal is almost finished. Most of the workmen are at the Deep Cut now. They're the ones who cause the trouble, and usually on Saturday night after they are paid. That's when they get drunk and start brawls."

"Then, unless Jack dreams up some new excuse to keep me here on the farm, I will plan to go with Luke," Clary said.

"Did he tell you not to leave here?" Sarah asked.

"No, not that I couldn't set foot off the farm," Clary said. "Nor has he refused to let me go into Bohemia Village. What he objects to is my wish to see Philadelphia and Wilmington with him. He doesn't give me any good reason why I can't go. He just says I can't and that's final."

"He always complains about the heat in Philadelphia," Sarah said. "So it may be that he thinks you wouldn't like it there in the summertime. As for you goin' to Wilmington, he probably plans to visit that woman and don't want you around when he does."

"I beg your pardon?" Clary stared at her. "What woman, Sarah?"

"Don't know who she is," Sarah said. "I only know he goes to Wilmington quite often, usually after one of his inspection tours along the canal. He finishes on the Delaware Bay side and then goes on to Wilmington."

"How do you know he visits a woman?" Clary asked. "Did he tell you?"

"Mister Jack?" Sarah laughed. "You know how tight-lipped he is. I accidentally heard Mr. MacKenzie talkin' to him one time, when I was servin' them dinner. Something about the lady needin' extra money that month."

"Jack sends money to a woman in Wilmington?" Clary sat down at the table, hoping thus to hide her suddenly shaky condition, which was caused by a sharp pain somewhere in the area of her heart. "He has a mistress?"

"Don't make much sense to me either," Sarah said, apparently oblivious to Clary's distress. "Wilmington's a long way for a man to go for a bit of pleasure, but I know better than to question Mister Jack. I wouldn't dare interfere in his private affairs, and you shouldn't either, Miz Clary. If you do, he'll just snap at you or tease you, and you'll never learn what you want to know. And sometimes, it's better not to know too much."

"But Sam MacKenzie knows."

"He must, 'cause they were talkin' about it. Miz Clary, you aren't upset about this, are you? 'Cause if you are, I'm sorry I told you."

"Don't be sorry. And, no, I'm not upset. It's no business of mine." She stood up, heading

for the kitchen door. "Mister Jack Martin can do whatever he damn well pleases."

"You goin' to check on him?" Sarah asked. "I think takin' those stitches out hurt more than he'd admit."

"I hope so," Clary whispered too low for Sarah to hear her. "I hope it hurt like hell. As for checking on him, let him rot!"

Not wanting to return to the house, she went for a long, rambling walk, which lasted more than an hour and ended at the sandy beach, where she stood staring at the upside-down rowboat in which her love affair with Jack had begun.

"Damn you!" she shouted, pounding on the keel of the boat. "You bloody bastard! I actually trusted you."

Dropping to her knees in the sand, Clary leaned against the rowboat and finally gave way to tears. After a while she dried her eyes and began to think over every moment with Jack since the day he had fished her out of the canal. She had always known instinctively that he was more than the simple gentleman farmer he pretended to be. There was some important secret in his life, and the woman in Wilmington was surely a part of that mystery.

Jack had sworn to Clary that he was not married and never had been, and she believed him on that subject. Though he had not mentioned love, she thought he cared about her. And she knew she was in love with him—enough to fight for him and for the relationship that had grown between them.

"I will be reasonable about this," she said to herself. "I won't make Jack pay for what happened with Rich. I will give him another chance to tell me what is going on and to prove he loves me. In the meantime, I will talk to Madam Rose. She may know something. And possibly Sam MacKenzie will be in Bohemia Village tomorrow. I might get some information out of him, too. If I'm going to fight for Jack, I will need to know who my competition is."

Rising to her feet, she dusted the sand off her skirts, then left the beach. She made her way up the hill, through the trees, and out onto the fields. When she reached the kitchen, she stuck her head inside the door.

"Sarah, are those peaches we preserved in whiskey ready to be eaten yet?"

"You could eat them now, but they'll taste much smoother later in the season." Sarah gave her a questioning glance, then went back to stirring the pot that was simmering on the cookstove. "Why do you ask? You want to make something with them?"

"I want to give a jar of them to Madam Rose." Sarah nearly dropped her wooden spoon.

"Why do you want to make friends with that woman, Miz Clary?"

"The peaches will be a thank-you gift for the clothes she gave me." Spinning around, Clary marched across the courtyard and into the house. Jack was in his room, packing a valise.

"I want to go to Bohemia Village with you tomorrow," Clary announced.

193

"My dear, I have told you several times that I must make this journey alone," he said.

"I didn't say I want to join you on your tour along the canal. I won't ask to go to Wilmington or to Philadelphia either." Her voice was strained, and he gave her a puzzled look. Ignoring his expression, Clary continued. "I just want to go into the village to look around and see how much it has grown since the last time I was there. I also want to take some preserved peaches to Madam Rose and personally thank her again for what she did on that first day."

"She did little." Jack's frown told Clary what he thought of her association with Madam Rose. "I paid her for your clothes. She even charged me for your bathwater."

"I don't care about that. She was nice to me when she didn't have to be. She also gave me some excellent advice, which I foolishly did not heed. I will ride into Bohemia Village in the cart with Luke, and I will come home with him in the evening."

"Home?" Jack repeated, his face lit with pleasure. "Has this farm truly become your home? You cannot know what it means to me to hear you use that word."

It was then that Clary's eyes fell upon the object in his hands. It was a square, flat package wrapped in clean white paper. Jack had been about to place it into his valise when Clary had walked into the room. She recognized it as one of several parcels that he had brought home from

his most recent day in Bohemia Village, where he had made purchases from the boats stopped there to unload their cargo. There had been a length of cotton fabric from which Sarah could make new shirts for Moses and Luke and yards of dark red calico for an everyday dress for Sarah. For Clary, Jack had brought a fresh supply of rose-scented soap and a patterned woolen shawl to keep her shoulders warm when the coming autumn evenings turned cool. She had assumed that this package contained some personal item for Jack's own use. Now she saw that one side of the package had come open, and from it spilled a corner section of something made of white lace. It was a delicate piece with a pattern of roses and leaves, and it had a scalloped edge. Jack saw her looking and glanced down at it.

"Are you taking that to Wilmington?" Clary asked.

"I am."

No explanation, no excuses—just two simple words. They broke Clary's heart. Her thoughts whirled forward in time to an icy January evening when she had also been betrayed by someone she had loved and trusted. The hurt and pain were infinitely more devastating—proof, if proof were needed, that she had grown to love Jack Martin with all her heart. And like Rich, Jack had betrayed her with someone else. Clary thought she would die from pain.

"Good," she said through clenched teeth. She nodded toward the white lace. "That ought to buy you a wonderful time."

As he stepped toward her, she slammed the connecting door between their rooms.

"I am asking you to trust me."

"Forget it, Jack. I wasn't born yesterday." Clary let loose a peal of bitter laughter. "But you would think I was, wouldn't you? In spite of the fact that I was born in an age when women were a lot more aware of what goes on in the world. In that time, one man already played me for a fool. Then I came here and let you do the same thing to me. Some people just never learn, do they?"

"How dare you insult me in that way!" Jack's eyes blazed. "I am not your former husband. In this time a gentleman's word is accepted as truth. I have not played you for a fool."

"That's a laugh and a half!" Clary watched him clench and unclench his fists. From the look on his face she thought that if she were a man he probably would have slapped her across the face and demanded that she meet him with pistols at dawn. In fact, he looked so furious that she took a wary step away from him. Beside her, their evening meal sat cooling on their untouched plates. For once Clary had no appetite for Sarah's delicious food. Her stomach was twisted into several different kinds of knots that made eating impossible.

"Clary." Jack appeared to be in better control of himself now. "I know you do not properly understand this time."

"Oh, so you think I'm dumb." She saw him grit his teeth and prepare to try again. He wanted

to reason with her when she felt like throwing a full-scale tantrum.

"Obviously, you are not dumb, since you refuse to stop talking long enough for me to finish a complete thought."

"Oh, do please finish your noble thoughts, my lord. I do most humbly apologize for interrupting you." Her words made him angry all over again. Clary knew well that tight, still look he sometimes got when she said the wrong thing. At the moment, she couldn't seem to help herself. Everything she said was wrong.

"In this time," he told her with exaggerated patience, "a gentleman's word is not given lightly and it can always be believed."

"Is that so? Are you claiming that no one of your exalted, lord-of-Afon-Farm social class ever tells a lie? Not even to a stupid little female?"

"Especially to a stupid little female." His tone of voice ripped across Clary's raw emotions like a jagged saw.

"I am well aware that people in this time don't think men and women are equal," she said. "But you are wrong, and I can prove it. Why, right here on your own farm women do heavy work—"

"Be silent!"

Never had anyone spoken to Clary in that way. In Jack's demeanor and in his low-pitched, quiet voice she recognized his inbred sense of his right to command and his certainty that his orders would be instantly obeyed. For a moment she saw herself through his eyes. Since walking into

the dining room half an hour ago she had been snapping and snarling at him like some petty, quarrelsome creature. And he was right. She had not given him a chance to explain. Her own past was getting in the way here, making her assume that he was having an affair with another woman when, for all she knew, that piece of lace might actually be a present for his elderly maiden aunt—or a business gift to the wife of a member of the board of directors of the canal project. She was talking too much and interrupting him because she was upset and she was giving way to her natural tendency at such times to babble without stopping.

"Go ahead, Jack. Say what you want to say. I will listen."

"When a gentleman gives his word, it cannot be broken. I have given my word not to speak on certain matters that are of the utmost importance to other people. I will not break my word, Clary."

"That's it? That's your explanation?"

"I am afraid it is."

"But it's no explanation at all!"

"You must be content with what I have said. Clary, from what you have told me about the future, I know that in your time a man's word is no longer his bond, but the change between your time and mine is not my fault. If you cannot trust me, then—"

"Then what, Jack?" Clary caught her breath, hoping he would tell her everything she wanted

to know about his past life. She should have known better. He uttered only one brief sentence.

"I have not been unfaithful to you."

"Yet." The moment she spoke she would have called the word back if it were possible. Then she saw the hurt on his face and saw how quickly and how well he disguised it. Jack Martin was used to hiding his feelings. That being so, how could she believe anything he said?

"Will you eat?" he asked coolly, indicating the food on the dining room table and the sideboard.

"After this argument? No way." She started for the door, hoping she would reach her bedroom before she began to cry.

"Perhaps a glass of Madeira then to settle your nerves." He filled two glasses with the pale wine she liked to sip after their evening meals together.

"No, thank you." She nearly choked on the words, fighting the tears.

"What, Clary?" His voice was soft and caressing, making Clary yearn to throw herself into his arms. "Will you not allow me to ply you with liquor?"

"Is there a key to that door between our rooms?" she asked.

"I can find it if that is what you wish." It was amazing the way his voice could change from tender to ice cold in an instant. "But you do not need to use a key. You have my word on it—I will not disturb you this night."

"I hope not, for your sake, because if you try anything, I plan to scream bloody murder until Sarah, Moses, and Luke all come running to the house to see what you are doing to me."

With that, Clary stalked out of the dining room. She was in the act of shutting her bedroom door when she heard the tinkling sound of a delicate crystal wineglass shattering against wood.

# *Chapter Eleven*

In the weeks since Clary had last seen it, Bohemia Village had indeed changed. There were new houses being built on Bohemia Avenue not far from Madam Rose's establishment, and behind her house two new streets had been laid out, with buildings in the process of being erected along them. On the shore of the cove at the south side of Back Creek the lime kiln was operating at full blast, no doubt to produce whitewash with which to paint the new buildings.

The most noticeable difference, however, was not in the village but along the sides of the canal and on the water, where there was a steady bustle of activity. There was a line of boats tied up, waiting to go through the locks. At the moment Clary could see two boats already in the first lock with the lock gates closed, and she could hear the steam engines in the pump house working hard to force water into the lock, which

would raise the boats to the next level.

Along the water's edge an informal market had been set up where fruits, vegetables, and sacks of grain were being sold. There were smaller vendors purveying baked goods, meat, milk, and butter to those who lived on their boats and who depended upon such salesmen to replenish their food supplies. A cart loaded with barrels of water rumbled past on its way to sell that vital commodity to the boatmen, for in the immediate area of the village and the locks, the water was much too dirty for drinking.

The village was noisy: loud voices, laughter, and the occasional curse mingled with the sounds of hammer and saw and the rattle of carts making their way along the rutted road, which had seen no improvement at all since Clary's first visit. On the canal boats babies cried, women chattered among themselves, and dogs barked. A team of mules stood waiting to be harnessed to the boats after the lock had been filled and the vessels were ready to move on. The animals would pull the boats through the canal to the next lock. The sudden braying of one of the mules added to the general clamor. When Jack spoke, he had to shout to be heard above the noise.

"Over there, Luke." From his seat on a fine black stallion, Jack pointed, and Luke turned the cart left toward the market, bringing the horses to a stop next to the long wall of Madam Rose's house. Looking across Back Creek, Clary could see a similar market set up on the opposite side of the water.

"Uncle Dancy!" Luke shouted, waving wildly, and a tall, muscular black man left one of the market stalls to join the group from Afon Farm. Incongruously, for such a huge man, he had the handle of a basket filled with fresh fruits and vegetables slung over one arm.

"Hello, Luke, Mister Jack. Good to see you." Dancy favored his former master with a broad grin. "Mr. MacKenzie's in town, too. He's over at the pump house on business, but he'll be back soon. Luke, you've been growin' again. Those overalls are too short for you."

"I know," Luke said proudly. "Mama says I'll be tall like you and my daddy." Seeing the curious glance Dancy turned on Clary, Luke hastened to introduce them while Jack found a place for the cart among all the others gathered at canalside with produce.

"I remember you," Dancy said to Clary. "You were almost drowned."

"I feel much better now." Clary allowed Jack to help her down from the cart, but she did not look directly at him, nor did she thank him for his assistance. She had refused to talk to him since their quarrel the previous night. "Dancy, is Madam Rose at home? I would like to pay her a visit."

"She's there, Miz Clary, but ladies don't usually pay her no visits. There's not many ladies here in Bohemia Village, but they mostly just ignore Madam Rose."

"Then she will probably be glad to have a little company." Clary shook out her skirts and

tilted her straw sunbonnet lower over her brow to shade her face from the sun. Dancy stared at her as if wondering what to do, then looked to Jack for direction.

"There is no stopping this determined woman," said Jack. "She cares little for the conventions of proper society, and she will visit Madam Rose whether I approve or not. If you will be good enough to conduct her to the front door, Luke and I will deliver our merchandise to those who have ordered it in advance. Then I will help him to set out the baskets of produce he plans to sell."

"Dancy has his own work to do." In her loftiest tone Clary objected to Jack's arrangements. "There is no need for him to escort me. I know where the front door is. If someone would just remove the jar of peaches from the cart before a customer decides to buy them," she finished, watching a pair of women looking with interest into the back of the cart.

"I'll take 'em." Slinging the handle of the market basket higher on his arm, Dancy picked up the large crock and started for the front of Madam Rose's house.

"Dancy, I can carry the peaches myself." Clary hurried to catch up with him. It was an uphill walk and Dancy was moving fast. Breathlessness soon silenced Clary's protests. She and Dancy rounded the corner of the house together and came out onto Bohemia Avenue just as Madam Rose herself appeared on the veranda.

She was wearing the same pink taffeta dress

Clary remembered from their first meeting, and her pale blonde hair was piled high in an elaborate style. The curls and waves and braids were apparently well lacquered, because they were not in the least disturbed by Madam Rose's present vigorous activity. She was holding a small, squawking man by the scruff of the neck, carrying him out of her house and across the veranda to dump him into the street.

"See that you stay out of my house in the future, Hezekiah Bartram," said Madam Rose. "I run a dignified, orderly place, and I will not have any man threatening me or my employees with physical harm."

A young woman with improbably red hair appeared on the veranda to hand Madam Rose a black felt hat. The redhead clutched a skimpy, transparent wrapper across her tightly corsetted figure,

"Thank you, Hermione." Madam Rose flicked her wrist and the hat flew into the street to land next to the hapless Hezekiah Bartram.

"You'll pay for this, you worthless bitch!" he snarled, scrambling to his feet with defiant glances toward several men who had paused to watch the scene. Clary was surprised to see that the expelled customer was well dressed in a full suit made from what appeared to be good dark fabric, a white shirt, a neatly tied cravat, and black leather gloves.

"Pay? Me? I think not. You are in the wrong here." Madam Rose dusted off her hands as though she were ridding herself of all traces

of her former customer. She straightened one of
the flounces on her pink taffeta skirt, and then,
catching sight of Clary, she nodded pleasantly.
"Good day to you, Miss Cummings. Were you
looking for me?"

"I came into town with Mr. Martin and Luke,"
Clary said. "If you're not too busy, I thought I
would pay you a short visit. I wanted to thank
you for your kindness and for the clothing you
gave to me."

"I was paid in full." Madam Rose frowned a
little, as if she could not quite comprehend what
Clary's true purpose might be.

"I know that," Clary said, "but kindness should
always be reciprocated. I have brought a crock of
preserved peaches for you and your—er—your
employees." She waved a hand toward Dancy,
who stood holding the crock along with the
basket still slung on his arm.

"For me?" Madam Rose looked baffled. She
recovered quickly. "Why, thank you, Miss
Cummings."

"May I come in?" When Madam Rose hesitated, Clary added, "I have been inside before,
you know."

"Of course." Madam Rose led the way through
the front door. The interior of the house was just
as Clary remembered it: smoky, smelling of beer
and stronger spirits, with half-a-dozen barely
clad girls lounging about the main room. Madam Rose looked around as if wondering where
to put Clary, and Clary decided to take the ini-
tiative.

"The table in the corner will be just fine," she said. "We can look out across the water and watch the activity while we talk. That is, if you are not too busy to take a break."

"A break?" Madam Rose's mouth quirked upward in a brief smile as she deciphered the unfamiliar term. "I think I would like a cup of coffee. Hermione, since Dancy is busy, would you be so kind as to bring us two cups of coffee please?

"Now, Miss Cummings," Madam Rose said when they sat at the table sipping the strong black brew, "perhaps you will tell me your real reason for this visit."

"I really did want to thank you," Clary said. "I appreciate what you did for me on that frightening day when I first came here."

"No one has come to Bohemia Village looking for you, if that is what concerns you," Madam Rose told her.

"I didn't even think about that," Clary said with complete honesty.

"Then there must be some other reason for your presence here today. Everyone who comes to this house wants something, if not from me, then from one or more of my employees."

"Can't we just meet like friends?"

"No, Miss Cummings, we cannot." Madam Rose fixed Clary with a level gaze and spoke bluntly. "I am the proprietress of the local whorehouse, where a respectable woman never sets foot except under the most dire circumstances. How can you and I ever be friends?"

"Perhaps because we are women alone, trying to make our way in a difficult world."

"Do you find life at Afon Farm so hard?"

"No. Actually, I'm very happy there. That is, I was until yesterday."

"What happened yesterday?"

"Sarah said that Jack visits a woman in Wilmington."

"Ah." With a satisfied air, Madam Rose sat back in her chair, coffee cup in hand. "This is why you are here. You want to know if I know who the woman is."

"Do you?" Clary leaned forward. "Madam Rose, if you know anything about her, please tell me. You can't imagine how important it is to me."

"On the contrary, I can imagine all too easily." Madam Rose shook her head sadly. "I did warn you about Jack Martin on our first meeting. It is plain to me that the man is harboring more than a few secrets. And now you have fallen in love with him. I suppose that you have been to bed with him?"

"Well—" Clary could feel a flush creeping into her cheeks under Madam Rose's unflinching observation.

"Oh, Miss Cummings, how foolish that was of you." Madam Rose clucked her tongue a couple of times, conveying dismay and just a touch of impatience at such naivete. "If you could not get a cash payment from him immediately, then you should have insisted that he marry you before you allowed him into your

bed. Now you have nothing left with which to bargain."

"At the time, I wasn't thinking very clearly," Clary admitted.

"That is perfectly obvious. It is a pity that no one informs young women about these practical matters at an early age. With a few pertinent words at the right time, much grief could be prevented. But then, of course, if all young girls were wise, I would soon be out of business for lack of ladies to work for me."

"How in heaven's name did an intelligent woman like you ever get into this business?" Clary asked, momentarily diverted from her quest to learn whatever she could about Jack's presumed mistress in Wilmington.

"I believe I explained it on our first meeting," said Madam Rose. "I was betrayed by a man. No one whispered those pertinent words into my ear when I needed to hear them, though whether I would have believed them is another matter."

"Where did you grow up?" Clary asked. "You seem to be well educated."

"I was born in southern New Jersey. My ancestors settled there from Sweden almost two hundred years ago. As for my education, I had it from my father."

"Are your parents still alive?"

"I do not know. If they are living, they would not be pleased to hear from me, not after I disgraced my family by losing my virtue to a local boy with whom I imagined myself to be in love."

"Couldn't you have married him? Wouldn't that have stopped any scandal?"

"Why would he marry me when he had already had what he wanted from me? No, he married a girl wiser than I. Thus, I learned a most important lesson. A clever girl never gives away what she can sell for cash or for a wedding ring."

"That's an awfully cynical attitude."

"I would say it is practical. I have done remarkably well. I own this house, you know, and the land upon which it stands."

"But you have to deal with rough types like Hezekiah Bartram."

"I can manage such men. I have learned how during the last ten years. The question is, Miss Cummings, how can you manage Mr. Jack Martin? Assuming you wish to manage him. What do you want from him?"

"Faithfulness, first and foremost."

"Then you want something that is nearly impossible to attain. Few men remain faithful to a mistress, and fewer still to a wife."

"I'm in no position to dispute either of those statements," Clary said. "Which brings us back to the woman in Wilmington. Do you know anything about her?"

"I have heard rumors. Sam MacKenzie once said something about his friend's peculiarly secretive personal life," Madam Rose responded thoughtfully. "I cannot imagine when he has time to see her, if she exists at all, for Mr. Martin is usually to be found at the canal or here in Bohemia Village or else at his farm."

"Sarah says he stops in Wilmington whenever he is at the eastern end of the canal."

"How does Sarah know this? More importantly, what is her purpose in telling you? Could she be trying to make trouble for you, perhaps hoping to drive you away from Afon Farm?"

"I don't think so. We are on very good terms," Clary said at once. "I like Sarah. No, I can't believe she would be that devious."

"Perhaps she hopes that you will win Mr. Martin away from his mysterious mistress and marry him yourself."

"You mean you think Sarah has chosen me as the future Mrs. Martin?" Clary gave a surprised laugh. "Good heavens, the thought never occurred to me."

"Miss Cummings, it seems to me that you never think at all about truly important subjects," Madam Rose said. "You ought always to question the motives of those people with whom you deal."

"You are right about that. If I had questioned my husband's motives before marrying him, my life would have been a lot happier. Madam Rose, I wish I'd had an adviser like you years ago."

"Then you appreciate the truth of all I have been telling you this morning," said Madam Rose. At a loud noise from the direction of the street outside, she turned her attention from Clary. "Whatever can that be?"

The two women hastened to the front door to find a crowd of about 20 men and women gathered in the street just beyond the veranda.

In the forefront was Hezekiah Bartram.

"There she is," the little man cried dramatically, pointing a finger at Madam Rose. "The Whore of Babylon. There ain't no place for her and her girls in a decent town like this."

Madam Rose stepped fearlessly to the edge of her veranda.

"Why, Hezekiah," she said, laughing, "you were not so determined to see me and my girls removed from town an hour ago when you were in an upstairs room threatening to cut the throat of poor Hermione if she did not perform certain unspeakable acts for your pleasure—and at a greatly reduced price, too. I will not tolerate violence, and the prices in my house are not open to bargaining. I had every right to remove you from the premises."

"He always was a tightfisted man," someone in workman's clothes shouted.

"Who always liked a tightfisted girl," another man shouted, this sally making those gathered in the street laugh aloud or titter behind their hands, depending upon their gender.

"Those of you who patronize my house know that it is clean, and so are my girls," Madam Rose said to the crowd. "We serve a useful purpose here by keeping the men who work on the canal content so that they do not bother the respectable ladies, and so that they drink inside rather than in the streets. Hezekiah, I think your unhappiness stems more from the fact that I personally ejected you from the house than from any true sense of moral outrage. Your

dignity was hurt when a mere woman lifted you off your feet and carried you outside."

"Sorry I missed that," one of the men in the crowd cried. "Madam Rose carrying Hezekiah. Haw, haw." The others began to laugh with him. Hezekiah Bartram's grim face turned a dull shade of red.

"I suggest that you good people return to your work now," Madam Rose said, smiling at them with all the ease of a star performer.

The crowd slowly dispersed until only Hezekiah Bartram was left standing in the street, glaring at Madam Rose and at Clary.

"You ain't seen the last of me," he growled. "Nor your girls neither. I'll see to it that you all get what you deserve and that everybody from Bohemia Village to Newbold's Landing knows about it." The look he sent Clary included her with the rest of Madam Rose's girls.

"You will not be admitted to my house again," Madam Rose told him. "You will have to take your pleasure elsewhere. Come, Miss Cummings." She spun on her heel and walked into the house, Clary following her. Dancy met them just inside the door.

"What's goin' on?" he demanded. "I heard the noise, and someone said there was trouble brewin'."

"I took care of it," Madam Rose told him. "It was only Hezekiah Bartram complaining again. I have forbidden him entrance here in the future."

"That man is mean," Dancy said. "I think it's

'cause he's so short. Short men think they have to prove they're just as good as us tall fellows."

"Be that as it may, we will not receive Mr. Bartram again, and," Madam Rose said, raising her voice so her employees could hear her, "any girl who has dealings with him away from this house will lose her job the moment I hear of it. Is that understood? He might have killed poor Hermione, and he could just as easily kill any one of you."

"What the devil happened here?" Jack appeared through a doorway that, as closely as Clary could tell, must lead from the kitchen into the main room. He looked around the room until he found Clary. "Are you all right?"

"Of course," she said. "Madam Rose and I can take care of ourselves."

While Madam Rose filled Jack in on the details of the incident with Hezekiah Bartram, Dancy went to the bar and poured out four big glasses of whiskey. One of these he handed to Clary.

"You better drink this," Dancy said. "You look like you're still scared. I sure am. That Mr. Bartram gives me chills." With that, Dancy swallowed an entire glass of whiskey in one gulp.

"I was not afraid," Clary declared.

"That's what she always says, too." Dancy looked toward Madam Rose. "But she always drinks one of these right down after a customer causes her that kind of trouble. I wish she'd give up this life and run an eatin' place instead."

"Sarah said something like that, too," Clary observed.

"Sarah knows what she's talkin' about." Dancy carried the two remaining glasses of whiskey to Madam Rose and Jack. Admitting to herself that Dancy was right and Hezekiah Bartram's vicious threats had unsettled her, Clary took a small sip of the liquor. It burned all the way down her throat, and she put the glass down on the counter without drinking the rest.

"Thank you, Dancy." Jack took the whiskey Dancy handed to him, and then he turned to Clary. "I have made all the purchases I intended to make here in the village and have packed them in the cart. Luke has sold just about everything we brought into town, so he is preparing to leave."

"But we just got here," Clary protested.

"With Hezekiah Bartram lurking about, I want you safely away from Bohemia Village," Jack said. "You should be able to reach the farm well before nightfall. No one would dare to bother you there. Madam Rose, might Clary borrow one of your guns for a few days? I want to take my own with me."

"Gun?" Clary echoed. "What for?"

"For protection, so you will be able to defend yourself if it should prove necessary," Jack told her.

"Guns terrify me. I don't even like to look at them. If driving back to the farm is going to be dangerous, why couldn't Luke and I just stay in town over night?" she asked.

215

"You would still have to go home tomorrow," Jack pointed out. "Nor is there a suitable place for you to sleep."

"Perhaps we could rent a room from Madam Rose." At once, realizing what she had said, Clary began to blush.

"Even if I had the space to accommodate you, my house would be a most unsuitable place, Miss Cummings," Madam Rose said. "Surely you understand that. If you were to spend a night beneath my roof, your reputation would be ruined. It is already tarnished by the time you have spent here today. Do not make matters worse for yourself."

"I don't give a damn about my reputation!" Clary cried.

"Well, you should," Madam Rose said. "Once lost, a woman's reputation is almost impossible to recover. I know of only one or two ladies who have succeeded in doing so."

"You cannot stay in town," Jack put in, "because Sarah and Moses expect you to return this evening. If you and Luke do not appear as planned, you will cause them considerable worry."

"I hadn't thought of that," Clary admitted.

"Miss Cummings, as I advised you earlier today, you really ought to learn forethought," Madam Rose said. "You speak—and I suspect you act—altogether too impetuously."

"And sometimes incoherently," Jack murmured, a wicked light in his eyes. Then, sobering, he said, "Clary, you will leave for Afon Farm

within the hour, and though I doubt that Hezekiah Bartram will come after you, I still want you to take a gun along, just as a precaution."

"Couldn't Luke have the gun?" Clary asked.

"Luke is not in the best of health at the moment. I do not believe he will be able to see well enough to fire a gun."

"Luke is sick?" Clary asked, instantly concerned. "He was fine this morning."

"He is not ill. Luke was involved in an altercation. It seems he is fond of Emmie, the girl who works in Madam Rose's kitchen," Jack told the women. "Unfortunately for Luke, one of the canal workers also likes Emmie and believes he has a prior claim on her affections. I am afraid their dispute came to blows."

"Is Luke badly hurt? Where is he?" Clary demanded.

"I would not interfere if I were you," Jack said. "At the moment Luke and the other young man are in the kitchen with Emmie and Lucy both tending to their somewhat minor injuries. I notice that Dancy has just been summoned. He will no doubt give his nephew and the other fellow a proper dressing-down." Seeing that Jack seemed more amused than worried about Luke, Clary relaxed.

"Mr. Martin," Madam Rose said, shaking a finger at him, "every time you visit my house, some problem occurs. If you are not more careful, I will be forced to refuse you entrance to the premises."

"If I go," said Jack, giving her a mischievous grin, "so goes Sam."

"You are all alike." Madam Rose raised her finger again. "Black or white, young or old, men are nothing but brawling little boys. Has any of my furniture or my precious china been damaged by this kitchen battle of youthful, would-be lovers?"

"The actual battle took place outside," Jack said. "Luke lost a basket of tomatoes when he fell on them and crushed them to a pulp, and some of his apples rolled into the canal. Otherwise, little harm was done. Luke has a bloody nose and he will have a swollen eye for a day or two. The other boy has only scraped knuckles."

"Disgraceful." Madam Rose shook her head at this story, but Clary could see how her eyes sparkled with humor.

"I will get the gun." Madam Rose stepped behind the bar. Reaching down she brought out a pistol and laid it on the counter. She gave Jack a shrewd look. "Since she professes a distaste for weapons, I suggest that you load it for Miss Cummings in order to lower the chance of a misfire if she has to use it."

"That looks like a real antique!" Clary exclaimed, hurrying across the room to look at it more closely. "Is it a flintlock?"

"What else would it be?" Madam Rose asked.

"It is certainly not the newest of pistols," Jack agreed, "but when properly fired, it is most effective."

"I don't know how to fire it." Clary bit her lip,

contemplating the weapon with unhappy fascination.

"I am going to show you how to do it. Hold it like this." Jack put the pistol into her hands. The stock was made of walnut wood worn smooth from years of handling. The barrel was iron, and the firing mechanism was brass, though it was in serious need of polishing.

"It is not loaded," Jack told her, "so you need not be afraid of it. Hold it out as though you were pointing at something. No, not so close to your face. If it misfires, it could blind you."

"Gee, thanks a lot!" The pistol was so heavy that Clary had to hold it in both hands. Feeling like a character from a costume movie, she put a finger on the trigger and held the gun straight out in front of her.

"That is a little better." Jack adjusted her grip and her stance. "You will have to cock the hammer before pulling the trigger." He took the gun from her and demonstrated.

"I really think I will need a lot more practice before I try to use this thing," Clary said.

"Nonsense." Madam Rose took the gun, pointing and cocking it with impressive ease. "You see how simple it is?"

"Have you ever had to use it?" Clary asked her.

"Occasionally, to threaten troublemakers," Madam Rose replied, "which may be all you will need to do. Or you may very well arrive safely at Afon Farm without having to touch the gun at all."

"I will load it," Jack said, holding out his hand.

"I do know how." But Madam Rose gave the gun to him and brought from behind the bar the supplies he would require. Clary watched while Jack poured powder down the barrel, inserted a cotton wad and ball, and used a rod to ram the ball against the powder.

"Now a little powder in the pan," he said. "If you find yourself in a situation where you are forced to use the gun, you will have only to cock the hammer, aim, and pull the trigger."

"Be prepared for the recoil," Madam Rose warned.

"Let's hope I don't have to use the bloody thing," Clary responded. "But just in case, how close do I have to be to my target if I'm going to have any chance of hitting someone? Oh, my God, I can't believe I'm talking like this!"

"Count on twenty feet," Jack told her. "Perhaps a little more, but since you are unskilled with firearms, your aim is likely to be undependable."

"You can say that again," Clary muttered.

"I have already said it," Jack replied. He cocked an eyebrow at her. "Is that one of your local phrases?"

Clary nodded. Holding the gun in one hand, Jack tilted her chin upward with the other. She thought for a moment that he might kiss her, but he ran a finger across her lips instead.

"I do not seriously expect that you will face any danger on your way home," he said. "It is

only that I do not want to take any chances with your life. Or with Luke's life either. Clary, you will have to drive."

"That will be a lot easier than handling a pistol," she said. "I have had a fair amount of practice driving the cart on the farm during the past few weeks."

"I know. I am depending on you, Clary." Again his fingertips traced her mouth.

"Have a good trip," she whispered.

"When I return, you and I will have a serious discussion." His voice was pitched too low for Madam Rose to hear him.

"Does that mean you will finally give me some honest answers about your past?" Clary asked.

"I will endeavor to make arrangements to do so," he said.

"What the hell is that supposed to mean?"

She spoke too loudly. Jack dropped his hand. Madam Rose frowned at her coarse language. Clary would have apologized, but Dancy returned to the main room, bringing Luke with him. The boy had a split lip and his nose and left eye were badly swollen. He had been cleaned up and was wearing one of Dancy's shirts and holding a cloth to his still-bleeding nose.

"Wait till your mother sees you," Clary told him.

"She won't be happy," Luke agreed, "but it was worth it. Lucy said I was wonderful."

"Lucy? I thought the fight was over Emmie!"

"Don't ask, Miz Clary." Dancy rolled his eyes and shrugged his shoulders. "After listenin' to

those four young folks in the kitchen, my poor old head is spinnin' in bewilderment. The boys that were fightin' are friends now. Anyways, what you said about Sarah is true. She'll want to take Luke's hide off him when she learns what he's been doin' here in town. Only trouble is, he's too big for her to spank anymore."

"If I know anything about Sarah," Clary responded, "she will do all the necessary punishing with one or two well-chosen sentences."

"Luke," said Madam Rose, "I strongly advise you to leave Bohemia Village at once before *I* decide to remove your hide and save Sarah the trouble. Do not return to my house until you are able to behave yourself in a more gentlemanly fashion."

"Yes, ma'am." Luke hung his head.

"Come on." Clary touched his arm. "Let's clear out of here before they run both of us out of town on a rail."

"Miz Clary, what's that mean?" asked Luke.

"Never mind. Just find the cart and get into it. I'm driving."

Jack brought the cart to the front of Madam Rose's house. He gave Clary a hand to lift her up to the seat beside him. There they sat for a minute, with their thighs pressed together and Clary's hand still in his. In spite of her disenchantment at his refusal to reveal his true self to her, the attraction he held for Clary remained as strong as ever. She swayed toward him.

"I regret that I cannot accompany you home," he said, "but there is not enough time. The boat

on which I have booked passage will enter the first lock in two hours and later today I am expected elsewhere for appointments."

"Including Wilmington?" Clary drew back, putting distance between them. She could not deny to herself that she wanted him still, but she could not trust him to behave honorably and she could not believe what he said to her. At the mention of Wilmington, she saw a veil come down across his eyes, and his handsome features grew tight and distant.

"I have several appointments in Wilmington," he said coolly, "and several more in Philadelphia."

"Philly," she murmured. He tensed, looking sharply at her before, just as suddenly, he relaxed.

"Of course," he said. "Your familiar name for the city. I remember now. Take care, Clary. I am depending on you to get Luke home safely."

He put the reins into her hands and jumped out of the cart. Luke climbed in beside her, where Jack had been. With a last wave to Madam Rose and Dancy, Clary drove away from Bohemia Village. They had not gone far before Luke doubled over.

"I don't feel so good," he informed her, "and this bouncin' don't help my stomach none."

"Do you want me to take you back to Madam Rose's?" Clary asked him.

"No. We got to get home tonight or Mama will be real worried. Maybe if I stretch out down there in the back and put my head on that sack

of flour and close my eyes for a while, I might feel better."

"That's a good idea." Clary slowed the horse until Luke climbed off the seat and lay down in the cart.

"Are you comfortable?" she asked, twisting around to see him.

"Yes, ma'am. I'm lying' in your shadow. It's cooler here. I might fall asleep."

"Go right ahead."

Clary urged the horse to move faster, hoping to get home before the cart ride could make Luke seriously ill. The road and the green landscape slipped quickly past. There was no chance that she would become lost. On the way to Afon Farm there was only one fork in the road, at which she would bear right, and there were no crossroads at all. There was no sound from behind her.

"Luke?" Clary looked around to discover him fast asleep. A light touch of one hand to his forehead assured her that he was not feverish. She returned her attention to the horse and the road.

The horseman came out of the trees at a gallop and did not stop until he was planted firmly in the middle of the road, his position forcing Clary to pull the cart to a full stop. She knew at once who he was, and a chill ran along her spine when she saw the hard and crafty expression on his face.

# Thrill to the most sensual, adventure-filled Romances on the market today...

## FROM  LOVE SPELL BOOKS

As a home subscriber to the Love Spell Romance Book Club, you'll enjoy the best in today's BRAND-NEW Time Travel, Futuristic, Legendary Lovers, Perfect Heroes and other genre romance fiction. For five years, Love Spell has brought you the award-winning, high-quality authors you know and love to read. Each Love Spell romance will sweep you away to a world of high adventure...and intimate romance. Discover for yourself all the passion and excitement millions of readers thrill to each and every month.

## Save $5.00 Each Time You Buy!

Every other month, the Love Spell Romance Book Club brings you four brand-new titles from Love Spell Books. EACH PACKAGE WILL SAVE YOU AT LEAST $5.00 FROM THE BOOK-STORE PRICE! And you'll never miss a new title with our convenient home delivery service.

Here's how we do it: Each package will carry a FREE 10-DAY EXAMINATION privilege. At the end of that time, if you decide to keep your books, simply pay the low invoice price of $17.96, no shipping or handling charges added. HOME DELIVERY IS ALWAYS FREE. With today's top romance novels selling for $5.99 and higher, our price SAVES YOU AT LEAST $5.00 with each shipment.

## AND YOUR FIRST TWO-BOOK SHIPMENT IS TOTALLY FREE!

### IT'S A BARGAIN YOU CAN'T BEAT! A SUPER $11.48 Value!

*Love Spell* ⊕ A Division of Dorchester Publishing Co., Inc.

# Get Two Books Totally
## F R E E —
## An $11.48 Value!

▼ Tear Here and Mail Your FREE Book Card Today! ▼

PLEASE RUSH
MY TWO FREE
BOOKS TO ME
RIGHT AWAY!

**Love Spell Romance Book Club**
P.O. Box 6613
Edison, NJ 08818-6613

AFFIX
STAMP
HERE

# *Chapter Twelve*

Hezekiah Bartram lounged forward in his saddle to lean on his horse's neck, but Clary knew he was not as relaxed as he was trying to appear. Her very first glimpse of him had shown her how determined he was.

"Well, now," he drawled, leering at her, "what have we here, drivin' down the road all alone? Ain't you the new girl at Madam Rose's?"

"I am not," Clary declared. "You are mistaken. Move aside, Mr. Bartram, and let me pass."

"You can pass when I'm done with you," he replied, "but that won't be for a long time. I got needs that Madam Rose ain't about to let me satisfy at her place, so I'll just have to do it elsewhere. You be a good girl for me, and maybe I won't send you back there. Maybe I'll just keep you for myself. That'd teach uppity Madam Rose a lesson, wouldn't it?"

"Luke," Clary whispered while Hezekiah Bar-

tram was still speaking, "are you awake?"

"Yes, ma'am," came a frightened answering whisper from down in the cart.

"Stay where you are until you have a good chance to jump up and surprise him."

"Miz Clary," Luke asked, "you plannin' to use that gun?"

"Let's hope I don't have to." Clary took a firmer grip on the reins and raised her voice, cutting across Hezekiah Bartram's continuing promises to have his lascivious way with her. "I said let me pass, Mr. Bartram. I am not who you think I am, and I have no intention of going anywhere with you."

"Ain't you the brave little lady?" Hezekiah Bartram kicked his horse, sidling closer. Leaning over he caught the harness at the cart horse's head. While his attention was momentarily diverted Clary shifted her position on the cart seat so her skirts would cover the gun lying on the floor at her feet. With one toe she gently nudged the gun along until it was just below her right hand. While doing this, she kept her eyes on Hezekiah Bartram and she tried to hide her growing apprehension behind a mask of righteous indignation.

"Let go of my horse," she ordered.

"I don't feel like it." The man gave her an insolent grin that set Clary's teeth on edge. She wanted to slap his face. "In fact, I think I'll just slip onto this horse and guide him right where I want him to go." He swung one leg up on his own horse's back as if he were preparing to

leap off it and onto the horse that was pulling Clary's cart.

"Don't you dare!" Dropping the reins, Clary lunged for the gun and came up holding it in both hands. She pointed it at Hezekiah Bartram.

"That old thing ain't loaded," he declared with considerable bravado. But he must have doubted his own words, because he took his hand off Clary's horse and put his foot back into the stirrup. Clary kept the gun leveled at his heart.

"It most certainly is loaded," she insisted, "and I know how to use it. Now move away."

"You ain't goin' ta kill me. You're just teasin'."

"I wouldn't bet my life on that if I were you," Clary warned. "Get out of the road and let me go by!" It occurred to her that if he obeyed her, he could easily pursue the heavily packed cart and she would not be able to outrun him. Nor could she handle the reins and a gun at the same time. She sincerely hoped Hezekiah Bartram would not think of that.

"I ain't goin' nowhere, 'cause you ain't got the strength to fire that thing," he said, laughing at her. "Look at you, your hands are shakin'!"

Clary sensed that the moment of truth was fast rushing upon her. She could almost hear Jack's voice telling her again how he was depending on her to get Luke safely home to his parents. She would do what was necessary to fulfill Jack's trust in her. She took her left hand off the gun and used it to cock the pistol as Jack had taught her. Then she put both hands around the stock again, with both index fingers on the trigger.

"Take one step nearer and I will shoot," she said. Unfortunately, her voice wavered and Hezekiah Bartram just laughed at her threat. Then he urged his horse directly toward her.

"I'm warning you!" Clary knew she had no choice. She had no doubt at all that Hezekiah Bartram would disarm her if he could, and then he would very likely turn the gun on Luke, who was still crouching unseen just behind her. And when Luke was dead, Hezekiah Bartram would rape her. She could not let that happen. Aside from the personal danger she faced, Luke—and Jack—were depending on her. Clary squeezed the trigger as hard as she could.

At the same instant that Clary fired the pistol, Luke leapt to his feet with a wild, earsplitting yell. There was a tremendous flash of light just in front of Clary and a deafening noise that seemed to her to rumble on and on, echoing and reechoing like thunder. The sound left her ears ringing. She saw Hezekiah Bartram tumble off his rearing, screaming horse like a figure in a slow-motion scene.

The recoil from the pistol forced Clary's arms upward and pushed her back off the seat and into the cart. She landed on top of Luke, with her straw bonnet knocked askew over her face.

"Miz Clary, are you all right?" Luke helped her to sit up and took the pistol out of her hands. Clary attempted to straighten her bonnet but she nearly fell flat again when the cart began to plunge forward along the road at breakneck speed. She tore at the ribbons, pulling the hat

off so she could see what was happening.

"The horse is bolting!" Luke yelled. He vaulted onto the seat to grab at the reins. They slipped out of his hands and he dove after them, reaching far over the front of the cart.

"Luke, be careful!" Clary stood up to catch at the straps of his overalls, pulling him back onto the seat.

"I got 'em!" Luke shouted.

"I can help!" Clary climbed onto the seat beside him and put her hands on the reins just below his. It took the combined efforts of both of them sawing hard on the reins to bring the panicked horse to a trot, then to a walk, and finally to a trembling, snorting halt.

"Oh, Luke," Clary gasped, "for a minute there, I thought we weren't going to make it."

"Me, too." Looking at her, Luke started to laugh uproariously. At first Clary feared he might be hysterical and she wasn't sure what she ought to do with him, but then she realized that he was genuinely amused. "Miz Clary, I wish you could see yourself. Your face and hands are so black. You look like a black lady."

"I do?" Clary looked down at herself. The sleeves and bodice of her gray cotton gown were liberally dusted with black, as were her hands and wrists. She rubbed at the backs of her hands. "Good grief, this stuff is like soot. It will take a lot of soap and hot water to get it off."

"What'll we do now?" Luke asked. "If you missed shootin' Mr. Bartram, he's goin' to come

after us, and he's goin' to be real angry."

"If I didn't miss him," Clary said, "he could be lying in the road bleeding. He's a terrible person, but we can't let him bleed to death."

"You mean you want to help him?" Luke gaped at her.

"I think we have to find out if he's hurt or not," Clary said. "If I shot him, then it's my responsibility to see that he gets the care he needs."

Luke considered this idea for a few minutes while Clary tried to steady her breathing and stop the shaking of her hands.

"If Mr. Bartram does need sewin' up," Luke suggested, grinning, "maybe you could let me practice on him. That would be a fine punishment for what he tried to do to us."

"Luke, that's awful!" She meant to be stern, but suddenly they were both convulsed with laughter. They leaned against each other, whooping and howling, while tears ran down Clary's face and she wiped them away with blackened fingers and then, for lack of a handkerchief, wiped her running nose on her dirty sleeve.

"I feel so much better now," she said when she could speak again. "I don't think I have ever been so frightened in all my life."

"Me neither," Luke agreed.

"It's not over yet." Bravely Clary straightened her shoulders. "Let's get this cart turned around and drive back to survey the damage."

They found Hezekiah Bartram lying sprawled on the road. He did not move when Clary pulled

the cart to a stop next to him. There was no sign
of his horse. Clary assumed it was finding its
own way back to its home.

"Is he dead?" asked Luke, sending a fascinated
look toward the immobile man.

"I can't tell from here. You stay in the cart."
Clary began to climb down to the road.

"Be careful," Luke whispered as if he feared
to waken Hezekiah Bartram.

"I will." Clary approached from the side. Cau-
tiously, she prodded at an ankle with her foot.
Hezekiah Bartram did not move. Still using her
foot, Clary pushed against his hip, and then gently nudged him in the ribs. Finally she crouched
down next to his head and put a hand against
his neck.

"He's alive," she reported with considerable
relief. "At least I won't have his death on my
conscience. I can feel the pulse in his neck, but
he is out cold."

Luke scrambled down to join Clary in the middle of the road. He stood with hands on his hips,
gazing down at the unconscious man.

"You're not gonna drive away and leave him
here," Luke said slowly. "You'd never do that. So
we got to get him into the cart."

"I can help you lift him," Clary said. "He's not
very big, so he can't be too heavy. We'll take him
back to Bohemia Village. Help me shift some of
those sacks and boxes so we can fit him into the
back."

Their preparations quickly made, Clary and
Luke lifted Hezekiah Bartram and shoved him

into the cart. They were not gentle with him, but that didn't concern Clary. She was just relieved to know that her shot had apparently gone wild, and the man's injuries were the result of the fall from his horse.

"Luke, I want you to sit in the back and hold the gun on him," Clary said, "just in case he wakes up along the way."

"But you fired a shot from the gun and we got no ball or powder to reload it," Luke protested.

"We know that," she said, "but Hezekiah Bartram is unconscious, so he can't know that we haven't reloaded it. Just pretend, Luke."

"I know." Luke grinned at her. "I'll tell him that, if he moves, I'll put a ball right in his chest."

"Maybe you ought to consider becoming an actor instead of a doctor," Clary retorted dryly.

Clary's second arrival in Bohemia Village in one day attracted considerable interest. Well aware that her blackened face and hands would cause curious comment, she kept her eyes fixed on the road and did not respond to the questions called out to her.

Sam MacKenzie had finished his business at the pump house and had started back toward the village. He met Jack Martin, who was about to step onto the footbridge just as Sam stepped off it. The two men stood talking until the racket of a cart racing down Bohemia Avenue and the sounds of loud voices caught their attention.

Clary saw Jack and Sam meet and shake hands. She drove the cart right up to them, bringing it

to a halt with a bit of a flourish. She definitely enjoyed seeing the incredulous look on Jack's face, and she liked even more the note of anxiety in his voice.

"My God, Clary, what has happened to you?"

Clary jumped from the cart into his waiting arms. Not until she felt him enclose her in a tight embrace did she believe the afternoon's ordeal was finished.

"I'll ruin your clean shirt," she murmured, pressing her powder-smeared face against his chest.

"That doesn't matter. Sweetheart, are you hurt?"

"No. No, I'm fine. Just a bit disheveled, that's all."

Jack shifted Clary in his arms. She looked up at Luke, who was standing in the cart. He still held the pistol pointed downward toward the man lying at his feet.

"Luke, give me the gun." Jack put up his hand and Luke laid the pistol in it with an air that suggested he was glad to be rid of both the weapon and the responsibility of standing guard.

"I think he's startin' to wake up," Luke said.

"Who do you have in there?" Jack asked. "Dare I guess?"

While they were talking, Sam MacKenzie walked around to the back of the cart. Reaching forward he dragged a groggy Hezekiah Bartram up by his shirtfront and stood him on his feet.

"Hezekiah, lad, I have a feeling that you are in serious trouble," Sam said to him.

Clary pushed herself out of Jack's embrace to start toward Sam and the man he was holding.

"Mr. Bartram stopped us on the road," Clary informed the mostly masculine crowd gathering around them. "He apparently believed that I was one of Madam Rose's girls and he wanted me to go with him. He was quite clear about what he expected of me."

"Did he touch you?" Jack's hands clamped hard on Clary's upper arms, holding her still. "If he laid one finger on you, I will personally—"

"He never got near the cart," Clary said. "Luke jumped up yelling to scare him, and I fired the gun. Then Mr. Bartram's horse threw him. That's why he was unconscious. I'm afraid my bullet missed him by a mile."

"That's exactly how it happened." Luke jumped down from the cart, grinning broadly. "Miz Clary was magnificent!"

"You were no slouch yourself, Luke," Clary told him, grinning back at him. "You were the one who stopped the horse when it bolted. I could never have handled it by myself."

"The horse bolted?" Jack's grip on Clary tightened.

"I told you," Clary said, "I am not hurt." She expected him to make some remark to the effect that he was glad she and Luke had come through the experience unscathed. Instead, he began to scold her.

"If you had remained on the farm, where I wanted you to be," he said, frowning at her, "this would never have happened."

"Don't start that again!" Clary raised both hands in a rapid gesture, breaking Jack's hold on her. "It's not my fault if Hezekiah Bartram is some kind of sex maniac. The man ought to be locked up!"

"She's right about that," Sam MacKenzie agreed. Raising his voice, he added, "Who'll take this reprobate into custody?"

"I will." A man dressed in plain dark garb and a flat black hat stepped forward. To Clary's eyes he looked like pictures she had seen of William Penn. Her assumption that he must be a Quaker was verified by his next words. "I am Josiah Grey. As a member of the Religious Society of Friends, I believe it is my duty to take this man into my care and to remonstrate with him about the error of his ways."

"I wish you luck with him," Clary said with some sharpness. "In my opinion, he's crazy."

"If indeed he is crazed, then he will receive good care until his wits are in order once more," Josiah Grey told her with polite gravity.

"If you are wise, sir, ye'll tie him up before ye take him away," Sam advised.

"Restraint will not be necessary. Gentle persuasion will do." Josiah Grey put a helping hand on Hezekiah Bartram's elbow. "Come along, friend. My house is on the north side of the canal. There I will care for your injuries and provide a room where you may rest."

"What this town needs," Clary said, watching Josiah Grey leading his still-groggy charge across the footbridge over Back Creek and then

235

on toward the canal, "is a jail and a couple of competent policemen."

"And what you need," Sam told her, forestalling what was apparently going to be a heated remark from Jack, "is soap and clean clothes. Lassie, it's back to Madam Rose's with ye for another bath."

"Now there I agree with you, Sam." Madam Rose shouldered her way through the onlookers who remained after Hezekiah Bartram was taken away. "Miss Cummings, I have just heard the news. I am most distressed by what has happened to you, and I feel a certain responsibility. I trust you are unharmed? And Luke, too?"

"We are both fine," Clary assured her, "though I think Sam is right and I will have to impose upon your hospitality once more."

"No." Jack broke into this conversation. "Clary and Luke are to go back to Afon Farm immediately. She can take a bath once she gets there. Sam, I want you to escort them. Use my horse. I won't require it while I am traveling by boat. You can ride the same horse back to town tomorrow and leave it here for my return."

Hearing Jack's imperious tone, Clary's frazzled nerves snapped. "Did it ever occur to you to ask my opinion before you start making decisions about my life?" she shouted at him. "I am not going anywhere until I get this black junk off my face and hands, and I want to change into clean clothes."

"Clarissa, you are creating a spectacle." Jack spared a quick glance at the onlookers, who

appeared to expect some new form of entertainment from the building argument. "I know Josiah Grey. He is an excessively kindhearted man and I believe his custody of Hezekiah Bartram will be entirely too lax. Bartram will find it easy to evade Mr. Grey, and he may come back into town looking for you. Therefore, I want you and Luke to reach the farm before nightfall.

"Luke may return to Bohemia Village in his father's company when necessary but you, Miss Cummings, are to remain at the farm until my return. Now you are both to leave at once, as will I. The boat on which I am scheduled to travel is delaying its departure for my benefit."

"Do you mean that you still intend to go on this ridiculous trip?" Clary was afraid she would break down and start to cry right there in public. She was still suffering from her frightening episode with Hezekiah Bartram and from firing a gun at another human being, and she wanted and needed comfort. Jack's first brief embrace and his concern for her had been gratifying, but she wished he would take her into his arms and hold her close. Instead, he planned to send her off to the farm with someone else. Sam MacKenzie was a nice man, but he wasn't Jack.

"I can't believe you are doing this to me," she said to Jack.

"I have little choice. I must be on that canal boat if I am to meet the Philadelphia-bound ship that is scheduled to leave Newbold's Landing on the Delaware at noon two days from now. It is important that I keep my appointments along

the canal and in Philadelphia. You will be perfectly safe in Sam's care."

"That isn't the point," she began.

"I think it is. You acquited yourself well this afternoon. I expect you to continue doing so. You will leave for Afon Farm as soon as Sam can saddle my horse." Jack gave her a hard look. "Clary, I have my reasons for what I am doing. You must trust me. I beg you, make no further protests." He brushed one finger across her lips as if to silence any words she might have spoken. With a nod toward Luke and Madam Rose and a quick handshake for Sam, he started across the footbridge to the canal and the boat that lay waiting in the filled lock.

"Jack!" Clary started after him.

"Let him go," said Madam Rose. "Men do whatever they please and you cannot hold on to a man who does not want to stay with you."

"He doesn't understand," Clary began.

"I think he understands all too well what you feel for him." Madam Rose put an arm around Clary's shoulders to keep her off the footbridge. The firm pressure she exerted slowly drew Clary away and turned her around so that she did not see Jack board the boat and thus she did not know whether he glanced back at her or not.

"Let him go," Madam Rose said again.

When Clary finally looked toward the canal as she mounted the step to Madam Rose's veranda, she saw that the lock gates were opened.

A mule had been hitched to the boat, and it was plodding slowly eastward along the towpath, pulling the boat. Jack was nowhere to be seen.

# *Chapter Thirteen*

They did not follow Jack's orders exactly or promptly. When Madam Rose pointed out to Sam that the cart horse deserved a rest after its hasty return to Bohemia Village, Sam agreed to delay their departure for an hour. During that time Madam Rose sent Luke to the kitchen to report to his Uncle Dancy—and, presumably, to Lucy and Emmie as well—all the details of his exciting afternoon.

"Tell Dancy I said to feed you," Madam Rose instructed the boy. "Nor would a cup or two of hot coffee be amiss, I think. You will find that coffee will lift your spirits in preparation for your homeward journey."

"Yes, ma'am. Thank you." Luke disappeared through the doorway to the kitchen.

"Now, Miss Cummings, I shall attend to you." Madam Rose led the way upstairs. "I fear the dress you are presently wearing is beyond

redemption. You will require a new one."

"Ruined or not, this is the dress I'll have to wear," Clary said. "If you remember, Jack refused to let me stop here to clean up and change. I don't have any money of my own to pay you with, and if you put another dress on Jack's bill, he'll know I disobeyed him."

"Are you so afraid of him?" Madam Rose gave her a quizzical look, as if she found that idea amusing.

"Of course I'm not afraid of him," Clary snapped. "It's just that we've been arguing so much lately. I don't want to cause any more problems between us."

"If you slept with him, then he owes you something in return," said Madam Rose, pausing outside the door to the wardrobe room.

"I wanted him, too," Clary said. "Putting a price on what we did would be immoral. I'm sorry if that insults you, but it's the way I feel."

"Amateur." Madam Rose spoke softly, and there was an odd glow in her eyes. She looked thoughtful for a moment, then said, "I believe the preserved peaches you brought to me earlier today would sell for the approximate value of the simple gown I have in mind for you."

"Those peaches were a gift!" Clary exclaimed, following Madam Rose into the room she remembered well. It was even more crammed with clothes than on the first occasion when she had seen it.

"The peaches will not, however, cover the cost of a full bath with heated water, a large towel, or

scented soap," Madam Rose continued. "I will instead provide you with a pitcher of hot water, a slightly used cake of kitchen soap, which will no doubt prove more effective for your present needs than the scented variety, and one small hand towel—all of which should be sufficient for cleaning your face and hands. Since the road to Afon Farm is dusty, you may prefer to wait until you reach your destination before changing your dress."

"I don't believe you," Clary said.

"I have spoken nothing but the truth," Madam Rose responded.

"I mean, I have never met anyone like you!" Clary explained.

"That is entirely possible. Here is the gown." Madam Rose held up a dark blue cotton dress that was not very different in style from the dress Clary was wearing. Tiny white flowers were woven into the fabric, the waist was a bit high, the skirt ankle length and full, the sleeves long and gathered into matching cuffs. This new dress also had a fichu of white linen trimmed in lace.

"It will make me look like the local school-marm," Clary said, fingering the blue material, "but it will be perfect for the cooler weather of autumn."

"That is what I thought. I will have Lucy wrap it for you." Taking dress, fichu, and a white cotton petticoat, Madam Rose left Clary, sending her off to the bathing room.

Clary found the black powder as difficult to remove as she feared it would be. Promising

herself a full bath when she got home, she did the best she could with the supplies Madam Rose had provided, and then she hastened to meet Sam, who displayed no great desire to leave. She found him in the main room on the first floor, talking to Madam Rose.

"Take my warnin', darlin'," Sam said to Madam Rose, "and hire a man to sit up there by the front door with a loaded gun. If Hezekiah Bartram slips loose from Mr. Grey's care, the man may come after you. I don't want ye harmed, lassie," he finished in the fake accent he usually reserved for his working hours.

"Extra help would be costly," Madam Rose objected.

"Not havin' it could cost ye yer life." Sam dropped the accent to speak with increasing and completely genuine emotion. "Rose, be sensible. That man is a dangerous lunatic. This isn't the first time he has caused trouble for you. He expects your girls to accommodate him in the most disgusting ways, and then he calls you and your employees Whores of Babylon. He's deranged, I tell you!"

"Perhaps Mr. Grey will prevail upon Mr. Bartram's better nature," Madam Rose suggested.

"That's not bloody likely and you know it! Hezekiah Bartram has no better nature!" Sam glared at her in exasperation. "Rose, I'm begging you to let me put one of the workmen from the canal in here tonight as a guard."

"You would put a fox in the henhouse," Mad-

am Rose told him. "I will handle the matter of Hezekiah Bartram in my own way, Sam.

"Ah, Miss Cummings, you appear to be quite restored." Catching sight of her guest, Madam Rose left Sam and hurried toward Clary. "Are you ready to leave? Lucy has placed your new gown in the cart."

"Once again I am beholden to you," Clary said.

"Not at all. Neither of us owes the other anything. I trust you will take care not to require my assistance again."

They found Luke sitting on the cart seat, reins in hand. Sam helped Clary up to the seat, Madam Rose waved a hand, and they set off for Afon Farm once more.

"Where've you been, Luke? Have you been dawdlin' along the way?" The tall form of Moses emerged from the evening gloom as the cart came to a stop in front of the barn. Moses stopped short when he caught sight of the mounted rider who accompanied the cart. "Mr. MacKenzie? What's wrong?"

"We had an adventure," Luke announced. "Miz Clary shot a man."

"What did you say?" Sarah appeared behind her husband.

"I didn't hit anyone," Clary assured her. She accepted Sam's helping hand to dismount from the cart and then she stood quietly while Luke and Sam between them provided an account of the day's events.

"Humph," said Sarah in disapproval when the tale was done. She looked from Sam to Clary, including both of them in her comments. "That's what comes of associatin' with fallen women—nothin' but trouble. Now you men get that cart unloaded and the horses rubbed down and settled for the night. Miz Clary, you come with me. I've got water heatin' that you can use for a bath, and I want to put that dress you're wearin' into a tub to soak overnight."

"Where I come from, a dress this damaged would just be discarded," Clary noted, but she obediently followed Sarah toward the house.

"That would be plain wasteful. I'm sure we can wash it clean tomorrow, and then you can wear it when you're workin' in the kitchen or doin' heavy housecleanin'."

Now, at last, Clary enjoyed the hot bath she craved, in the bathing stall next to the kitchen. Then, feeling greatly refreshed and wearing the blue dress Madam Rose had given her, she met Sam in the dining room for the meal that Sarah had concocted with less than an hour's notice.

"Fried ham slices, pickles, sweet potatoes, greens, hot biscuits and sweet butter, apple pie." Sam surveyed the sideboard with anticipatory pleasure. "Sometimes, when I am far away, I dream about Sarah's cooking."

"Speaking of going far away," Clary said, allowing Sam to hold her chair for her, "did Jack mention to you why it is so important for him to be in Philadelphia this week? He was so insistent about keeping to his mysterious schedule."

"There's no secret about it," Sam answered. "Jack must have told you that he was one of the contractors for several portions of the canal as well as for the Summit Bridge. He wanted to make his last inspection well before the official opening of the canal. If there should prove to be any problems, he wanted to allow time to correct them. As for his visit to Philadelphia, I understand that he holds a fair number of shares in the canal company. He deals with the board of directors in his capacity as contractor and then he attends meetings of stockholders. From what he said to me I gather that his appointments in Philadelphia this week have to do with the grand opening next month and with final work on the canal. It won't be completely finished on opening day, you know."

"Why couldn't he just tell me all of that himself?" Clary asked.

"Didn't he?" Sam slanted a knowing look at her, letting Clary understand that he knew perfectly well that she was pumping him for information. In response, Clary gave up all pretense of making polite conversation in favor of asking more probing questions. She went directly to the heart of her unhappiness with Jack's absence.

"What kind of meeting will Jack attend in Wilmington?"

"I don't know." Sam busied himself with cutting the piece of ham on his plate.

"You must know," Clary insisted. "You are his friend."

"Friends don't pry."

"Are you telling me to shut up?"

"To do what?" Fork halted in midair, Sam looked at her, openly puzzled by her twentieth-century slang.

"Even after all these weeks, I still forget sometimes." At once she knew he would not understand those words because he was unaware of her coming back from the future. "Forgive me, Sam. I come from a place where women sometimes speak out of turn and use unseemly language. I know I have no right to interrogate you about Jack. It's just that he seldom tells me anything important, and I can't help wondering about his life before I met him."

"I have known Jack Martin for more than five years," Sam said. "We have worked together, eaten at the same table often, and sometimes drunk too much together. On several occasions we have traveled together. I consider him my best friend, and I know I am his friend. But there is always some part of him that remains hidden. Now it's my experience that a man will be willing to leave certain areas of his friend's life private if that's the way the friend wants it. But a woman keeps asking questions. Women pry until they learn everything there is to know about a man, and sometimes they use what they learn against him. So a man has to be careful in what he reveals."

"You are talking about betrayal," Clary said. "I would never do that to him."

"Perhaps not. But he hasn't known you very

long, so it could be that he's not sure of you yet. Give him time. He hasn't sent you away from Afon Farm, has he? That means he wants you there. Judging by the way he acted this afternoon, I'd say he does care about you."

Clary could see that Sam was embarrassed to find himself speaking so intimately about his best friend with someone he had met only twice, so she decided to switch to a slightly different subject. She did it with a teasing laugh.

"What about you, Sam? Do you have deep, dark secrets?"

"Dozens of them." Sam laughed back at her. "I'll tell you one. I want to own a ship that will carry cargo from Baltimore through the canal to Wilmington and on to Philadelphia or even upriver to Trenton. I'm a seafaring man at heart, but at this time of my life, I would be content to sail a safer course."

"Jack did mention something about this," Clary said, hoping to encourage him to include her favorite subject in his conversation once more.

"We've discussed becoming partners, but I haven't seen the right ship yet," Sam told her.

"If you come through the canal regularly, you could see Madam Rose during your stopovers," she noted.

"Ah, yes, Rose. I worry about her, you know. Bohemia Village is changing fast. The canal workers are beginning to move on to other projects and respectable businessmen are coming into town and bringing their families

248

with them. There is sure to be a church built before long, and clergymen don't approve of Rose's kind of business. Neither do the wives of businessmen. Rose may soon discover she has no place in Bohemia Village. Hezekiah Bartram's antics were just the beginning of what I fear could become persecution."

"Not while I have breath left to say anything about it," Clary declared. "Madam Rose has been nice to me, and I have to tell you, Sam, I admire her for not giving in when her life fell apart back in New Jersey. She picked herself up, came here, and started her own business. While it's sure not the kind of business I would want to run, she has made a success of it."

"You are her only female champion," Sam said. "Nor are there many men who would stand up for her. They visit her house after dark, but by daylight they like to pretend they are above spending time with that kind of woman."

"You'd stand up for her," Clary said. "That's another of your secrets, isn't it, Sam? You care deeply about her. Where I come from, we would say you are in love with her."

"Ah, well, lassie, let's allow that secret to remain between the two of us, shall we?"

"My lips are sealed," Clary told him. "But I think Madam Rose already knows that particular secret about you. And I wouldn't be surprised if half of Bohemia Village and most of the canal workers knew it, too."

\*     \*     \*

Sam left early in the morning, and Clary went back to her by-now-familiar routine of helping Sarah in the kitchen or with the housekeeping or working in the fields when she was needed. She expected Jack to be gone for at least two weeks, so she tried to keep herself busy, hoping to make the time go faster. One of the projects she intended to get underway during the autumn and winter was that of teaching Luke to read and write. She began by speaking to Sarah on the subject. She had scarcely begun before Sarah reminded her of everything that Jack had done for his former slaves, who had become his valued employees.

"What Moses and I have here on this farm is much more than I ever dreamed of having," Sarah said. "Now I dream of Luke having still more. But I also want him to be safe, and he can't be that if he starts pushin' himself up above folks who won't take kindly to an educated black boy."

"I understand," Clary said. "There is no easy solution to that problem, Sarah, not even where I come from, though we like to think we are much more enlightened than people are here. Luke is eager to learn and we can't deny him that pleasure, though his eagerness may diminish as he realizes how difficult it will be. I could try to teach him to read and write and do numbers, and we'll just see how he progresses. At the very least, if he can read, he will possess a skill that will enrich his life."

"I wish I could read," Sarah said. "I memorized some Psalms when I was little, 'cause the master

in the house where I was used to read them to the family and the house slaves every evening. I say those Psalms over and over on Sundays, but knowin' how to read would be much better."

"I could teach you, too," Clary offered.

"Not me, I'm too old now for school," Sarah replied in a voice that allowed no argument. "But you have my permission to try with Luke. I know Moses won't object. Then Luke could read new Psalms to us on Sundays."

Clary began teaching Luke that same evening after his chores were done. She sensed in him the impatience she would expect of any teenager who was set to a task he believed a younger boy should do, but she repeatedly reminded him of his desire to be a doctor and, buoyed by that dream, Luke persisted.

The golden September days ran into each other, and save for the loneliness caused by Jack's absence, Clary was content. He came home a day early, on a Sunday afternoon.

With Moses, Sarah, and Luke occupying themselves in quiet Sabbath pursuits in their cottage, Clary felt at loose ends. The day was warm and sunny, drawing her to the little beach and the river, where a faint haze drifted above the water as a forewarning of the cooler autumn days soon to come. Clary was wearing her work shirt and overalls, which she removed as soon as she stepped onto the beach. Underneath she wore her old bra and bikini briefs. While trying to adapt to the undergarments that belonged with her nineteenth-century dresses, Clary still clung

to her twentieth-century underwear when she
was in her working clothes. Each night she
washed her bra and briefs and hung them to
dry over the towel bar of the washstand in her
room. Both garments were beginning to look a bit
bedraggled, but they would serve as a makeshift
bathing suit. Not that anyone would see her. Luke
came to the river to fish as often as he could, but
Sarah would not allow him to do so on a Sunday.
There were farms on the other side of the river,
but they were far enough away for Clary to be
confident that she would be all but invisible to
observers on the farther shore.

She walked across the beach carefully, avoiding the gumball seeds that had dropped from
the trees edging the beach. The little brown balls
were covered with sharp projections and were
painful to tread upon.

When she stepped into the water, soft mud
oozed up between Clary's toes and a small
silverfish darted away from her. The river was
shallow, so she was well into the water before
it was deep enough for her to swim. Once she
was past the mud along the shore she found
the river perfectly clear and clean. She swam
for a long time, and she was refreshed by the
first faint hint of autumn chill in the water.

She was finished with her swim and ready to
leave the water when she saw Jack move out of
the trees onto the beach. He had discarded his
coat and cravat and was clad as she had first
seen him, in an open-necked white shirt, a wide
leather belt, light tan breeches, and high black

boots. However, his hair now barely reached his earlobes. Presumably, he had visited a barber while in Philadelphia or Wilmington.

Treading water, Clary waved to him, then started toward the shore. She knew that he saw her, though he did not return her greeting. When she was close enough to shore to stand up and walk out of the water she was also near enough to see the look of astonishment on his face—and the way his eyes took in every detail of her exposed body.

"My God, Clary, what are you doing?" he demanded. "Why are you naked?"

"I have been swimming. I'm not naked. This is a bikini." Amused by the mingling of horror and desire she discerned on his face, she turned slowly around so he could see her, front and back. "Actually, I am more covered up than some women I have seen at the seashore."

"It is worse than wearing nothing!" he declared.

"Why, Mr. Martin, I am surprised to know that a man of your undoubtedly worldly experience can be shocked by a mere bathing suit." She came out of the water to stand before him, looking up into his usually unfathomable gray eyes. Today she could easily read those eyes. They were dark with desire.

Clary experienced a moment of thrilling triumph. Whoever he had been with and whatever he had done during his absence from Afon Farm did not matter. Jack wanted her now. And she was frighteningly glad to see him again. She forgot that she was angry with him, forgot her

resentment at his refusal to take her with him on his travels. All Clary wanted in that breathless moment, when they stood less than a foot apart, looking into each other's eyes and souls, was Jack's arms around her. When his hand stroked along her cheek and into her hair, Clary stopped breathing, waiting for what she knew he would do next.

With a muffled oath he caught her to him, his arms hard around her, the sharp edges of his belt buckle stabbing at her sensitive skin. Clary did not care if his embrace hurt. His mouth was warm on hers, her fingers were winding through his newly shorn hair, and she was almost as close to him as she wanted to be.

Almost. But he was going to remedy that shortcoming as soon as possible. He released her just long enough to unfasten his breeches and push them downward. Then they were lying on the sand and Jack was pulling at her flimsy garments.

"Be careful," Clary gasped, still trying to hold onto her wits. "If you tear them, I can't get another set. Then I really will have to swim naked."

"Only if you let me swim with you." His hands were on her bare breasts, caressing until she cried out at the hard tightness he created.

She managed to pull off his shirt so she could stroke her hands across his broad chest, but it seemed there would be no time to undress him further. They were both too eager to join together to waste a moment more than was absolutely necessary.

"I would be jealous of the fish that swim between your beautiful legs," he murmured, his fingertips like the fluttering fins of those same fish upon her thighs. Quickly his fingers moved higher into an exquisitely sensitive place.

"Oh, Jack," she cried, "I want you inside me."

"Do you, Clary?" He knelt between her thighs. She saw the dark intensity of his face and knew how hard he was trying to control his own need until she was fully aroused and ready for him.

"Yes, I'm ready now." She lifted herself to meet his forward thrust and moaned in pleasure when he surged into her.

"I have missed you." He held himself still, his face slick with perspiration, his mouth hard with the effort to restrain himself for a few moments more. "You feel so wonderful. I dreamed about you every night. Don't move like that. Clary, I can't wait!"

"I don't want you to wait." She pulled his face down to hers and kissed him hard, and she kept on moving because she knew he liked it in spite of his protest. Then he was moving, too, moving in hard, almost violent strokes that told her far more clearly than words could ever reveal just how much he had missed her and how desperately he desired her. She met his passion with her own, met and melted together with him into one searing, joyful whole. And in his shout of passion fulfilled she heard the echo of her own softer cry.

When it was over she clung to him still, not wanting the moment to end, not wanting to

separate from him. She lay upon the sandy beach, only now becoming aware that there were at least two spiny gumballs pressing into her back. And only now understanding how much she loved him. Jack Martin filled her heart in the same passionate, tumultuous way he filled her body. And she was terrified, for she remained unsure of his exact feelings toward her. She had to learn whether he loved her— or whether she was but a temporary interval in a life in which someone else mattered more to him than she did.

With the late-afternoon breeze ruffling the water and making Clary shiver, they lingered only a short time on the beach. Once back at the house, Clary rinsed river water out of her hair and sand off her back and legs, and Jack piled a tray with food and took it to his bedroom.

"Join me," he invited when Clary appeared in the connecting doorway wearing only her ruffled cotton nightgown. "I note that you are properly clad for the occasion, my dear."

"As are you, sir," Clary returned, indicating his blue dressing gown and bare feet. The tray of food sat in the middle of his bed. Clary perched at one corner of the mattress, her back against the carved bedpost. She reached for a slice of ham, but he slapped playfully at her fingers.

"I shall feed you, madam, and when you are full I shall make love to you again, albeit more slowly this time."

"Is that a promise?" Clary opened her mouth

for the piece of ham he placed between her lips.

"You may depend upon it." Jack sank his teeth into the other end of the ham slice so that their lips were touching.

Startled, Clary drew back. "What are you trying to do?" she demanded.

"You still have much to learn," he murmured, unabashed by her reaction. "In many ways you remain remarkably innocent, my sweet."

"Perhaps that is because you keep me ignorant," she replied, recognizing the opening for which she had been waiting.

"It will be my great pleasure to enlighten you, Clary."

"Will it?" She regarded him through narrowed eyes. "All right then, enlighten me, Jack. Tell me what you have been doing while you have been away."

"That is not precisely the enlightenment I had in mind," he murmured, smiling a little.

"What was the weather like in Philadelphia?" she asked. "What did people talk about at the board of directors meeting? What sort of celebration do they plan for the grand opening next month?"

"I had hoped for a somewhat more intimate conversation." He was peeling an apple, his long fingers quick and graceful with fruit and knife. Clary thought about those fingers stroking along her thighs or her breasts. She closed her eyes, telling herself to keep her mind on the important subject. She could not afford to let this opportunity slip away. When she opened her

eyes again Jack was looking at her in a questioning way.

"Why won't you tell me anything about your life beyond Afon Farm?" she cried.

"I have not asked you for every detail of your previous life, Clary. Grant me the same privacy."

"If you really cared about me, you would open up a bit."

"I have told you a great deal about myself."

"You haven't really told me anything at all."

"Clary, why can't you understand that there are some stories that are not mine to tell?"

"What the hell does that mean?"

"Do you know," he said smiling, "that I have not heard you swear for a long time? I have almost missed the sound of your sweet voice cursing." Then, with complete seriousness, he said, "Leave this subject alone, Clary. There are things I can never tell you."

"Then how can you expect me to trust you? I want to trust you, Jack, but you make it almost impossible."

"When have I ever proven untrustworthy to you?" he demanded. "Or to anyone else you know in this time? Clary, my dear, I do care deeply about you. Surely you know that by now. There are promises I have given that I cannot and will not forswear. If my refusal to break my word does not prove to you that I am an honest man, then there is little hope for us."

He reached for her, and unable to stop what she wanted so much, Clary went to him willingly.

"Tell me you believe me," he whispered against her lips. "Tell me that you do trust me. Say you care for me as truly as I care for you."

"I do, Jack." She felt completely at home in his arms, safe and secure there. Never before had she known this kind of hot, drugging desire for any man.

How could a man who was not completely trustworthy make her feel this way? Loving Jack as she did, how could she not trust him? As his lips came down on hers in a heated rush she knew that even if every word he spoke to her was a lie, she did not want to learn about it. All she wanted was to love him and to hope that one day he would love her in return.

# Chapter Fourteen

"We have done remarkably well this year." Jack sat at the dining room table, his account book open before him and coins in four neat piles of varying sizes arranged on the table's glossy surface.

"The harvest isn't over yet," said Moses.

"Nevertheless"—Jack looked from Moses to Sarah to Luke and finally to Clary—"with the coming festivities when the canal is officially opened I thought you might be glad of an early payment, in case there is something you want to purchase in preparation. I will divide profits again at the end of the year and give you a second payment then."

"I would like a new bonnet to wear for the grand opening," Sarah said. "Moses tells me a woman in Bohemia Village was selling hats and shawls the last time he was there. And Moses ought to have a new dress shirt for the occasion.

I really should go into the village with him the next time he takes produce to sell."

"Well, then, here you are." Jack pushed a pile of coins toward Moses, another toward Sarah's hands. A third pile he gave to Luke. He picked up the fourth pile, which was considerably smaller than the others. "Clary, you have not been at Afon Farm for very long, but certainly you have earned this much."

Clary was so surprised that she took the money without protest when he gave it to her. She stayed where she was as the others left the dining room, waiting until she and Jack were alone before she spoke.

"I can't accept this." She held out the coins to him. Rising from his chair he put both his hands over hers, preventing her from returning the money.

"You have earned every penny," he said.

"Doing what?" she cried and felt herself beginning to redden under his warm and tender gaze.

"Everyone on this farm knows how helpful you have been," he said. "It is only fair to pay you. Why do you object, Clary? I pay Sarah for her work, and she does not take it amiss."

"Sarah doesn't sleep with you," she whispered.

"I want you to have some money of your own. I have paid you only for household chores and for fieldwork. As for the rest, that is between us, and what you give me in private is something far beyond my ability to repay. Nor would I want to pay you, for an exchange of money would only cheapen the dearest, sweetest hours of my life."

His hands tightened on hers. "I think you do not fully appreciate what you mean to me. You have crept so quickly into my heart and banished a terrible loneliness. Clary, I pray you will never have to return to your own world, for I do not know how I could exist without you."

She gazed up at him through eyes blurred by sudden tears. This was the closest he had yet come to declaring that he loved her. Her lips parted in a silent invitation to a kiss, but he shook his head.

"I will not kiss you now," he said, "nor embrace you either, lest you misunderstand in the slightest degree. The coins you hold you earned by honest work. The sweetness we share together each night is something separate from our daily routines.

"Separate," he repeated, speaking almost to himself, "and yet that sweetness permeates every moment of my days. Clary, I wish I could tell you—" He stopped, shaking his head again. "I cannot say more."

She knew his reticence had something to do with his mysterious past and the promises he had made to people she might never meet. But she did not doubt the sincerity of his declaration to her, and she gave in return her own declaration. Taking her cue from him, she did not mention love in so many words.

"I don't want to return to the twentieth century, Jack. There would be nothing for me in that time. Everything I care about is here." Her voice was choked with emotion.

"Thank you, my dear."

She believed that he was exerting a great deal of willpower in his effort to contain strong passion. For once she was grateful for his restraint. If he had taken her into his bedroom to make love to her then and there, she might still have wondered exactly how much of the money he had given her really was for her work and how much for what they did together in bed. Silently she scolded herself for her inability to completely trust and believe in the man. Were it not for her own unhappy past, the last hour would have buried all her doubts about him.

When he released her hands and returned to his books, Clary left the dining room to store her wages at the bottom of the blanket chest in her bedroom. She could think of nothing she wanted to purchase with the money, not even clothing for the grand canal opening. Jack had brought her a new straw bonnet from Philadelphia to replace the one so badly battered during her encounter with Hezekiah Bartram. The new hat had a wide brim in front, and it was lavishly trimmed with flowers and embroidered ribbons. Gray leather gloves and a small purse on a chain completed his gifts to her. Clary planned to wear all of them and her new blue dress, without its fichu, to the canal opening. If the weather were cool, she would add to her ensemble the patterned shawl that was Jack's first present to her.

Recalling the days just before her marriage to Rich, when her closet and bureau drawers had

bulged with clothing, she could only shake her head in amazement. Thanks to Sarah's help at the washtub, the well-worn gray cotton gown was cleaned of the black powder and restored to wearable condition. It was Clary's serviceable dress for every day. She donned her overalls and work shirt for really dirty jobs. She wore the green-and-white formal gown on most evenings, which left the new blue dress for special day-time occasions. This was her entire wardrobe, and for the moment at least, she felt no need to add to it.

"Well, perhaps some twentieth-century under-wear," she muttered, smoothing the ribbons of her new bonnet. "Half-a-dozen pairs of white cotton briefs would be lovely. But if I want them, I'll have to make them myself, and they'll have drawstrings at the waist, because there is no elastic yet."

Thinking that elastic was a minor luxury to give up in return for the contentment of her present life and the joy she found with Jack each night, Clary laid the bonnet back in its box, along with her lingering doubts about the man she loved. Then she went to help Sarah prepare the evening meal.

October seventeenth, the day appointed for the official opening of the Chesapeake and Delaware Canal, dawned bright and clear, and both carts from Afon Farm set off early for Summit Bridge. In the back of the cart driven by Moses, Luke guarded the picnic meal prepared by Sarah. A

second basket of food rested in the cart Jack was driving.

"Why aren't we going by boat?" Clary asked as they jolted their way along an incredibly bad trail. "Wouldn't it be easier?"

"No doubt," Jack answered. "But the canal will be so crowded with boats that we would not be able to get close enough to see or hear well, and the actual ceremony is to take place at the bridge. Clary, I plan to introduce some of the important men and their wives to you. I also hope I have convinced—well, let us wait to see if all my wishes for this day are fulfilled."

As they drew nearer to the bridge, they were joined on the way by other farm carts, by a few carriages, and by folks on horseback or traveling by foot. All wore their best clothes. Peddlars carrying their souvenir wares or food for sale made their slow way toward the site of the festivities. More economically substantial vendors drove colorfully painted carts packed with commemorative merchandise, which they intended to sell to the holiday throngs. Nearly all of these salesmen sported decorations of bright red, white, and blue bunting, and flags were freely displayed on backpacks, on carts, and on carriages.

"Where did all these people come from?" Clary wondered, gazing around at the colorful scene. "I thought you said the countryside around Afon Farm was only sparsely populated."

"So it is," Jack replied. "These folk have come from all over the peninsula, some of them traveling for two or three days. This is a great event,

my dear. There is the bridge just ahead."

"Good Lord!" Clary stood up to see better. Bracing one hand on Jack's shoulder, she stared at the sight before her. They were not approaching from the State Road, which led directly across the bridge and continued northward on the other side of the canal. Instead, Jack was driving them eastward along one of the trails used for transportation of supplies during the construction of both bridge and canal, so Clary first saw the entire vista at an angle. There before her was a wooden covered bridge that spanned empty space in a single arch almost 250 feet long. Below the bridge gaped the famous Deep Cut, where workers had carved out solid granite to a depth of nearly 90 feet. "To think all of that was done by hand. No bulldozers, no backhoes, no jackhammers—just picks and shovels and buckets!" Clary exclaimed.

"And a bit of black powder for explosive. Clary, please sit down before you fall out of the cart," Jack warned.

"I can't see when I sit. There are too many people between me and the bridge." But she sat anyway, convinced to follow Jack's order by the continued rough motion of the cart. Eagerly she turned to her companion. "I have to tell you, Jack, that what I see here is an incredible accomplishment. Did you build this?" She waved a hand that included both the bridge and the Deep Cut beneath it.

"Some of the workmen I hired did," Jack responded with a laugh. "And I contracted to

supply a good portion of the materials."

"Anyone who had anything at all to do with it should be very proud," she told him.

"Why, thank you, Miss Cummings." Having found a place to leave the carts, Jack pulled to a stop with Moses beside him in the other cart. Jack helped Clary alight.

"Look at all the boats!" Luke shouted, rushing forward to see the vessels crowded into the water below. "I see three big steamboats!"

"You stay away from the edge," his mother warned, "and don't get lost. We'd never find you in this crowd."

Sarah was not exaggerating by much. There were hundreds of people present, and the crowd was growing larger as the passengers from the steamboats disembarked and slowly made their way upward to the spot next to the bridge where a platform had been erected. Gay red, white, and blue bunting was hung on both the platform and the entrance to the bridge. A band was assembling nearby to provide music for the event.

After seeing Sarah, Moses, and Luke to a good vantage point, Jack took Clary's arm and led her forward toward the speaker's platform, but their progress was soon blocked by the crowd. Jack began politely but insistently pushing his way through the throng until he and Clary stood next to the platform.

"Mr. Martin!" cried a jovial voice from above them, and a hand came down to shake Jack's. "Welcome, sir! Welcome, ma'am! Step up here

onto the platform and greet the committee before the speeches begin!"

In the next ten minutes so many men were introduced to Clary that she quickly lost track of who each one was, though a few did stand out in her memory later.

"Mr. James Fisher, who is the president of the canal company," Jack said, shaking the man's hand as he presented Clary. Jack turned to the person standing next to Mr. Fisher. "This is Mr. Robert Lewis, chairman of the committee of works for the canal. And this is Nicholas Biddle." This last man's name Clary did recognize. She tried not to gape at the famous banker, whose family had played an important and continuing role in the history of Philadelphia right down to her own time.

All of the men on the platform, in dark frock coats and trousers and neatly tied cravats—the successful businessman's outfit of their day— were genial. Their overdressed ladies were cool toward Clary. She noticed a few of the women gazing at Jack with shining eyes, then sending speculative glances in her direction as if they were curious about her relationshp with him. Jack cut a romantic figure in his dark gray coat and trousers, deep blue silk brocade vest, and spotless white shirt. He moved among these important men with ease, yet it seemed to Clary that he held himself a bit separate from them. There was about Jack a quiet reserve that contrasted with the open, hearty, sometimes boisterous American men.

After a few quick looks at the women in their brightly colored, flounced, tucked, pleated taffetas and figured silks, their bonnets and shawls, parasols and jewelry, Clary knew she was greatly underdressed for the occasion. In the eyes of this group of well-to-do ladies, only her fine leather gloves and her overdecorated Philadelphia bonnet saved her from fashion disaster. She noticed more than one pair of puzzled feminine eyes moving from contemplation of her plain blue cotton gown to that hat, and she could not help wondering what those very proper ladies were thinking about Miss Clarissa Jane Cummings.

"Ah, good day to ye, Miss Cummings." Sam MacKenzie appeared out of the surrounding crowd. "Glad I found ye, Jack, me lad." The two men shook hands, then several of the directors also cordially greeted Sam.

"Where is Madam Rose?" Clary asked Sam, ignoring a look from Jack that plainly warned her not to mention Sam's romantic interest while they were with the officials of the canal.

Sam, however, did not appear to mind the question. His blue eyes alight with mischief, he gave her an honest answer. "Rose is much too busy to attend this affair. There are celebrations taking place all along the canal, and a long line of boats tied up at Bohemia Village waiting to enter the locks. Rose's establishment will be heavily patronized today, so she will doubtless spend a happy hour or two later, counting all the money she will make." Sam's sigh suggested to Clary that he

was not as pleased at the prospect as Rose might be.

"Look there," Sam said. "It appears the program is about to begin. Jack, me lad, can we find the lady a seat?"

As Jack assisted Clary to a chair in the front row and took his place beside her with Sam on her other side, there came from the direction of Fort Delaware, out on Delaware Bay, the sound of distant guns firing a long salute.

"Three rounds of twenty-four guns each," Sam whispered to Clary, adding with a chuckle, "They decided twenty-one guns wouldn't be enough for this grand achievement of American engineering."

"It is a great achievement," Clary responded. "I am overwhelmed when I think about all the work that was done by hand."

Apparently the dignitaries assembled at Summit Bridge were of the same opinion as Clary, for their speeches were long and flowery. Mr. Lewis began by officially announcing to Mr. Fisher the fortuitous completion of work on this most remarkable canal. Thereafter, transportation to Philadelphia was expected to be greatly expanded, thus vastly increasing profits for all who used the canal and for the shareholders.

This claim, as Clary knew from Jack's remarks on the subject, was not quite accurate. In addition to a large landslide within the Deep Cut just a few days before the opening—which was barely cleared in time for the opening ceremonies—there remained a fair amount of work still

to be done on the canal, mostly in shoring up the sides, which had an unfortunate tendency to collapse and fall into the water, thus blocking all traffic.

While Mr. Lewis held forth on the history of the canal and the difficulties of its construction, Clary let her eyes and her thoughts wander. Where she, Jack, and Sam were sitting, most of the people were expensively dressed, and one lady in particular. That lady was clothed in a pale gray taffeta gown of simple but elegant design that put to shame all the bedizened women sitting beside their husbands on the platform. Tall and slender, she had blonde hair showing beneath the brim of her tastefully decorated bonnet and a delicate, beautiful face.

She was looking right at Jack. Clary realized that Jack was looking back at the woman, who favored him with a brief, tiny smile. Clary thought the woman must have been aware of her own steady gaze, for she removed her eyes from Jack's face to look at Clary. The woman glanced away at once, transferring her attention to the speaker.

"So she did come after all," Jack murmured. "I am glad to see it."

"Who is she?" Clary whispered.

"Who?"

"You know who. The lady in the pale gray outfit."

"A lady," he replied.

"You haven't answered my question," she persisted.

271

"I hope I will be able to answer it later. Be patient, sweetheart."

But later, the speeches were finally over, the bands had finished playing marches, and the two military units sent from Philadelphia had finished their drill and marched smartly off. The official party was starting to make its way to the steamship *William Penn*, where a banquet was scheduled to be served along with more speeches and a lecture on internal improvements by Mr. Nicholas Biddle. When those seated in the front rows began to stand up and move about, speaking casually to friends, Jack turned to Clary.

"I must ask you to excuse me for a short time," he said. "There is someone to whom I must speak."

"The lady in gray?" Clary asked. Jack's next words surprised her.

"I would like you to meet her, but she is excessively shy. Let me speak to her first, to ask her permission to present you."

"Present me to her?" Clary cried. "What is she, a duchess?"

"Not quite." Jack's mouth twitched with humor. "Please wait here with Sam." He moved off through the crowd.

"I'm going, too," Clary declared to Sam. "If I'm right there beside Jack, she can't refuse to meet me."

"No." Sam put a gently restraining hand on her arm. "Wait here as Jack told you to do."

"Why should I?" Clary demanded.

"If he intends to bring the lady back with him to meet you properly," Sam said, "then it would make a better impression upon her if you were to wait."

"Do you know who she is?" Clary cried. "Is she the woman he sees in Wilmington? Is she his—" Clary broke off. She could not bring herself to say the word mistress, and something in her heart told her that if the woman were his mistress, Jack would never introduce her to Clary. He had too much class to try a shabby trick like that.

"I don't know the lady," Sam said, "but it would be ill-bred of you to rush up to them while they are talking and demand an introduction. Leave this to Jack." But Sam was frowning, too, as he and Clary watched the couple.

Jack's head was bent toward the slender woman. He appeared to be pleading with her. The woman sent a hasty look in Clary's direction, then turned her back, still speaking to Jack while she shook her head. Jack caught her arm, talking to her with an air of intensity that conveyed itself to Clary all too clearly.

"It seems the lady doesn't want to meet me." Clary turned her own back toward the pair so neither Jack nor the woman would be able to see how hurt she was. "Sam, would you be good enough to escort me to the carts? Sarah has prepared a cold meal. Since we are not important enough to be invited to the grand banquet, perhaps you would care to join us?"

"I would be honored." Sam offered his arm and Clary took it.

"Am I behaving like a proper lady now?" She could barely keep her voice from sounding like the snarl of a painfully wounded animal.

"There may be a very good reason for what we have just seen," Sam said.

"Well, I wish someone would tell me it," Clary cried. "Sam, don't think I am angry with Jack. It's pretty obvious that he tried to get her to agree to meet me. I guess I just didn't pass her social test."

Moses, Sarah, and Luke had taken their basket of food and found a place with three or four other families with whom they were apparently on friendly terms. Clary saw them talking and sharing their food.

"Let's find a shady place," Sam suggested, picking up the basket from Jack's cart. There was a blanket in the cart, too. Sam handed it to Clary, and then he pointed toward the ground overlooking the Deep Cut. "Over there perhaps. We can sit beneath those two big trees and watch the boats passing below us on the canal while we eat Sarah's wonderful food and listen to the band that has been engaged to play for the pleasure of those of us not honored with special invitations to dine aboard the *William Penn*. I am glad to be here and not there. I can all too easily imagine the overheated room, the heavy meal, and the long speeches. If I were there, I would most likely fall asleep and embarrass

myself. Your kind invitation to eat with you has saved me from an irredeemable social error."

Clary knew he was trying to make her feel better. She went with him as cheerfully as she could and helped him to spread out the blanket beneath the trees as he wanted. She was laying out the cold fried chicken, bread and butter, and sliced tomatoes on a checked tablecloth spread atop the blanket when Jack rejoined them.

"Shall I leave?" Sam asked, springing to his feet.

"There is no need, my friend," Jack replied. "Thank you for staying with Clary. I do not mind if you hear what I have to say to her.

"Clary, I am sorry." Jack turned to her. "I hoped she would be present today so the two of you could have the opportunity to meet in an informal way. But the lady is retiring by nature and her emotions are in a delicate state. She wished to return to her cabin aboard one of the steamships."

"What you are really saying," Clary retorted, stung by the unknown woman's rejection, "is that she took a good look at me and decided she didn't like what she saw."

"I promise you, it is not that," Jack said. "I am convinced that, if only the two of you could meet, you would soon discover how much you have in common."

"Apparently, she didn't think so." Clary could not be annoyed with Jack. She had seen him trying to bring together two separate parts of

his life—for she was certain after watching them talk that the woman in gray was important to him. It was not Jack's fault if the woman refused to meet someone she might consider a rival for Jack's affections. "I still don't know who she is," Clary said.

"I am not at liberty to tell you her name," Jack replied.

"For God's sake, man!" Sam exclaimed. "Clary deserves a better explanation for the insult she has just received." He might have said more except for the hard look Jack sent him, which stopped his words.

"If you are my friend, Sam MacKenzie," Jack said in a cold and distant tone of voice, "then you will drop the subject of that lady at once."

"As you wish," said Sam. "I make it a habit never to tread into areas where I am not welcome."

"Please, Sam, eat a piece of chicken." Clary offered the napkin-wrapped platter to him. "Let's just try to forget everything but the lovely day and this delicious food and the band playing. That is a familiar song I hear." She lifted her head, listening.

"It's *Anacreon In Heaven*," Sam told her. "'Tis a difficult tune. It's well nigh impossible to sing the words and hit every note on key."

They got through the remainder of the afternoon under the pretense of enjoying themselves. Sam spoke with expectation about the profits to be made as soon as the canal was fit for heavy traffic.

"I am still looking for a good ship," he told Jack. "I will let you know as soon as I find one."

After they finished eating, Clary strolled across the Summit Bridge between Jack and Sam, so they could admire the view from the northern side of the Deep Cut. They even descended to canal level to walk along the towpath for a short distance. Along their way they were stopped frequently by men who knew Jack and Sam and who wanted to introduce their ladies. Clary found these women much more friendly than the wives of the important and wealthy officials, and in the guise of a lady visiting from New Jersey she managed to carry on pleasant conversations with several of them. But the strain of pretending to be someone she was not was tiring. By the time Jack and she made their farewells to new acquaintances and to Sam and started off on the road back to Afon Farm, Clary wanted only to lie down and sleep. She did in fact doze for a while with her head on Jack's shoulder and his arm around her.

"Wake up, sweetheart." Jack steadied her on the seat. Opening her eyes, Clary realized that they were in the barn. "Just sit there and keep me company while I take care of the horse. Then I'll see you into the house."

Resisting the desire to crawl into the back of the cart and go to sleep again, Clary did as she was told until Jack spoke again.

"Come to me," he said softly, raising his arms. Clary let herself fall into them. The next thing

she knew, she was in her own bedroom and Jack was undressing her.

"You will sleep more soundly here than with me in my room," Jack said, unfastening the hooks at the bodice of her gown as he spoke. "I can see you are overtired. Sleep late tomorrow if you want."

He slipped her nightgown over her head and tucked her beneath the covers as if she were a sleepy child who had been kept up too late. Clary did not protest what he was doing, nor his decision to let her sleep alone. As soon as he snuffed the candle, went into his own room, and closed the door, she fell into a deep slumber.

Later, in the middle of the night, she wakened to the sound of Jack's footsteps on the gravel by the front veranda and to the breeze-borne scent of his pipe tobacco. In the few moments before she drifted back into oblivion she wondered why he should be pacing and smoking that night when he had done neither since the first time they had made love.

# Chapter Fifteen

It was difficult to wake up. For a long time Clary lay still with her eyes closed, too lethargic to move. All the while, she tried to dismiss a sense of growing unease in the vicinity of her stomach. When she finally rolled over she knew at once that moving had been a mistake. She kept on rolling, right off the bed and onto the floor, where she grabbed the chamber pot from under the bed just in the nick of time. She was violently sick.

Afterward, she poured water into the basin on the washstand and splashed her face with it. Her reflection in the small mirror on the wall was drawn and pale, and her stomach was still so queasy that she feared she would be sick again before long. She crept back into bed, huddling there in a miserable, curled-up ball until Sarah tapped lightly on her door.

"Maybe you were in the sun too long yester-

day," Sarah said when she learned of Clary's illness.

"That jolting cart didn't do much for my digestion either." Clary did not say what she really thought—that unrefrigerated fried chicken might be the cause of her illness.

"You stay in bed," Sarah ordered. "I'll bring you a cup of tea."

Clary moaned, feeling ill again at the very thought of tea. But when Sarah brought the pot of steaming brew the tray also held thin slices of dry toast and two small apples.

"I put some quieting herbs in the tea," Sarah told her. "Sip it slowly and nibble on the toast and the apple, too. It'll settle your stomach."

"Seasickness food." Clary pushed herself up against the pillow to accept the cup of tea from Sarah. "I remember Doctor—well, someone I used to know always advised just this diet for seasickness."

"I wouldn't know about that," Sarah replied, "but toast and apples always help Luke when he's feelin' unwell."

Clary drank half a cup of the tea and swallowed a mouthful of toast, then went back to sleep. She wakened to Jack's hand smoothing her hair and his lips on her brow.

"Too much excitement yesterday," she murmured.

"That's what Sarah said. She doesn't think it's serious."

"A good thing, too," Clary said, still feeling groggy, though her stomach was calmer. "I'll

bet there aren't any doctors around here."

By noontime she felt well enough to be up and dressed, and by evening she was ravenously hungry.

"Which only proves," Jack teased, watching her devour a slice of ham and a large spoonful of corn pudding, "that you ought to remain here on the farm for the sake of your own well-being."

"You really are a male chauvinist," she told him. "The strange thing is, it doesn't matter as much as it would have when I first came here. Perhaps I am becoming emotionally acclimated to this time. Do you suppose my change in attitude means that I am going to stay here permanently?"

"Let us hope so." His hand touched hers.

"What will happen now?" she asked, half to herself.

"We will finish the harvest and prepare for winter." His smile was warm and caressing. "Would you like a glass of Madeira?"

"I think I'll stick to tea tonight, thank you."

Clary watched him pour a glass of wine for himself. Outside the open windows, it was already dark and in the tall grasses the crickets sang their end-of-summer song. Clary had the odd sensation that a phase of her life was ending with the summer. Perhaps it had ended the previous day with the opening of the canal—or more accurately with the refusal of the woman in gray to meet her. There were so many questions she wanted to ask Jack about that

moment, about the woman's identity, and about his previous life, yet she knew she would ask none of them. He accepted her as she was, with a past too distant to matter in his day. It could well be that for him, his own past was equally distant. Clary discovered that she wanted only to think about the present. It seemed to be all that mattered.

"The only time we have," she murmured, "is now."

"Very true." Jack finished his wine, the crystal glass sparkling in the candlelight when he lifted it. His face was pensive, his eyes shadowed. When he rose to hold Clary's chair for her, she put a hand on his arm, then reached upward to kiss him on the mouth. He drew in his breath, and she saw the ready flare of desire in his eyes.

"I do not want to impose myself on you if you are feeling unwell." His voice was so husky that she knew he wanted her badly.

"You are never an imposition. Don't you know that by now? I do believe that my health would be greatly improved by the treatment only you can provide."

He did not respond to her gentle teasing in his usual lighthearted way. His next words were serious, and she could tell they were heartfelt.

"You cannot know what you mean to me." His hands cupped her face. "Clary, I will say only this and then not speak of the incident again. I am truly sorry for the snub you suffered yesterday. I was angered by it and hurt for your

282

sake. I beg you to understand that the lady was motivated not by malice, but by fear."

"Fear?" Clary pulled back a little so she could see him better. "Who could be afraid of me? Jack, I promised myself I wouldn't ask any more questions about your past, but isn't there anything you can tell me about that woman?"

"I am sworn to silence."

"I am beginning to understand what your word of honor means to you. I won't press you for answers you cannot give. I do understand that what happened yesterday was not your fault. By the way, that incident isn't why I was sick this morning. I wasn't pouting or sulking. I think the fried chicken disagreed with me." She smiled at him, hoping to lighten his somber mood. "Tell me, sir, were you planning to take me to bed in the next couple of hours?"

"Madam, I was planning to take you to bed within the next few minutes." Solemnity gone, he laughed at her. "And to keep you occupied for several hours at least!"

"I have just discovered from Jack," Clary said to Sarah, "that his birthday falls on Halloween. It's one of my favorite holidays."

"On what?" Perplexed, Sarah looked up from the pie crust she was rolling out on the kitchen table.

"You don't know about Halloween? How funny. It never occurred to me that you wouldn't, but perhaps it is still a purely religious holiday. I'm sure Halloween isn't promoted here the way

it is in my old hometown. Well," Clary said, "one week from today we are going to have a surprise birthday party for Jack. Would you mind making a cake? I'm not too sure yet about my ability to bake something delicate in that brick oven and have it come out fit to eat."

"A pound cake," Sarah decided, "with plenty of butter and a dozen eggs in it and just a touch of grated lemon rind. That is, if there are lemons available in Bohemia Village."

"Ye gods!" Clary began to laugh. "Poor Jack's arteries will be totally clogged after eating that. Oh, never mind, Sarah, it sounds delicious. I am going to Bohemia Village with Moses tomorrow, so I'll look for lemons for you." She was also planning to search for a present for Jack. It was nice to have money she had earned for herself that she could spend on him. She could think of nothing Jack might want, but she was sure she would find just the right thing among the market stalls and the new shops springing up in the once quiet village.

She was not disappointed. On the north shore of Back Creek she found a flat-bottomed canal boat tied up just before the lock entrance. The owner had set out on the deck a row of dusty odds and ends that reminded Clary of the merchandise to be found at a twentieth-century tag sale. Among the items displayed was a slender volume of poems by Lord Byron in only slightly used condition. Clary knew Jack liked poetry, for he kept several books of verse in his bedroom. She bought Lord Byron's poems for a

penny and came away from the transaction with the feeling that the seller thought he had the better part of the bargain.

Returning along the footbridge to the south side of the canal, Clary purchased the lemons Sarah wanted for Jack's birthday cake and then searched out a few other provisions needed for the kitchen at Afon Farm. These were mostly spices that Sarah would use to enliven winter and holiday fare. Clary bought two long vanilla beans, a whole nutmeg, some sticks of cinnamon, and a fabric bag packed full of whole peppercorns.

She took her time, enjoying the sights, the smells and sounds, and the lively atmosphere. Children played games between the carts and around the wooden bins of produce. A dog chased a fat tabby cat across Bohemia Avenue and up a tree. Clary was so intrigued by the bustle and color surrounding her that she did not even mind the occasional brief outburst of unpleasantness. She quickly sidestepped a canal worker and a vendor whose dispute over price had escalated into blows. Seeing the soberly clothed figure of Josiah Grey approaching, she felt certain that the responsible Quaker gentleman would admonish the combatants to treat each other with respect and honesty instead of resorting to physical force. She spared a brief thought for the deranged Hezekiah Bartram, wondering if Josiah Grey's reasonable kindness had succeeded in taming the unpleasant man before continuing on her way.

She found Moses in his usual place in the sprawling market, just west of the foot of Bohemia Avenue. He was finishing the sale of the current load of autumn produce.

"I would like to speak to Dancy before we leave," Moses told her, taking the filled basket from her arm and tucking it into the back of the cart.

"Good," Clary said. "That will give me time to pay a call on Madam Rose."

Disregarding Moses's grim expression, Clary walked up the hill and around the corner to the front door. She found the main room of Madam Rose's house almost empty. Only three girls sat at the tables and there was just one male customer.

"Has business fallen off since most of the canal workers have moved on to other jobs?" Clary asked after greeting Madam Rose.

"There is also the problem of the traveling preachers who too often succeed in their attempts to drive would-be customers away," Madam Rose replied. "Those self-righteous men stand in the street outside my house and preach against the wicked whores within. Last week, one of them so affected Terpsichore that she packed up all her belongings and left with him. One does wonder what a preacher will do with a harlot on his arm."

"Perhaps he'll put her on display as an example of what his preaching can do. You are missing more than one girl," Clary noted, looking around the room.

"Cleo accepted a proposal of marriage from one of the canal workers and went west with him to his next job in Ohio," Madam Rose explained. "Zenobia decided to return to her home when she received a message that her mother was sick. Thus, I am left with only Hermione, Calliope, and Sinope—a deficiency in numbers which scarcely matters since I have few customers each day."

"Madam Rose, I must tell you that I hope your business continues to deteriorate until you are forced to move into a new line of work," Clary said.

"Miss Cummings, you sound exactly like Sam MacKenzie." Madam Rose's voice was weary and her face was strained when she glanced toward her girls.

"Is Sam in town today?" Clary asked.

"I believe he is at the pump house," Madam Rose murmured. "Some difficulty with pumping water into the locks. It seems as though this canal will never be in perfect working order."

A short time later Clary left, and as she was waiting for Moses to bring the cart around to Bohemia Avenue, she caught sight of Sam MacKenzie.

"Hello, Sam!" She waved to him. Two passing ladies looked at her in disgust and stuck their noses into the air, pulling their skirts closer to their bodies as if they feared contamination from anyone having anything to do with Madam Rose's house. Clary ignored them and waved to Sam again.

"I'm so glad to see you," she said to him. "Could you join us for dinner at Afon Farm on the thirty-first of the month? You are welcome to stay the night if you like. I want to surprise Jack for his birthday."

"As it happens," Sam said, "I was thinking of riding that way one day soon. I just may have news for Jack that will come as a fine present for his special day."

"I would invite Madam Rose, too," Clary began, but Sam stopped her.

"She would not leave her house just now," he said. "Have you seen her? She's not taking well to the latest changes in Bohemia Village. Last night she was talking about moving to western Pennsylvania or Ohio, where there are still canals being built. Good-bye, Clary. I'll see you next week." Sam helped her climb onto the cart seat and then waved his farewell.

Clary held tightly to the seat as she and Moses lurched and jolted along the road. She hoped the ride would not make her sick. Her stomach was upset much too often of late, and she was aware that the problem had nothing to do with tainted food. She had not had a menstrual period since just before Jack's return from his September trip to Philadelphia. She was glad enough not to have to deal with the sanitary problems—she hated having to use folded cloths for napkins and hated even more having to wash them out by hand afterward. But she was frightened by the new problems a pregnancy would entail. She was not sure what Jack's reaction

would be, but she was going to have to tell him before long—not only because he had the right to know she was carrying his child, but because Sarah would soon begin asking why Clary had no soiled cloths to launder.

Clary decided that, if no signs to the contrary appeared before Jack's birthday, she would tell him on Halloween night after his party was over. If he was happy about her news, then it would be like another birthday present. If he was angry, she would just have to deal with it as best she could. She put a protective hand on her abdomen, hoping that what she thought might be actually was true, and praying that Jack would be pleased. She did not know if he liked small children or not. The subject had never come up in their conversations. But surely he would love his own child.

The beginning of the birthday party was a great success. Jack was genuinely surprised to see Sam ride up to the house in late afternoon and delighted to learn that Clary and Sarah had anticipated Sam's arrival. Since Jack and Moses had been out hunting during the past few days, the women were preparing a roast turkey feast for the first course at dinner.

Clary discovered during the evening meal that wild turkey meat was tougher and had a much more gamy flavor than the farm-bred birds she was used to eating. But the men seemed to enjoy it, and Jack announced that he would commandeer the best feathers to use as quill pens.

Flora Speer

To further enliven the party, Sam had brought with him several bottles of port wine and a fresh supply of Madeira.

"We will open the Madeira tonight," Jack decided. "The port we will allow to rest from its travels for a few weeks."

"Why?" Clary asked, looking with some curiosity at the dusty bottles.

"So the sediment can settle," Sam told her.

"Sam, you must return later in the year," Jack said, "to sample your gift."

"I was hopin' for the invitation, Jack, me lad." Sam winked at Clary. "I accept with pleasure."

When the men began to open a bottle of new Madeira, Clary excused herself. In the kitchen she found Sarah, Moses, and Luke awaiting her.

"Are you ready?" It was a needless question. They were all well rehearsed in Clary's plans for the celebration.

Sarah's pound cake rested on a silver tray, surrounded by bright autumn leaves. After Clary had described birthday cake candles to Luke, he had devised a single long wick of braided straw dipped in tallow. It burned with a smoky flame and did not smell especially nice, but it stood boldly upright in the center of the cake, lending it a festive look.

"Sarah, you carry the cake in," Clary instructed. "You made it, after all."

"I'll take the fruit." Luke lifted a crystal bowl filled with the peaches Sarah and Clary had preserved in spices and whiskey.

"I have our present for Mister Jack." Moses

held a flat, round object covered with a clean flour sack.

"And I have the book I bought for him," Clary said.

They marched from the kitchen through the still, cool autumn night, across the courtyard, and into the house, where Jack sat at the dining room table, drinking Madeira with Sam. Jack looked up as they came into the room, surprise changing to astonishment and then to pleasure at the cake with its makeshift little candle.

"Happy birthday." Sarah set the cake down in front of him.

"Happy birthday, Mister Jack." Luke presented the bowl of peaches. "These are delicious. I tasted them to be sure."

"Clary, was this your idea?" The look Jack gave her was one of pure love.

"Everyone contributed something," she replied, her heart rejoicing at his delight.

"You must all stay and partake of this delicious surprise," Jack said.

"Are you sure you want us here?" Moses glanced toward Sam, then back to Jack's face.

"You have helped to make the celebration for my benefit," Jack responded. "It will not be complete unless you participate now."

"Thank you." Sarah graciously inclined her head. "We would be happy to join you."

"Clary." Jack returned his attention to her. "What is the order for this ceremony? Am I expected to cut the cake?"

"Before you do," Clary said, "you are supposed

to make a wish and blow out the candle. It's a tradition."

"That's the strangest candle I've ever seen," Sam remarked. "If it burns for much longer, it may well set the house on fire."

"Then I ought to blow it out at once. I wish—" Jack paused, looking at Clary, and behind the warmth of his expression, she detected a seriousness that made her blush.

"Don't tell us what the wish is," she cried, "or it won't come true."

"I understand," he said. "This tradition involves magic. I am surprised at you, Clary. I thought you did not believe in such superstitions."

"Sometimes I do," she murmured, her eyes gazing deep into his.

With Jack's silent wish made and the candle safely extinguished, the extra chairs along the wall were pushed up to the table, and the six of them sat down to enjoy the cake, fruit, tea, and for the three men, a glass of Madeira.

"I'm old enough for wine," Luke declared.

"You hush and drink your tea," his mother told him.

"I'm sticking to tea, too, Luke," Clary said.

"You have refused wine for more than a week now," Jack mused. "Have you taken a dislike to Madeira?"

"Not at all. I will explain later," Clary replied.

Jack raised his brows in a questioning way, but did not press her. Clary's nervousness over what she would tell him later began to dissolve. Jack was so relaxed, he looked so contented, and

he treated her with such warmth that she could not think he would be angry when he heard her news.

"Ma'am," Sam said as soon as he had polished off the last of his cake and peaches, "since you are mistress of these festivities, tell us please, may we now present our gifts to the guest of honor?"

"Whenever you like," Clary replied. "Moses, will you go first?"

When Jack unwrapped the cloth bundle, the gift from Moses and Sarah proved to be a fine new straw hat, flat crowned and wide brimmed to shelter his face from the sun.

"Your old one is fine for workin' in the fields," Moses explained, "but when you go into town, you ought to have a new hat to wear."

"I thank you both." Jack tried on the hat to a chorus of approval.

Luke's gift was hidden behind the sideboard.

"I made it myself," he said, giving the fishing rod to Jack.

"Thank you, Luke. I will see to it that we go fishing together in the next few days," Jack said.

"Your turn next, Sam," Clary said, fully aware that, caught up in the spirit of the occasion, he was bursting with eagerness.

"My gift isn't a package," Sam said to Jack. "It's news. I have located the ship we have been talking and dreaming about owning. The *Venture* is big enough to hold plenty of cargo, but not too large or too deep in draft to pass through the canal."

"At last!" Jack's eyes gleamed with pleasure. "Where is she berthed, Sam?"

"In Wilmington. I thought we might leave tomorrow and go together to see her before anyone else can make an offer for her. The owner has agreed to wait until I contact him again."

"Yes, you are right. If she is what we have been looking for, then we ought not to risk losing this chance."

"Could I go with you?" Clary asked.

"Not this time," Jack answered. "But if we do purchase the ship, and if you would like, I promise you may sail on our first voyage to Philadelphia."

"All right." Clary agreed at once, thinking of her unsettling morning sickness. In a few weeks the illness would be over and she could travel without feeling nauseated every day.

"I almost forgot." Sam jumped to his feet. "Jack, there is another package for you. Excuse me for a moment. It's in my saddlebag." He left the dining room, returning a minute later with a parcel wrapped in rough cotton cloth and tied with twine.

"This was left at Rose's house by a messenger who was traveling through the canal on his way to Baltimore," Sam said. "Rose promised to send it on to you, and she asked me to deliver it."

"Thank you." Jack took the parcel and began to open it. Clary, watching him, was briefly distracted when Sarah and Moses rose from the

table and Sarah began to collect the dishes. When Clary looked back at Jack again, he was lifting out of the wrappings a fine white linen shirt. As he did so, a folded piece of paper slipped from the linen and drifted to the floor. Clary bent over to retrieve it. When she picked up the paper she could not avoid noticing the signature: *My love always, Philly.*

Into Clary's mind came the memory of Jack's delirious ravings as he tossed on his bed in a fever after injuring his arm. Philly, he had cried. Philly. And she had stupidly imagined that he was thinking of business in Philadelphia! She recalled his surprise when she had used the nickname Philly for the city.

Sam said something to Jack and Jack faced toward his friend while he answered.

Clary still held the note in shaking fingers. After only an instant's hesitation and before Jack could see what she was doing, she opened out the folded paper and glanced down at it again. She had time to decipher only snatches of the message, which was written in an elaborate hand with many swirls and flourishes. But what she read was more than enough to destroy the happy mood of the evening for Clary, along with her certainty of Jack's true affection for her.

*Dear Jack . . . How I hate that false name. If only . . . I regret . . . could not meet her. . . . My dearest, you will understand . . . discretion necessary. . . .*
*My love always, Philly.*

When Jack turned his head to look at Clary after speaking to Sam, she gazed back at him as if he were a stranger to her.

"Is something wrong?" he asked.

"You didn't notice this." She gave him the letter. With his eyes on it, she made her escape into the hall. Sarah came after her.

"Are you sick again?" Sarah whispered, giving her a knowing look. "Or did something upset you in there?"

"I am just a little tired. Shall I help you in the kitchen?"

"You stay here and attend to your problems," Sarah ordered, keeping her voice low. "'Cause I think you have a serious problem, Miz Clary. If you have anything to tell that man, tell him now."

"You know," Clary whispered.

"'Course I know. You think I'm stupid and can't count just 'cause I don't know how to read? You've got his baby in your belly, and he deserves to be told about it." Sarah faced her with narrowed eyes. "You didn't give him that book you bought for him. What changed your mind?"

"A love letter from another woman." The lump in Clary's throat cut off further explanation. She spun around and raced to her bedroom. Sarah followed her.

"Can I bring you anything?" When Clary just shook her head, Sarah went on. "Get a good night's sleep if that's what you need, but you

take my advice, Miz Clary, and tell him right away. If you can't do it tonight, then do it first thing tomorrow."

"First thing tomorrow," Clary hissed at her, "he is going away. Didn't you hear him talking with Sam? He is going to Wilmington, and while he's there, he will certainly see her. He will want to thank her for his lovely, handmade birthday present!"

"You already know what I think about this. I'm not goin' to repeat myself."

After Sarah left her, Clary undressed, got into bed, and snuffed the candle. Sam would be sharing Jack's room with him for the night, so she did not have to fear that Jack would appear, wanting to make love to her. She was assured of an entire night in which to think.

What her thoughts revealed to her only upset her more, for Clary believed she could recognize a recurring pattern to her relationships with men. Her husband Rich's habit had always been to ignore her until she made a great fuss that precipitated a quarrel, at which point he doled out a small ration of affection. Afterward, with Clary temporarily pacified, Rich could resume ignoring her while she carried the emotional weight of their relationship. She now understood all too well his reasons for this peculiar behavior.

Unlike Rich, Jack did not ignore her, but he did keep the most important parts of his life hidden from her. When she insisted on information about his past or his life away from the

farm, Jack calmed her with a sentence or two calculated to give her just a crumb of knowledge. Then he asked her to trust him—and he made love to her as if he really cared for her, thus ending the dissension between them until the next incident occurred to make her question his motives. Because Jack was the only one who knew she was living in the wrong time, she was emotionally dependent upon him, and therefore particularly vulnerable to this treatment.

"The same pattern over and over again," Clary muttered, sitting up in bed in the dark with her arms around her legs and her forehead down on her knees while she tried to make sense of the wrong turns her life had taken in two different centuries. "I have been too passive. I have let the men I care about manipulate me into causing them the least possible amount of trouble, and both Rich and Jack have betrayed my naive trust. Well, no more. This situation is going to change. I am going to change! I have a baby to think about now, and my child deserves a responsible adult for a mother. I finally know what I want and need, and by heaven, I am going to find a way to get it." She lay down again, a grim smile on her lips.

"Jack Martin, you are about to discover what real trouble is."

# *Chapter Sixteen*

"I am going to Wilmington," Clary announced the next morning, one hour after Jack and Sam departed from the farm.

Wooden spoon in hand, Sarah turned from the cookstove to stare at her. "And just what do you plan to do there?"

"I intend to find out exactly who this Philly person is and what she means to Jack."

"You may not like what you learn."

"Sarah, I have to know. I can't go on in complete ignorance of Jack's real life."

"If you ask me, this farm is his real life. That and now maybe the ship he's plannin' to buy with Mr. MacKenzie." Sarah gave the soup in the kettle a stir. "I told you before, Mister Jack's got no free time to spend with loose-livin' women."

"We don't know what he does when he's away on those business trips of his," Clary declared, remembering another man who had used such

trips as a disguise for unfaithfulness. "I am not going to sit here obediently until Jack comes back, hoping that just possibly he will then deign to reveal to me a few more facts about himself. I have to know more before I can tell him that I'm carrying his baby. Sarah, can't you understand how I feel?"

"No," Sarah admitted, "I can't imagine what it's like not to trust your man. I've always been able to trust Moses. Even when we were still slaves, when we had nothin' else, I had that much.

"You can't go alone," Sarah said after a moment's thought. "What'll happen to you if you get sick along the way? You better take Luke with you."

"Thank you. I knew you'd help me."

"Moses isn't goin' to like this, but I'll talk to him and he'll give in after a bit of an argument. At least most of the harvest is finished, so he can make do without Luke's help for a few days. You got enough money for this trip?"

"I think so. I haven't spent more than a few pennies of the wages Jack paid me. I can't think of a better cause to spend that money on."

"Well, then." Sarah laid down the spoon. "You go get ready, and I'll talk to Moses and Luke."

Clary never learned what Sarah said to Moses. Though he did not look pleased, he made no objection to her about her planned trip or about Luke going with her. They rode into Bohemia Village with Moses that morning, Clary on the cart seat beside him, an excited Luke perched

on a box of produce that was scheduled for loading on a schooner bound eastward through the canal. Within half an hour of their arrival in the village, Moses had secured passage on the same ship for Clary and Luke.

"You won't have to search for space on a second boat after you reach Newbold's Landing," Moses said. "You can stay aboard this one all the way to Wilmington. I've sold produce to Captain Peter Schyler for the last two summers, so I know he's an honest man. Now, Luke, you stay right with Miz Clary. Don't leave her side, and take good care of her."

It was still well before noon when their ship left the second lock at Bohemia Village and, pulled by a pair of mules, moved into the canal. Their progress was slow but steady, and even with time for filling the lock at St. George's and then the fourth and final lock at Newbold's Landing, they were through the canal and into the man-made harbor that opened into Delaware Bay well before the early setting of the sun on that first day of November.

"We will anchor here in the harbor and cast off on the incoming tide near dawn," Captain Schyler told his passengers. "With the tide and the wind helping us, we should drop anchor in Wilmington shortly after noon tomorrow."

While the other passengers went ashore to take their chances on an evening meal at a local tavern, Clary and Luke opened the hamper Sarah had packed for them and feasted on cold slices of ham, bread and butter, pickles, and apple tarts,

all washed down with mugs of hot coffee they purchased from the schooner's cook.

Moses had booked a small cabin for Clary. At Luke's insistence, the boy slept lying across the deck just outside her door.

"My daddy told me to pretend to be your personal servant," Luke said, "and that's what a servant would do, so don't you argue with me, Miz Clary."

"I am sorry to say that I have to agree with you," Clary replied. "It's probably the safest thing for you as well as for me if you appear to be guarding me."

The passage up Delaware Bay to Wilmington the next morning was a bit rough, with a strong incoming tide and a stiff wind from the southeast. Clary was surprised not to suffer from either morning sickness or seasickness. But her stomach was still far from calm, for she dreaded what she might discover when the brief voyage ended.

With the schooner tied up at the wharf in Wilmington, Clary and Luke began to search for the ship that Sam MacKenzie wanted to buy.

"I thought you didn't want Mister Jack to know you were in town." Luke knew only that Clary had extremely private and personal business to conduct in Wilmington. Clary felt certain that once Luke and Jack were both at Afon Farm again the boy would mention this excursion, but by then it should not matter. One way or the other, the issue of Clary's relationship with Jack would soon be settled.

"I can only tell you this, Luke," she said. "I need to find out where Jack will go after he is finished with the business having to do with the ship." She did not add that she was sure Jack would take this opportunity to visit the mysterious lady who had appeared at the Summit Bridge for the grand-opening celebrations.

A short while later, Clary stopped to ask a sailor for directions, and he said, "The *Venture*?" The man pointed. "Down that way, ma'am."

"Thank you. Come on, Luke."

"Are you goin' to just walk right up to Mister Jack and say good morning to him?" Luke asked.

"I am not going to say anything at all to Mister Jack," Clary responded. She put out a hand to stop the boy. "Careful, Luke. There he is, and Sam, too. Quick, come this way." She pulled Luke behind a pile of crates waiting to be loaded onto a nearby barge.

Jack and Sam came walking along the dock in company with a third man. With her finger against her lips cautioning Luke to silence, Clary listened to their conversation.

"I can have the papers drawn up at once," the third man said to the other two. "Then, as soon as you deliver the money to me, you are free to take possession."

"We'll want a lawyer to make it legal on our side, too." That was Sam speaking. "I know just the man. I'll see to it, Jack. We can have the sale completed by noon tomorrow and begin refitting the ship the next day."

"Excellent. I leave the choice of lawyer to you." Jack shook hands with his friend and with the other man. "In the meantime, if you will excuse me, I must pay a call on a friend. Sam, I will meet you at our rooms later this evening." The three men separated.

"Come on." Clary pulled at Luke's sleeve.

"Where are we goin'?"

"We are going to follow Mr. Jack Martin," she told him. "It shouldn't be too difficult. Wilmington is not a very large city."

Jack was walking fast. Before long Clary developed a severe cramp in her side and was forced to stop and catch her breath.

"Go on, Luke," she ordered. "Don't lose him. I'll catch up with you as soon as I can."

"No, ma'am. I can't do that. My daddy said not to leave your side. This isn't the nicest part of town for a lady to be alone in." Luke looked around at the docks behind them, the ships berthed there, the sailors moving purposefully along on errands of their own. More than a few rough-looking characters were in sight and some of them were eyeing Clary with interest. "I'd never leave you here even if my daddy hadn't told me to stay with you. We could stop at that tavern over there and ask for a cool drink for you, and you could sit down till you feel better."

"If we do, Jack will get away. Oh, hurry, Luke, he's just gone around that next corner! We'll lose him for sure." When Luke still hesitated to leave her, Clary knew she would have to disregard the pain in her side. Picking up her long skirts, she

began to run. At once, Luke was running, too. They passed several men who turned to stare, but with Luke right beside Clary, no one tried to stop her.

"There he goes." When they reached the corner around which Jack had vanished, Luke paused, pointing. "Miz Clary, you look sick. You can't keep runnin' like this. You got to stop and rest."

"I will rest when I find out where Jack is going. Hurry up, Luke!"

"Stop tellin' me to hurry." Luke sounded remarkably like his mother. "I'm goin' as fast as I can, and you're goin' faster than you should."

Now well out of the dock area, Jack slowed his pace and so did the two following him. When Jack paused, Clary and Luke dodged between buildings or hid in doorways. This peculiar behavior occasionally elicited frowns or questions from alert citizens as to what the two were doing. Clary responded to these queries by pretending that she had been momentarily confused, but suddenly remembered her way. Wilmington proved to be larger than she had realized. It was a surprisingly long walk to a square of red brick houses with a small park in the center.

"This part of town looks almost like London." Clary noted neatly pruned bushes and a few trees, the latter dropping the last of their leaves onto the paths that criscrossed the grass of the quiet little park. "Perhaps that's why he chose it."

"Chose it for what?" Luke asked.

"That is what we are here to discover," Clary told him.

As they watched, Jack walked quickly across the square. Doing their best to stay out of his sight, Clary and Luke stayed as close behind Jack as they dared. They were hiding behind a thick holly bush when Jack mounted the sparkling white steps of one of the brick houses and lifted the gleaming brass knocker on the front door. The door opened at once and a tall, thin, man appeared.

"Good afternoon, Gilbert." Jack's voice carried clearly to unseen watchers in the park.

"Good afternoon, my lord. Lady Philippa will be pleasantly surprised to see you." The door closed, cutting off the rest of the elderly man's welcoming words.

"Miz Clary," Luke whispered, "you better sit down. You look like you're goin' to faint. There's a bench." He led her to the seat and Clary gratefully sank upon it.

"My lord?" she whispered. "Lady Philippa? What the hell is going on?"

"I don't know," Luke answered, "but if you're usin' words like that, it must be somethin' bad. You just rest here for a while, and then we'll go back to the docks and find a boat to take us home to Bohemia Village. If my daddy isn't in the village when we get there, we'll talk to Dancy and he'll get Madam Rose to help us reach the farm."

"I am not going back to Afon Farm until I have some answers," Clary said. "I wanted to

learn the truth about Jack's secret life, and I am going to stay right here until I do. Sooner or later Jack will have to leave that house to meet Sam."

They waited for an hour or so. A few people passed them—a nursemaid with two small children, a well-dressed woman followed by a maid carrying packages, two men deep in conversation—and all spared only a quick glance for the young woman in her dark blue dress and fashionable bonnet, accompanied by a black servant who stood just behind the bench, guarding his mistress.

Just as Clary began to wonder if perhaps Jack was planning to remain inside the house all night in spite of his promise to meet Sam, an open coach drew up in front of the house where he was. A moment later the elderly Gilbert, whom Clary had decided must be the butler, opened the door, holding it wide while a woman stepped out of the house. She was the same slender blonde woman who had spoken to Jack at the opening ceremonies at Summit Bridge. She was dressed in pale blue silk cut in the same kind of simple, elegant style that had made her so notable on that earlier day. Her dainty bonnet was decorated with blue flowers to match her gown. Behind her, chatting with ease and good humor, was Jack. And between them, holding on to the hands of both grownups, was a boy about six years old.

"Oh, God, no!" Clary's hands flew to her mouth as she attempted to smother her own anguished cry. "He has a son!"

There could be no mistake. The boy's handsome face, though still youthfully plump, bore the imprint of Jack's own fine bones. Moreover, his hair was the same shade of burnished mahogany as Jack's hair. Unable to take her eyes away from the scene, Clary watched Jack hand the blonde woman into the carriage. Then he lifted the boy up to join his mother. Clary heard the adults laugh together when the boy scrambled to sit beside Jack. The carriage drove off.

Clary remained sitting on the wooden park bench, too numbed by shock to move, unable to weep or scream or do anything else to alleviate the incredible pain tearing her bosom. She knew what the pain was. Her heart was breaking in two, and when it was completely broken, she would die. She was sure of it. No one could endure such pain and live.

"Miz Clary." She heard Luke's voice speaking as if from a distance. "You got any of those smellin' salts in your purse? 'Cause I think you need 'em now."

"No salts," she said, gasping. "Madam Rose has all the salts. A real salty character, Madam Rose. I should have listened to her advice about Jack Martin." She gave a half-hysterical laugh, and to her horror, she began to cry uncontrollably. The tears ran down her face unchecked.

"You goin' to be sick?" Luke asked, concerned. "You sure look awful pale."

"Sick?" Clary could not stop crying. "I am more likely to die than be sick."

Jack had sworn to her that he was not married. But he had obviously lied to her about having another woman, so he could have lied about his marital status, too.

"Oh, God!" she wept. "Two kids by two different mothers. It's just like a family in the twentieth century!

"Honor. Truth. Trust," she went on bitterly, still crying as she spoke. "Just see what trusting a man has gotten me. Sarah was right. I don't want to know this particular truth, and now that I do, I can never put it out of my mind. Damn him! Damn Jack Martin!"

"You stop this!" After a quick look around to be sure there was no one in the park to see what he was doing, Luke grabbed Clary by the shoulders and shook her hard. "Stop this cryin'! I'm sorry to be rough with you, but that's what Mama would do if she were here. Now you take a deep breath and shut your mouth and think for a while! You can't sit here cryin' your eyes out till Mister Jack and that woman come back. You know you wouldn't want them to see you this way. You got more pride than that."

"Have I? Or has pride gone where honor and truth and trustworthiness have gone?" But she did as Luke ordered, taking several deep breaths.

"You feelin' better now?" Luke was regarding her closely.

"I am calmer, if that is what you mean." Clary took another long breath. "I can't stay here."

"That's just what I've been sayin'. It's time to go home, Miz Clary."

"I don't think I have a home anymore." Clary put a hand to her forehead. "You'll never understand this, Luke, but as a famous man once said, it's deja vu all over again. The same thing keeps happening to me no matter where—or when—I am."

"Let's go back to the docks." Luke took her arm, helping her to rise from the park bench and then turning her toward the street from which they had entered the square. "Captain Schyler said he's sailin' back to Baltimore as soon as he reloads the ship. Maybe we can take passage home with him."

Clary was in such a miserable emotional state that she let Luke guide her through the streets of Wilmington with no protest. After her rush not to lose sight of Jack and the trauma of discovering that he had a son, she was inexpressibly weary.

"Was it such a long walk when we came this way before?" she asked at one point, vaguely wondering if they were lost. They might wander around for days, until they dropped from hunger or thirst, and she would not care. Or would she? The thought of the child she was carrying kept her walking and made her believe Luke's assurances.

"It's not far now," Luke said.

In fact, it was a long time later when they stumbled onto the docks some distance away from Captain Schyler's ship. Clary was convinced that they had been lost, but it didn't matter. They could board the schooner and

sail away from Wilmington, away from Jack and his blonde woman, whether she was his wife or his mistress. Clary wanted only to put as much distance as possible between herself and Jack. Thus, as she and Luke walked along the docks, she was horrified to recognize, pulled up near the *Venture*, the carriage in which Jack, the blonde woman, and the child had been riding. The carriage was empty, but at the sight of it an unreasoning anger erupted in Clary's breast.

"How the hell did he get that thing down on the docks without someone stopping him?" she demanded in a loud voice. "The bastard ought to be fined for blocking traffic!"

"Good evening, Miss Cummings." Captain Schyler answered her. He was on his way to his own ship and had overheard Clary's outraged exclamations. A hearty chuckle acknowledged her unladylike choice of words, but his response to her question was polite. "No doubt some wealthy man is showing off his latest acquisition to his lady who, unlike yourself, is too dainty to tread upon these docks for more than a few paces. I understand the *Venture* was sold this afternoon. She's a fine ship, one any man would be proud to own."

"Captain Schyler, can you take us on as passengers for the return trip to Bohemia Village?" Clary asked.

"I'm not leaving until dawn," he said. "You would have to stay on deck for the entire trip. All the cabins will be in use. I am surprised to

hear that you want to return home so soon. Most people, having made the voyage, remain in Wilmington for a few days at least, or even sail up the river to Philadelphia or Trenton."

"I was able to complete my business in Wilmington in just one day." Clary tried to sound as if she were pleased by this accomplishment. "Now I am so eager to return home that I am willing to sleep aboard ship, even on the deck." She did not add that she also wanted to be off the open dock before Jack spotted either her or Luke. She was keeping her back turned toward the *Venture* and was pleased to note that Luke was doing the same. She hoped Jack and his guests were deep in the bowels of the *Venture* inspecting the ship and would not step above deck until she and Luke were safely out of sight on Captain Schyler's Baltimore-bound schooner.

"It promises to be rough weather," the captain warned, looking skyward, "but if you are determined, then come aboard. Deck space is half price, payable in advance."

Captain Schyler was a kind man. He found a protected spot on deck for Clary and even ordered one of his men to bring blankets for her and Luke.

"I won't charge you extra for them," he said.

"Thank you." Clary's voice was low. "I don't have much money left."

"Are you in some kind of trouble?" Captain Schyler gave each of them a hard look.

When Clary discovered she could not speak because of fresh tears, she merely shook her head, and Luke answered for her.

"Miz Clary's upset right now. She got some bad news today."

"Indeed?" Still that hard, searching look. "When did you two last eat?"

"This mornin' before we left the ship." Again Luke spoke for Clary. "We brought our own food aboard."

"Oh, yes, the straw hamper I was to drop off at Bohemia Village on my return trip. Well, you can take it ashore yourselves when we get there. I suppose there is nothing left in it?" The captain walked away, leaving Clary and Luke alone.

"My mama gave me a little extra money to bring with me," Luke said. "I could go ashore and get some food."

"What would you do if Jack should see you and demand to know why you are in Wilmington?" Clary cried. "I can't face him right now, Luke. At this moment I'm not sure if I can ever face Jack Martin again."

"Then I'll just wait till we reach Newbold's Landing to eat." Luke sat down on the deck next to Clary. "You better wrap up in that blanket. It's goin' to be a cold night with the wind blowin' the way it is."

"I'm sorry, Luke. You must be hungry."

"Maybe not for long." Suddenly, Luke was grinning. A seaman squatted beside them with two plates in one hand and two mugs in the other.

"With the captain's compliments," the seaman said, "but you are to return the crockery to the galley when you've finished. Captain doesn't want it broken when the ship starts to roll early tomorrow morning."

Each plate contained a serving of tasty stew and a large chunk of brown bread. The mugs held coffee. There were no forks or spoons provided, but neither Clary nor Luke was in a mood to complain. They ate the pieces of meat and vegetables with their fingers and mopped up the gravy with the bread.

"Glad to see you're eatin'," Luke said.

"I have good cause to eat." Clary's hand rested on her abdomen for a moment. "I want to stay as healthy as possible."

"That's a good sign. You know," Luke went on, "I don't think that lady we saw is Mister Jack's wife. If she were, she'd be livin' on the farm with him, wouldn't she? But I've never seen her before."

"Then you missed her at the big canal celebration," Clary told him. "She was there, and she refused to meet me."

"That wasn't very nice." Luke paused, thinking. "You mean, Mister Jack wanted her to meet you? Why would he do that if he's—you know, if he's seein' her instead of you? But the thing is, if she's not married to Mister Jack and you want to marry him, then you could, couldn't you?"

"Why would I want to marry a man who lies to me all the time?" Clary asked bitterly.

314

"I don't know," Luke answered. "But I think that's what you want to do. Otherwise, why'd you follow him all the way to Wilmington?"

Clary fell silent, thinking about what Luke had said. In the straightforward way of many youths, he had just hit upon a crucial point. Why should Jack Martin, who was sleeping with Clary, want her to meet the other woman in his life? Something about that scenario was wrong. It was out of character for Jack. He would want to keep his wife and his mistress—or his two mistresses if that were the case—separated from each other.

Clary might not know everything she wanted to know about Jack, but of one thing she was certain. He was a fastidious man. His house was kept clean, his food elegantly served, his farm was remarkably neat and well cared for, and his person was always spotless. When he came home dirty after a hard day's work, he always scrubbed himself clean before the evening meal. A man so scrupulously clean would not be likely to keep two women. The idea would offend him.

The only explanation that Clary could think of for this puzzle was that perhaps the woman in Wilmington was a former mistress and Jack was still seeing her because of his son. Perhaps the woman stilled cared for him. That would explain the affectionate tone of her letter to him, and the reason why she would send him a hand-made birthday present. But it did not explain why Jack had not simply told Clary about his former affair and asked her not to talk about it to others.

Her thoughts in a whirl, physically and emotionally worn out by the day's events, Clary scarcely noticed when Luke gathered up the plates and cups to take them back to the galley. She huddled into her blanket, and despite the cold night and the hard deck beneath her, she fell fast asleep. She did not waken until near dawn when the ship got under way.

# *Chapter Seventeen*

Clary and Luke reached Bohemia Village late on the following day. The skies were gray, the wind was blowing, and rain was falling steadily.

"We're goin' to have to stay in town tonight," Luke said while he and Clary stood by the ship's rail awaiting the word to disembark.

"Is there a place where you can go?" Captain Schyler gave them one of his piercing looks. "I would allow you to remain on board until I sail tomorrow morning, but it will be wet as well as cold on deck tonight and all of my passengers are continuing on to Baltimore, so there are no spare cabins available."

"I have a friend," Clary said, "and Luke's uncle lives in town."

"I'm mighty glad to hear that. There goes the gangplank now. Good luck to you, Miss Cummings."

Clary was sorely tempted to ask Captain Schyler if she could remain on his ship until he reached Baltimore. It would be so easy just to sail away from all her problems and never return to Afon Farm.

You can't do that anymore, she told herself sternly. You have run away too often in the past, and on the most recent occasion, you ended up at the bottom of the canal. This time you will stay and fight for what you want, because no matter what he has done or who the woman you saw him with is, Jack is the man you love.

Once ashore, Clary marched right up to the front door and into the main room of Madam Rose's house, with Luke following her. Dancy was behind the bar, redheaded Hermione was sitting on the lap of the only customer in the place, and Calliope and Sinope, the other two girls who still worked there, were drinking together at another table.

"You back already?" Dancy saw them at once. "Moses said you went all the way to Wilmington."

"Miz Clary finished her business there real quick." Luke glanced at the girls, who were staring at him and Clary. He looked away as if he were embarrassed.

"You shouldn't keep comin' here," Dancy said to Clary. "It don't look right for a lady to be in a place like this. Somebody might think you're one of the girls.

"Calliope," Dancy went on, his dark eyes searching Clary's face as he spoke, "find Madam

Rose, will you? I got a feelin' Miz Clary wants to talk to her."

"Thank you, Dancy." Clary sank down into the nearest chair and put her head down on the table.

"Luke, if you're hungry, go to the kitchen and ask Emmie for something to eat," Dancy said. "Take that hamper with you. Didn't you have any luggage?"

"No, sir."

Clary lifted her head as Luke disappeared into the passageway that led to the kitchen.

"You want a drink?" Dancy asked her, offering the whiskey bottle and a glass.

"I'd rather have coffee."

Dancy nodded and a moment later set a large cup in front of her. Clary was still sipping it when Madam Rose appeared. Madam Rose said nothing at first, but sat down next to Clary. Dancy gave her a cup of coffee, too, and then withdrew to his post behind the bar.

"I seem to come to you whenever I am in trouble," Clary began.

"Many young women have done so in the past. You are carrying Jack Martin's child."

"How did you know that?"

"It is my business to know such things. I notice the dark circles beneath your eyes, your pale face, the way in which your figure has recently blossomed. Yet I do not think you have come here to make the request of me that some other women in your position do." Madam Rose paused, waiting for Clary's

response, and Clary understood to what she was referring.

"I want this child," Clary said. "I want its father, too. The problem is that he appears to have previous obligations." Within the next few minutes she revealed all that she and Luke had seen and done while in Wilmington.

"As usual, you have acted impetuously and without considering the consequences," Madam Rose commented, "although, under the circumstances, your actions are understandable. What do you now expect me to do to help you?"

"I would like to stay here overnight," Clary said. "Luke, too. We'll go back to the farm tomorrow when the rain has stopped."

"Jack Martin might object to the mother of his child spending the night in a whorehouse," Madam Rose said bluntly.

"He's not in a position to complain about anything I do," Clary responded. "I don't have much money left, but I'll give you what I have." She opened her purse, took out the few remaining coins, and pushed them across the table toward Madam Rose.

"Like so many otherwise intelligent women, you have no idea what it costs to maintain a business. This is not enough." Madam Rose flicked the coins with her fingertips, sending them back across the table toward Clary, who sat staring at the woman, unsure what to do next. She had not expected to be refused a room.

"Do you know," said Madam Rose as if to herself, "that you are the only respectable woman

to speak pleasantly to me since I was sixteen years old? You are also the only person to repay a kindness I have done by giving me a gift in return." She paused, taking a deep breath as if steeling herself to perform a task that was close to unacceptable to her.

"Tonight and every night recently, there are several empty rooms in this house. You might as well sleep in one of them since your presence can have no effect on my profits.

"However, I think Luke ought to spend the night with Dancy rather than upstairs where the girls are. His parents would have my head if he were corrupted while in my house."

"Thank you," Clary whispered. She reached for the coins on the table. Madam Rose stopped her.

"I will accept just one of these." Madam Rose picked up a 25-cent piece. "To cover the cost of clean sheets."

For the first time in days, Clary laughed with real humor.

"You are the most remarkable woman I have ever known," Clary said. Madam Rose actually smiled back at her. Then they both sobered, listening to sounds outside the house.

"What is that noise?" Clary asked.

"They are singing hymns," said Madam Rose. "There are certain religious folk in this area who are determined to shut down my house. They sing and pray in front of it every night, hoping thus to discourage prospective customers from entering. Pay them no heed. They are perfectly

peaceful and will disperse soon enough." Madam Rose stood. "It is late and you are plainly weary. I will show you to a room."

As the two women walked toward the stairs the singing outside stopped, the slightly off-key music being replaced by loud shouts, as if someone were haranguing the protestors, though inside the house the words were muffled. Just as Madam Rose started up the steps leading to the second floor, a rock crashed through one of the front windows and landed on the table where she and Clary had been sitting just moments earlier. The chairs and the table were showered with broken glass.

"My God!" Clary gaped at the sudden mess. "Those guys mean business."

A second rock splintered the other front window, and this time the missile hit one of the two girls who were sitting together.

"Sinope!" Madam Rose hurried to the girl, whose forehead was bleeding. "Dancy, bring a towel!"

While Madam Rose tended to her injured employee, the man with Hermione on his lap got to his feet so fast that he dumped her onto the floor. He headed toward the front door.

"Where are you going, you coward?" Clary yelled at him. "You take your pleasure, but when things get a little rough, you leave."

"I sure ain't stayin' here," he responded and rushed out of the house. A loud cheer greeted his exit.

"Miss Cummings, get away from the door!" Madam Rose came after her. "Please I don't want you to be hurt, too. Jack Martin would never forgive me."

"I wasn't going outside. I just wanted to make certain of something. I thought I recognized the loudest voice out there, and I was right." Clary went back into the main room, where Calliope, Sinope, and Hermione huddled together while a grim-faced Dancy worked busily behind the bar, his hands out of sight. "Hezekiah Bartram is back. He is probably the reason why peaceful hymn singers have taken to throwing rocks."

"He has escaped the gentle confinement of Josiah Grey?" Madam Rose shook her head. "That is a pity. On the subject of my business, Mr. Bartram is quite mad. I do believe you are right. He would not be above taking some violent action or instigating violence on the part of others."

"I'll stop 'em all." Dancy revealed what he had been doing below bar level. He had been loading a gun. He brandished a pistol that Clary recognized at once.

"A shot into the air might well encourage them to disperse," Madam Rose agreed. "But first, before we resort to firearms, let me remonstrate with them."

"Are you as crazy as Hezekiah Bartram?" Clary asked. "That's a mob out there. They won't listen to you."

"Nevertheless, I must try." Madam Rose started for the front door.

"I can't let you do this alone." Clary went with her.

"Miss Cummings, this is not your quarrel," Madam Rose said.

"Yes, it is," Clary declared. "Hezekiah Bartram is a former customer here. You told me once that he favored Hermione but that she was afraid of the physical harm he threatened her with. As I see it, this is just one more example of a man using a woman and then turning against her or hurting her or, at the very least, walking out and leaving her to face the consequences of what he has done. It happened to Hermione, to you when you were a young girl, and at present it is happening to me for the second time in my life. We face them together, *Rose*."

"*Clary*." Madam Rose's eyes were suddenly suspiciously bright. "My given name is Astrid. But don't tell them." She inclined her head first toward the girls in the main room, then toward the noise of the crowd outside.

"Never. I promise." Clary smiled at her.

When they opened the door and stepped onto the veranda, they were greeted by a roar. There were only 15 or 20 rain-soaked men and women standing in the street, but their mood was so ugly that Clary was grateful for Dancy's presence just behind her and for the knowledge that he still held the loaded pistol concealed by his side. As usual, Dancy would let Madam Rose do the talking, but he would be there to back her up if necessary.

"There she is!" Hezekiah Bartram shouted. In the light of the torches held by a few of the men his face was aglow with a wild, fanatical fervor. "That's the wicked woman, and her lewd and unprincipled friends are with her! Drive them from our town! Into the wilderness with them!"

It was then Clary noticed that Hezekiah Bartram was holding an ax in one hand. He drew back his arm and with a high-pitched shout let the ax fly. It struck Madam Rose on her right shoulder, then continued on to imbed itself deep in the doorframe. Madam Rose reeled from the vicious blow, then recovered to stand straight and stiff, facing the crowd with blood running down her arm. Clary gestured as if to help her, but Madam Rose shook her head.

There was no time to argue the matter. The crowd pulled back for a moment, as if the sight of the two women, one of them bleeding, had given them pause. Hezekiah Bartram, perhaps comprehending that the crusading spirit was wavering, combined exhortation with further action.

"Follow me!" he shouted, rushing forward. "Destroy the whores and their house!"

Clary was watching Hezekiah Bartram, so she did not see who threw the torch, but whoever did it had perfect aim. The torch flared through the night, sizzling in the rain. It fell through one of the broken front windows and into the main room. Clary heard someone screaming inside the house. Dancy chose that moment to step in front of Madam Rose and fire the pistol, but it

was already too late to stop what was happening. Frightened, but determined not to give way, Clary braced herself to withstand the coming attack.

Just as the protesters moved toward the veranda in a seething body bent on wreaking destruction upon the two women, Dancy, and anything else that stood in their way, a stout figure in dark clothing mounted the steps to stand beside Dancy.

"I came as quickly as I could," Josiah Grey said.

"It wasn't fast enough," Clary snapped at him. "Why didn't you keep that madman locked up?"

"We will discuss the terms of his confinement later," Josiah Grey told her. "For now let me do what I can to put an end to this disgraceful scene."

"You'd better do it fast," Clary said, "because there are six people inside this house. We need to get them out now, and not into the arms of a raving mob either."

"Good people, listen to me." Josiah Grey stepped forward, raising his arms. The townsfolk paused in their forward push, to hear what Josiah Grey might have to say to them. "Do not allow a poor madman to rob you of your common sense. It is far better to change the activities that occur in this house by gentle persuasion and by righteous example than by ugly violence. Hezekiah Bartram has lost his wits, but you have not lost yours. I ask you to disperse before serious harm is done to life and property—harm

that will torment your consciences for the rest of your lives."

"Don't listen to him," Hezekiah Bartram yelled. "You all know what goes on inside that house. I say, burn it to the ground!"

"It's already burning," Clary muttered. Just then, she heard a youthful voice calling to her from inside. "Oh, my God, Luke! Why didn't you go out the kitchen door? Luke! I'm coming!"

With no thought for her own safety, Clary hurried into the house. Smoke stung her eyes and a roaring noise accompanied the bright flames attacking the bar. A glass bottle cracked from the heat and a momentary whoosh of blue flame identified burning alcohol before the flames consumed the liquid. Over the noise of the flames Clary heard Dancy's low-pitched voice and knew he had followed her. And then she heard Luke again.

"Miz Clary, where are you?"

"Luke, I'm here. I'm all right." She reached him and touched his shoulder.

The next few minutes were a smoke-filled, chaotic nightmare. Sinope's hair was on fire. Luke was beating at the flames with a towel while he shouted to Clary to get out of the house. Emmie and Lucy burst from the kitchen hallway to run screaming through the smoke and fire until Clary caught them and pointed toward the door. Dancy was roaring for Luke to get outside. Madam Rose appeared to push Hermione and Calliope to safety. Dancy picked up Sinope and carried her out of the house, catching Luke's hand and dragging

him along, too, onto the veranda and then down to the street.

Clary raced around the main room, checking the hallway into the kitchen one last time, shouting up the stairs, trying to locate anyone who might have rushed inside to help and then become dislocated in the smoke. She was having difficulty with her own sense of direction. Her eyes and throat were burning, and there was an acrid taste in her mouth. It was Captain Schyler who finally pulled her from the house when she could not find the door.

"Miss Cummings, what are you doing in a place like this?" he demanded, pounding her on the back to clear her lungs of smoke.

"I was trying to help," she sputtered, coughing hard. Then, looking at the house, she said, "We need more water."

"It's all right. I came ashore as soon as I saw the fire, and I brought with me a band of my seamen and some of my male passengers, too. They are helping the townsfolk. If you are certain you are uninjured, and if there is no one else inside that building, I will rejoin my men."

After thanking Captain Schyler, Clary sent him off to help; then she looked around at a surprising scene.

Immediately after discovering that the house was on fire, Josiah Grey had formed a bucket brigade to carry water from the canal to the house. Thanks to the well-respected Quaker's efforts, the same men and women who a short time before had been ready to do violence to Madam

Rose, Dancy, the girls, and the property now worked to save the house. Other people, seeing the flames and hearing the commotion, arrived to ask if they could help. Two women in plain dark Quaker dress, who identified themselves as Josiah Grey's wife and sister, were treating an assortment of cuts and burned hands. Madam Rose stood quietly, letting Mistress Grey tear off the sleeve of her rose taffeta dress so her shoulder could be bandaged. Clary went to Madam Rose.

"How are you?" Clary asked.

"Alive, but ruined," Madam Rose said, her eyes on the flames.

"Perhaps this is a sign from God," murmured Mistress Grey.

A heavyset woman appeared on Bohemia Avenue, accompanied by three teenage children who were pulling a small cart. From it the woman and her children began to dispense coffee to those who had been fighting the fire. Someone else arrived with blankets and covered the damp, weeping girls from Madam Rose's house.

When dawn arrived, Clary stood arm in arm with Madam Rose in the still-falling rain, watching the smoke and steam rise from the ruins of the house. The veranda and the main room were gone. The kitchen and a good portion of the second floor still stood, though many timbers were blackened and charred. Josiah Grey was there yet, directing the final firefighting efforts.

"While I am sorry for your financial loss," he said to Madam Rose, "I cannot regret the

end of so reprehensible a business as yours. We can at least be grateful that no one was seriously injured. I trust your shoulder will heal quickly."

"This is all your fault," Clary accused him. "You let Hezekiah Bartram get loose after you promised to keep him under control."

"The townsfolk have him well tied up now," Josiah Grey said. "They will transport him to Elkton, where a physician resides who deals with such unfortunate cases."

"You should have taken him there weeks ago." Clary was not appeased.

"I am aware of my culpability in this affair, and I intend to make what amends I can. Madam Rose, it would be foolish of you to attempt to establish another house such as the one you have been maintaining when public opinion is so strongly opposed. Is there no legitimate and respectable business that you would care to manage? You have but to ask and my resources are at your disposal."

"Who would patronize me?" Madam Rose asked in a listless voice.

"That piece of land is in a prime location." Josiah Grey gave the smoking ruin a sharp glance. "Perhaps when you have had a few days in which to recover from this most unfortunate incident, heaven will send the proper response into your thoughts."

"Perhaps." Madam Rose sounded doubtful. After a minute or two, Josiah Grey bowed to the women and moved away.

"You are welcome to stay at Afon Farm for a while," Clary offered. She did not care that the farm was not hers to offer, nor did she care what Jack's response might be. All she wanted to do was ease the pain and loss her friend must be feeling.

"I could not leave my girls and Dancy," Madam Rose replied. "They will need me to find lodging for them and to see to it that they have food and new clothing. In any case, if I were to leave town, someone might place a claim upon the land and what remains of the building. It cannot have escaped your notice that I am not well liked in Bohemia Village," she finished in a dry voice.

"That might not be entirely true today," Clary said. "Last night the entire village turned out to help you. I'd be willing to bet that everyone who was here fighting the fire will feel a proprietary interest in what you do next." She fell silent, watching Madam Rose.

The woman looked beaten, her face smeared with smoke and grime, her pale hair falling down her back, the only gown she had left torn and wet and stained. Someone had draped a coarse blanket over her shoulders. Madam Rose held a coffee cup in her hands, her head bowed as she stared silently into the cold dregs. As Clary looked at her, wondering what she could possibly say in encouragement, Madam Rose drew a long breath and lifted her face to the rain.

"If I give up now," she said, "then Hezekiah Bartram has won—and so have those townsfolk

331

who are so sympathetic this morning, the same ones who allowed my house to be set ablaze last night. They are probably hoping that I will run away, that I will leave town so they can forget about me."

"Running away never helps," Clary said. "Stay and fight for what you want. That's what I intend to do."

Then, before Clary's eyes Madam Rose began to change, drawing strength from some inner well of courage. She shrugged off the blanket and straightened her shoulders and spine. She kept her chin high. On her face there was a look of new determination. Even her torn, dirty rose taffeta dress seemed to have improved in condition.

"Emmie and Lucy are good cooks," Madam Rose said, as if she were thinking out loud. "As Sam has so often told me, and as Josiah Grey has more recently remarked, my house is in a wonderful location. All the ships going eastward through the canal stop here before entering the locks, and those traveling westward stop after leaving the canal. Passengers and crews alike are often weary of ship food. Then there are those who must wait several days for their ships to arrive. Clary, you must return to the farm at once. In your delicate condition, you need Sarah's care."

"My delicate condition?" Clary repeated, stunned by the sudden change of subject. "I feel better this morning than I have for weeks. No morning sickness at all."

"Still, rumors fly quickly, and Sarah is certain to hear of last night's fire. She will worry about Dancy and will wonder if you and Luke were in town during the excitement. You and Luke, arriving home safely, will put her mind at ease—and my mind, too, for I will be much too busy to look after you."

"I don't need looking after," Clary said.

"Jack Martin would disagree. Clary, please do as I ask."

"Only if you tell me what you intend to do," Clary said.

"I shall change my life," Madam Rose responded, a faint smile curving her lips. "I did it once before when I left my childhood home. I can do it again now. And when I do, I will change this town, too."

Before Clary and Luke could locate horses for hire or find anyone with a cart who might be traveling in the direction of Afon Farm who would give them a ride, Moses drove into town with a load of late-season produce. Having assured himself that his son and Clary were unhurt, he at once demanded to see Dancy.

"You better come back to the farm with me," Moses said to his brother.

"I can't do that," Dancy told him. "You and I both know I'm not a farmin' man. I'm a town man. Besides, I couldn't leave Madam Rose now. She'll need me to help her start a new business."

"I sure hope it's a more decent one than her last business," Moses replied. "If you're certain

you won't go, then I'll deliver this produce and leave right away. Sarah will want to know what has happened, and she'll be glad to have Luke and Miz Clary home safe and sound."

By the time she got to the farm and Sarah had been told all about the fire, Clary was too tired to eat. She went to bed and slept until late the following morning.

"Luke told me everything that happened in Wilmington," Sarah said when Clary was seated at the kitchen table devouring eggs, fried potatoes, and homemade bread. "At least, he told me as much as he knows. He was more excited about the fire."

"Could I have more potatoes please?" Clary polished her empty plate with a piece of buttered bread.

"Glad to see your mornin' sickness is gone," Sarah said. "Luke tells me you think Mister Jack has a son."

"I'm not hungry anymore." Clary pushed her plate aside.

"You got some reason why you're not talkin' about this?" Sarah asked. "Or are you just plannin' to make yourself sick over it?"

"Luke and I saw them together," Clary said. "Jack, the woman—you might remember her from the canal celebrations—and a little boy who looks just like Jack."

"You sure you're not jumpin' to conclusions?"

"How could I be? I know what Luke and I saw. Oh, God, I'm going to be sick!" Clary rushed out of the kitchen, heading for the privy.

"Here," Sarah said a few minutes later when she pushed open the privy door to hand Clary a damp cloth. "I knew you were eatin' too much and too fast. After what you've been doin' over the last few days, you better be careful or you'll lose that baby."

"Jack wouldn't mind," Clary muttered into the warm cloth she was holding over her face.

"Don't you talk that way! I'm tellin' you, there must be somethin' you don't know about. Mister Jack's an honest man. I know that, even if you don't."

"At this moment," Clary said, "I don't know what I think or what I feel."

"You go take a rest till your stomach settles," Sarah advised. "And while you're restin', you think about what I've said. When Mister Jack comes home, you talk to him and give him a chance to explain. Seems to me, you got a bit of explainin' to do to him, too, when he finds out where you've been."

Back in her room, Clary found that she could not sleep, nor could she lie quietly on her bed. Too driven by conflicting emotions to be still, she paced restlessly around the house, straightening a chair in the dining room, picking Jack's pipe off the parlor mantel, then replacing it, and finally walking into Jack's room.

She knew what she was going to do and she knew she ought to be ashamed of herself, but she was too distraught to stop. If Jack would not tell her anything about himself, then there was only one way for her to discover the truth.

She pulled open the bottom drawer of his high-boy, where she knew he kept his ledger. She lifted out the heavy book and another below it that she saw was a record of the crops planted at Afon Farm and how much each crop had yielded for every growing season since Jack had come there. Beneath the two bound books were loose papers and a few letters.

Clary found the letter that had been in Jack's birthday present. After carefully rereading the letter, she discovered it contained little information. It was mostly an apology for Philly's refusal to meet Clary at the Summit Bridge festivities.

Three other letters were from a Mr. Benjamin Wilmot in Philadelphia. They dealt with canal business and with the shares that Jack owned in the canal company—and with additional shares owned by someone in England referred to as the marquess. A fourth letter from Benjamin Wilmot was folded around another letter. Clary started to read the letter from Benjamin Wilmot.

*Sir, I forward to you unopened the enclosed missive from your father. I trust you remain in good health—*

Clary put aside Mr. Wilmot's note and opened the letter it contained, noticing as she did so that this second letter had originally been sealed with wax into which a design was imprinted. Clary could make out the shape of a bird and what looked like a sword, but

the seal had been broken open across the middle. The cramped letters and the flourishes and slashes of the handwriting inside suggested to her that the letter had been written in either haste or anger. She had to study it for a while before she could make any sense of the old-fashioned handwriting, and by then she knew it was pure rage that had possessed the writer.

*Justin, I have learned from Mr. Wilmot that you took with you to America a woman and that you have installed her in a house in Wilmington. For shame! How can you give yourself over to lustful pleasures when your family is in such dire need? Your poor sister-in-law has been so deeply distressed by your despicable actions that she has suffered another miscarriage. You, and you alone, are responsible for the loss of the child who should have been my next heir. Damn you, Justin, you've killed my grandson! I curse the day you were born, and I blame your mother for cosseting you when you should have been beaten regularly. You are no true son of mine—*

The letter went on and on in this vein, filling a large page, with more invective squeezed into the margins. Almost lost in all the imprecations, curses, and promises of future punishment was a scrawled signature written out in full as if to give greater weight to the angry words preceeding it:

*William James Quentin Martynson, Marquess of Huntsley.*

Clary put the letter down on the bed, where she was sitting. Her first reaction was anger for Jack's sake, followed by a rush of understanding. No wonder Jack did not want to talk about his past life, if he had a father who hated him as much as the Marquess of Huntsley seemed to hate Jack. But his name wasn't Jack, it was Justin.

"Justin Martynson," she whispered. "No wonder that butler called you my lord. You are a nobleman."

# *Chapter Eighteen*

Jack came home two days later. He was in the best of humors, so he did not at first notice that Clary's excitement over the ship he and Sam owned did not match his.

"We sailed through the canal," he said. "Imagine our astonishment when we saw the condition of Madam Rose's house. Poor Sam was thunderstruck and terrified that she might have been injured."

"Did you speak to Rose?" Clary asked.

"I did, and I was surprised to learn that you were present during the fire. Clary, I am so grateful that you were not hurt." He would have put his arms around her, but Clary moved away to the other side of the fireplace. Outside, a cold November rain was falling, though a cheerful fire warmed the parlor. Jack stood watching Clary move around the room as if she could not find a spot on which to settle. Intensely conscious of

him as she was, Clary knew the exact moment when his glance sharpened and his attitude took on a new wariness.

"Why were you in Bohemia Village? Moses did go in for produce that day and took Clary home," Jack said. Madam Rose said only that you were there and that I would have to ask you about the circumstances of your visit."

Clary went still then, looking into his eyes to watch his reaction to what she would tell him. For it was going to be the truth, and then she intended to hear the full truth from him.

"Luke and I were on our way home from Wilmington," she said. "It was late when we came through the canal and the weather was bad, so I decided to stop with Rose for the night."

It was Jack's turn to stand immobilized, gaping at her. "You followed me to Wilmington?" he said in a harsh whisper.

"And to your precious Philly's house," she added.

"You had no right to intrude into my private affairs." His suddenly arrogant tone was too much for her.

"I had every right!" she exploded. "You would tell me nothing. You evaded every question I asked about your life or about her, and when evasions didn't work, you lied to me."

"You are the one who lied to me!" he declared. "While you so charmingly surprised me with a party for my birthday and waved farewell to me the next morning as if you really cared for me—

all the time you were plotting this deceit."

"I didn't plan a thing until I saw the love letter Philly tucked into the birthday present she sent you. And a remarkably intimate gift it was, too. A handmade shirt? 'My love always, Philly?' Give me a break, Jack! What kind of a fool do you think I am?"

"You read her letter to me?" Jack's eyes were pools of silver-gray ice. "It seems I was the fool here—a fool to believe that you might ever trust any man or to think that you could comprehend the requirements of honor. That was not a love letter."

"If you will remember, my lord," Clary said, taking great pleasure in the way he winced at her use of the title, "the paper fell out of your shirt and onto the floor. It was unfolded when I picked it up. I could not avoid seeing it."

"A lady would never have read it."

"We both know I am no lady," she said. "If I were, I never would have gone to bed with you, would I? But then, your precious Philly isn't a lady either since she has borne you a son who looks remarkably like you."

"A son?" Jack's jaw fell open, and then he burst into laughter. "Oh, Clary, is that why you are so angry? It serves you right for not trusting me and for devising that mad voyage to Wilmington. My dear, you have it all wrong."

"Have I?" She glared at him, her fists clenched, her teeth set. "Then suppose you explain to me exactly who that woman is and who the boy is. And by heaven, if you lie to me one

more time, I swear I'll do something desperate."

"Philly is my widowed sister," he said. "The boy is my nephew. If you think he resembles me, then I am honored, for he is a fine young lad."

"Do you really expect me to believe such a lame excuse?" she screamed at him, deeply hurt by this new deception.

"I do because it is the truth." He caught her by the shoulders, holding her still when she would have flung away from him. "Clary, do you realize how foolish it was of you to make that trip? A young woman and a boy traveling alone that way might have fallen into serious danger."

"Don't change the subject. You do that all the time when I'm getting too close to the truth, and I won't stand for it anymore. If Philly really is your sister, which I don't believe for a minute, then why isn't she living here with you?"

"Because she is delicate, damn it! This farm life is too hard for her. She is used to luxury and to all the pleasures of London. Wilmington is a poor substitute for what she has lost, but at least she is safe there and respected." He stopped, and Clary saw something down deep in his eyes close like a slammed door.

"I heard the butler call you my lord," Clary said, "and I heard him refer to her as Lady Philippa. Why would an English nobleman come to America and change his name and pretend to be a humble farmer? Why would his sister live in Delaware?"

She wanted him to tell her that his father, the marquess, had sent him to the United States to make certain that every penny of profit from both farmland and canal stocks was sent home to England. She had gathered that much information from the terrible letter in the bottom drawer of the highboy in his bedroom. And from that letter she knew that he was still lying to her, for the marquess had made it clear that Lady Philippa was not Jack's sister. She was his mistress. She might not even be an aristocrat, though that detail mattered little to Clary.

"My dear, there are certain things that, in honor, I cannot tell you," he said. "I can only ask you to have faith in me."

"You keep saying that. You keep asking me to trust you, but you don't trust me enough to tell me the truth. You can't even tell me your real name."

"My name is Jack Martin."

"No, it's not! I've known that much since I first met you. For God's sake, tell me something that's true! Give me something I can hang on to. Can't you see how lost and frightened I am?"

"Sweetheart, there is no need for you to be frightened." He gathered her into his arms and Clary was so desperate for comfort that she went to him unresisting to lean against his strength. Jack went on as though he was instructing a recalcitrant child in the simplest facts of life. "I have given a promise I cannot break. You will just have to take me

as you find me and accept that, whatever I may once have been, I am now simply Jack Martin, gentleman farmer. You have told me how proud your countrymen are in your own time to be the descendants of people who came to this land and remade their lives, changing their circumstances and often their names, too. Why can't you accept that this is what I am doing?"

"Because I know from personal experience that when lies are uncovered—and they almost always are uncovered at some point—the truth that is revealed can result in terrible emotional devastation." Clary pushed herself out of his arms. "I lived a lie once, in the twentieth century, because I chose to believe without question everything a man told me. I can't do it again. If you won't tell me the truth, then we are finished."

"I would give everything I have if I could tell you," he whispered, and even through her own despair, she sensed his pain and the conflict to which she was subjecting him. "I would give my soul, Clary! But I cannot, I will not, break my word."

"Then I can't continue to live here at Afon Farm." Clary turned toward the door so he would not see the tears she could not prevent from running down her cheeks. "The next time Moses drives into Bohemia Village, I will go with him, and I will not return."

"You have no means of support," he protested. "You are still a stranger in this time."

"There you are," she said. "That's the difference between us right there. I told you an incredible truth. I trusted you with my life. You won't even tell me your name. Don't worry about me, Jack. Perhaps Rose will give me a job." She heard his outraged gasp as she went out of the room.

"You will think better of this in the morning," he called after her.

"No," she said. "I won't."

Clary spent a sleepless, tormented night, and as a result, her morning sickness returned with a vengeance. When she did not appear in the kitchen for breakfast, Sarah came to see what was the matter.

"Stay in bed," Sarah ordered. "I'll mix up some of those herbs I gave you the last time. They stopped the heavin' right away."

Clary was sitting up in bed drinking a cup of the hot herbal tea, with Sarah watching to be sure she swallowed all of it, when Jack opened the door between their rooms and entered.

"I didn't invite you to come in here." Clary did not care if she sounded rude.

"You are sick," he said. "I heard you earlier, but I didn't want to intrude."

"How very honorable of you, my lord." Noticing Sarah's bewildered expression, Clary added, "I am sorry to tell you, Sarah, that I will be leaving Afon Farm shortly. I want you to know that I appreciate everything you have done for me. You have been a good friend."

"You can't leave," Sarah protested.

"My sentiment, precisely," Jack said.

"You can't stop me, Jack," Clary snarled at him. She seemed to be making a habit of rudeness this morning, but again she did not care. She was too unhappy to be concerned about anything but her own pain and her uncertain future once she left the farm.

"Mister Jack." Sarah stood with hands on hips, sending a look toward Jack that ought to have curled his toes. "Why can't you see what's right in front of your eyes?"

"Don't talk in riddles, Sarah. If you have something to say, then say it straight out."

"I can't do that," Sarah told him. "It's not my riddle to explain."

"Now you know how it feels," Clary said to Jack, taking a perverse pleasure in his obvious confusion and his concern over her illness. She almost laughed, but she choked on her tea instead and began coughing. Sarah took the cup from her and waited until Clary had recovered.

"You have to tell him," Sarah said. "If you don't, it will be a terrible mistake."

"Tell me what?" Jack demanded. "Clary, is something seriously wrong with you?"

"She's as healthy as that chestnut mare of yours," Sarah told him and walked out of the room.

"But the mare is—" Jack gave Clary a long, searching look. "This is not the first morning when you have been sick. The day after the

affair at Summit Bridge you were ill. When Philly was carrying Justin, she was sick every morning for weeks. Clary, are you bearing my child? Is that what all this quarreling is about? Of course it is. You want your baby to have a name."

"I want my baby to have an honest father," Clary said. "I want to know who the father is."

"Why should you doubt it when I am certain? I am the father!" He was laughing. "Do you know how wonderful this news is? Clary, we are going to have a child. We'll make a family, you and I and the baby, and Philly and Justin. It's a new beginning for all of us. And I will resolve any doubts you have about your child's name." Taking her hand, he grew serious. "Clary, will you marry me?"

"I can't because I don't know who you are." She snatched her hand away.

"Let us have an end to this nonsense about my identity. I am Jack Martin." Bending over the bed he caught her face between his hands. "How many times do I have to say it? Since the very first day I stepped ashore in this land, that has been my name—in Philadelphia, in Wilmington, in Bohemia Village, and here at Afon Farm. Like all those other immigrants about whom you have told me, in these United States, I have no other name."

She was too nauseated and too heartsick to continue fighting this particular battle. Betrayed by her heart into loving him when her brain kept telling her she should not, pregnant and

347

frightened in a time not her own, she saw that her only alternative to marriage would be to follow the course Rose had once taken. But she was not as brave as Rose. The thought of giving her body to anyone other than the man she loved made her even more nauseated, and she knew she could not pursue such a life for more than a few months before she became too large to sell herself.

"Well?" Jack asked, his hands still at her face. "Will you marry me?"

He did not mention love. Clary, wanting truth from him in all else, found herself wishing that he would lie about this one issue. When he did not, she decided to bargain before giving him what he—and she—wanted. If she could not have love, then she would have her own way on a few matters at least.

"I believe you have asked me to be your wife solely out of a sense of honor," she said, fully aware that her words would sting him in a tender spot, "but I come from a different tradition. You will have to grant me three promises before I accept your proposal."

"You know the promises I cannot grant," he said.

"I also know the ones you are capable of granting. I want to be married here at the farm, so Sarah, Moses, and Luke can attend. I don't know what foolish rules may be in effect about blacks going into churches used by white people. We will avoid any problems on that score by holding the wedding here, on

your territory, where those good people will be welcome."

"Agreed." He began to smile. "I hope all the promises you want from me will be as easy to accept."

"They are not. I asked the easy one first. The second thing you must promise is that Dancy, Rose, and all the girls from Rose's house must be here. I am assuming that you plan to ask Sam, but if not, then I want him here, too."

"Of course Sam will be invited. But the rest is impossible." When Clary would have protested, Jack put a finger on her lips while he continued. "Two of the girls have gone away. According to Madam Rose, they have gone to Baltimore to work. Only the red-haired girl is left."

"Hermione," Clary said. "I want her here, along with Emmie and Lucy, who work in the kitchen at Rose's. And Dancy, too."

Jack studied her face for a while, smiling as he considered her demand.

"I will go this far," he said. "We will invite all of them, and the invitations will be sincere. Whether they accept or not is up to them."

"All right," Clary said. "That's fair. But I really do want Rose to be here. I know you think it's highly improper of me, but I like that woman in spite of her profession."

"I like her, too," Jack said, "though not as much as Sam does. What is the third promise you require of me?"

"I want you to invite Philly and her little boy to our wedding."

349

"No, Clary," he began, but she stopped him.

"I will accept no excuses on this one," she said. "That's why I saved it for last, because it is the most important promise I want from you. If she really is your sister, then she ought to be here. Her presence at our wedding will make up for the way she slighted me at the canal ceremony."

"You are testing me," he said.

"You're damn right I am. I'm testing her, too. She snubbed me. Now I want her to be polite to me."

"What you want," he said, turning his back and walking away from the bed, "is for Philly to come here and make some mistake, to give away a clue to our mutual past."

"Perhaps I am hoping for something of the sort," she replied. "You are always talking about honor, so here's a chance for you to accept a challenge. Invite her and see what happens."

"You are extending the challenge to Philly, not to me," he said. "You have no idea how unfair you are being to her by insisting on this condition to our marriage."

"Perhaps if I knew more, I'd have a better idea about it," she responded.

"Good God, Clary, is it always going to be like this between us? Will you never stop prying and trying to learn things that are not your concern?"

"If I am going to be your wife, then everything about you is my concern," she said. "That's the deal, Jack. Take it or leave it."

"Do all twentieth-century women bargain like this about marriage?" he demanded.

"If they don't, they ought to," she said.

"It is most unbecoming in a lady. Fathers, brothers, uncles, or other guardians may bargain over the marriage settlement, but for a woman to lay down conditions in such a way is unheard of—and inappropriate—and indelicate."

"Gosh," Clary said, hoping the gleam in his eyes was humor and not anger, "all these complaints and we haven't even started haggling about my dowry yet."

"You don't have a dowry," he protested.

"Oh, yes, I have." She laid a hand over her abdomen.

"If I were not so found of you," he said in a soft and dangerous voice, "I believe I would hate you at this moment."

"If I were not so fond of you, I wouldn't be bargaining at all," she retorted. "You are the one who has driven me to this unseemly behavior. I am only fighting for what I want. Men do it all the time. Why shouldn't women?"

"You are not going to get along well with my sister," he warned her.

"Make her come to our wedding and we'll find out about that."

"Clary!" Unexpectedly, he gave in. "Very well, I will write to her, but as with the other guests you want, I cannot be responsible for her acceptance of the invitation."

"Yes, you can," Clary said. "Furthermore, I will read the letter you write, and I will add my

own note to it. And you had better make damn sure she does accept."

"You don't trust me at all, do you?"

"You got it, Jack."

Clary knew a moment of pleasure at his reaction to her slangy response. Immediately afterward his irritation changed to a sadness so profound that Clary almost gave up the fight then and there. Such sharp insistence on having her own way was foreign to her, but she believed this was the only method by which she could have Jack and the truth about him, too. And the awful truth about her own feelings for him was that, no matter who he really might be, or what he had done to so anger his father the marquess, or whether Philly was his sister or not, Clary loved him and wanted to marry him.

"I wonder," she mused, "if Rose was able to salvage any of those gowns from her house. That wardrobe room was better than a costume store. I'm sure I could find a perfect wedding dress in there."

At that point, shaking his head in disbelief, Jack walked out of her bedroom.

# *Chapter Nineteen*

Not only did Philippa come to Jack and Clary's wedding, but she also traveled in the ship Jack and Sam had purchased, and in Jack's company, for he had gone to Wilmington to escort her to Afon Farm. They arrived just an hour before the ceremony was scheduled to take place, at a time when Clary was beginning to wonder if Jack would show up or if he would leave her to explain to their guests why the bridegroom was missing. After weeks of strained politeness between them and no show of affection from him, Clary was increasingly uncertain of Jack's feelings toward her. She feared she might have pushed him too far with the demands she was making. She was, after all, living in a time when women were expected to be meek and submissive, and she was sure Jack knew she intended to keep on prying and insisting until he told her everything about his life. In the meantime, she

prayed he would understand that marrying him without knowing all she wanted to know on that subject was an act of great faith on her part.

Hearing the crunch of cart wheels on the drive, Clary ran outside, still clad in her dark blue cotton dress. The woman beside Jack on the cart seat was tight-lipped, her chin held high. The little boy with her was dressed like a miniature man in a dark suit. His burnished hair was perfectly smooth, apparently unruffled by the drive from Bohemia Village—or perhaps, Clary thought, his mother had combed it at the last minute.

"Hello. I'm glad you got here safely." Clary tried to sound welcoming. The woman simply looked down her nose at Clary and did not respond. Immediately, Clary transferred her attention to the little boy.

"Are you Justin?" She bestowed a wide smile on him and received a shy, faltering smile in return.

"Yes, ma'am." When Clary held up her arms, Justin jumped from the cart.

"Justin, mind your manners," his mother admonished with a frown. Jack helped her to alight from the cart, and then tucking her hand into his elbow, he brought her to Clary.

"This is my sister, Mrs. Philippa Gordon," he said. "And my nephew, Master Justin Gordon."

"I am very glad to have you here," Clary said.

"It is my understanding that you refused to marry Jack unless I was present," Philippa responded in a cold tone.

"Your presence was very important to me."

Clary was determined to be polite. "I have no family at all, and I wanted a female relative with me on such an important day." Did she imagine it or was there a faint thawing of Philippa's glacial demeanor at those words?

"Justin," asked Jack, "would you like to come with me while I drive the cart around to the barn? I feel certain the ladies would prefer to discuss bridal gowns and trousseaux without men present."

"Yes, sir. Thank you, sir."

Clary almost called coward after Jack as he drove off, leaving her alone with her unwilling guest, but she restrained the impulse. Philippa would probably resent the slur on her brother's honor.

"He forgot to unload your luggage," Clary said.

"We have none. We are not staying overnight."

"Oh, what a shame." Clary struggled to remain polite. "Sarah and I prepared my room for you and Justin to use."

"I prefer to return to Wilmington at once." Philippa pursed her lips. "My son and I will drive to Bohemia Village this evening with Mr. MacKenzie and spend the night in our cabin aboard the *ClaryRose*. We will sail with Mr. MacKenzie tomorrow."

"*ClaryRose?*" Clary let out a gurgle of laughter that made Philippa look at her with surprise. "Are you telling me that those two serious businessmen renamed the *Venture* in honor of Rose and me?"

"Apparently so. I do wish Jack were not involved in trade."

"Why, because he was born an aristocrat? In this country a title is a disadvantage, and anyone who wants to eat and keep a roof over his head has to have at least a minor involvement in some kind of trade. Besides, didn't Napoleon once call the English a nation of shopkeepers? But it was those same ordinary shopkeepers who finally defeated him at Waterloo."

"Actually, it was the Duke of Wellington who— no, you are quite right, Miss Cummings. Jack frequently reminds me that we are living in a different country now and he tells me that I must try to lose my prejudices."

Clary showed her guest into the house and they entered the parlor while they were talking. For lack of flowers, since it was so late in the season, the parlor and dining room were decorated with long-needled pine branches, stems of bright berries brought in from the surrounding woodlands, washed and polished apples and pumpkins, and small sheaves of wheat. A white cloth was spread over Jack's recently acquired desk, which would serve as an altar for the occasion. Silver candlesticks stood at each side of the desk, with a matching pair on the mantel. Philippa looked around at the simple furnishings.

"I must tell you, Miss Cummings, I once hoped that, when Jack finally chose to wed, the ceremony would take place in a grand cathedral with the most important members of society in attendance."

"Everyone who will be here today is a dear friend," Clary said. "That is what matters most to me, and I believe to Jack, too." She paused a moment, then plunged on with the speech she was determined to make. She had detected a few cracks in Philippa's snobbish, aristocratic veneer and she decided to take advantage of the fact that they were alone.

"Mrs. Gordon, I am going to be blunt with you. I know Jack is withholding a lot of important information about his past from me, and I won't pretend that I don't resent the way he is keeping me in the dark. We have had some pretty vigorous discussions about it. But none of that can change the fact that I love him with all of my heart. There are, however, a few questions I have to ask you before I marry him, and I must insist on honest answers.

"Is Jack really your brother? Is Justin his nephew? Or do you and your son have some other relationship to him?"

Philippa had gone chalky white during this speech. She stood, a slender figure in palest lavender silk, one delicate hand at her throat, her gray eyes wide with astonishment. It was her eyes that caught at Clary's heart. Facing her at close range for the first time, Clary could see how similar those eyes were to Jack's and she knew the answer to her questions before Philippa answered them.

"This is why you were so determined that I should be present today, isn't it? So that you could ask and watch my reaction while

I answer?" Philippa whispered. "What courage you have. I would not dare to speak so boldly to a stranger who might hold my lover's heart in her keeping. Your courage deserves an answer.

"Jack is indeed my brother, and I love him at least as much as you do, perhaps more, since I have known him longer and therefore I have greater reason to know how good and true he is. Justin is my son, and Jack's nephew. Like Jack, Justin bears a strong resemblance to my father, while I am more like my mother in appearance."

"Thank you." Clary closed her eyes in relief.

"Jack told me that you believed I might be his mistress," said Philippa. "Well, why shouldn't you wonder about us when you have been told so little of our circumstances? Yes, Jack did tell me that you made a daring excursion to Wilmington and that while there you saw the three of us together.

"Miss Cummings, allow me to provide a piece of information that may ease your concerns about my brother's emotions in regard to you. In late August, Jack visited me in Wilmington, and during those few days, he repeatedly begged me to let him tell you everything concerning our situation in this country and about our past lives. I would not agree. I still cannot agree. I am sorry if my reticence has made you unhappy, but once I decided to live in quiet retirement, I had no other choice but to insist upon maintaining my privacy."

"Your privacy," Clary repeated, staring at

her. "Not knowing your real relationship to Jack nearly destroyed me. It almost killed my love for him. I do not like people lying to me."

"Will you believe me if I tell you that Jack's deepest wish is to make you happy? You may trust him completely, Miss Cummings. He is the best of men, and he has been unfailingly loyal to me during a time of great tribulation. You see—" She paused as if gulping back tears. "You see, my son's father is dead and I—we three have no family but each other. If Jack had not insisted that I come with him to America, I would be living alone in England, unaware that my dear brother has found a woman who is courageous and warmhearted enough to love him in spite of her doubts."

"And this is the deep, dark secret that Jack has been keeping from me?" Clary asked, knowing there was more—much more—that ought to be told to her.

"Every word I have spoken is the truth," said Philippa. "I swear it."

"I do believe as much as you have told me," Clary said, "because I have the feeling that you are not the kind of woman who can live easily with secrets. But I still don't understand—"

"Excuse me, Miz Clary," Sarah said, interrupting them. "If you're goin' to get dressed in time for the weddin', you better start now. There's more horses and carts comin' up the road, and you don't want folks seein' you before it's time for your entrance."

"Thank you, Sarah. You are right. Mrs. Gordon, we will talk more about this later. Perhaps you would like to wait here in the parlor?"

"I always hoped," said Philippa, "that, when my brother married, I would be invited to attend his bride. May I help you to dress?"

"Thank you. And just so there won't be any secrets on my part, and knowing that you are certainly able to count and will soon figure it out for yourself, I ought to tell you that I am going to have Jack's baby."

Clary wasn't sure exactly why she suddenly felt compelled to mention her pregnancy. It wasn't obvious yet, so she could have waited until after the wedding. She did wonder if such a startling announcement might make Philippa reveal still more about her life and about Jack's, for Clary did not know all of it yet. She had not heard any explanation for that furious letter from the marquess, nor a reason why the marquess had referred to an unknown woman who had accompanied his son to America, when the woman was in fact his own daughter. Or was Philippa Jack's half sister by another father?

"Jack's child?" Philippa's pale, delicate face blushed bright red and then, amazingly, became suffused with pleasure and with another emotion that Clary could not identify. Philippa looked from Clary to Sarah for confirmation.

"It's true," said Sarah, nodding, "though I do think she ought to keep it quiet for another month or two, so people won't talk. Call me if

you need me, Miz Clary. I'll be in the kitchen till the preacher gets here." With that, she left Clary alone with Philippa.

"Jack did not tell me this," Philippa said. "But then, as you and I have cause to know, he is the very soul of discretion. Oh, Clary—may I call you Clary? And you shall call me Philly. I am so happy for you. If you love Jack, then you must want—and he must be so—he loves children, he has always been so good with Justin. Oh, dear, I fear I am not making much sense. Clary, how brave you are to be so cheerful. But then, you could not be frightened with Jack to sustain you. How fortunate you are to have him."

"This is very strange," Clary said. "I was afraid you would be offended, but I wanted to be completely honest with you. I put great stock in honesty. I never imagined that you would take the news this well or that you would be happy for me."

"You will be married in just an hour," Philippa said, "so there can be no question about the child's legitimacy. No, I do not think there will be any problem."

"What kind of problem were you thinking of?" Clary asked, still intrigued by the woman's unexpected reaction.

"Well, inheritance rights, of course—this farm, that fine ship—"

"Let us both hope that we won't have to worry about inheriting anything from Jack for decades," Clary said sternly.

"Oh, no, I did not mean—that is—oh, Clary,

we are truly sisters now. Both mothers, you see. I feel quite certain that we shall be the very best of friends."

"I would like that," Clary said, pushing to the back of her mind all the questions she still had about Jack's life and his sister's.

Clary could hear the voices of guests arriving and she knew she would have to get out of the parlor before Moses or Luke began showing people into it. Taking the arm of the still-chattering Philippa, Clary drew her across the hall and into her bedroom. As she shut the door she caught a glimpse of Luke on the front veranda.

"Luke," she called, and when he turned to answer her, she said, "When Rose comes, will you send her to my room? I have a feeling that I am going to be grateful for her company, not to mention her help with all the hooks on my dress."

"Yes, ma'am," Luke answered, grinning. "But you better hurry up. Mister Jack looks awful impatient to me. If you don't come out of that room on time, he just might charge in there and pull you out!"

When Rose appeared, she in no way resembled the erstwhile madam of the local house of ill repute. Her hair was pulled into an elegant coil at the back of her head and topped by a small straw bonnet trimmed in pale pink flowers to match her dress, which was made in the simplest design possible, with a shallow neckline and long sleeves. Her gloves were cream

kid, her earrings and brooch were made of seed pearls set in swirls of gold wire.

"Good heavens, aren't you dressed yet?" Stripping off her gloves, Rose set to work on the recalcitrant hooks at the front of Clary's bodice, which Clary had been trying to fasten with the fumbling help of Philippa.

"My hands won't stop shaking," Clary confessed.

"Brides are supposed to be nervous," said Philippa, "but not their sister-in-laws. I fear I have been of no assistance at all."

"You are Jack's sister?" Rose shot her a questioning look. "I didn't even know he had one till Sam told me this morning. So you are the lady from Wilmington."

"I have been living in retirement," said Philippa.

"So I understand. We will be seeing more of each other in the next day or two. I am traveling to Philadelphia on the *ClaryRose*."

"You are leaving Bohemia Village?" Clary pulled away from Rose's assisting hands. "Please don't go!"

"It will only be for a week. I want to order new furniture from a cabinetmaker in Philadelphia. And you, dear Clary, ought not to miss me at all. You are expected to be completely occupied with your new husband. Now stand still and let me finish those hooks."

Clary's wedding gown was pale blue silk. It did not come from Rose's stock of costumes, for all the clothing in the wardrobe room was ruined

by smoke and water. Instead, Rose purchased the fabric from a shipment passing through the canal on the way to Philadelphia, and she gave the material to Clary as a wedding present. A seamstress who had recently opened a shop in Bohemia Village had made the dress, cutting and fitting it on Clary during one long visit and adding the final touches in a second fitting only the day before the wedding.

Because Clary wanted to be able to wear the gown again it was simply made, with a low, round neckline filled in with removable white lace that ended in a narrow ruffle at the throat. The sleeves were puffed to the elbow and finished with a wide lace ruffle, which was also removable. The waistband was set a good two inches above Clary's own waistline—which would be an advantage in the coming months as her figure expanded—and the full skirt was gathered to it with tiny cartridge pleats. The skirt was supported by a stiff petticoat.

Instead of wearing a hat Clary parted her dark hair in the center and pulled it back in the style of the day, fastening it with combs decorated with blue silk roses. Elbow-length white kid gloves and flat blue silk slippers completed her wedding outfit.

When she was fully dressed and beginning to be nervous, Clary heard a knock on the door between her room and Jack's.

"Philly," Jack called through the door, "may I speak to you for a moment?"

After Philippa hurried into her brother's room, Clary and Rose looked at each other.

"I must say," Rose remarked dryly, "that you appear to be every bit as shaken now as you were on the first day I met you."

"This is a different kind of shaky," Clary responded. "Rose, you have been my friend since that day. That's why I wanted you with me this morning."

"I wonder if you understand what your friendship has meant to me," Rose said, touching her hand.

"Clary?" Philippa had returned. "Jack asked me to give these to you and to tell you that he is eager for the ceremony today." She held out her open hand. There, on the pale lavender kid of her gloves, lay a pair of sapphire-and-diamond earrings, the stones set in gold. "These belonged to our mother. Jack and I are agreed that you should have them."

"Very nice." Rose picked up one of the earrings, holding it up to the light so she could see it better. "These are real stones, Clary."

"Of course they are." Philippa appeared to be offended by Rose's businesslike assessment of the jewelry.

Clary thought if Philippa were not so well bred she would have snatched the earring out of Rose's fingers. Seeing the mercenary gleam in Rose's eyes, Clary repressed a laugh and, at the same time, discovered that much of her nervousness was gone.

"I am glad I had my ears pierced a couple

of years ago," Clary said. "If I can just get my gloves off, I will put on my wedding present and wear the earrings to the ceremony."

"Let me." Rose attached the earring she was holding. She put out her hand with a regal gesture and Philippa surrendered the other earring. Wondering if ever another bride had had two such disparate attendants, Clary repressed a fresh giggle and tried to stand still. Rose stepped back, inspecting her handiwork. "Jack always did have excellent taste." She pulled on her gloves and, after a sly grin at Clary, went to the door. "Are you coming, Philippa?"

"Yes." Philippa's eyebrows went up a notch or two at the familiar use of her given name. "I ought to find Justin. He may be up to some mischief."

Left alone, Clary closed her eyes, trying to calm the sudden frantic beating of her heart and acknowledging that with the moment close at hand she was afraid—afraid that Jack was only marrying her because she was pregnant with his child, afraid that all the secrets in his past might prevent them from living happily together. And still, in some deeply hidden corner of her mind, lay the fear that she would without warning be returned to the twentieth century and never see Jack again. Her terror at that possibility only confirmed to her how much she loved him. Doubts and secrets did not matter in that moment. All she was certain of was her deep and abiding love for the man who would that day become her husband.

"Are you ready?" Sam opened the door a crack and peeked around the edge of it. "Rose said you were dressed, and Jack is waiting for you."

"Yes." Clary took his arm. "Let's do it."

"Ye'll be happy, lass. He's a good man."

"That's what everyone keeps telling me. It's what I believe in my heart." Impulsively, she kissed him on the cheek. "Thank you, Sam, for everything you have done for me. You are a good man yourself and a true friend."

"Ach, lassie, ye're embarrassin' me now." Sam slipped into his fake accent and Clary snapped out of her overly emotional, close-to-tears mood to grin at him, which, she knew, was the reaction he hoped for. Still smiling, she let Sam propel her out of her room and across the hall to her wedding ceremony.

She saw her friends in the parlor, all of their faces turned toward her. Moses, Luke, and Dancy wore dark suits and white shirts. Sarah was in her Sunday-best gray gown with white fichu and a spotless white scarf wound around her head. Emmie in yellow and Lucy in pale peach stood next to Sarah.

Clary smiled at Sarah and the others. Then her glance moved on to Hermione in a soft green gown with her outrageously false red hair hidden beneath a very proper straw bonnet—Rose's doing, Clary was sure—and to Rose herself in her ladylike pale pink gown, and Philippa in lavender silk with a hand on her son's shoulder. There were a dozen or so other people present, men with whom Jack had worked on the canal,

neighboring landholders, most of them with their wives, the preacher in his black suit and white collar. Clary's gaze skimmed over all of them quickly and came to rest on Jack.

He was wearing a perfectly tailored gray suit she had never seen before. The fit and the cloth suggested that it had been made in London. Jack's eyes were shadowed and Clary thought he looked nervous.

There was no music. Clary and Sam simply walked across the parlor to where Jack was waiting. Sam removed her hand from his arm and placed it into Jack's hand. The ceremony was brief. The ring Jack slipped onto Clary's finger was plain gold, but then he added a second ring, this one a ruby surrounded by diamonds.

"Your betrothal ring," Jack murmured, just before he kissed her.

Afterward, while bride and groom accepted the congratulations of their guests, the witnesses crowded up to sign the documents. A few minutes later Clary took the opportunity to glance at the names. Right next to the name Samuel James MacKenzie, Rose had signed herself as Astrid Rose Andersdottir. On the line above was written Philippa Gordon. And Clary's new husband had signed himself as simply Jack Martin.

Clary saw Jack watching her and knew he knew that she had been hoping for some clue in his legal signature or in his sister's.

"This is not a day for questions. This is a day for rejoicing," he said to her. Then he added

with a glance toward the dining room, "From the meal that you and Sarah have prepared, I expect our guests to go home well satisfied."

When she first realized that her wedding day was set for the fourth Thursday in November, Clary had been pleased. She knew there would be no official Thanksgiving until President Lincoln proclaimed the holiday decades later, but for her wedding reception she and Sarah produced a menu of roast wild turkey, baked ham, sweet potatoes, relishes, mashed turnips, corn bread and biscuits, pumpkin pie and apple pie, with Sarah's lemon pound cake iced and decorated with frosting flowers for the wedding cake. There was cider to drink, some of it hard and fizzy, Kentucky whiskey for the men, Madeira wine or sherry for the ladies, and a large pot of coffee.

Clary intended to celebrate each anniversary of her marriage with a roast turkey dinner, thus unofficially keeping a holiday she cherished—and especially celebrating it on those years when it fell on a Thursday. She would tell Jack what she was doing, but no one else.

The wedding having taken place shortly before noon, the celebration ended some four hours later as darkness began to fall, the guests hastening to leave so they could reach their destinations before night.

"Philippa, wait." Clary stopped Jack's sister as she was preparing to get into the cart Sam was driving. "Jack and I would like you and Justin

to join us for the Christmas holiday. Please say you will."

"I am not certain," Philippa began, but Jack stopped her protestations.

"I will accept no indecision," he said. "Now that you and Clary have met, I would like you to become friends. It would be good for Justin to be able to run freely about the farm. He is too much restricted, Philly. So are you, for that matter."

"Do you really think it would be wise for me to spend so much time here?" Philippa still looked doubtful. "I might say—that is, I cannot always— Jack, are you sure you want us here?"

"I will answer for my husband." Clary slipped her arm through Jack's in a fond gesture. "We both want you to come and stay for at least a week. How can we be friends, as Jack hopes, and as I hope, too, if we don't know each other?"

"I am afraid—that is—it is difficult for me— Jack?"

It seemed to Clary that Philippa was appealing to her brother to cancel the invitation. Clary waited to hear what Jack would say.

"I want you here, Philly. We have been separated too often in these last six years. I am beginning a new life. I would like to see you do the same."

"Well, if you are certain—that is, if you don't think I might accidentally—I mean—" She stopped, obviously flustered, and took refuge in good manners. "Thank you very much. If the weather

holds so that travel through the canal is not stopped, Justin and I will be happy to accept your invitation."

"Uncle Jack," said Justin, who was sitting on a temporary seat in the back of the cart between Emmie and Lucy, "will you take me hunting? Luke says you take him when you go after squirrels."

"If the weather is fit, we will all go together," Jack promised. "Now, Philly, don't say he can't. It is time for him to begin his manly training. I will teach him to ride a horse, too."

As they drove away, Justin looked back, his small face alight with excitement at these promises.

"Pray that the weather does hold," Clary told Jack, "or that is going to be one disappointed little boy."

"If they cannot come for Christmas, I will see to it that they visit early in the new year," Jack said. "Philly needs to get out more, too. I have been remiss in my care of them."

"From what I've seen, you have taken very good care of them," Clary told him.

"I don't want to talk about my sister and her son any longer," Jack said. "This night is for you and me, Clary." He drew her across the veranda and into the house where Sarah, Moses, and Luke were carrying the last of the food out of the dining room.

"I left a tray of food here on the sideboard just like you wanted, Mister Jack," Sarah said.

"Thank you for everything you've done today,"

Clary told them all. "Sarah, I feel as though I should help you with all these dishes."

"No, you won't!" Sarah's response to this suggestion was characteristically tart. "This is your weddin' night. Your place is with your husband, not in the kitchen."

"Thank you for that, Sarah," Jack said, laughing. After he and Clary were alone, he added, "You are a lovely bride. I am glad I chose the sapphire earrings to give you today. They are most becoming with that gown."

"Rose thought so, too, after she checked the stones to be sure they weren't paste." Hearing his chuckle, she asked, "Do you mean to say that there is more jewelry?"

"You must allow me to keep a few surprises for the future," he teased.

Clary opened her mouth to ask another question, then closed it again. This was not the time to interrogate him and she was suddenly remarkably nervous. Jack seemed to understand what she was feeling.

"Would you like a little time alone?"

"I think so. It has been such a busy day."

"Do you need help with your dress?" When she shook her head, he tilted her chin up to kiss her lightly on the lips. "Clary, you must know that I will do everything I can to keep you safe and happy."

"I do know." Just as you've kept Philippa safe, she thought with a surge of tenderness.

In her room Clary discovered, spread out upon her bed, a lacy white nightgown and matching

robe trimmed with white satin ribbons.

"Oh, Jack." She lifted the gown. It was gossamer light and sheer as a cobweb. Letting it fall onto the bed again she quickly removed her gown, petticoat, chemise, and the light corset the seamstress who had made her wedding dress had insisted she must wear. She washed her face and hands and brushed out her hair. When she was finished she donned the nightgown and robe. Glancing rather uncertainly toward the connecting door, she noticed that it was not fully closed. It sprang open at the touch of her fingertips. Inside his bedroom, Jack was waiting for her.

"You have a new robe, too," she said, noting the dark red brocade in which his tall figure was wrapped.

"A gift from Philly. She insisted that I could not go to my bridal night wearing my old blue dressing gown," he said. "I thought it only good manners not to inform her that I have no intention of wearing it for more than a few minutes."

They stood less than a foot apart, gazing at each other.

"Are you nervous, Clary?" He raised his hands to clasp her fingers lightly in his.

"I shouldn't be, but I am," she admitted.

"Perhaps that is because you understand what this night means. Before dawn comes, you and I will be bound together for all time. If you have any reservations, this is your last chance to leave."

"I have a great many reservations," she said,

"and you know what they are. But I will not leave you, Jack. What I want most in this world is to stay with you and to be your wife."

"Do you have the slightest notion how much I love you?" His voice trembled a little as he spoke.

"Love?" Clary gasped. "You do?"

"You are my very heart," he whispered, "and all the more because I know the depth of your love for me."

"You know that?"

"How else could you come to me like this, trusting me so much, though until now you have had little proof of my love?"

"A wedding ring," she said. "A betrothal ring. Your mother's sapphire earrings. New night clothes for this special evening."

"Those are not proof. They are only symbols. The real proof is in your heart, which understands my heart without words." He bent his head to touch her lips with his. "I will always love you, Clary."

She went into his arms, banishing all questions and doubts and differences between them for one blessed night. Although it was less than a month since they had lain together, Clary felt as if it had been years. She wanted Jack with a steady, fervent need, and from the way in which he embraced her, she knew his desire matched or, possibly, surpassed hers.

She wound her arms around his neck and lifted herself up onto her toes, pressing against him. The edges of his robe fell apart and Clary's

sheer garments provided no serious barrier to the sudden heated pressure of his hard arousal. She moaned when he released her, but it was only to shift position so he could lift her off her feet and carry her to his bed.

A short time later her nightgown and robe drifted through the air like the wisps of fog they resembled to land beyond Clary's line of sight. Jack tore off his robe and came down beside her, overwhelming her senses with his wild, passionate kisses and his erotic caresses. He knew how to stir her to her very soul. From the first time they had made love, Jack had instinctively done all the right things to make certain that she would be as satisfied as he was. But on this night there was a new tenderness to his lovemaking.

"Never has anyone trusted me as you do," he whispered, his lips upon her throat and then on her breast. "Your faith in me and your willingness to overlook what I cannot tell you show me that you love me, too. I will spend the rest of my life proving to you that your trust is not misplaced."

If she suspected for a moment or two that his words were deliberately chosen to prevent further attempts on her part to penetrate the mystery still surrounding him, she did not allow those thoughts to remain for long. Nothing could destroy the love she felt for him. When Jack rose above her, looking deep into her eyes, she was conscious only of her husband and his passion, which was her passion, too.

With one swift, sure movement he made her his, and Clary cried out in joy and pulled him closer.

"Don't leave me, Clary." They were fused together and Clary began to tremble with impending ecstasy. "I could not live without you."

"Jack." There was no time to say anything more before she dissolved into him, into his hot, driving love. She knew he was right, and one of her questions was answered. She could not return to the twentieth century, for she and Jack were bound together forever as he had said they would be, and if they were separated, both of them would surely die.

# *Chapter Twenty*

"You need not have spent these last few weeks keeping to your own room at night," Clary said.

"I thought it was necessary, though it was unbearably difficult to stay away from you. You may have noticed my vile humor." Jack pressed a kiss just below her navel.

"Then why did you stay away?" She sighed with sensuous pleasure as his hand slid along the inside of her thigh.

"First, because you needed time for your anger to cool. You do recall how furious you were when I returned from Wilmington?"

"I am not likely to forget it, nor how angry you were in response." Clary supressed a gasp when Jack's lips moved lower, seeking a particularly sensitive spot.

"I also thought that a period of abstinence would make our wedding night more special," he murmured.

"It has been that. Jack, stop—oh, no, don't stop. Oh, my God!" Clary responded to his touch and his knowing laugh with a loud cry. "I've married a madman. How can you make me feel this way so often?"

"How can you keep on talking at a time like this?"

But her talking had just ceased. Clary was beyond answering him. Waves of intense pleasure washed over her, leaving her unable to do anything but cling to Jack. It was not until much later, when he lay with his head on her abdomen and her hands were laced through his hair, that she spoke again.

"We never did settle that argument after you came home from Wilmington," she murmured.

"I thought we did. The three demands you made of me were met, and so we have wed. You and my sister are well on your way to becoming friends. I see no further cause for discord between us."

Clary chewed on her lip, debating whether or not to tell him about the day when she had opened the bottom drawer of the highboy just across the room from the bed where they lay, the day when she had found and read the letter written by his father, the marquess. She thought about all the questions raised by that letter, and then decided not to spoil a perfect wedding night by mentioning it. The letter could wait. But she could not resist giving him the opportunity to volunteer what she wanted to know.

"Neither you nor Philippa has told me everything," she said.

In response to her words, Jack lifted his head and looked directly at her.

"My love, I am going to give you a little husbandly advice. Do not poke into dark corners where you ought not to be. Your trust means the world to me, Clary. Do not break my heart by withdrawing it."

"I won't." She smoothed back his hair and let her fingers trail along his cheekbones and down to his lips. "My problem is, I love you so much that I want to know everything about you. But I don't want to hurt you, Jack."

"Then let well enough alone, sweetheart, and believe that you know everything you need to know. I love you and I will never stop loving you."

"All right." Her hands smoothed their way across his shoulders and he lowered his head again with a contented sigh. "From this night on, I will do as you want."

Jack and Clary did not return to Bohemia Village until the Saturday two weeks after their wedding. The intervening days were quiet ones as the warm autumn weather stretched on. Clary had never known such peace or such happiness. Her morning sickness was all but gone, her nights were spent in Jack's arms, and her days were busy with the last chores of the harvest season. Both Jack and Sarah insisted that she must rest each afternoon.

Sometimes Jack joined her in her own bed-room.

"I would like you to ride into town with me tomorrow," he told her on one of those after-noons when the sun outside their window was pale gold and low in the sky and the bare tree branches rustled and creaked in a sudden gust of wind. "There is something I want to show you. I think you will be pleasantly surprised."

"I will go anywhere with you," she replied in lazy contentment. "Is it about the *ClaryRose*? Will she be berthed at Bohemia Village? I would like to go aboard her."

"The *ClaryRose* ought to be at or near Balti-more tomorrow," Jack replied. "Sam is taking a cargo south from Philadelphia."

"Then is your surprise something to do with Rose?"

"You are the most persistent woman I have ever known. Do not tease me any more or I will do terrible things to you." He illustrated his point with a caress that made Clary catch her breath.

"Do you realize that I have forgotten how to blush?" she murmured, touching him in a simi-lar way. "And it's all your doing."

Just before they left the farm the following morning, Jack presented her with a dark blue woolen cloak. There was no mystery about where he obtained the frequent gifts he gave to her. On Jack's instructions Sam bought them on his voyages and dropped them off at Bohemia Village when he passed through the canal. But

Clary never could decide just how Jack got the packages to the house without her seeing them or where he hid them until the time when he put them into her hands.

"You will need this if you are to stay warm today," Jack said, folding her in the thick fabric.

"You have become an overprotective husband."

"I hope that remark is intended as a compliment." He fastened the clasp at her throat and kissed her.

"Yes, it is," she said, smiling at him. "Since my parents died, I have pretty much had to fend for myself. I've only recently discovered that I like having you care enough about me to want to protect me. I like being self-sufficient, but I like being loved, too."

Clary was glad of her new cloak, for a cold wind whipped about them on the drive to Bohemia Village, and streaks of clouds high in the atmosphere suggested the possibility of rain or snow in the near future.

"Here we are." Jack pulled up in the usual place at the market along the canal. There was not much produce left from the farm to sell so late in the season—a few baskets of apples, some pumpkins—though there was the usual bartering of other merchandise going on. Clary wasn't paying attention to the market or to the fact that Jack immediately sold off their produce to a man on a canal boat. She was too busy staring at Rose's house to notice what was going on around her.

"Good heavens!" she exclaimed. "I don't believe it."

The repairs to the fire-damaged house had been completed since she had last seen it on the day before her wedding. A new and more elaborate veranda graced the front, with carved wooden pillars to support the veranda roof and wide front steps leading up from the street. Where the old house had been unpainted, this remodeled version was neatly whitewashed and every window boasted a pair of gleaming black shutters.

"Jack, is this the surprise?"

"It is. Miss Andersdottir is now running a respectable inn and dining room."

"She really ought to change that last name," Clary said thoughtfully.

"Perhaps Sam will convince her to do so." Jack's eyes were dancing with humor, and Clary knew he had divined her thoughts.

"Is Sam completely finished with his work on the canal?" Clary asked. Jack's own involvement in the canal project had ended shortly after the grand opening, and whenever he spoke of Sam these days, it was in connection with the ship they jointly owned.

"He is. The canal will be completely finished by spring, with all those famous collapsing sides properly shored up to prevent further mud slides. The locks are already functioning well. Thus, Sam is once more the seafaring man he has yearned to be."

"With regular stopovers here in Bohemia Village," Clary added, "which is all to the good."

"Sweetheart, you have the soul of a match-maker," Jack teased. "I can only assume it is because you are so happy with me that you want your friends to be as happily married."

"Whatever gave you that idea?" Clary teased him back and he laughed.

Clary found the new interior of Rose's house as different from what it had been as the outside. In the main room, the bar had been removed in favor of tables and chairs placed to take full advantage of the fine canal view.

"There is a new taproom on the lower level," Rose explained. "It opens at the back of the house, so people can enter directly from the market area or just cross the road from the canal."

Rose's own appearance was altered, too. Gone were the pink taffeta ruffles and laces, the corded decorations, the curls and waves and braids of her former costumes and hairdos. This new version of Astrid Rose Andersdottir was dressed in a deep, muted shade of rose. Her gown was modest in style and simply ornamented. Her pale hair was swept into the smooth coiled arrangement she had worn at Clary's wedding. However, Rose showed Clary around the remodeled house with the same confident air she had always displayed.

To the left of the front entrance was Rose's office. Behind the office was a small private sitting room, and then Rose's bedroom, which was decorated in shades of pale pink with ecru lace.

Out near the front door, the old, rickety steps to the second floor had been replaced by a wide

stairway with a polished mahogany banister.

"The upstairs rooms are filled every night," Rose said in answer to Clary's question about the state of her new business. "Travelers don't know or care about the original use to which this house was put. I must confess, I found it a bit disconcerting at first to see men bringing their wives and children here and to have them remain over night when I was previously accustomed to a more frequent turnover of guests. However, not as much furniture is broken these days, and we no longer have to change the sheets as often as in the past, which is a great monetary savings. I am also able to charge more for family groups than I dared extract from a man for the privilege of taking one of the girls into a room for an hour or two."

"I am glad to know that you haven't changed entirely," Clary responded, laughing at these crisp and practical comments.

She and Jack ate a late midday meal in the public dining room and discovered that Hermione—whose flamboyant red hair was slowly growing back to its natural dark brown shade and who was as soberly dressed as Rose in a brown outfit with black braid trim— was acting as Rose's assistant manager. Dancy still ruled over the bar in the taproom and made occasional forays into the upper room as a warning to customers to keep order. And Emmie and Lucy, turned loose in the kitchen, were producing a remarkable array of delicious food.

The newlyweds returned to Afon Farm with their cart loaded with packages that Clary intended as Christmas presents. Fearing that the weather would change and she might not be able to travel into town again before the holiday, she spent the afternoon in the new shops and at the booths along the canal.

"Just where, may I ask, do you intend to conceal these gifts until Christmas Day?" Jack asked as they drove along.

"Under my bed or in the blanket chest," she replied.

"They won't all fit, my dear."

"I suppose we could store a few in the highboy in your room." Clary sent a sidelong glance his way to see what his reaction would be to this suggestion. "I seem to remember that there was a lot of empty space in the bottom drawer."

"When did you look into the bottom drawer?" A note of sharpness crept into his voice.

"On the day after you cut your arm," she replied easily. "Perhaps you were too feverish to recall it, but you spent that day in bed working on your ledger."

"I haven't forgotten." An oddly tense little silence fell between them until Clary spoke again.

"Do you think I might find space in there to hide some of these packages? Just until I wrap them up for Christmas, you understand. Perhaps you could remove those big books until then."

"I do not think so." It was as firm a dismissal as Clary had ever received.

"I see. Well, then, I shall have to find some other place."

"That would be best." Another silence followed his words. Then Jack said, "Clary, you have not opened that drawer more than the one time, have you?"

"What reason could I have to go through your ledgers?" she said, evading a direct answer. "What are you hiding in there, Jack? The crown jewels, stolen from the Tower of London and smuggled into this country? My Christmas present? The shrunken head of some former wife?"

"What a bloodthirsty idea." But he did not laugh, nor was he diverted from the subject. "So you have been rifling through my private papers. I do not take kindly to having my privacy invaded."

"I do not take kindly to people who deceive me," she retorted, hurt by his sudden coolness.

"What did you discover, Clary? Evidence that I did murder some previous wife? Or were you more interested in how wealthy I am? Did you read the ledgers?"

"Certainly not." She was glad that this statement could carry conviction. "I don't think I could figure out those long columns of figures that I saw you working on while you were recuperating from your wounded arm." She hoped mention of his arm would call to his mind the way in which she had cared for him. Gratitude on his part might serve to defuse the

battle she saw shaping up on the subject of that cursed bottom drawer. She wished with all her heart that she had never opened it. If she had not seen the letter from the marquess, she could have believed every word that Jack and Philly had said to her.

And you would be living in a fool's paradise once more, she told herself. You decided you weren't going down that path again. You wanted openness and honesty. Perhaps it's time for you to be honest with him.

"Jack," she said aloud, "it's true that I didn't do more than glance inside the ledger and then flip through the other book you keep about the crops you grow. This was just after I returned from Wilmington, and I was hurt and angry and frightened by what I had seen there. I thought there might be something in your papers to tell me who Philly was and whether or not Justin was your son."

"I see." Jack's mouth was a thinly compressed line of controlled rage. "Is prying into other people's private affairs a common practice in the time from which you come?"

"I'm afraid it is," she replied, thinking of supermarket tabloids and the popularity of tell-all television talk shows. "But I know better than to do something like that. My only excuse is that I wasn't thinking clearly."

"What did you discover?" He rapped out the question so coldly and his face was so set and hard that Clary felt a small thrill of fear. Still, she answered him honestly.

"I found a letter from the Marquess of Hunt-sley. I couldn't decipher all of it because his handwriting was so atrocious, but I could tell he was furious with you. What he said indicated that Philly was your mistress." Clary stopped because Jack was glaring at her with such blazing outrage in his eyes that she began to be seriously afraid of what he might do.

"Did it ever occur to you," he ground out, "that this secret you are so determined to uncover could destroy the lives of innocent people if it were revealed?"

"I never thought of that."

"Perhaps you should think more often in the future." His voice was deadly cold.

"Rose says I too often act impulsively on important matters," she said, "and without considering the consequences."

"That is certainly the case in this instance."

"I'm sorry. I have never spoken about what I found in that letter, not even to Philly when we talked."

"If you ever say a word of this to Philly," he grated, "by God, I will beat you!"

"No one hits me!" she exclaimed. "No one! If you lay one hand on me in anger, Jack Martin, I will leave you and you will never see me again."

"You have no idea of the seriousness of your interference." They were by now at the farm. Jack pulled the cart to a stop in front of the barn, and Clary saw Moses coming toward them to take the horse and to help unload the packages. Jack caught her chin so she could not turn

her face away from his furious gaze. "As your husband, I order you not to speak one word about this matter to anyone. Do not question me about it again. And do not, under any circumstances, open the bottom drawer. Do you understand me, Clary?" he thundered.

"Who do you think you are?" she snarled at him. "Bluebeard? Do you know the story, Jack? 'Don't use this one key. Never open this particular door.' We know what happened to Bluebeard's wife when she disobeyed, don't we?"

"Unlike Bluebeard," he said in a gentler voice, "I have only one wife, so I have not killed the woman I love—yet."

She pulled away from him and got out of the cart without assistance, though Moses was standing beside it.

"I mean what I say, Clary," Jack told her. "My tolerance is at an end."

"Fine! Keep your damned secrets." She spun around, her skirts swirling, and ran for the house. Once in her own room she slammed the connecting door shut so hard that Jack must have heard it out in the barn.

No sooner had Clary pulled off her new cloak and her bonnet than Jack and Moses appeared with the packages she had purchased in town.

"Just put them down there in the corner," Clary instructed. "I'll sort them out later." She noticed Jack's quick glance at the closed door to his room, but he said nothing about it.

"Sarah left your evening meal in the kitchen," Moses said. "And there's enough cooked food in the pantry for tomorrow."

"Thank you." Clary responded with a some-what-forced smile so Moses would know she wasn't angry with him. "I forgot that it's Saturday night."

"I better see to the horses," Moses said, leaving.

"I'll come with you." Jack followed him out of the room.

Left to herself with no one upon whom to vent her frustration, Clary stood wondering what to do next. She was not in any mood to deal with the pile of Christmas presents, nor was she hungry enough to do anything about an evening meal.

"I think it's time for the traditional Saturday-night bath," she muttered to herself. "Maybe afterward I'll be able to think more clearly."

In the kitchen she found the kettle of hot water on the cookstove, where Sarah always left it. Pouring the water into a bucket, she carried it to the bathing stall. The weather was almost too cold to use the stall. Jack had told her there was a large tub that could be moved into the warm kitchen for baths during the winter, but Clary wasn't ready to give up the privacy, or the freedom to splash water around carelessly, that the outside stall allowed. After pumping a second bucket of cold water for rinsing, she hung her clothes on the hook and then entered the stall. She washed quickly, shivering a bit, and it took

some nerve to rinse off the soapsuds with the cold water.

She was twisting her hair over one shoulder to wring out the excess water when Jack appeared. He was completely naked and he looked remarkably grim.

"I'll be finished in just a minute." Clary reached for the towel he was holding.

"Let me." He spread out the towel, holding it in both hands. Thinking that he was going to wrap it around her, Clary did not protest when he reached toward her. An instant later the towel was doubled up across her back and she was pushed hard against the brick wall.

"Jack, what are you doing?"

"Making certain that you know who I am," he said.

He came against her, holding her where she was with the full length of his strong body. He did not hurt her and the towel provided sufficient padding to keep the uneven bricks from bruising her back, but Clary could not move. She pushed against Jack's shoulders and then against his upper arms, but to no avail. He stayed where he was.

He kissed her hard, insistently demanding her response until she unlocked her tightly clenched teeth and gave his tongue access to her mouth. The familiar stroking heat was irresistible. Nor could she ignore the stiff erection trapped between their bodies. After weeks of pleasurable lovemaking with Jack she was exquisitely atuned to his needs and accustomed to having

all her own desires fulfilled by him. Not even his outraged anger could stiffle the sensual urge that so easily flared between them. In fact, that violent emotion only intensified her usual reactions to him. Jack's skin pressing so agressively against hers was more than she could bear. When her arms went around his neck and she was no longer fighting him, Jack loosened his tight hold on her enough to allow one of his hands to slide down between them.

Clary leaned her head back against the brick, trying to see his face, but it was too dark. She could hear his quick breath and smell his familiar scent. She could feel his hand as he guided himself to the heated spot between her thighs. His hand skimmed quickly over her hips, then along her thigh, lifting her leg, pulling it upward. With a choked cry she gave herself over to him.

"Ah, Clary." He held her so tightly that she could not move; she could only stand trembling on one foot, leaning back against the wall, accepting what he was doing to her. Always before he had been gentle with her, even during their most intensely passionate moments. Tonight she could feel his anger in his every rough stroke into her yielding body. He was hard, tough, boiling over with rage and desire—and with a particular fear. "Clary, don't leave me. I need you. Stay with me. Stay with me!"

He went rigid, shuddering with the approach of his climax. In that moment Clary found his mouth and kissed him, loving him, needing to reassure him that she was his and always would

be. A moment later, much too soon for her, he withdrew from her and leaned against the wall beside her, his arms at his sides, breathing in deep, gasping breaths.

"Jack, my darling." She put her arms around his waist and her head on his chest. Slowly he embraced her. They stood locked together in the winter darkness until Clary began to shiver.

"Come." He led her out of the bathing stall.

"My clothes," Clary protested, shivering more violently.

"Here." He thrust them into her hands, along with the damp towel and his own garments. Then he swung her up into his arms and carried her to the house, walking naked through the chill December night.

In his bedroom he took the clothes from her and tossed them aside, then tucked her into his bed and got in beside her. She was by then thoroughly chilled and so she went eagerly into his arms to let him warm her, but she had the oddest sensation that she was the one who was warming him and that it was not his body that was cold, but his soul, and the cold was for him a constant, aching pain.

When, a short time later, their embrace turned warmer still, she opened her thighs and her heart. He came into her gently this time, softly and tenderly, all the anger between them left outdoors in the bathing stall. And this time he stayed with her until she sobbed her sweet release, and when he was finished, too, he smoothed her hair and kissed her

face and told her repeatedly that he loved her.

"I can't stand fighting with you," she murmured, snuggling against him. "Not even when the making up is so lovely."

"Then let us stop quarreling. Clary, you must cease this eternal questioning of my past. I do not continually worry at your secrets to uncover them."

"Mine?" she cried. "What secrets do I have?"

"You have never told me the full story of your husband's infidelity."

"I don't want to talk about that," she cried. "It was so long ago, so far away. What does it matter now?"

"Perhaps I feel the same way about the events in my life about which you are so curious." When Clary did not answer, he went on. "So, my love, both of us have areas of our lives into which we do not want others poking—not even those we love. Perhaps especially those we love."

"I hadn't thought of it that way," she admitted.

"Think of it now," he said. "Think hard and long because, I warn you, if you persist in the way you have been going, you will destroy our happiness and our future together. Let us have an end to this constant bickering and to your curiosity."

"Perhaps you are right."

"I know I am right. Shall we make a bargain? I will not demand to know your secret if you will refrain from asking about mine."

She held on to him, lying there in his bed with the quilts warm around them, and she thought about how much she loved him and how the character he revealed to her in his everyday behavior was above reproach. His honor meant so much to him, he was such a good and true man, that whatever the mystery of his past might be it could be nothing very terrible.

"Clary?" His arms tightened around her as if he feared she would take flight.

"You just told me to think long and hard," she whispered. "That's what I am doing."

"And?"

"I will agree to your bargain because I love you and because, much as I hate to admit it, you are right. No more questions, Jack. We will live honestly day to day and try to make each other happy."

"You do make me happy." His mouth was on her throat. "Without your love, my life would be a desolate place. Never leave me, Clary, and never take your love from me, for if you did, my heart would break from loneliness."

# *Chapter Twenty-one*

With just two weeks left before Christmas, Clary and Sarah plunged into holiday preparations. They were by now used to working together and Clary's household skills were greatly improved since her first days at the farm. They baked fruit-cake, made pies with Sarah's homemade mince meat—which was liberally laced with whiskey as a preservative—and finished the last of the preserving and pickling. Then they cleaned the house, giving special attention to Clary's room, which would become the guest room during Philly's stay at Afon Farm. Luke set up a small trundle bed for Justin to sleep on, while Clary dusted the furniture and mopped the floor and Sarah made up the beds with freshly ironed sheets and the spare quilts from the blanket chest.

With the cleaning finished, it was time to decorate. Jack, Luke, and Clary hiked into

the nearby woods to gather long-needled pine, holly bright with red berries, pine cones, and wild nuts.

"I want to cut down a tree," Clary insisted. "We'll put it in the parlor."

When Jack and Luke both looked at her as if she had taken leave of her wits, she explained the tradition of a Christmas tree as if it were a custom confined to her own family.

"There is more to it than that," Jack said in a low voice, while Luke tramped about looking for a tree matching Clary's specifications.

"In the twentieth century, it's a big part of the holiday celebration," she said.

"Then you shall have what you want."

"Thank you. Jack, you are so good to me."

"Just remember this when I ask something of you." The kiss he planted on her ready lips clearly indicated to Clary what his payment for the tree would be.

"I never heard of such a thing," Sarah protested when they dragged the chosen tree into the parlor and set it in a bucket of wet sand. "It'll only drop all its needles and make a mess for us to clean up afterward."

"That's part of the holiday tradition in my family," Clary said, winking at Jack. "Now we have to decorate it."

She used dried grasses and milkweed pods. Luke brought her a long vine that was covered with purple berries, and this she draped around the tree like a garland. Because there was no fancy holiday paper available, Clary was

planning to wrap the presents she had bought in plain white paper. She had purchased a large roll of it in Bohemia Village. In the shop owned by the seamstress who had made her wedding dress, Clary had bought a spool of narrow red ribbon to tie up the packages. The leftover scraps of paper and ribbon she fashioned into tree ornaments, teaching Luke how to cut out snowflakes, which they attached to the tree with red ribbon. A white paper star topped the tree. When she was finished, Clary wrapped a sheet around the bucket holding the tree, and on the sheet she set out the presents.

She and Sarah laid pine and holly branches on the parlor and dining room mantels, tucking pine cones in at strategic spots. Clary hung red-ribboned swags of greens on the front and back doors. A bowl of greens dotted with tiny red ribbons sat on the dining room table, flanked by the silver candelabra holding long white tapers. As a finishing touch Clary put a small bowl of fragrant greens in the guest room.

"It does look nice," Sarah said, agreeing with Clary's admiring exclamations. "Mister Jack never bothered much with Christmas, though I can tell he's pleased by what you've done. But come January, you and I are goin' to have one heavy cleanin' to do."

Philly and Justin arrived two days before Christmas, traveling on Captain Peter Schyler's sloop, since Sam was presently in Philadelphia on yet another trip and was not expected in

Bohemia Village until Christmas Day. Jack and Clary drove into town to meet their guests.

"I am very glad to see you again, Miss Cummings," said Captain Schyler. "I have often wondered how you fared since our last parting."

"It is Mrs. Martin now," Clary said. "I recently married Jack."

"Did you?" Captain Schyler shook Jack's hand. "Sir, you have found yourself a most enterprising lady. You ought to enjoy an interesting life with her."

"I expect to, and I look forward to it," Jack replied.

"Is it too late for a fond acquaintance to kiss the new bride?" the captain asked. Having obtained Jack's permission, he bent to kiss Clary on the cheek.

"I hope you've told him all about that trip to Wilmington," he whispered in her ear.

"It was because of Jack that I went there, and he does know about it," Clary responded. In a louder voice, she added, "Captain Schyler, if you are ever in Bohemia Village for more than a day or two, you are most welcome at Afon Farm. You were good to me at a time when I was unhappy, and I won't forget it."

"He is a very nice man," Philly remarked when Captain Schyler left them to return to his duties. "He showed Justin all over the ship and even let him hold the wheel for a time. One would not expect to discover a seaman who is so well bred."

"What, Philly!" Jack exclaimed in pretended astonishment. "Are you by any chance voicing approval of a man who is in trade?"

"He is a very superior sort of tradesman," said Philly, blushing a little.

"And a very wealthy one," Jack added.

"Indeed?" Philly cast a speculative gaze upon Captain Schyler's trim schooner.

It snowed that night, so in the morning Clary took Justin out to build a snowman and to show him how to throw snowballs. When they became chilled and their hands were red and raw, they retired to the kitchen to drink warm cider and eat Sarah's freshly baked sugar cookies.

"How vigorous you are," Philly said when she, Jack, and Clary were sitting in the parlor and Justin was napping in the guest room. "Clary, ought you to be running about while you are in such a delicate condition?"

"I am far from delicate," Clary protested. "I have never felt so well."

"You are fortunate." Philly sent a glance Jack's way, and her cheeks turned bright pink. "I was ill every day before Justin was born. Morning sickness added to seasickness. It was a most unpleasant time."

"I am sorry to hear that." Clary responded sympathetically. Jack was looking hard at her. She smiled and shook her head, determined not to ask questions that would violate the promises they had made to each other not to pry into their respective past lives.

For all the warm affection between brother and sister, Philly was openly nervous and Clary thought she knew why. Philly was afraid she would slip and reveal too much, as she had just done with her remark about suffering from sea-sickness as well as having morning sickness, for now Clary knew that Philly had been pregnant during the crossing to the United States.

Jack had given his employees Christmas Eve and Christmas Day off from work, so Clary and Philly did the cooking, though much of the preparation was done beforehand.

"Miz Clary," Sarah warned on the morning of Christmas Eve day, "please don't let Miz Philly burn down my kitchen. That woman don't know a thing about cookin'."

"I will confine her to slicing, placing food on platters, and carrying things to the dining room," Clary promised.

"She'll probably slice off her fingers," Sarah predicted.

No such catastrophe occurred, in part because Philly fluttered about the kitchen trying to help, but never actually accomplished anything.

"I have always depended upon servants," she said. "I have never learned to be practical. I envy your skill, Clary."

The ham Clary baked for Christmas Eve dinner proved to be delicious, as were the candied sweet potatoes, the corn bread, all the pickles and relishes, the fancy cookies, pies, and cakes.

After dinner they opened their presents because Justin insisted with all the ferocity of an

overexcited six year old that he could not be expected to sleep that night if he had to wait until Christmas Day, and he therefore intended to keep the grownups awake all night with his weeping.

"What a little monster you are," Jack said affectionately, handing him a package. "This is from Clary."

It was a book, which Clary promised to read to him as soon as possible. She also gave him a wooden wagon and three brightly painted wooden soldiers to ride in it.

"Tell me, Justin," Jack said, "did you like the pony I let you ride earlier today while the women were preparing that wonderful feast for us?" When Justin nodded enthusiastically, Jack went on. "Then I think you must have it for your very own. We must prevail upon your mother to allow you to visit Afon Farm more often so you will be able to ride him."

"I can have Brownie?" Justin's eyes were wide.

"He is all yours," Jack replied.

"Mama, a pony!"

"Yes, dear, I heard." Philly turned upon her brother eyes almost as wide as Justin's. "Jack, are you quite sure it is safe for him to ride? I do not want him to be injured."

"You cannot coddle him forever, Philly. He's not a baby anymore. Bring him back to the farm in the spring and let him spend a few days in the sunshine and fresh air."

"If you would like," Clary added, "You could leave him here for a week or two."

"We'll turn him into a farmer," Jack threatened, laughing at Philly's expression of horror at this idea.

"My son will be a gentleman," she insisted.

"Like your brother?" Jack asked, still teasing.

"Yes!" Philly's voice was unexpectedly fierce. "You are the finest gentleman I know."

"We can also hope that Justin will resemble the gentleman his father undoubtedly was," Clary said, ruffling the boy's hair.

"Never!" The cry seemed wrenched from Philly's deepest heart. "Do not say such a thing. My son will be nothing like his father." Philly burst into tears.

"I'm sorry. I didn't mean to upset you." Clary wasn't able to finish her apology because Philly rushed out of the parlor. "Jack, what have I done? Should I go to her?"

"It is not your fault," he said. "Stay with Justin. I will see to Philly." He followed his sister out of the room.

"Mama's sad," Justin said.

"I know, dear." Clary put an arm around the boy, wondering how words intended as a compliment could have produced such an effect, wondering, too, and not for the first time, why Philly never mentioned her late husband.

"Mama cries sometimes," Justin remarked.

"Does she?" Clary hugged him absentmindedly, her thoughts on Philly and Jack. For all her good intentions and her determination to do as Jack wanted, the past constantly intruded on the present.

"She cries when Uncle Jack goes away," Justin informed Clary. "Every time."

"I suppose she misses him. I know how much I miss him when he leaves the farm." She sat with her arm around Justin until Jack returned to the parlor.

"Philly is washing her face," he reported. "She says she is sorry she caused such a fuss and asks that we not reopen the subject."

"Justin," Clary said, "perhaps you will pick up that large flat box from under the tree. When your mother comes back, you may give it to her. It is a surprise from me."

Thus, when Philly stepped into the parlor a few minutes later, she was met by the sight of her son attempting to balance a box far too large for his small arms to encircle. The ensuing laughter relieved any embarrassment between the two women.

Later, when they were alone in his bedroom, Jack put his arms around Clary to whisper his appreciation of her tactful handling of the incident. Then he gave her his gift, a necklace and brooch to match the sapphire-and-diamond earrings that were his wedding present to her.

"Oh, my." Clary let the stones slide through her fingers. "It's gorgeous. I have never owned anything like this."

"Like the earrings, these belonged to my mother," he said, answering the question she had carefully left unasked. "She gave them to me shortly before she died, so I would have them to present to my bride when the time came."

"I will treasure them because you gave them to me and because they once were hers," Clary said.

"Wear them tonight," he urged, mischief overcoming seriousness. "I have long imagined you wearing those sapphires and nothing else."

"An intriguing notion." As always she warmed to the sensual light in his eyes and to his humor. "However, in your charming fantasy, you have overlooked one small detail. Where shall I place the brooch?"

"While I can think of several interesting locations for the piece," he said, considering the question in mock solemnity, "for the sake of my personal safety, I would suggest that on this occasion you place it in the hair upon your lovely head."

And so Clary went to bed that night clothed only in sapphire-and-diamond earrings and necklace, with the brooch glittering among her dark curls. Jack, otherwise quite naked, insisted on matching his wife's jeweled formality by donning the fine silk cravat that was one of her gifts to him. They made love with much laughter, which they tried to muffle under the quilts so Philly would not hear them in the next room. They also tried not to make the ropes that held the mattress creak too loudly. In this attempt they were not altogether successful, though Clary voiced no complaints about any other aspect of Jack's Christmas Eve entertainment. Nor did she object to the encore with which he delighted her shortly before dawn on Christmas Day.

# *Chapter Twenty-two*

Three days after Christmas, while Philly and Justin were still at the farm, an unexpected visitor arrived. Benjamin Wilmot was in his late fifties, gray haired, rotund, and obviously suffering from the effects of his cold ride. Clary had never met him before but she knew that he lived in Philadelphia, where Jack often dealt with him on canal business.

"Mr. Wilmot, I am surprised to see you here." Jack pulled the front door wide to admit the shivering man. "Ah, here comes Moses, who must have seen you ride in. He will take your horse to the barn and see it well cared for during your stay with us."

"Come into the parlor," Clary urged Mr. Wilmot, leading him and Jack into the room where Philly was sitting. "Let me prepare a glass of whiskey or rum with hot water in it. I have the water handy, having just brought

it from the kitchen so I could make a hot drink for my husband before our midday meal. Perhaps you would care to join us when we eat?"

"A hot rum toddy would be most appreciated on such a bitter day. As to the meal, I thank you, madam, and accept most gratefully." Mr. Wilmot rubbed his hands together, holding them toward the fire. He spoke to Jack. "Sir, I had hoped to find you in Wilmington for the holiday, but your butler Gilbert informed me that you were here at the farm, so I took leave to seek you out at home."

"Here you are." Clary handed him a mug filled with rum and hot water with a dash of freshly grated nutmeg on top. "This will help to warm you. Mr. Wilmot, you look terribly serious. Nothing has happened to the *ClaryRose*, has it? Is Sam all right?"

"Clary, if you will but give Mr. Wilmot a chance, I believe he will explain to us why he is here," Jack said.

"When I disembarked from the *ClaryRose* this morning, Mr. MacKenzie was planning to spend the rest of the day at the tavern in Bohemia Village," Mr. Wilmot told Clary. "His ship is safely anchored in Back Creek.

"Now, sir," he went on, turning to Jack, "this is, as your wife has noted, a most solemn occasion. Sir, I have the melancholy duty of informing you that your father, the Marquess of Huntsley, has died."

407

Philly made a startled sound at this announcement and looked as if she wanted to say something, but Jack silenced her with a gesture.

"I am very sorry to hear this," Jack said to Mr. Wilmot. "May I ask how you received the news?"

"In my capacity as the late marquess's agent in the United States, I received formal notification from your family solicitor in London. The letter to me accompanied this packet. Both items were brought to Philadelphia on a ship that arrived there on Christmas Day." He held out a packet that looked to Clary like a thick letter sealed with red wax. "I thought you would want to know as soon as possible," Mr. Wilmot said.

"Then William has succeeded to the title." Jack took the packet. "While I am most appreciative of your consideration toward me, Mr. Wilmot, it was scarcely necessary for you to travel so far during the holiday season. You could have written to me and sent this packet with your letter."

"No, sir, I could not. According to the letter I received, you are the heir to the marquessate."

"Oh, no!" Philly cried, her hands flying to her suddenly pale face. She looked as if she might faint.

"There has been some mistake." Jack was openly horrified by Mr. Wilmot's words. "William has been married for more than seven years. Surely by now he and Lady Chastity have several children to their name who will inherit in time, and William himself is young

and healthy. So you see, I cannot possibly be the heir."

"Sir, I can only tell you what was in the letter sent to me. You will, of course, wish to read your own letter in private." He started to leave the room. Clary would have followed him out, but Jack stopped them.

"Mr. Wilmot, I must ask you to remain. And you, too, Clary. Don't leave me now, my dear."

Clary saw naked need in his eyes, along with a strange glimmer of fear. It was unlike Jack to be afraid of anything. With her heart beating hard, she sat down on the settee next to Philly.

"Oh, Jack," Philly cried, "what shall we do? This new life we have made for ourselves and for Justin will fall into ruin now."

"I do not think so, Philly, which is why I want Mr. Wilmot to stay while I read the letter from Huntsley's solicitor."

Clary watched her husband break the seal and unfold the letter with hands that shook for a moment. It was not an unnatural reaction for a man who had just learned of his father's death, but Jack did not seem to be grieving. Clary thought he was deeply worried, and the glance he sent toward Philly, as if to tell his sister to buck up and be strong, convinced Clary that the moment of fear she had seen in him was not for himself but for Philly. Clary saw Philly lift her chin and give Jack a little nod, at which signal he lowered his eyes to the letter and began to read aloud.

*My lord, it is with the deepest sorrow that I inform you of the recent tragic events in your family. Your father, the Marquess of Huntsley, and your older brother, Lord William Martynson, Viscount Martynson, have died as the result of an epidemic of diphtheria which has lately been raging near and at Huntsley and which has also killed more than a dozen tenants and several of the household servants.*

*Your sister-in-law, Lady Chastity, fell ill of the disease and has miscarried as a result, though she is slowly recovering under her mother's care. As a consequence of these untimely deaths and the loss of Lord William's expected child, the title of Marquess of Huntsley has now devolved upon you. My lord, I respectfully request your return to England at your earliest convenience, as the finances of the estate are in sad condition and will require your full attention.*

There was more, mostly descriptions of the aforementioned sad condition of the Huntsley estate and the need to replace lost staff as soon as possible.

"Poor Lady Chastity," Philly murmured, her eyes upon Jack as they had been during the entire reading. "I knew her when I was in London. She is a sweet girl. Jack, we cannot continue in this way any longer."

"Of course you cannot," Mr. Wilmot said to

Jack. "Sir, you must return to England at once. I will make the arrangements for you."

"No," Jack said, his eyes on Clary. "I am not returning to England. Not now, not in the future."

"But you must!" Mr. Wilmot cried. "Sir, your responsibilities—"

"Are ended by that letter," Jack said.

"This is outrageous!" Mr. Wilmot looked as if he would explode. "As a loyal citizen of the United States, I care nothing for foreign titles. But for a man to refuse to take up the duties left to him by his dead father and brother is unconscionable."

"If you will be patient, I can explain." Jack turned from the fuming Mr. Wilmot to Clary. "In order to pay a debt of gratitude, my sister and I have practiced a deception upon Mr. Wilmot and upon you, Clary. But you, Clary, have always known that, though not the nature of the deception nor the reasons for it."

"It is my understanding from letters the late marquess wrote to me," Mr. Wilmot declared, "that the woman who accompanied you to these United States is not your sister at all, but your mistress. I must confess that I am shocked to find her here in company with your wife."

"You do her an injustice, Mr. Wilmot." Striding to the settee where she still was, Jack put a hand on Philly's shoulder. "This woman is indeed my sister and as fine a lady as I have ever known. However, I am not Justin Martynson."

411

"Then who are you, in heaven's name?" Mr. Wilmot took a long swallow of his rum as if strong spirits would help him to accept what he was hearing. Clary began to wish that she had prepared a stiff drink for herself.

"I was baptized Percival Gordon Henry Cadell," Jack said. "My sister, who is known in Wilmington as the widow Philippa Gordon, is in fact Lady Philippa Augusta Henrietta Cadell. Our older brother, so far as we know, is alive and in happy possession of his earldom and his lands. And he, Mr. Wilmot, has three strong sons to his name. I am heir to nothing, as you shall hear if Philly agrees and if you care to listen."

"Your real name is Percival?" Clary asked.

"Yes, tell them everything, Jack," Philly cried, speaking right over Clary's words. "I am so weary of subterfuge, and you know I am not good at it. I have been most dreadfully nervous every day of my visit here. Clary deserves to know, and I am certain we can trust Mr. Wilmot's discretion. He has never failed us yet, though I am aware that he does not hold me in very high regard, believing me to be your mistress for all our claims to be brother and sister."

"Indeed, sir, I think you had better make a thorough explanation!" Mr. Wilmot declared. In a quieter voice he added, "I will admit to a considerable personal curiosity. To practice and continue a deception of this magnitude for so long a time is not only reprehensible, it is most remarkable. I should like to know how you did it."

"It was done for my sake," Philly said. Laying one hand over Jack's on her shoulder, with her other hand grasping Clary's fingers and holding on tightly to them, she continued. "Jack, you have borne so much for me. There is no need for you to fabricate yet another tale for my benefit when I know you hate lying every bit as much as I do. My dear, sweet brother, I release you now from every promise of secrecy I ever extracted from you. For your honor's sake, for the sake of your marriage, you must tell everything."

"For heaven's sake!" Clary cried, exasiprated. "Stop beating around the bush and tell us what this mysterious everything is!"

"Indeed," agreed Mr. Wilmot, who had entirely regained his composure during Philly's speech. "Please do, and without further delay."

"If you are sure?" Jack gave Philly a hard look until she nodded, pressing her lips together as if to quell some emotional outburst. Jack's hand tightened on her shoulder for a moment. "Thank you, Philly. It will be a great relief to tell the truth, especially to Clary."

Moving away from the settee where his sister and Clary were, Jack walked to the fireplace to lean an arm along the mantel. He looked relaxed while staring into the fire as if deciding exactly how to proceed, but Clary knew him well enough to see the tension in him.

"Almost seven years ago," Jack said, straightening to meet Mr. Wilmot's eyes, "Lady Philippa Cadell spent her first season in London. She was a great success for her beauty and charm, though

she was not an heiress. Despite her small dowry, there were several men who paid their addresses to her, among them a notorious, highborn rake who was the son of a wealthy and powerful earl. Our older brother Richard believed Philly had the chance to make a great match with this man, so he allowed the association.

"One evening, at a ball held in a large London house, the rake danced with Philly and afterward lured her into the dark garden. There he proceeded to ravish her despite her struggles and her pleas. In the process, he blackened her eyes and bruised and bloodied her body in unmentionable places.

"My friend, Justin Martynson, happened to be present at the same ball. It was he who discovered Philly wandering distraught in the garden with her ball gown torn and bloody. Justin got her away through the garden entrance and took her to his house, which was nearby. He then sent for me and for Richard. When Richard learned of the incident, he was most unsympathetic to Philly, though her distress and her battered physical condition were sadly evident." At this point, Jack's voice turned savagely bitter. "The good earl, my brother Richard, decided his sister must at once marry the man who had ravished her. The fellow was, after all, the son of an other earl and in line for the title. I disagreed most vigorously to this plan and Philly refused ever to see the man again, much less marry him. As a result of the quarrel that followed, we parted company

with our brother that night and have not seen him since."

"Good heavens, sir, this is an appalling story!" Mr. Wilmot exclaimed.

"Richard being unwilling to do so because he was still hoping for a marriage, I challenged the guilty man at once," Jack said. "Justin acted as my second. We met at dawn two days after the incident at the ball, by which time the scandal was all over London."

"You fought a duel?" Clary cried. "My God, Jack!"

"I put a bullet in his heart," Jack said, looking right into Clary's eyes. "And from what I know of what he did to Philly, and of all the women he ravished before her, and the women he doubtless would have harmed in the same way in the future if he had been allowed to live, I cannot say that I regret what I did."

"Oh, God!" Clary said again. She put an arm around Philly, who leaned against her as if seeking courage.

"I believe dueling is against the law in England." Mr. Wilmot did not seem especially shocked by this aspect of the story. In fact, he looked at Jack with considerable admiration. "Under the circumstances you describe, no honorable man could fault you for what you did. Was the duel the reason why you left England?"

"I did not at first intend to leave. Justin helped me to reach a safe place away from London, and I took Philly with me, since after our quarrel

with Richard she had nowhere else to go. No family members and none of her former friends would receive her, and the earl was bent upon vengeance for his son's death. We thought it our good fortune when, only a day after the duel, Justin's father commanded his immediate presence at Huntsley Hall and there ordered him to come to America to watch over the family's financial interests in this country. Justin at once decided that Philly and I should travel with him."

"Where is Sir Justin now?" asked Mr. Wilmot.

"I am coming to that. I want to be certain that Clary understands the situation in which my sister and I found ourselves. After the attack on Philly, and then when the results of the duel became common knowledge, my sister had no hope of a respectable future or a good marriage in England. Because of the scandal and our quarrel with him, Richard disinherited both of us, leaving us penniless. But Justin came to our rescue for a second time. He paid our passage, and so we three and Justin's faithful valet, Gilbert, boarded a ship bound for the New World."

"Only two of you and the servant left that ship when she docked in Philadelphia," Mr. Wilmot said. "I must ask you again, sir, where Justin Martynson is?"

"He contracted a fever during the voyage and died of it," Jack said. "I have in my possession his death certificate, signed by the captain of our ship and the ship's doctor. If you require

further proof, I will give you the name of the ship and the captain's name. He will have an entry in his log for the date in question, for there were more than a dozen seamen and passengers who fell ill of the same fever and five of them died. I was sick myself for several days, though not so ill as Justin. Philly and Gilbert together nursed both of us."

"By then, Justin was almost like another brother to me," Philly put in.

"And so you assumed Justin Martynson's identity," Mr. Wilmot said to Jack. "Tell me, sir, is this why you have always refused to accept the income from his personal estate in England and sent that money back to the marquess instead, calling it profit from the farm?"

"I could not take the money," Jack said. "I already owed Justin a debt too great ever to be repaid in full."

"For that gesture alone, I must think better of you," Mr. Wilmot said. "But still, to take over another man's life—"

"It was Justin's own idea," Jack said, interrupting the other man. "He knew he was dying and—admittedly in the throes of a fever—he concocted the plan. I was to pose as Justin. Philly could continue to be my sister, since no one in America knew Justin personally or knew that he had no sister. Thus, Philly and I could begin a new life, free from the taint of scandal. By the end of the voyage we knew that Philly was carrying the child of the man who had attacked her, so we agreed that she should pose as a recent widow.

"For my part, I was to fulfill Justin's mission in this country. I promised my friend that I would cultivate the land once owned by Justin's uncle, Roger Martynson—this farm—and send to the marquess as much money as possible from it and from the canal stocks the marquess had inherited from Roger. Apparently, the marquess believed the canal company was withholding dividends, though in fact the company has not paid any money to its shareholders yet. You must admit, Mr. Wilmot, that I have faithfully discharged my promise to Justin."

"Yes, you have." Mr. Wilmot was thoughtful. "I begin to understand many things that have puzzled me about you for years. This is why you assumed new names immediately upon your arrival and required me to see to it that those names were legally yours."

"Then you really are Jack Martin?" Clary asked her husband.

"It is what I have been telling you for months," he responded. "Mr. Wilmot, there was never any question of my attempting to assume the title of marquess. Justin knew his brother and then his brother's children would inherit. Also, the old marquess had such an intense dislike for Justin that my friend believed his father would not care if he remained in this country indefinitely. Which is why, at almost the last moment before leaving England, Justin managed to wrest the title to this farm from his father in return for a written promise to remit a large percentage of the yearly profit from it to the marquess for the

rest of the marquess's life. Like Justin, I think the old man hoped that this plan would keep his son permanently out of England. In that at least, father and son were in agreement.

"When he knew that he did not have long to live, Justin said that he wanted me to have the same security he would have enjoyed, and so he willed the farm to me. The ship's doctor and Justin's valet, Gilbert, served as witnesses to this will. For obvious reasons, I never informed the marquess of the change in ownership, nor you either. I just sent all the money I possibly could to Justin's father each year."

"And made a fine job of it, too," Mr. Wilmot said. "What an extraordinary agreement. There can be no question that you have more than fulfilled your part of it."

"You will understand why I have no desire to return to England," Jack said, looking at Clary. "My home is here now."

"I can foresee no reason why anyone would dispute your claim to this farm," Mr. Wilmot said. "Good heavens, sir, it was a wreck before you came here. You are the one who has made this land productive." He paused, his eyes meeting Jack's. After a long, considering moment, Benjamin Wilmot put out his hand.

"Thank you," Jack said softly and shook hands with him, thus sealing their unwritten agreement to keep this strange story between themselves.

Clary could see that Jack was clamping down hard on his emotions, and it suddenly struck her

just how much the farm meant to him. It was his own piece of the New World, soil that he tilled and planted and harvested with his own hands. He had made the difficult transition from idle aristocrat to disinherited younger brother to hardworking American entrepreneur. Clary's heart swelled with pride in him and with love.

"We do, however, have a problem to solve," Mr. Wilmot said, returning briskly to business. "Some response must be made to the London solicitor's letters."

"You are right," Jack said. "The debt I owe to Justin extends to the tenants and the land that would have been his today, had he lived. It is my duty to make certain that Justin's heritage remains in his family."

"What do you suggest?" asked Mr. Wilmot.

"Justin had a distant cousin or two on his father's side of the family. He used to joke that if the main branch of the Martynsons should ever die out, there would still be relatives aplenty to claim the title. Why don't we inform the solicitor of the truth of this situation? He will then be required by law to notify the next nearest relative that he is in line to be the new marquess. It will be a better solution all around than just ignoring the letters from London and leaving the solicitor to believe that Justin has no interest in his heritage."

"The truth of the situation, sir? What truth would that be?" There was an appreciative sparkle in Benjamin Wilmot's eyes.

"Before you leave Afon Farm I shall write a letter to that solicitor," Jack said, "informing him that Justin Martynson has unfortunately died of a fever. I shall add that he willed his farm to me, his best friend and business associate. I will be grateful if you would reiterate these indisputable, perfectly truthful, facts in your accompanying letter to London. However, I see no reason for either of us to mention the exact date of Justin's death or my original name."

"Sir, you have a touch of the scoundrel in your nature." Benjamin Wilmot smiled, thinking. "But your suggestion will serve the Huntsley estate well, and considering the distance between Philadelphia and London, I do not think anyone across the ocean will trouble to probe too deeply into our account of the way in which you acquired the farm."

"This arrangement will get you as well as Jack off the hook with the Huntsleys, Mr. Wilmot," Clary said.

"I beg your pardon, madam?" Mr. Wilmot swung around to stare at her in astonishment.

"You will no longer be responsible for collecting and transferring money from the farm to England," Clary explained. "Now you will only have to deal with the English solicitors about the canal stocks, and since they won't pay any dividends for at least twenty years, you won't have to do much work on the Huntsley account."

"My dear Mrs. Martin, since I hold more than a few shares in the canal company myself, I

do sincerely hope you are wrong!" Mr. Wilmot exclaimed.

"She is more likely to be right," Jack said, laughing. "My wife is remarkably insightful about the future. Clary, my love, have I time to write my letter before we eat? Or shall I wait until afterward?"

"I think it would be best to wait," she said. "I detect a wonderful fragrance wafting this way from the dining room, which means Sarah is about to call us in to dinner."

When the midday meal was over the men retired to the parlor to write their respective letters to London. With young Justin off to the barn to tend to his new pony under Luke's supervision, Clary and Philly were left alone in the dining room.

"Clary, I must know," Philly whispered. "Do you despise me?"

"Because some brute raped you?" Seeing Philly flinch at her use of the blunt word, Clary put her arms around her sister-in-law. "Of course I don't despise you, and now that I know the truth I understand why you wanted that whole affair kept secret. But, Philly, it wasn't your fault. It wasn't."

"I thought afterward that it was in part my doing because I accepted his invitation to dance, and I willingly agreed to go into the garden with him in order to cool ourselves when the dance was over. I did not know what he intended until it was too late. Before that night I was always

treated kindly by men and so I never expected what he did to me.

"After that night," Philly went on, "I knew that everything had changed, and I would henceforth be treated only with contempt and derision."

"Considering the time and place where you were living," Clary said, "leaving the country was probably the smartest thing you could do. Philly, I can't begin to imagine what you must have felt when you realized that you were carrying that terrible man's child. He was Justin's father, wasn't he? There wasn't anyone else?"

"Oh, no." Philly gasped. "I could never—the thought of anyone touching me that way—I would rather die."

"It doesn't have to be painful and terrifying," Clary said. "Not when the man and woman love each other. I hope someday you will have the chance to learn that for yourself."

"When I see you and Jack together I do begin to believe that not all men are as cruel as that one wicked person."

"One is the operative word here," Clary said. "Just one man raped you. Think of the good men who have taken care of you since that night. Philly, what are you going to tell Justin when he asks about his father? He will, you know. Children are curious about such things."

"He must never be told what happened to me," Philly said. "The knowledge could only hurt him. It might even destroy him. In spite of everything, I love my son and I do not want him ever to think he is to blame for any unhappiness I have

suffered. I have decided that when he wants to know who his father was, I shall describe to him the man for whom he is named and hope that with the older Justin's fine example set before him, and with Jack to provide guidance as he grows up, my son will prove to be completely unlike the cruel person who was only accidentally his father.

"Though Justin Martynson did not live long enough to have his own children," Philly added, "perhaps my son can in some way become the spiritual son of the man who did so much for Jack and me when there seemed to be no future at all for us."

"This is all very nice," Clary said, "but can you keep up such a deception for a lifetime? You admit you aren't very good at lying, and I have seen firsthand how nervous pretence makes you."

"For my son, I will do it." Philly spoke with so much determination in her voice that Clary could not doubt that she would at least make a good try. "I must ask you, Clary, not to speak of this again, to me or to Jack, who long ago promised me that he would never discuss the events that led to our leaving England. I do not want to risk Justin ever overhearing one single word that might cause him to doubt his parentage."

"Fine. This is your choice," Clary told her. "I don't entirely agree with you, because I think the truth usually comes out, and almost always at an inconvenient or a dangerous time, but I will go along with your decision. I have to admit

that I wouldn't want a child of mine to know his father was a rapist. That's a hideous burden to lay on any child, and it is just the kind of burden a loving mother would take onto her own shoulders. You know, Philly, in your own way you are every bit as strong and remarkable a person as your brother."

"Thank you, Clary. I am so glad Jack married you." Philly threw her arms around Clary and kissed her, but Clary's thoughts had already jumped ahead to imagine Jack's response to what she would say to him when he and she were at last alone together.

# *Chapter Twenty-three*

Wrapped in her warm cloak Clary stood beside Jack on the gravel drive watching Benjamin Wilmot ride away toward Bohemia Village on the first leg of his return journey to Philadelphia. He carried with him the two letters he and Jack had composed that afternoon, which he would send on from Philadelphia to London.

"There goes the very last trace of the best friend I shall ever have," Jack said on a sigh. "What a pity. The Martynsons were an ancient and noble family. I hope the younger branch proves as noteworthy as the older one was."

"Shall we walk?" Clary asked. "I have a few things to say to you and we can be more private here than in the house."

She linked her arm through Jack's and together they set off across the open field, their boots crunching through a thin layer of snow, their breath two white clouds in the damp cold. While

Clary was still trying to decide how to begin, Jack spoke, dealing directly with the events of that day, his thoughts still on his friend.

"Are you sorry not to be a marchioness?" he asked. "Sorry that I am not Justin Martynson after all?"

"Certainly not. I would far rather be Jack Martin's wife."

"Sweetheart, you cannot know how glad I am to hear you say it. I have worried over that detail since I first learned that you had read the marquess's letter to Justin."

"You will be even happier when you hear what else I have to say. Jack, I owe you an apology for the way I continued to nag you and ask leading questions when you kept begging me to desist and also an apology for snooping among your private papers. It was wrong of me to behave that way. I should have known that whatever your secret was, it would be an honest one."

"Your past history would hardly lead you to trust any man without substantial proof," he said.

"That's just the point. I did have proof. It was all around me, in what you've done with this farm, in the way you treat Moses and his family, in your friendship with Sam. Good grief, Jack, even the way you acted toward the madam of a whorehouse only proved what an honest and decent man you are! And I was too blind to see it."

"Oh, Clary, I do love you." Jack threw back his head and laughed at her words. "Promise

me that you will never stop speaking so plainly. I find I particularly like the words no marchioness would ever dream of using."

"And that's another thing," Clary went on. "Ever since that fascinating conversation with Mr. Wilmot this morning, I have been thinking about the way you moved from one kind of life to another, protecting your sister all along the way. It must have been a major dislocation for you, to go from being an English nobleman living in a mansion to a farmer and to actually harvesting and selling the farm produce yourself. Philly once said something snobbish about people in trade, and you must have been raised to think the same way. I want you to know how much I admire you for handling a difficult transition so well."

"My life on Afon Farm does not represent as big a change as you might imagine," Jack replied. "I have always preferred the country to the city, and when I was a boy, I especially enjoyed market days in the town near where I grew up. I suspect, if I were the older son and had inherited the "family title" I might have spent my life very much as I am doing now. I might even have been involved in building a local canal in England," he finished with a chuckle.

"Tell me about your family," Clary begged, delighted to have him speaking so freely at last.

"You know already about Philly and about our older brother," he said. "I adored my mother, who died when I was twelve. My father regarded me in much the same way as old Huntsley did

Justin, and with some justification in both cases.
I believe Justin would have taken to this life, too,
if he had survived that voyage. He and I were not
suited to London society life. We were always
bored with the endless parties and routs—and
with all the rules. In short, we were a pair of
youthful troublemakers. If we hadn't sailed to
America, we might well have gone to India in
search of adventure and a fortune. Many younger
sons do."

"I am glad you came here instead," Clary told
him. "I cannot imagine what would have happened to me if you hadn't been present when I
arrived in this time."

"If I were in India, perhaps you would have
appeared there," he said, "for I do believe that
you and I were meant to meet and love. I also
believe that you will remain in this time."

"So do I." After a minute she added, "I have
no desire to return to my old life. I belong here
with you."

"Then," he said, "believing as you do, and in
view of the fact that you now know all there is
to know about me, don't you think the time has
come for you to reveal your deepest secret to
your loving husband?"

"Jack, I would never for a single minute
dream that I know everything there is to
know about you," Clary said. "Learning to
know you is going to take me the rest of
my life."

"I feel the same way about you, sweetheart,
which is why I need to know the truth."

"What truth?" Clary could not look at him. She was frantically trying to think of a way to avoid saying what he was going to insist on knowing. She told herself she should have expected this turn of events.

"About your husband's infidelity," he insisted gently. "I have known since the first time you spoke of it that you were not telling me the complete story."

"I would rather not talk about it," she murmured.

"You are evading my questions, just as I used to evade yours," he said, "and I am certain you are doing it with less reason than I had, for there is no one in this time who can be hurt by what you might say. Clary, surely you know there is nothing you cannot tell me. You are the one who has always insisted on a marriage based on honesty. Be honest with me now."

She heard the slight crack in his voice that betrayed how important this was to him. Because she loved him, she felt compelled to do as he asked, to describe the scene that had shattered her old life.

"It's not a pretty story," she said. "It is the reason why I have always found it difficult to trust you completely, though I knew from the beginning that you are a very different kind of man from Rich."

The short December day was ending, and in the gathering twilight, Clary found the courage to say what might have been too embarrassing to reveal in the bright glare of noon.

"I have already described to you how I found Rich in our bed with a lover."

"A close friend to both of you," Jack added, giving her a verbal nudge when she paused. "She could not have been a true friend to you if she would lie with your husband."

"Not she. He." It was hard to say those first few words, but once started, the story poured out of her. "He was a mutual friend, whom we had known for years. He was Rich's best man when we were married. He visited our house frequently on Sunday afternoons or Monday evenings to watch the football games with Rich. I even tried to match him up with some of my unmarried girlfriends. And all the time he and Rich were a pair. And I never guessed.

"In the twentieth century, we are a lot freer about such things than you are in these days, but even so, I cannot describe the shock I felt when I walked in on them and saw what they were doing. Within a second or two my entire life shifted so that I saw myself and my marriage from a new perspective. Incidents and remarks I hadn't understood before suddenly made sense to me and I realized how stupid I had been."

"Not stupid. Honest and trusting, and your trust was abused. Clary, you should not have been witness to such a scene." Jack made no move to touch her, apparently understanding that she needed to stand alone while she finished what she had to say.

"I thought I was going to die. I couldn't breathe, my heart was banging against my rib cage, and I

couldn't see straight. I don't know how I got to my car or where I drove before I found myself on the bridge." She stopped, looking up at him through the blue twilight. She was filled with a sense of surprise and mounting joy. "It is absolutely amazing, Jack, but telling you after holding all of this inside for so long, I have just realized that it doesn't matter anymore. I can remember feeling those terrible emotions, but all I feel about that night right now is indifference. I am cured of caring about Rich and of blaming myself because my marriage went wrong. All of it happened literally in another lifetime. I guess you could say that, as of this day, you and I are free of our pasts."

"Of the harmful effects," he said. "Not of the lessons learned."

"I feel lighter," she said.

"I have recently experienced a similar phenomenon. Truth telling does wondrously improve one's vitality and one's hopes for the future."

She took his hands, standing there in the snow, and when she smiled at him, she saw his wide smile flash in response.

"I love you, Jack Martin, and I thank God you found me in time," she said. "You saved my life in more ways than one."

"Sweetheart." He bent his head to kiss her. "'Twas you who found me by driving into the canal on the most fortunate day of my life."

432

# *Epilogue*

The combined christening celebration and
Fourth of July picnic was a great success.
The best of Sarah's food was set out upon the
tables placed on the lawn in front of the house. A
few of the men who had worked with Jack on the
canal and who had then chosen to settle down in
the area rather than move on to some other canal
project were present with their families, as were
two neighboring landholders, with their wives
and children, and several businessmen from
Bohemia Village. Even Benjamin Wilmot and
his wife and daughter had come from Philadelphia. They all spread out across the open
field, sitting on chairs or on blankets spread
on the ground, eating and talking while their
children ran about chasing butterflies or taking
turns riding on Justin's pony.

Clary sat in the shade beneath a tree
with James Gordon Martin, the three-week-old

guest of honor, sleeping peacefully in his cradle beside her.

"Do not allow yourself to become overtired, Clary," Philly warned, stooping to look at the baby.

"I am completely recovered. Sarah makes a wonderful midwife."

"She has just told me that Jack is planning to hire more employees for the farm and to put Moses in charge of them."

"That's right. Jack won't have time to help much with the harvest this year," Clary said. "The *ClaryRose* has been so successful that he and Sam are talking about buying a second ship, which means he will have to spend longer hours with the account books. I will be occupied with Jamie, so I won't be much use in the fields, though I can still help Sarah in the kitchen. And then, of course, Luke will be leaving in August." Clary looked across the meadow to where Luke and Justin were leading the other young people in a rather disorganized game with a large ball.

"I know my brother had something to do with Mr. Wilmot offering to arrange a place for Luke at that school in Philadelphia," Philly remarked.

"Luke has made such rapid progress that I can't teach him anything more," Clary said. "That young man is bright. He just needs a chance to show what he can do."

"I hope he will make the most of the opportunity Mr. Wilmot is offering." Philly shaded her eyes, looking toward the road. "Clary, here come more guests. Is that Mr. MacKenzie?"

"Sam!" Clary hurried forward to meet the cart pulling up where the gravel drive divided and one branch led behind the house to the barn. "Rose! I was beginning to think you weren't coming."

"We dropped anchor in Back Creek earlier this morning." Sam helped his passenger to alight as he spoke. "Rose wouldn't let me miss this great event." He broke off to shake Jack's hand and congratulate him on the birth of his son.

"We have, however, missed the baptism itself," Rose snapped, "which is most improper of us."

"Ah, would ye listen to her?" Sam said to Clary. "Wed less than a week, and already she's naggin' at her poor husband. I tell ye, Clary lass—"

"Married?" Clary asked, interrupting him.

"Aye." Sam's grin nearly split his face in two. "She decided to sail up to Philadelphia with me to order more furniture for the inn, and just as we arrived she finally agreed to marry me. So I insisted we do the deed right there in port before she could change her mind. Madam Rose is now Mrs. Samuel MacKenzie and completely respectable at last."

"How wonderful!" Clary embraced both Rose and Sam.

"Madam Rose?" Philly repeated, looking toward Clary with a puzzled expression.

"It's a long and complicated story," Clary told her sister-in-law. "I will explain it to you when we have more time."

"We've brought another guest with us," Sam told Jack. "I didn't think you'd mind. He left

Bohemia Village after we did, but he ought to be along soon."

"There is a horseman coming down the road now," Philly said. "Oh, my. Is that Captain Schyler?"

"He reached Bohemia Village this morning on his northward run," Sam said, "and since he has to wait for some cargo to arrive, I suggested that he join us."

"He is very welcome." Clary noted the interesting shade of pink that suddenly suffused Philly's cheeks. "Philly, perhaps you would see that he has something to eat."

When Philly and Jack moved off together to greet this latest guest, Clary turned to the man still standing beside her.

"All right, Sam," she said, "it's time for you to tell me everything."

"If it's about the weddin' yer askin', better quiz Rose," Sam advised, giving his wife a look of complete adoration.

"I will later," Clary said. She linked her arm through Sam's to keep him from leaving her alone with Rose before she was ready to let him go. "At the moment, I have another subject in mind. I have finally learned about Jack's mysterious past, but I still don't know anything about your life before I met you. If we are going to be close friends—and we ought to be, because Rose and I are friends—then I want to know who you really are."

"There isn't much to tell," Sam said evasively.

"Then stop prevaricating and tell it," Rose ordered in a tart voice. "If you do not, I will. Clary has a right to know your true identity."

"Ah, Rose, how can I resist yer sweet blandishments?" Sam grinned at her, then spoke to Clary. "I was born Samuel Lachlan MacKenzie, the youngest of five sons in a family of old Scottish blood, but my parents were far too poor to allow their children to live on inherited wealth. There wasn't any wealth. Even my oldest brother, the heir to our father's title, was forced to make his own way in the world from an early age.

"I went to sea for a while," Sam continued. "My last voyage was as a junior officer on a ship transporting Irish laborers across the Atlantic to work on the canal. I was successful in putting down a few disputes amongst the men while we were still aboard ship, and after we reached Philadelphia, I was offered the job of supervising the same men while they dug the canal. The laborers trusted me, ye see."

"Yes," Clary said, smiling at him, "I do see why men coming to a strange new land would trust you. I trusted you right away. When did you meet Jack?"

"During my second day at the canal. We took to each other at once."

"That makes sense, too, and your story explains why you called Jack my lord from time to time. You recognized a fellow nobleman when you met one."

"My friend Jack is a nobleman? My, my," Sam said, a definite twinkle lighting his blue eyes. "Fancy that! And he never said a word to me!"

An hour later Clary and Jack finally had a chance to speak alone.

"Do you think Philly likes him?" Clary glanced toward where Philly and Captain Schyler sat on a blanket talking while the captain devoured a plate piled with fried chicken, ham, biscuits, and assorted other foods.

"I hope so. I know I like Peter Schyler," Jack said. "My dearest wish for Philly is that she will find a man who will treat her as she deserves to be treated and who will make her happy again."

"What about Rose and Sam? Were you surprised by their marriage?"

"They richly deserve each other. They will be happy." Jack caressed Clary's cheek in a tender gesture. "So many changes have taken place in all our lives since this day last year."

"Early America was known as a place where people could make over their lives to suit themselves. We have all done that, haven't we?" Clary said. "You, Sam, Rose, even Hermione, who manages the inn when Rose is away. Especially me. Now Luke will have his chance. And perhaps Philly's turn will come soon."

When the baby began to whimper Clary lifted him into her arms. Cuddled against his mother's bosom, he fell quiet at once. Standing behind Clary, Jack put his arms around both of them, holding them against his heart while together they watched their family and friends enjoying

438

the celebration they had made possible.

"Allow me to inform you, madam," Jack murmured into Clary's ear, "that you are the very heart and soul of my new life."

"You are mine, too," she responded. "Allow me to tell you, sir, that you found me just in time—literally. Without you, I had no time left at all. With you, I have eternity."

Their guests politely pretended not to see the kiss Jack and Clary exchanged then—except for Philly, who blushed and hid her face behind her hands and then glanced with shining eyes at Peter Schyler's laughing face.

# BELIEVE
## Victoria Alexander

Tessa thinks as little of love as she does of the Arthurian legend—it is just a myth. But when an enchanted tome falls into the lovely teacher's hands, she learns that the legend is nothing like she remembers. Galahad the Chaste is everything but—the powerful knight is an expert lover—and not only wizards can weave powerful spells. Still, even in Galahad's muscled embrace, she feels unsure of this man who seemed a myth. But soon the beautiful skeptic is on a quest as real as her heart, and the grail—and Galahad's love—is within reach. All she has to do is believe.

___52267-5                                  $5.99 US/$6.99 CAN

# FLORA SPEER
## Rose Red
## A Faerie Tale Romance

*Once upon a time...they lived happily ever after.*

**"I HAVE TWO DAUGHTERS, ONE A FLOWER AS PURE AND WHITE AS THE NEW-FALLEN SNOW AND THE OTHER A ROSE AS RED AND SWEET AS THE FIRES OF PASSION."**

Bianca and Rosalinda are the only treasures left to their mother after her husband, the Duke of Monteferro, is murdered. Fleeing a remote villa in the shadows of the Alps of Northern Italy, she raises her daughters in hiding and swears revenge on the enemy who has brought her low.

The years pass until one stormy night a stranger appears from out of the swirling snow, half-frozen and wild, wrapped only in a bearskin. To gentle Bianca he appears a gallant suitor. To their mother he is the son of an assassin. But to Rosalinda he is the one man who can light the fires of passion and make them burn as sweet and red as her namesake.

\_52139-3                           $5.99 US/$6.99 CAN

The Magician's Lover — Flora Speer

Determined to locate his friend who disappeared during a spell gone awry, Warrick petitions a dying stargazer to help find him. But the astronomer will only assist Warrick if he promises to escort his daughter Sophia and a priceless crystal ball safely to Byzantium. Sharp-tongued and argumentative, Sophia meets her match in the powerful and intelligent Warrick. Try as she will to deny it, he holds her spellbound, longing to be the magician's lover.

___52263-2                                    $5.99 US/$6.99 CAN

# Lady of the Night
## Cordia Byers

Manacled to a stone wall is not the way Katharina Fergersen planned to spend her vacation. But a wrong turn in the right place and the haunted English castle she is touring is suddenly full of life—and so is the man who is bathing before her. As the frosty winter days melt into hot passionate nights, she realizes that there is more to Kane than just a well-filled pair of breeches. Katharina is determined not to let this man who has touched her soul escape her, even if it means giving up all to remain Sedgewick's lady of the night.

___4404-8 $5.99 US/$6.99 CAN

**Dorchester Publishing Co., Inc.**
**P.O. Box 6640**
**Wayne, PA 19087-8640**

# Heart's Magic

## Flora Speer

**Bestselling author of *ROSE RED***

In the year 1122, Mirielle senses change is coming to Wroxley Castle. Then, from out of the fog, two strangers ride into Lincolnshire. Mirielle believes the first man to be honest. But the second, Giles, is hiding something–even as he stirs her heart and awakens her deepest desires. And as Mirielle seeks the truth about her mysterious guest, she uncovers the castle's secrets and learns she must stop a treachery which threatens all she holds dear. Only then can she be in the arms of her only love, the man who has awakened her own heart's magic.

___52204-7                               $5.99 US/$6.99 CAN

# BITTERROOT

TIMESWEPT

## VICTORIA CHANCELLOR

### Bestselling Author Of *Forever & A Day*

In the Wyoming Territory—a land both breathtaking and brutal—bitterroots grow every summer for a brief time. Therapist Rebecca Hartford has never seen such a plant—until she is swept back to the days of Indian medicine men, feuding ranchers, and her pioneer forebears. Nor has she ever known a man as dark, menacing, and devastatingly handsome as Sloan Travers. Sloan hides a tormented past, and Rebecca vows to use her professional skills to help the former Union soldier, even though she longs to succumb to personal desire. But when a mysterious shaman warns Rebecca that her sojourn in the Old West will last only as long as the bitterroot blooms, she can only pray that her love for Sloan is strong enough to span the ages....

\_52087-7                                   $5.50 US/$7.50 CAN

# FOREVER & A DAY

## VICTORIA CHANCELLOR

When Linda O'Rourke returns to her grandmother's South Carolina beach house, it is for a quiet summer of tying up loose ends. And although the lovely dwelling charms her, she can't help but remember the evil presence that threatened her there so many years ago. Plagued by her fear, and tormented by visions of a virile Englishman tempting her with his every caress, she is unprepared for reality in the form of the mysterious and handsome Gifford Knight. His kisses evoke memories of the man in her dreams, but his sensual demands are all too real. Linda longs to surrender to Giff's masterful touch, but is it a safe haven she finds in his arms, or the beginning of her worst nightmare?

__52063-X                                  $5.50 US/$7.50 CAN

# DON'T MISS OTHER LOVE SPELL TIME-TRAVEL ROMANCES!

*Tempest in Time* by Eugenia Riley. When assertive, independent businesswoman Missy Monroe and timid Victorian virgin Melissa Montgomery accidentally trade places and partners on their wedding day, each finds herself in a bewildering new time, married to a husband she doesn't know. Now, each woman will have to decide whether she is part of an odd couple or a match made in heaven.
_52154-7                          $5.50 US/$6.50 CAN

*Miracle of Love* by Victoria Chancellor. When Erina O'Shea's son is born too early, doctors tell the lovely immigrant there is little they can do to save young Colin's life. Not in 1896 Texas. But then she and Colin are hurtled one hundred years into the future and into the strong arms of Grant Kirby. He's handsome, powerful, wealthy, and doesn't believe a word of her story. However, united in their efforts to save the baby, Erina and Grant struggle to recognize that love is the greatest miracle of all.
_52144-X                          $5.50 US/$6.50 CAN

> "Flora Speer opens up new vistas for the romance reader."
> —*Romantic Times*

# PASSION'S FURY

"No," Clarissa whimpered.

"Yes," Jack whispered. "Now, once more, just to be sure."

This second kiss was not a test. It was the real thing. Her hand with the wineglass still in it was crushed between them, but that didn't stop him. He held her so she could not pull away while his mouth worked a long, slow magic on hers. Clarissa was so amazed by her own welcoming reaction to him that she did not try to stop what was happening until his tongue slid along the edge of her lower lip. Only then did she begin to fight him. He released her at once.

"How dare you?" she cried. "I do not want to be kissed or handled in any way at all by any man."

"Now you begin to sound like a woman of my time," he said. "What a pity."